Isabelle Broom was born in Cambridge nine days before the 1980s began and studied Media Arts at university in London before a 12-year stint at *Heat* magazine. When she is not travelling all over the world seeking out settings for her escapist novels, Isabelle can mostly be found in Suffolk, where she shares a home with her two dogs and more books than she could ever hope to read in a lifetime.

To find out more about Izzy and her books, read excerpts, view location galleries and gain access to exclusive giveaways, you can sign up to her monthly newsletter via her website, isabellebroom.com.

Isabelle Broom

The Beach Holiday

HODDER

First published in Great Britain in 2023 by Hodder & Stoughton
An Hachette UK company

2

Copyright © Isabelle Broom 2023

A CIP catalogue record for this title is available from the British Library

Paperback ISBN 978 1 529 38372 0
eBook ISBN 978 1 529 38370 6

Typeset in Plantin Light by Hewer Text UK Ltd, Edinburgh
Printed and bound in Great Britain by Clays Ltd, Elcograf S.p.A.

Hodder & Stoughton policy is to use papers that are natural, renewable
and recyclable products and made from wood grown in sustainable
forests. The logging and manufacturing processes are expected to
conform to the environmental regulations of the country of origin.

Hodder & Stoughton Ltd
Carmelite House
50 Victoria Embankment
London EC4Y 0DZ

www.hodder.co.uk

For my readers.

I

Every good story needs a strong opening. Mine was the letter box.

The clunk as the post hit the mat was punctuated by an enthusiastic yapping, as the dog that had been snoozing peacefully across my feet shot up and hurled itself from the room.

'Dodie,' I called, in the half-hearted tone of someone who knows they will be ignored. She was not my dog, and even if she had been, I doubted she would have paid much heed. Authority was not a trait that came naturally to me.

From the snarling sounds I could now hear drifting up the stairs, it seemed likely that whatever Dodie had discovered in the hallway was at imminent risk of destruction and so, with a sigh that seemed to come from a very long way inside, I threw back the covers and set off on a rescue mission.

'Drop,' I commanded a few moments later, reaching gingerly for the end of the rolled-up magazine that wasn't obscured by brown, curly muzzle.

Dodie eyed me with disdain.

'You can have a treat,' I coaxed, noticing the lift in her ears as she registered the last word. She watched me back away towards the kitchen, and then I heard the soft tap of her paws against the lino as I levered open the fridge door. There was a half-empty packet of cocktail sausages inside, and I took one out and held it up so she could see.

'Drop,' I said again, and Dodie, all wide-eyed and wagging tail, did as she was told, accepting her reward with what I could have sworn was a smile. Either that, or she was reminding me how many teeth she had. Picking up what was left of the magazine, I placed it on the table and was in the process of filling the kettle when a key sounded in the front door.

'Honeys, I'm home!'

Such was Dodie's determination to greet her owner before I did, that she almost concussed herself on the pedal bin in her haste to exit the room. I smiled to myself as I listened to Jojo making a fuss of the dog, calling her by every other bizarre name she seemed to have inherited over the past two years – Mrs Dodieson, Doja Prat, Doodle Pup, Betty Doo. No wonder the poor mutt had a personality disorder.

'Tea?' was how I greeted her, and she nodded gratefully as she put down her bag.

'Please. The inside of my mouth feels like the crater of a volcano that's been dormant for a century.'

'Right.' I grimaced in sympathy. 'I'm guessing there was wine involved last night, in that case?'

Jojo groaned. 'Champagne first, and then wine – and I'm pretty sure we cracked open the gin when we got back to his place. And you know when you stay at someone's house for the first time and feel weird about helping yourself to a glass of water?'

'Somewhere in the dusty archives of my mind, I think there's a vague recollection, yes,' I told her, stirring in the milk.

'Well, that's what happened. I woke with such a raging thirst in the night that I seriously considered sticking my face in his fish tank.'

'He had a fish tank in his bedroom?'

She laughed, showing even more teeth than Dodie had. I put the tea in front of her and pulled out a chair.

'Thanks, Your Honor,' she said, grinning as I tutted. She'd been adding the word 'your' to my name ever since we were teenagers, arguing that it gave me gravitas. 'And thanks for staying over to mind this one.' She nudged the now-snoozing Dodie with a foot. 'I would have invited Nemo over if the silly girl didn't get so jealous.'

'We're calling the man you're dating Nemo, are we?'

Jojo shrugged. 'It's better than Fish Boy.'

My best friend approached dating in much the same way she did wine tasting, by trying as many different flavours as she could until she happened across one that warranted buying the bottle. As she had pointed out numerous times, it was only right that she did something to redress the balance that I, in my current state of self-imposed celibacy, had upset. My last relationship had ended over four years ago, and aside from a few ill-advised brief encounters in the pubs and bars of Cambridge, I had chosen to keep romantic entanglements of any kind at a distance.

Jojo spotted the magazine and began tearing off its cellophane wrapper. She did not mention the fact that it was part-shredded, so I could only assume Dodie's treatment of any incoming mail must be standard practice. Despite her disturbed night and the lingering effects of alcohol, my friend had a high colour in her cheeks and her blond hair fell in neat swirls around her shoulders. The black dress I'd seen her toddle off in the previous evening was obscured by a creased blue-and-white striped shirt, the bottom of which she'd knotted together around her waist. She might have been too shy to ask her date for a glass of water, but Jojo was presumably brazen when it came to pinching his clothes. I wasn't sure whether I admired or despaired of her. It was probably a bit of both.

'Ooh!' she said now, tapping a finger at whatever she was reading.

Leaning across the table, I saw that she had *Idol* magazine open at the reviews page and I recognised the book jacket immediately. It was the latest in my father's series of bestsellers, each centred around a character called Benedict Stamp, a former US marine-turned rogue agent who went underground in order to catch the people who killed his wife. This original vengeance mission had consumed the narrative of the first three books, while in the twenty-one that followed, Stamp had fought battles on every continent, before heading into space to foil a plot to destroy the Moon. The books were far-fetched but well researched and Stamp himself was a likeable enough, if slightly unpredictable, hero. There was also a lot of sex in the books – a fact that had rendered me mute with discomfort the first time I'd read one, aged just twelve. His newest novel, the twenty-fifth in the series, introduced Stamp's long-lost son, Marty, who the eponymous hero is hoping will take over the family business, such as it is. According to *Idol* magazine's book reviews editor, it was a 'gut-churning thrill ride'; they had awarded it five stars.

'It's a good one,' I said loyally. 'There's a scene where Benedict manages to have sex while skydiving, which is quite a feat given that he's in his fifties.'

Jojo glanced from me back to the page, momentarily confused. 'Oh,' she said, 'that's one of your dad's, is it? I didn't even notice; I was too busy reading this.' She turned the magazine around so I could see the small boxout at the bottom of the page. A headline asked: *Do you have a bestseller in you?*, below which there were two photos, one of the New York skyline, and another of Big Ben in London. According to the copy that followed, the UK's largest publishing house was celebrating the fact it had just opened a North American office by launching a novel-writing competition. Entrants were invited to submit a full synopsis plus first three chapters of a work in any genre, as long as the story was inspired by the locations pictured. Three runners-up would each win a session with a literary agent and editor, while one winner would be granted a fifty-thousand-pound two-book publishing deal.

'Gosh,' I said. 'That is . . . wow.'

'I know, right?' Jojo bounced up and down in her seat. I often wondered if I had become more sedate over the years simply to act as her pacifier.

'This competition is tailor-made for you, Honor. You have to enter.'

I peered at the small print. 'But the deadline is the end of August,' I said. 'It's almost June.'

'Buckets of time.' Jojo flicked a casual hand. 'It's only a few chapters.'

'I don't think that I—' I began, but Jojo had not finished.

'Honor,' she went on, 'this is a gift. I'd go so far as to say that it was a sign from the universe. What are the chances of a writing competition explicitly asking for novels inspired by both England and New York – the two places you know better than any other? Not even you can deny that it's a brilliant opportunity.'

I could not, so I said nothing.

'This could be the catalyst you need to finally write that novel you've been talking about for as long as I've known you.'

What Jojo did not know was that I had already started plenty of novels. The first thirty thousand words of at least ten were languishing on my laptop.

'Thousands of people will enter this competition,' I pointed out. 'I don't stand even a sliver of a chance.'

'Don't give me that "I'm no good" modest spiel.' Jojo had adopted her stern voice. 'Even if you don't win, you'll at least be getting your work under the noses of the right people. It's a way into the industry, although I have never understood why you don't just ask your dad to—'

I glared at her, and she pulled a face.

'I know, I know – you want to make it on merit alone. I get that. Hell, I even admire it. But this, *this* – ' she tapped a finger once again against the page ' – is your way in.'

I took a moment to imagine what it would feel like to win, to have my writing heralded as prize-worthy, to be paid real money for a story I'd created, to be able to call my father and say, 'Look what I did. I finally made a success of myself.'

Sitting back in my chair, I reached for my mug of tea and did my best not to catch Jojo's eye over the rim of it.

'So?' she demanded.

I had my excuses ready, but before I could reel them off, Jojo had rolled up the magazine and whacked me with it.

'Oi,' I said, rubbing the side of my head. 'What was that for?'

'That,' she said grimly, 'was me knocking some sense into you. Because you know I'm right, Honor – this *is* your chance. Promise me you're not going to let it pass you by.'

It would be so easy to agree, to reassure her I would try, but it wouldn't be honest. To enter this competition would be to risk losing it, and coming anywhere other than first place would feel like a loss to me. I had to be sure that the book I was writing was worthy of a win, and in order to do that, I would need a good idea.

A really, really good idea.

2

It took me less than twenty minutes to cycle the short distance from Jojo's cluttered terrace on the north side of the city to my equally jumbled abode, which was situated along a narrow, cobbled lane not far from King's Parade. Given that I earned only the rather meagre salary offered by the student liaison offices of Cambridge University, there was no way I could have afforded to live in such a sought-after location if it were not for my mother, who had taken ownership of the flat when she purchased the bookshop below.

I secured the front and rear wheels of my bicycle to some railings – a necessary precaution I'd learned the hard way – and let myself in through the peeling-paint mess of a side door. Another job I needed to add to my ever-growing to-do list. Ordinarily, during my annual summer recess from work, I would catch up on all the mundane domestic tasks that had built up over the intervening months, but this year they would have to wait. I was due to visit my father at his New York home in just a few days' time.

Opening the inner door to the flat, I sighed as I always did when confronted with the chaos that lay beyond. Piles of books covered most surfaces, as well as a large portion of the floor, while a pinboard groaned under the weight of flyers, postcards and illegible scribbles reminding me to do things that I shamefully never got around to. The clean but damp laundry that I'd tossed across the back of the sofa yesterday meaning to hang up was still there, as was the bag of groceries I had dumped on the small kitchen table. Checking inside, I was relieved to find no perishables, although I did discover an errant sock by the washing machine and a deflated string of tights draped half-in and half-out of the drum. A vase of near-dead flowers was festering on the coffee table in front of the settee, and it looked as if the wardrobe in my bedroom had suffered a bad case of clothes poisoning, because it had spewed most of its contents across the carpet.

Using my foot to push half-heartedly at the mess, I closed the bedroom door and made straight for the fridge, helping myself to a Diet Coke before slumping in my favourite chair beside the window. From here, I could just make out the majestic soft-gold spires of King's College Chapel, and it was a view that never failed to lift my mood. I loved living this close to the heart of the city, not remotely put off, as many would be, by the constant stream of tourists, students and cyclists. Noise had never bothered me, and while solitude was often mooted as an ally of any aspiring writer, I found it unnerving; all that silence spilling in and suffocating my inspiration. *Or lack thereof*, whispered my subconscious.

I longed to retrieve my laptop from beneath whichever pile of stuff it was buried and start writing something – anything – but the truth was, I had no idea where to start. Every novel I began, only to abandon, represented another fissure in the foundation of my self-confidence, and over the years it had broken down into little more than rubble. I was incapable of completing anything – not the washing, not the door repainting, not even a simple text message half the time. The only thing of note I had been involved in finishing since university was my relationship with my ex, Felix. As achievements went, it fell so far short that it barely reached the kerb.

I could still recall the events of that day in cruel detail: Felix's features crumpling, the tremble in his hand as he realised that no, I wasn't joking; his eyes, pale and serious, pleading with me to see sense. I'd told him how I felt, and he'd tried to barter, to come up with a timeline, a plan, a 'do or admit defeat' schedule that we could both agree was fair. But I wouldn't. *Couldn't.* And in the end, I had left him with no choice.

I stood abruptly, my agitation fuelling me into action, and began to work my way methodically through the household chores. I tidied and wiped, sorted and arranged, removed bins and organised recycling. I cleaned my teeth to rid my mouth of the dusty Diet Coke aftertaste, then promptly drank another, wincing as the sweeteners clashed revoltingly with the spearmint. The more tasks I ticked off, the better I felt. I had gained back a modicum of control over my life and I clung to the sensation, coming up with more and more outlandish jobs in order to maintain it. I pushed around the vacuum cleaner, refolded the towels, went through the teetering stack of unopened post and watered my gasping collection of plants. It was only when I was considering tackling the ironing that the fog mercifully cleared. Glancing around at my much tidier surroundings, I allowed myself a small smile of triumph and went to prepare some lunch. I was halfway through constructing a cheese and pickle sandwich when my mum rang.

'Are you in?' she asked, hanging up as soon as I confirmed that I was. A few seconds later, the door on street level was opened, and she hurried upstairs into the flat.

'Never know if you might have company,' she said, as breezily as she could. My mother worried about me being alone – it was one of many things the two of us had in common.

'How's Jojo?' she asked, shaking her head to the offer of a drink. 'One more coffee and I'll be ready to compete in the Boat Race singlehandedly.'

I explained about fish tank man, and she shook her head in bemusement. 'At least Jojo continues to try, I suppose.'

'Before you say anything, remember that I choose not to date,' I said, between mouthfuls of sandwich. 'Too much else going on.'

My mum was diplomatic enough not to argue with me. I watched as she twisted her dark hair around a finger, going to chew the ends and then thinking better of it. I had inherited my colouring from her, but the shape of my face and the features within it were all my father's. Like her, I was shorter than average at a little over five feet, but while a stint on the university hockey team followed by over a decade of daily cycling had helped me compile a fair amount of muscle, my mum had remained willowy. Not that she wasn't tough, however. Nobody spends their entire career lugging around crates of books without gaining some strength.

'Looking forward to your trip overseas?' she asked. My mum always stoically referred to the time I spent with my father as a 'trip overseas'.

'I'm hoping it will inspire me,' I admitted. I hadn't meant to tell her about the writing competition, but for some reason I felt compelled in the moment to do so, even though I knew exactly what her response would be. Nobody wanted me to achieve my ambition of becoming a published author more than my mum. Her passion for reading and writing had led her into her first job as a book publicist, which in turn had set her on the path to meeting my father and eventually having me. When single motherhood had warranted a change in lifestyle and living arrangements, she'd returned from London to the city she grew up in and found part-time work as a bookseller, eventually taking over the business when the elderly couple who ran the shop retired. Books, she was fond of telling me, had given her everything.

'I worry that I'm not going to have a good enough idea in time,' I confided, gripped by the same fear that I'd tried so gallantly to push back against all morning. 'What if I try only to fail?'

My mother smiled at me rather sadly, then reached across and took my hand in hers. 'I'm sure there are many quotes by people far more intelligent than me about failure,' she said. 'But I'm guessing platitudes aren't what you need right now?'

I shook my head.

'In that case,' she said, 'all I'll say is this: failure is only guaranteed if you don't even try. The only way you can know for sure if anything will work out is by giving it your best shot. That's all any of us can do. If you never try, you'll never know.'

'I'm pretty sure that last part is a song lyric,' I told her.

My mother's smile withered a fraction.

'If I were you,' she went on, 'I'd put the competition out of your mind. Just start writing a book that feels right to you; write it for yourself and no one else.'

I nodded in agreement, made all the right noises, and praised her for being so wise, yet inside I was conflicted. I didn't know how to do what she said. The very concept felt childlike to me, a rule decreed by someone who had no authority to make it. The fact was, I would not be writing this or any other book for myself, for her, or even for a competition. I would be writing it as a means to an end, for someone else entirely.

3

I was eight years old the first time I met my father.

It happened on a Saturday. I knew it was a weekend because Mum had let me have Coco Pops for my breakfast. On school days, she insisted on Weetabix. She told me it was because I needed proper fuel for my developing brain, but all I knew was that I much preferred the chocolatey cereal – especially when the box came with a toy hidden inside. On that morning, I had tipped the box over the bowl and a plastic monkey figurine had toppled out.

'He's green for luck.'

Mum smiled at me, although her expression did not match her tone of voice. I often noticed this when I was a child and wondered if it was an unavoidable symptom of getting older, like hair falling out or wrinkles forming. Luck also struck me as a strange thing to need on the day you were going to meet your dad, who I had no doubt would love me. And so, I fished the toy out of the bowl and handed it to her.

'I don't need it, Mum. You can have it.'

We took the train from Cambridge down to London, me in the window seat and Mum beside me, holding open a novel but never turning a single page. The countryside hurried past, a green blur interrupted by flashes of grey road, red-roofed houses, and the white smears of sheep. I wanted to play I-Spy, but everything flashed out of sight too quickly, so instead we started a game of storytelling. Mum said, 'Once upon a time, there was a blue cat who loved balloons,' and I continued by saying, 'but he never had them for very long, because his claws were too sharp,' and on we went. Even then, I understood that stories were like magic. I had boarded the train knowing nothing about that blue cat, but by the time we rolled into King's Cross station, he had a name, friends, a topsy-turvy house, and had learned how to knit anti-balloon-bursting mittens. I liked him so much that I wanted to get out my pens and notebook and write the story down, but Mum said there wasn't time.

'We don't want to be late for Jeff.'

That was she called my father. I wasn't sure what to call him. It had always been 'Dad' inside my head, but whenever I attempted to say it out loud, it made me feel strange, as if my tongue had grown three times too large for my mouth. As I thought about this, my earlier resolve that I had nothing to worry about abandoned me, and I had to stop walking in order to breathe properly.

'Honor?' Mum crouched until her nose was level with mine. 'Nervous?' she guessed, and I nodded. I didn't want to speak in case I started to cry.

'There's nothing to worry about,' she soothed. 'I bet Jeff is every bit as jumpy about meeting you as you are him.'

From the little I knew about my father, who was already successful enough to have his books displayed in shop windows, this did not seem right.

'Are you sure he'll like me?' I asked.

Mum's face seemed to collapse inwards. 'Of course he will,' she said. 'You, Honor Butler, are one of a kind. Just be you, and the rest will take care of itself.'

Like a fool, I believed her, and off we went.

The restaurant had high ceilings and a polished floor that made a pleasing sound beneath the soles of my smart red shoes. Mum had taken me to get them specially, and then we'd chosen a skirt that matched. I usually wore shorts and trainers, but I was grateful she'd insisted I make an effort in this instance, because all the other diners were very smartly dressed. The men were in suit jackets and ties, while the women wore strings of pearls and silky-looking blouses. Almost every table we passed was occupied, but nobody appeared to be talking very much and nobody so much as glanced at me.

I opened my mouth to say something, only to fall silent as a man stood up just ahead of us. This was he, my dad. I could feel it, in the same way I felt a cold edge in the air moments before it rained. I took him in, absorbing his height, his dark eyes, his neatly combed hair, and the mouth that only seemed to smile on one side. He was familiar yet unknown, and I was unnerved.

I dropped my gaze to the floor, listening in silence as he greeted my mum. He called her 'Jennifer', and I wanted to tell him that was wrong, that her friends called her 'Jenny' or 'Jen', but never Jennifer. When he turned his attention to me, I stiffened.

'You must be Honor,' he said, his American accent making my name sound longer than it was.

I made myself look at him. 'Your smile is wonky,' I said, to which he laughed. A great, big, loud laugh.

'It sure is,' he replied. 'Will you show me yours, so we can compare?'

I may only have been eight, but I knew what he was doing, how he was attempting to tease a reaction from me. All the same, I smiled.

'Darn it!' he cried, slapping a hand against his leg. 'Well yours is about as symmetrical as they come.'

He had scaled the first awkward hurdle and elicited a giggle from me. We sat at the table, and he asked me all sorts of questions about my school, my friends, and my hobbies. When I told him that what I enjoyed most was writing, he looked pleased.

'Honor actually won a school prize for a poem she wrote,' said Mum. She had turned very pink, and I wondered if the soup she'd ordered was too spicy.

'She did?' My dad turned to me as he forked up some salad.

'Her teachers think she has real raw talent.'

'That's just great, honey,' he said. 'Although, if you want to be rich when you grow up, you're probably better off writing novels. Not much money in poetry.'

'She does stories, too,' Mum said. 'Show him your book, Honor.'

She nodded at me encouragingly, and I reached under my chair for my rucksack. The notebook inside was something I was very proud of. The top half of each page was blank, to add a picture, while the lower part was lined, ready for the words to be filled in. So far, I'd written over thirty stories, and after flicking through it for a few minutes, I selected one involving a time-travelling penguin before passing it across.

My father took the book and fell into silence as he read. I waited for him to chuckle as he came to the part about my feathered hero's legs being too short to ride the penny-farthing, but his expression did not so much as flicker.

'Cute,' he said eventually, closing the book and putting it down on the table.

'Cute' was the word people used to describe kittens or newborn babies. I shifted uncomfortably in my chair, unsure what to say.

'Honor did all the research into the Victorian era herself,' Mum told him. 'Took a book out from the library and noted down all the things that interested her. I think it's a marvellous story,' she added, and I wasn't sure which of us she was addressing.

'I can see that a lot of thought went into it,' said my dad. 'But there's too much in there about how Mr Penguin feels, rather than descriptions of what he gets up to.'

Discomfort, like creeping ivy, spread through my body. I felt hot and sick and angry.

'People read stories because they want to feel excited,' he told me. 'It's your job to take them on an adventure, which you could have done with Mr Penguin here, if you hadn't spent so long telling the reader how much he missed the friends he'd left behind. Nobody is really going to care about that.'

I'd cared about the penguin, had worried that his decision to travel through time would mean he ended up lonely, but I had clearly got it wrong. My dad was the proper author, after all. I snatched up the exercise book and stuffed it back into my bag, not caring when it caught on the zip and some of the pages ripped. I resolved that I would throw it in the bin the first chance I got and start a new one.

My shame receded as our lunch continued, but the anger I felt towards my mum hardened. I tallied her lies as I solemnly ate my chips, recalling all the occasions she'd told me how gifted I was at writing, how if I put my heart and soul into my stories people would love and admire them no matter what. She had made me believe that my interpretation of the world was enough – that I was enough. But I wasn't, not in my father's eyes. I had disappointed him, and that left me with only one option.

I had to become someone else, someone new, someone better.

For him.

4

I had, for quite some time, been in love with New York.

I loved the contrasts of the city, the sprays of green park nestled between concrete towers; modern sculptures arranged on plinths in the courtyards of 19th century churches; how you could listen to birdsong and sit among nature up on the High Line before emerging moments later into a world of car horns, rising steam and the vibrations of trains hurtling past underground. She was grandeur and grime, friendly yet challenging, and every moment thrummed with possibility.

When I'd first visited as a teenager, it was the lights and sounds that enthralled me, but as I grew to know both the city and myself better, I realised it was more the attitude of New York that appealed to me – it was a place where things happened because people believed that they would. And on this trip, more than any other, I needed to put my faith in her.

Congenial as ever, my father had offered to send a car to the airport to collect me, but as usual I politely declined. After sitting for over seven hours in a plane, the last thing I wanted was to be trapped for another ninety minutes on the highway, as the heavy commuter traffic crawled its way towards the city. Instead, I took the Air Train to Jamaica station, then caught an F line Metro down to West 23rd Street and walked the final few blocks to where my father lived, in relative luxury, across the top two floors of a five-storey apartment building.

It was nearing eight p.m., but the sweltering heat of the day had carried through into the evening. I could feel its humid mass pressing against me as I waited to cross the road. My hair, carefully blow-dried the previous day, hung lank around my shoulders, while the jeans I'd travelled in clung uncomfortably to my legs. I could smell dust and exhaust fumes, the rich and doughy scent of baked bread, and as I trundled my case past a local pizzeria, I picked up a note of paraffin from the small lamps on each outdoor table.

From all around there was the sound of voices, some raucous, others subdued; a tinkle of laughter and an obscenity shouted in jest. An elderly man asked me if I needed directions, his smile when I said I was fine genuine enough to raise one of my own in reply. I knew I was seeing, hearing and sensing the unfurling bud of another night in the world's most enigmatic city, and wondered how I could ever hope to condense it into words, how anyone could really hope to capture the essence of a constantly evolving beast such as New York.

I strayed so far into my own meandering thoughts that I barely registered I'd arrived at my destination. After hoisting my case up the steps to the imposing front door, I located the panel with 'J. Butler' embossed in gold and pressed the buzzer.

Nothing.

I tried again.

Still nothing.

I was gearing up for a third go when there was a crackling sound, followed by what sounded like a woman's voice and then a low whirring clunk as the locking mechanism sprang open. Assuming I must have been let in by a well-meaning neighbour, I took the lift up to my father's apartment half-expecting nobody to be in, so was surprised to find the door standing ajar.

'Hello?' I called over the threshold, unwilling to go inside until expressly invited. I was being ridiculous, of course – I was this man's daughter, not a vampire out to drain his blood.

'Hey,' called a voice, definitely female. 'I have a pan on the stove – come on through.'

My father lived alone; of that I was fairly certain. Mystified, I took a step backwards and examined the number on the door, checking that I hadn't somehow ended up on the wrong floor. But no, I was in the right place.

'OK,' I called back.

Making my way inside, I closed the door quietly behind me. The hallway that led into the main body of the apartment was decorated with framed book covers, and there was also a photograph of my father at his graduation ceremony, sporting that strange, half-masted smile of his. There were no pictures of me, nor of the two of us together, and I tried not to let that sting me as I parked my case against the wall and stepped tentatively through the open-plan lounge. Tan leather sofas were arranged around three sides of an enormous jute rug, each angled not towards a television but the windows, all of which offered floor-to-ceiling views across the city. A Great Dane-sized cactus lurked menacingly beside a bar trolley, upon which a number of bottles gleamed in the soft light of a Tiffany lamp. The lid of my father's treasured record player was propped open, but the stylus was poised upwards, the turntable below it bare. I worried fleetingly of dust and made an instinctive move to lower it. During one of my visits here as a clumsy seventeen year old, I'd accidentally scratched one of his prized Sinatra records, and the resulting sulk had lasted the best part of a week.

A crash emanated from the kitchen, followed by a cheerful volley of swear words. Bemused by this and more than a little intrigued as to the identity of the mystery cook, I ceased my dithering and went to investigate, opening the door to a wall of steam.

'Hello,' I said, waving a hand in front of my face. Through the fog, I could just about see the figure of a tall, slim woman, clutching the handle of a saucepan.

'Just a second!' she said, without looking up, and I waited while she gingerly carried the pan to the sink. There was a loud hissing sound, and another cloud of steam filled the room.

'Here, let me help you.'

I crossed to the window before she had the chance to reply, levering it open and watching with satisfaction as the hot air funnelled out into the night.

'That's better,' I said, turning to face her and finding a bright smile waiting to greet me. She looked to be around my age or perhaps few years older, although the facial bone structure below her piled-up nest of tawny hair was exquisite enough to render any contouring palette redundant.

'You must Honor,' she said. 'I'm Tallulah.'

It was clear from her expression that she presumed some sort of prior knowledge on my part, so it was with a certain amount of embarrassment that I then had to ask her to elaborate.

'JB didn't tell you I'd be here?' she asked.

I leaned against the worktop, hands twisting together as I shook my head. 'No, I'm afraid not.'

She laughed at that, wiping her hands on the front of her cream linen trousers before gesturing to the sink.

'You hungry at all? I made pasta and some tomato sauce. I mean, it might well be inedible, but I figure it's better than chomping on thin air.'

'Sounds good,' I said. 'Do you need any help?'

Tallulah considered. 'There's some Pinot Grigio in the fridge,' she said. 'Why don't you pour that while I attempt to salvage something out of this mess?'

'How many glasses shall I—?'

'It's just us two for now. JB's out at some talk, but he won't be long.'

She still hadn't told me how she knew my father, or why she was apparently living with him. The only assumption I could make was that she must be his partner, but in all the years I'd known him, he'd never moved a girlfriend in. Either Tallulah was a very special case, or there was another explanation for her being here. She certainly seemed very at home, and I could tell from the casual way she navigated the kitchen, sourcing a jar of capers from the fridge, a grater for the Parmesan, and the pepper grinder from beside the toaster, that she was more than just a dinner guest.

We took our plates through into the dining area and sat together at one end of my father's long oak table.

'To not setting the place on fire,' Tallulah said, raising her glass towards mine.

There was nothing about her demeanour that suggested she was nervous, as one might assume a romantic partner would be around the daughter of their new love interest, but that could be explained away by the fact she was American, and therefore born with bundles of confidence slipped in among strands of her DNA.

I clinked my glass against hers and took a large sip. The wine was ice cold and delicious, its faint lemon undertone rousing my taste buds from their plane-food-induced coma.

'So,' I said, deciding to forego any more small talk, 'how long have you and JB been an item?'

Tallulah gawped at me. 'Oh, no. You thought that—? That's hilarious.'

'You're not together?'

She laughed with such force that it caused her forkful of tagliatelle to wobble.

I sorted through my mind for alternatives: housekeeper? Long-lost relative? Work colleague? None seemed plausible somehow.

'You're going to have to help me out here.'

Tallulah smiled. 'JB's been helping me with my writing. He's . . . I guess you could call him my mentor.'

It was my turn to gape incredulously. 'Your mentor?'

'Yeah. He really didn't tell you about it?'

I shook my head.

'Typical JB,' she said, apparently privy to my father's every quirky trait. 'And there was me thinking that I was a special case.'

'I'm sorry,' I said, putting down my cutlery, 'but I'm still not sure I understand.'

'Well, the thing is,' she began, leaning towards me conspiratorially, 'I've always been a huge fan of his, and I've been trying for years to get my own writing career off the ground, so I thought I would message him, you know? Just a little tweet to say how much I admired him. JB then got back to me, we started talking, and a couple of days later he asked if he could take a look at my stuff.'

Knowing how abrasive my father could be when it came to critiquing someone's writing, I winced in preparatory sympathy.

Tallulah, however, could not have looked more content as she then said, 'Imagine my surprise when he told me how much he'd enjoyed reading it. I mean, come on – *the* Jeffrey Butler, emailing to tell *me* that he could see real potential in my work. I honestly thought he was pulling my chain.'

'He doesn't really do jokes,' I remarked, but if Tallulah noticed my rather droll tone, she didn't let on. Instead, she merely shrugged and helped herself to more wine.

'How did chats about writing lead to you moving in?' I asked. 'Because you are living here, aren't you?'

'Only temporarily,' she replied. 'JB and me, we got to talking a lot more often as the weeks went by, and then he asked if I had any free time over the summer. I didn't at that stage, but I managed to move some stuff around after I heard what he was offering.'

'Which was?' It was an unnecessary prompt, because I could tell that Tallulah was enjoying relating her story.

'Get this,' she confided, 'he said he'd take me on as his live-in assistant for a few months, and as well as paying me for my time, he'd also give me feedback on my writing, so it works really well for both of us.'

I was in the midst of processing this information when Tallulah switched topic and began telling me about her current work-in-progress, a darkly humorous modern tale about the warring factions of a wealthy American family. It sounded so much more ambitious, intellectual and grown-up than any of my pathetic attempts, and I burned with shame as I pictured all the half-finished flimsy romcoms gathering the cyber equivalent of dust on my computer. The contrasts between myself and Tallulah could not have been more pronounced. She had all the gusto that I lacked, not to mention the self-belief required to make something of herself, and she had also secured the one thing that I had been reaching for my entire life.

My father's undivided attention.

5

'Shall I grab us another bottle?'

Tallulah had just watched in bemused fascination as I upended what was left of the first one into my glass.

Whatever the speaking version of writer's block was, I appeared to have developed a severe case of it in the past few minutes and could no more answer her question than I could have tap-danced up the side of the Empire State Building.

Taking my continued silence as an affirmative, Tallulah pushed back her chair only to pause halfway to her feet. I had, like her, heard the muffled ding of the elevator doors, and so we were both staring towards the hallway when my father came into sight.

Jeffrey Butler wore his sixty-five years well, the Harrison Ford good looks enduring despite the greying of his once-dark hair. He was still lithe and broad-shouldered, the eyes behind his tortoiseshell-framed glasses every bit as steely, while the chinos and shirt he wore were impeccably cut. I had never been able to look at him and not marvel at the fact that he was my father. And I doubted that would ever change.

'Ladies,' he said.

I found my voice. 'Hi.'

'Great to see you, honey.' He crossed to the table and kissed me briefly on the cheek. 'How was the journey – awful? Poor Honor has to fly coach,' he told Tallulah. 'One of these days, she'll agree to let me bump her up to premium.'

'I still can't believe you actually have a grown-up daughter,' Tallulah observed. 'You don't look old enough, nowhere near.'

I drained what was left in my glass.

'I'll go get that bottle.' Tallulah strode towards the kitchen. 'Shall I fetch a glass for you, JB?'

'No, thanks. Think I'll hop on the bourbon. Long night,' he said to me, making his way to the bar trolley. 'The event ran over, and then I had to stay on and do a signing.'

'Right,' I said, watching as he selected a whiskey tumbler and held it up to the light. 'Grubby,' he muttered, pulling out the bottom of his shirt to give the rim a polish. I searched for something interesting to say.

'Book going well?'

My enquiry was superfluous. None of my father's novels ever had a sales trajectory line that did not go straight up. I found the idea of even five people reading a book I'd written miraculous, yet my father sounded coolly blasé as he reeled off first full-week's sales figures that were well into the tens of thousands.

'And that's just over here in the States,' he said, pouring a measure of amber liquid over the ice in his glass before swiftly topping it up with a second. 'The international numbers are projected to be far higher.'

'That's incredible,' I told him honestly. 'Mindboggling.'

Tallulah had returned with the wine, and a third helping of the pasta, but my father shook his head.

'Better not,' he said, tapping a hand against his flat stomach. 'Not now I have confirmation on the beach house.'

'You do?'

Tallulah, rather disconcertingly, jumped up and down and clapped her hands together. 'That's so great.'

My father took the seat closest to hers and removed his glasses, placing them on the table beside his glass of bourbon as he rubbed his eyes.

'It had better be,' he said, 'given how much green I had to lay down to get it.'

My father was inordinately fond of telling people how much 'green' he'd had to lay down on various things. Money did not embarrass him as a topic of conversation – a quirk I'd always attributed to the fact that he had plenty of it.

'What beach house is this?' I queried, as Tallulah sat down and put her bare feet up on the edge of my father's chair. A lock of her red-gold hair had come loose from its clip, and I watched as she attempted to tuck it away behind her ear. She was one of those people who seemed to move constantly, while in contrast, my father preferred to sit still and quiet, ruminating over what he should do or say next as opposed to letting his actions speak for him. I often found myself twitchy in his presence and wondered if Tallulah – who was now drumming her fingers against her chin – had been similarly affected.

'Your dad's managed to get a summer rental,' she enthused, not waiting for him to confirm before she continued, 'which is really hard to do this late in the season. He's a regular miracle worker.'

My father, I noted, accepted the compliment with a knowing smile.

'What can I say?' he said. 'Lady luck has long been on my side, and clearly she hasn't grown tired of me yet.'

'When you say beach?' I prompted, and again it was Tallulah who replied.

'We mean The Hamptons,' she said. 'Southampton, to be precise.'

I'd seen depictions of The Hamptons in films and television shows and knew that it was a playground for the rich and famous, but not much beyond that. The south fork of Long Island might only have been a few hours' away from New York City, but my father had never suggested visiting before, and it had not occurred to me to do so either. When I was in the States, it was to spend time with him – or at least be close by if and when his schedule allowed him to factor me in.

'And when you say summer rental,' I went on, 'how long do you mean?'

Tallulah blinked at me as if confused. 'The whole summer,' she said. 'Often folks will just spend the weekends over there, but when you're lucky enough to take your office with you wherever you go . . .' She trailed off, demurring at last to my father, who was making short work of his bourbon.

'We'll be spending most of the next two months out there,' he told me, and again Tallulah clapped her hands together with ill-disguised glee. 'I have a deadline and Tallulah here is writing the next Oprah Book Club hit, so I figured it made sense to get out of the city for once.'

This from the man who once told me that all self-respecting writers should base themselves in the most densely populated places on Earth because 'cities are human zoos, and you don't have to pay for a ticket to gawp at the animals'. I decided against reminding him of this.

'Sounds like a good plan,' I said loyally. 'When do you go?'

For the first time in my living memory of him, my father's expression turned sheepish.

'Yeah, about that,' he said, swirling the ice around in his glass and not looking at me. 'Unfortunately, honey, you might have to cut your trip short. The house will be ready by the end of Friday, and I'd like to be in and settled ready for the working week.'

Today was Wednesday. I frowned. 'You want me to leave?'

'No, God no.' He reached across and patted my hand. 'You can stay on here in the apartment if you want. I just figured that you wouldn't want to, not on your own.'

'But I only just got here,' I began, aware of a crushing sensation inside my chest. 'It will cost me loads to change my flight.' My voice had gone up an octave, and there was a whining undertone that became more pronounced with each word.

'I can take care of that for you,' he said easily. 'Maybe treat you to that first-class ticket at last.'

I'd been in the city less than four hours, and already he was rejecting me. In desperation, I glanced towards Tallulah; saw her flinch as she recognised the anguish in my pleading eyes. Putting down her glass, she cleared her throat noisily.

'I'm sure Honor doesn't have to go, does she?' she said slowly, thinking on her propped-up feet. 'Why can't she just come out to the beach with us? It's simple enough for her to catch a train back to JFK from there, and that way I'll have a girlfriend to hang out with while you're busy working. It won't affect my work,' she added, when it looked as if my father was going to argue. 'And if anything, it'll help you with yours. Do you really want me hanging around all day long, distracting you?'

'But Honor came to see the city, didn't you, honey?'

He was trying to lead me away from accompanying them, and it rankled. I barely ever questioned my father's decisions, but on this occasion, I had an ally on my team for once.

'I came to see you,' I told him. 'New York is a bonus, of course, but it's not the reason I'm here.'

'You see!' Tallulah stood up and started clearing away plates. 'And this way, we all get what we want. You two get to spend time together, and I get someone to help me put tanning oil on my back. It's a win-win, JB.'

She had said the magic word, his favourite above all others. I had practically seen the lights go on in his eyes as she uttered it.

Because, as I knew only too well, there was nothing that mattered more to my father than being the best. It was just a shame that for every win in life, there must also be a loss. And it always seemed to be mine to bear.

6

The Long Island Rail Road train departed from Jamaica station at a little after midday, its gentle lurching motion soothing Tallulah off to sleep just as we cleared the outskirts of the city.

She had spent most of the night writing, she explained, as she kicked off her trainers and shuffled into a more comfortable position, and would not have been awake at all if not for the three cans of energy drink she'd consumed before we left the apartment. My father, who had several meetings lined up with movie executives, would be driving out to join us in The Hamptons the following day. This, he claimed, would give us time to settle in, although I guessed what he meant by that was it would give Tallulah time to get things just as he liked them. On the single occasion that I'd invited him to stay with me on the Cambridge stop of a UK book tour, he had found fault with practically everything. My mattress was too soft, my windows too small, the shower too weak, the coffee even weaker. He'd vowed never to stray from hotel accommodation again, and I'd cried for two days straight.

It was a searingly hot day, the sun so far obscured by a thick duvet of cloud. Tallulah had promised me it would be cooler by the coast, explaining that the main reason people packed up and went to The Hamptons every weekend was to escape the cloying humidity that permeated New York City in the summertime. I'd spent the previous day revisiting some of my favourite haunts – Strand Books on Broadway, Bryant Park in Midtown, Los Mariscos in Chelsea Market for a ceviche tostada lunch followed by a leisurely stroll through Battery Park – and collected an unfortunate backpack tan line in the process.

Tallulah had started to snore, and I smiled as I took in the slack-jawed expression of contentment on her face. It was impossible not to be envious of her, but there was a genuine fondness there as well. We'd not spent enough time together yet for me to know her in a meaningful way, but I was intrigued to find out more, to slow down the positive spin she put on everything and examine all her details.

People had always fascinated me. I wanted to understand who they were, how they had been shaped, and what made them unique. I'd long studied everyone I came into contact with, whether that was close friends, family members, or the train conductor who had checked my ticket moments ago, his jaunty cap positioned just so. When I couldn't ask for a potted history of their lives, I built one in my mind, constructing a possible personality from the clues I had picked up. Tallulah, I decided, was overcompensating for something, perhaps a sad or traumatic event from her past that she was doing her best to forget. Either that, or she was deeply insecure, her sole reason for commandeering every conversation a kind of armour to protect her from any subjects she did not have the confidence to discuss. She was full of sweet bravado, but I sensed a disquiet that she was battling to hide.

Almost without realising it, I'd taken a notebook from my bag and started to write, sketching out the beginning of a character that was rapidly taking shape in my mind. A woman, young but world weary – someone who had experienced the sharper tip of life far too soon and had been emotionally scarred as a result of it. I wrote down what she looked like, which musical artists she listened to, who her best friend was, and the kind of food she made to comfort herself. I listed her political beliefs, her academic achievements, her go-to sandwich filler of choice, and with every addition I made, she became larger, fuller and more real. I filled one page, then another, a white noise descending until I was wholly consumed by her, this new person, a beginning of a story that could be something. My hand began to ache, and I shook it, rubbing it against my leg to get the circulation flowing.

One thought slithered through my defences, and I settled on it until it flashed in neon brightness through all the others. 'Look at you, Honor,' it said. 'You're writing.'

I paused and began to read back over everything I'd scribbled down, pleased with my progress save for one small detail – I'd yet to give my character a family. Who she was would ultimately be determined by those who had raised her, but as I brought my pen down to fill in the gaps, I froze. I did not want this person I'd created to have the same issues that I had, but the only faces I could see as I stared downwards were those belonging to my own parents. There they were, the barricade I could never hurdle, the suffocating truth of them as impenetrable as stone.

Groaning, I slumped in my seat. I could feel the compulsion to write draining away, but I had no fight in me to claw it back. It was a start, I told myself. Proof that when inspiration struck, I did have the potential to create something worthwhile.

Stowing my notebook back in my bag, I took out the dog-chewed copy of *Idol* magazine that Jojo had given me and flicked to the competition page, reading once again through the terms and conditions, the requirements for entry, and details of that incredible prize – one with the power to change someone's life. I had convinced myself that I not only wanted to win it, I needed to win it.

'Where are we?'

I'd not noticed Tallulah rousing from her nap, and almost threw the magazine across the carriage in fright.

'I don't know,' I admitted. 'I haven't really been paying attention.'

Tallulah shifted across to the window seat, rubbing her eyes as she did so. 'Don't worry,' she said a few seconds later, 'we're just about to pull into Westhampton – not quite there yet.'

'Phew!' I pretended to mop my brow. 'Thank goodness you woke up.'

'Yeah,' she agreed, delving into her slouchy suede bag and extracting a small tube of hand lotion. 'We might have ended up stranded in Montauk for the night.'

'Would that have been a bad thing?'

'I guess not.' She shrugged, rubbing cream into her knuckles. 'Montauk is nice and all, but Southampton is neater, you know? Like, tidier.'

'I'll have to take your word for it.'

'Must be a good magazine, if it's distracting you from peering into people's backyards,' she said, gesturing to the view. She was not wrong – from our position up on the second deck of the train, it was indeed possible to see into the rear gardens of every property we passed. Most contained some kind of pool, and I saw a deer standing in the shade of a tree in another.

'It's a great read if you happen to be interested in celebrities,' I replied, flipping the magazine over so she could see. The cover featured a blurred photo of a man, a baseball cap pulled down over his eyes and a hand raised to shield his face. 'NIGHT FLIGHT OF MR RIGHT' declared the headline, below which was a lurid pink squiggle informing us that the full story was on page ten.

'Oh my God – is that—? May I?'

Tallulah took it from me and located the feature. 'I knew it was him,' she said, and began to read aloud.

'Following an eight-week stint at the Second Chances Centre in Malibu, Hollywood heart-throb Cellan Thomas is back out and ready to live his best hot guy summer.

'In these pictures – obtained exclusively by Idol magazine – the British-born actor, who recently turned 35, can be seen doing his best to remain incognito as he sneaked out of the rehab facility under cover of darkness last weekend.

'(Sorry, Cellan, but we would recognise those razor-sharp cheekbones anywhere!)

'Idol can also exclusively reveal that his long-term on/off girlfriend – Californian model-turned nutritionist to the stars, Wylie Brooke – will likely be joining him at his luxury East Coast home very soon. The pair split shortly after having a public spat in New York over the Easter weekend, but a source close to both parties tells us, "Wylie loves Cellan deeply and is looking forward to helping him heal with her new diet plan, Clean & Supreme, which focuses on curing the body from the gut up. She is a forgiving person with a pure soul and understands that Cellan was not himself at the time of their break-up. Friends are hopeful of an engagement announcement by the end of the summer, after which Cellan is keen to return to his busy acting schedule."

'Idol spoke to an industry insider, who explained, "Cellan entered rehab not long after winning his first Academy Award for Mr Right, so many of the offers he may have received as a result of that could well have expired by now. If he wants to maintain his place at the top of the 'hottest property in

*Hollywood' list, he'll need to take on a big blockbuster project
sooner rather than later."*

*'Cellan – who pronounces his name "Keff-lan" – has never
revealed his reason for seeking treatment at Second Chances,
but Idol understands that his widely reported issues with
alcohol are the likely cause. Given that the star himself looks
like a long, tall drink of something deliciously dark and stormy,
we can't say that we're surprised – or that we could resist his
charms any more than he can apparently resist the bottle.*

*We hope you're feeling better soon, Cef! And don't worry
– if you fall off the wagon again, Idol magazine will be more
than happy to catch you . . .'*

Tallulah lowered the magazine with a sad sort of sigh. 'Poor
guy,' she said.

I nodded. I could see why she might feel sorry for this
actor, but I found it all a bit dramatic. Cellan Thomas had to
be one of the most famous people in the world at the moment,
yet apparently no amount of untold riches, critical acclaim
and Oscar statuettes could make him happy. He was probably
a man into whose lap everything had always landed neatly.
There seemed to be a lot of them around.

'I'm sure once he's in his luxury mansion, relaxing in a
bath full of bank notes, he'll feel much better,' I said, and
Tallulah smiled.

'I guess that's true.'

The train was beginning to slow again. I could hear the
weary wail of the brakes as a water tower came into view, the
name Hampton Bays emblazoned across its front.

'One stop to go,' Tallulah announced. 'I'm going to go and
use the restroom.'

I watched her weave away along the carriage, long skirt
rippling, and started to check that I'd repacked everything

into my bag. The magazine was on the empty seat beside me, still open at the story about Cellan Thomas, and for a moment I found myself drawn in by the haunted expression behind his dark eyes. I knew that look, and recognising it made a coldness steal over me.

Turning to the page that featured the writing competition, I carefully tore it out and slipped it inside my notebook for safe keeping. The rest of the magazine I screwed up and shoved resolutely into the nearest bin.

There was nothing else in its pages that I cared about.

7

Southampton charmed me from the moment I stepped off the train.

The small platform was decorated with pots of bright red azaleas that had begun to wilt in the heat, although I had to allow that Tallulah was right – it was markedly cooler here than it had been in the stifling city. The breeze that greeted us was fresh, determined, and a little salty, and I did that thing all British people do when arriving by the seaside, and breathed in great gulps of it.

'Ah, the sea air,' I said, and Tallulah wrinkled her nose.

'Is that what it is?' she said. 'The only thing I can smell is the train.'

We dragged our luggage down the ramp and, after consulting the map on Tallulah's phone, turned right and followed the road down and under a low bridge. Immediately, I was struck by how different the pace of life was. The cars that passed us did so at little more than a crawl, and the walking pace of the few pedestrians we encountered was more of a meander than the bustle I was accustomed to back in New York. I could hear birdsong, the cicada-like fizz of sprinklers, and the rustle of wind in the trees, the only other sound our shoes against the asphalt of the path.

A large proportion of the surrounding houses were set back from the road behind swathes of immaculate lawn, and most had a star-spangled banner fixed either to pole or porch.

White picket fences marked the boundary between sidewalk and garden, and mailboxes stood sentry beside open gates. I understood why Tallulah had settled on 'neat' as her adjective of choice, because it was exactly the word I would have chosen. There was an overwhelming sense of everything being in its correct place, and of there being time to make it so.

'Over there.' Tallulah had stopped and was pointing across the road towards the opening of a narrow driveway. 'I think that's it.'

There was no need to wait for a break in the traffic because there wasn't any, and a few minutes later, the two of us were standing together staring up at our new home. I would only be here for ten days, but Tallulah would presumably remain until the season came to an end. The house was English-countryside-jigsaw-puzzle pretty, with a faded timber facade, white picture windows, and a gable roof that slanted lower on the far side. The grounds that encircled the property were an attractive blend of tidy, well-tended beds and shrubs, and there was a rustic swing hanging docile from the branches of a splendid oak. The grass underfoot was soft and springy, and rather than drag the wheels of my case across it, I lifted it up and carried it over to the front door. After rooting under several plant pots that were stacked to one side, Tallulah produced a large brass key, and we were in.

Given my father's love of heavy wooden furniture and musty old books, I was not surprised that he'd chosen to rent a place like this – with exposed floorboards, mustard walls, and antiquated fittings – rather than one of the sleeker, more modern properties that had been purpose built along the seafront.

While Tallulah headed off in search of the kitchen, I prowled along the upper landing, then ventured into the attic rooms, which included a sizeable lounge, a bedroom complete with walnut four-poster, and a bathroom that boasted a beautiful roll-top tub.

'Oh, this is adorable.' Tallulah had appeared in the doorway, one hand on her hip.

'Will you sleep up here?' I asked, but she shook her head.

'Afraid I've already staked my claim on the one with a shower in the en suite,' she said. 'I can't function in the morning without properly powerful jets of water pounding against my body, you know? Why don't you take it?'

I hesitated. I desperately wanted to take over this lair, but it was only fair that my father had the option, given that he was paying for the house. When I pointed this out to Tallulah, however, she waved a dismissive hand.

'JB's like me,' she said. 'He'll prefer to be closer to wherever the coffee is kept – trust me. And while I'm on the topic,' she added, as I flopped down happily on the bed, 'one of us is going to need to pop to the store. There's nothing in the fridge except bottled water.'

'I'll go,' I said. 'I'd like the opportunity to explore the place a bit.'

'It'll take you about twenty minutes to walk down to South Main Street,' she said, 'but I read that there's a bicycle in the outhouse.'

'Now that,' I said, bouncing back up onto my feet, 'sounds perfect.'

Pausing only to smear some sun cream onto my shoulders and fish out a Cambridge-branded baseball cap from my heap of belongings, I retrieved the decidedly rusty-looking steed from the garden shed and pedalled out into the sunshine. It felt glorious to be back in the saddle, even if the stuffing inside it had long since rotted away, and I felt the corners of my mouth twitch into a wide smile as my hair ribboned out behind me. The bike was a classic Dutch shape, with upright handlebars and a large wicker basket, and the tyres were in a surprisingly good state given how old the frame must be.

I pushed on, resting my feet as the road began to slope, allowing me to freewheel all the way down to the heart of the village. Tallulah had told me that the food market was on a road off to the left, but I decided to cycle the length of South Main Street first to get my bearings.

The road was wide – far wider than the spindly cobbled backstreets I was used to navigating in Cambridge – with ample space for cars to park on either side. Local cafés and restaurants were easy to spot on account of the tables and chairs that were arranged on the pavement in front of them, while clothing stores and gift boutiques did their best to draw in customers with stunning floral arches and colourful window displays. Wooden crates crammed with Aegean blue hydrangeas sat by benches next to foxgloves of the purest pastel pink, and painted fire hydrants in the brightest yellows and reds perched by the kerb. Bunting was strung between the plane trees that lined each side of the street, and I could see twists of fairy lights wrapped around the trunks. So much thought, care and consideration had gone into the tiniest details, and it made Southampton seem cared for and respected. I'd yet to see any dropped litter or graffiti, and even the rubbish bins were clean. It was about as far removed from my beloved New York City as it was possible to be, but I found the change of pace pleasantly calming. Perhaps, I dared to hope, The Hamptons would turn out to be an ideal setting for me to write without distractions.

Having reached the far end of the street, I dismounted at the crossing and wheeled the bicycle over to the opposite side, thinking that I would walk back up to the corner. I whistled as I strolled, taking it all in and smiling at the friendly greetings from passers-by. There was a bakery up ahead and I decided to buy some fresh bread. Readjusting my grip on the handlebars, I was momentarily distracted by a woman walking past with a Chihuahua that appeared to be wearing minuscule booties and didn't see the door to the hardware shop next to me being flung open. Nor did I see the man emerge through it at speed. In fact, all I did see was a dark blur of movement, followed by a shout of alarm. But it was too late to move, and a few seconds later I, the man, and the bicycle were all lying face down on the pavement.

8

'What the f—?' I cried, the last word swallowed up by the blood that was pooling into my mouth. Kneeling up, I gingerly raised a hand to check for broken teeth.

'Shit. I'm so sorry. Are you OK?'

'Of course I'm not,' I snapped, rooting in my bag for a tissue.

'Here.' The man stretched out the bottom of his T-shirt and offered it to me.

Glaring at him, I bent over to dab at the blood and wiped away the tears that had sprung out as my chin connected with the tarmac.

'I bit my tongue,' I said.

'Sorry, didn't quite catch that?'

'I. BIT. MY. TONGUE.'

'Oh. Well, shit. My bad. I might have been going a little fast.'

'You think?' I stormed, wincing as I stood. My right knee must have been under the pedals as I fell because there was a nasty scrape that was already beginning to bruise. The bike itself seemed mercifully to have survived intact, although the temptation to kick it was strong. Leaving it on the ground, I hobbled over to the nearest bench and sat down to inspect my stinging elbows.

'I really am sorry.'

The man was hovering behind me. He was British, I realised, with the hint of an accent I couldn't place. Turning to look, I saw that he wasn't staring at me, but towards the store he'd just come out of.

'Are you a shoplifter?' I asked.

That got his attention. 'No. Do I look like a thief to you?'

I considered him, took in the scruffy beard and the cap pulled down over sunglasses. 'You look like someone who's trying to hide.'

He smiled at that, a flash of straight, white teeth that looked very un-British to me. 'Truth?' he said, and I nodded. 'I was trying not to be seen. The thing is,' he went on, crouching so his face was level with mine, 'I get recognised sometimes, and most of the time I don't mind, but today . . . Let's just say, I can't face it.'

I frowned. Had I hit my head harder on the concrete than I thought, or had this man just admitted to me that he was a recognisable somebody?

'There are a couple of girls in there that I'm sure are on my tail,' he said, then, 'Oh shit!' Scuttling around to my side of the bench, he sat close beside me and threw a cautionary glance over his shoulder. 'I think they saw me through the window.'

'Are you taking the piss?' I asked. 'Is this one of those dumb hidden camera shows?'

'No. Although that would be preferable.'

'For you maybe,' I hit back.

The man did not reply, he was still too busy checking behind us for his apparently ardent fans. The front of his pale blue T-shirt was a mess of bloodstains but given that all the wounds were on me rather than him, I didn't feel all that bad about it. My mouth had stopped bleeding thankfully, but my tongue still throbbed.

'Who are you?' I asked. 'And don't tell me to guess because I haven't a clue.'

'You'll think it's weird,' he replied, hunkering down until only the very top of his cap would be visible from the hardware store.

'Try me. Oh, unless you're a porn star. I think I can cope with not knowing that.'

He chuckled. 'Definitely not a porn star. Chance would be a fine th—'

'OK, OK.' I held up a hand. 'I think I get the gist.'

'I'm a stuntman,' he confided, not without a certain amount of pride.

'Right.' I drew the word out, registering his ripped Vans, tatty jean shorts, and bitten-down fingernails. 'Is that why you felt the need to roll your way across the street like Indiana Jones straight into me? Were you getting a bit of practice in?'

He appraised me. 'You're funny.'

It had been a long time since I'd talked to a man in this easy back-and-forth way, and it felt nice to flex my flirtatious muscles. That said, I thought, wincing as I examined the torn skin on my knee, flexing anything was probably going to hurt for a while.

'You might need a bandage,' he said, leaning so close to me that the peaks of our caps collided. 'Can I see?'

Reluctantly, I started to raise my leg only for screaming to erupt behind us.

'There he is!' cried a girl, and we swung round to see two teenagers advancing, each with a mobile phone held aloft.

'Bollocks,' he said. Then, grasping my hand, 'Can I have your bike?'

'What do you mean have it? No, you can't have it. It's not even mine.'

'I'll give you five-hundred dollars for it,' he pleaded, reaching in his pocket and producing a fistful of notes.

'It's not worth that much,' I protested, but he was already on his feet, dragging me and the bike after him. The two girls were clutching each other and one looked close to tears. It seemed absurd that he wouldn't say a quick hello to them.

'There's about seven hundred here,' he said, shoving the wad of cash towards me. 'Take all of it.'

'You're being ridiculous,' I said, trying to steer the bike out of his grip, but this only made him hurry us along the street faster.

'Fine,' I said in exasperation. 'I'll help, but I'm not selling my bike to you. Just get on – I'll take you home.'

I couldn't see his eyes, but it was obvious that both brows were raised.

'What?' he said. 'Like a backy?'

'Yes, now get on before I change my mind.'

Not needing to be told twice, he swung a leg over the saddle as I positioned my feet on the pedals.

'Hold on,' I instructed, relinquishing a groan of effort as my thighs struggled against our combined weight. My injured knee burned, but we were away, speeding past a toy shop and thudding down the kerb onto the road.

'Oof!' I heard from behind me, and grinned.

'Which way am I going?'

'Turn right and go down to the traffic lights, then hit another right,' he said. 'You're looking for First Neck Lane on the left.'

I had not bothered to get changed out of the dress I'd worn on the train and was horribly aware of how low-cut it was at the back. There was no doubt that this stuntman, whoever he was, was currently being treated to a clear view of my gnarly old bra, and it occurred to me then that I could have simply ridden him a short distance away from his pursuers before letting him off, rather than taking him all the way back to his house. Then again, it was a nice excuse to explore a bit more of the area, and as I followed his instructions and headed along wide, tree-lined lanes past grand gated houses, the overriding feeling was one of exhilaration.

'It's right again just here,' I heard, and checking behind to make sure there were no cars, I swung onto Great Plains Road, narrowly missing a gardener as he stepped out from behind a parked van.

'Whoa!' said my passenger, grabbing my waist as I swerved, his legs flailing. 'Steady.'

'Steady?' I scoffed. 'I'm not a carthorse.'

'No, a carthorse would be a much safer ride.'

I braked sharply. 'Careful,' I warned. 'Or I may buck you off.'

'Promises, promises,' he drawled, then took his hand off my waist to tap me on the shoulder. 'It's just here.'

He had stopped me at the entrance to what I guessed must be a long drive, but I couldn't see either that or the house beyond on account of the huge, metal gate barring the way. There was a coded keypad set into a pillar to one side, and an intercom below it.

I held the bike still while he clambered off, then pushed it forwards and leant it carefully against the tall privet hedge that ran along the boundary of the property. A good proportion of the houses in this area were designed in the same way, the thick spruce providing the type of concealment desired by the incredibly rich. And I didn't need to work in real estate to know that only the exceedingly wealthy could afford to live here.

'How's that knee feeling?'

I lifted my foot from the ground to get a better look. 'Sore,' I admitted. 'But I think I'll be back to my Russian Cossack dancing ways pretty soon.'

'Is that something you do often?' he asked, head on one side. 'Cossack dancing?'

'Only when I'm drunk,' I said happily.

He nodded. 'I used to be more of a worm guy.'

'Arthritis put paid to that, did it?' I joked, and he laughed.

'Nope. Sobriety.'

He'd said it casually, but I felt immediately awkward. Sharing tales of drunken antics was something that traditionally bonded British people, but it was a completely stupid behavioural trait. It wasn't even as if I drank alcohol that often anymore. The days of sneaking bottles of vodka into nightclubs and topping up glasses of coke in the ladies' toilets with Jojo were a very long way behind me, and aside from the occasional glass of wine, I managed to abstain.

'Don't worry,' he assured me, catching sight of my mortified expression. 'But if you really wanted to make it up to me, you'd give me a demonstration of your best Kazotsky kick.'

'I don't know what that is,' I told him. 'But I know I'm not doing it.'

We smiled at each other, and I had the sense that I had seen him somewhere before.

'So, stuntmanning . . .' I began, changing the subject. 'How does that work? Are you a body double for all the big-name stars, or are you one of those YouTubers with a huge following, who films themselves Pogo-sticking onto telephone boxes, that sort of thing?'

He laughed. 'Is that a thing?'

'It could be.'

'I dabble,' he said evasively. 'Do a bit of everything.'

'Come on,' I pressed, 'you must be fairly successful if teenage girls are crying over you.'

'They're not crying over me,' he said. 'They're crying over the person they think I am.'

'Ooh, cryptic.'

'I look a lot like someone famous,' he explained.

I took a step closer, and he lowered his sunglasses to reveal hooded brown eyes flecked with gold. His lips were thin but shapely, his nose slim and neat. I was near enough to feel the heat of his breath. He smelt faintly of mint and the sweet coconut scent of sun lotion.

'The only person coming to mind is Tom Hanks in *Castaway*,' I said. 'After he'd been stranded on that desert island for a few years.'

He tugged at his beard. 'You think I should lose the fuzz?'

'Definitely,' I agreed. 'Do you want me to go back and ask that gardener if he has a hedge trimmer you can borrow?'

He rolled his eyes at me in amusement before pushing his sunglasses back into place.

There was a beat of silence, and then we both started to speak at the same time.

'You go,' he said.

I hesitated for a moment. 'I was just going to say that I should probably get going. I was on my way to get essential supplies when you crashed into me, and my friend will be extremely caffeine deprived by now.'

He nodded. 'I know how they feel. Do you think you can find the way back to town?'

I glared at him in mock outrage, and he raised his hands, backing away.

'OK, silly question. Please don't kick me in the balls – they're still recovering from the bike ride.'

'At least we have injuries in common now,' I replied, and again, he laughed.

Fetching the bike, I wheeled it down to the road and mounted, turning to see the large metal gate creaking open. I wanted to follow him along the pristine driveway, insist that he apply antiseptic cream to my cuts and bruises, bring me a glass of homemade lemonade and a plate of cookies. I wanted, I realised with a jolt, simply to spend more time with him.

'Well,' I said. 'Bye, then . . . ? What is your name?'

He smiled. 'You really don't know?'

'If I did, I wouldn't be asking.'

'OK, let's agree on Tom.'

'As in Hanks?'

'As in Tom. And you are?'

'Honor,' I called.

'It was nice to meet you, Honor.'

The gates had closed, blocking him from view and I listened to the crunch of gravel as he walked away from me.

'Ditto,' I whispered, aware of something potent beginning to churn inside me.

'It was nice to meet you, too.'

9

That night, I started writing.

Not just notes and ideas, but prose. I sat at the desk by the open window in my attic room, laptop in front of me, and wrote about a chance encounter between two people, a woman not like the one I had conjured up in the train, but someone as far removed from myself as I could imagine, and a man exactly the same as Tom.

The idea had come to me as I cycled away from where I'd left him, realising as I did so what an incredible gift I'd been given. Not only did I have a great leading man, but he was a stuntman, accustomed to living an exciting life. In all the other novels I'd started before, I'd been missing that element; I'd always created characters who said plenty but did very little; ordinary souls, living mundane lives. The words of wisdom that my father had shared with me the first time we met had never left me, and I knew from him that what readers wanted was to be taken on an action-packed adventure. Thanks to the mysterious Tom, I finally had the inspiration required to write one. Perhaps, I thought, as I tapped away, my New Yorker stuntman could be content with his status as the most daring guy in Hollywood until a new, London-born stuntwoman arrived on the scene and promptly managed to outshine him. The two could enter into a friendly contest, each suggesting increasingly dangerous stunts in a bid to beat the other. I would have them run through fire, leap off cliffs, and wrestle with crocodiles, all the while falling in love with each other, of course.

I wished I'd thought to ask Tom more about what his job entailed, rather than teasing him about his beard. The internet was helpful to an extent, but nothing would be more convincing than authentic detail, and to win this competition, I was going to need a novel that stood out from the rest. Anything I didn't know, I made a note to add in later, for once not letting these small hiccups slow me down.

Writing an account of what had happened earlier came easily, and I found myself laughing as I tapped away at the keys, describing how the two of us had ended up sprawled across the pavement. It felt refreshing to be drawing inspiration from something I'd experienced first-hand, and thinking about Tom – or Patrick, as I'd decided to name him in my story – was no hardship. I was already conjuring up the romantic scenes that I'd be able to write once I brought my two characters together. Tom may have joked about chance being a fine thing, but I would be willing to bet more than a rusty old bike that I had been single far longer than him. And it wasn't because I was particularly discerning, it was simply down to prioritising. I'd chosen to put my own pursuit of love on hold in order to write a fictitious one. I'd reached the conclusion that only by achieving the latter would I stand a chance of being able to give the former the commitment and energy that it required.

When I'd tried to explain my reasoning to Felix, he'd not responded well.

'We've been together for eight years, Honor,' he'd said. 'You're my best friend. I want us to build a life together.'

'I want that, too,' I'd told him. 'But first, I need to build something for myself – a career. A proper one, as a writer.'

Felix had made a noise of exasperation. 'You are a writer, Honor. You don't need a book deal to prove that.'

I'd stared at him incredulously, saw that he was serious, his pale gaze direct and unwavering. Felix knew me, had said he understood why I needed to make a success of myself, and had always supported me in that. But when I pointed this out to him, he'd grimaced. For Felix, with his childhood sweetheart parents, his first-class law degree, and his ability to cruise easily into whatever port in life he chose, it must have seemed unfathomable that I, the woman he'd selected to share it all with, would turn down his offer of a happily ever after. Nobody had ever said 'no' to Felix.

'What if you never get a book deal, Honor?'

I had glared at him then, wounded by the suggestion.

'It's a possibility,' he'd argued. 'What if five years go by and nothing has changed? Will we be honeymooning in our fifties and having children in our sixties?'

'Now you're just being facetious,' I'd grumbled.

'Why can't we just agree on a date?' he'd pleaded. 'A cut-off point, where we agree to move forward with the next stage of our relationship.'

'And if I say no?' I'd replied. 'What then?'

Felix had sighed. I thought he would pull me into his arms as he always did, tell me that everything would be OK and that it was foolish to argue. But he didn't. Instead, he'd taken my hand and squeezed it.

'I love you, Honor,' he'd said quietly. 'But I can't wait forever – not even for you.'

All it would have taken to keep him was one promise, a declaration from me that, of course, I loved him too. But in that moment, I'd found that I could no longer pretend. I'd let him go, and he'd gone on to find someone else, marry that someone else, and start a family with her. In the simplest terms, he'd won, and I'd lost, but even now, I could not regret the steps I'd taken. Felix knew that for me, success was as necessary as oars were on a rowing boat – yes, I would stay afloat without it, but I would never get anywhere, not in either the real or figurative sense – yet he had lost sight of the fact when it threatened his own trajectory. Losing Felix was far from easy, but his lack of faith in me was the point I came back to whenever regret resurfaced. Eventually, I'd resolved that if achieving my goals meant putting love to the back of my to-do list, it was a bargain I was prepared to strike – although, I thought, as I finally fell into bed in the small hours, there was nothing to stop me writing about it.

I must have slept soundly because the very next thing I became aware of was a hammering on my bedroom door. Bleary-eyed, I stumbled across to open it and was greeted by Tallulah, looking peppy in green yoga pants and a matching crop top.

'What's happened?' I croaked, standing to one side to let her in.

'Oh, nothing special,' she said breezily, wandering across to the desk and peering down at my open notebook. 'Working on something?'

'Not really.' Hurrying after her, I reached down and covered my scribbles with a hand.

Tallulah looked surprised. 'I didn't know that you're a writer, too,' she said.

'I'm not. I mean, I'm not published yet. I do write, though – or I try to.'

'That's so great. Why didn't you say?'

I yanked down the hem of the T-shirt I'd worn to bed and bent to stow the notebook in my backpack.

'I guess because I had nothing to tell. I didn't even have an idea until yesterday.'

'Aha,' she said, a smile of delight spreading across her face. 'Let me guess – the stuntman?'

I'd told Tallulah about my encounter with Tom when I'd returned from the shop, basket laden with goodies that we had spread across a rug in the back garden and shared as the sun set behind the trees.

'Maybe,' I allowed, shuffling towards the bathroom and closing the door on her.

'So, it's a romance novel then?' she hollered.

'Can't a woman pee in peace?' I called back.

Tallulah didn't reply, but when I emerged a few minutes later, she was still there, sitting on the edge of my unmade bed.

'What?' I said, seeing the mischievous look on her face. 'What's so funny?'

'I'm not laughing,' she protested. 'I'm psyched. JB prefers to write alone, but I like being around other people. Usually, I just go and sit in a café somewhere, but now you and I can write together. That's if you want to?' she added, uncertainty making her seem younger somehow. She'd told me her age last night, and as I'd suspected, she was in her mid-thirties – three years older than me.

'Sure,' I said, crouching to examine the contents of my case, which I'd yet to unpack. Tallulah joined me, fishing through the pile of clothes until she located a bikini.

'Put this on,' she instructed. 'We're going to the beach.'

'We are?'

'That's why I came to wake you. I thought it would be nice to have a day out before JB arrives this evening, demanding all our attention be on him.'

I thought privately that it was unlikely my father would expect or even want any attention from me, but I had to agree that a walk along the beach sounded nice.

'Perhaps we can call it a plot walk?' I suggested. 'That way we're working and playing at the same time.'

Tallulah clapped her hands together. 'See,' she said, 'I knew that you coming out here with us was a good idea. JB wasn't sure, but I was convinced before I even met you that we'd be friends. I mean, he and I get on well, so it stands to reason that you and I would.'

'Wasn't sure?' I echoed, seeing her face fall as she registered her slip-up. 'The two of you discussed it prior to my arrival?'

Tallulah chewed her bottom lip. 'I think he was just worried that you'd be bored,' she said, not meeting my eye. 'You know what it's like when you have a house guest? You feel obligated to entertain them at all times. I guess he just wants to squirrel away down here and write, but we can both relate to that, can't we? He's going to be so thrilled when he finds out you're working on a book, too.'

'No,' I said, more sharply than I had intended. 'I don't want him to know – not yet. It's' – I searched fruitlessly for the right word – 'complicated between me and him.'

Tallulah's expression softened. 'OK,' she said. 'I won't say a word if you don't want me to, but I really do think you should. JB has been so supportive of my work, I'm sure he'll be the same way towards you – probably even more so.'

'Are we going to the beach or what?' I asked, cutting a deliberately cheerful swathe through the conversation. Tallulah looked for a moment as if she might argue, but then decided against it. I understood her confusion. It was strange that my father showed little to no interest in what I chose to do, but he only behaved that way towards me because I'd never impressed him. In order to gain his pride, I had to deserve it, and if Tallulah couldn't see that, then she didn't know my father even half as well as she thought she did.

And that, at least, provided a small measure of comfort.

IO

Coopers Beach, I soon discovered, was the undisputed feather in Southampton's cap.

According to Tallulah, who stored facts she'd read in magazines like rodents did nuts for winter, it was consistently voted as one of the top ten beaches in America, and as soon as we'd clambered out of the free shuttle buggy that we'd flagged down in the village and strode the few metres from car park to wooden walkway, I understood exactly why.

White sand stretched away in both directions, the east and west horizons dancing with heat, while ahead of us the Atlantic Ocean crashed its mighty waves against the shore. Terns circled overhead, their shrill cries interrupting the chatter of the gulls that hulked in shallow pools below them. Shaggy tufts of grass pushed through the pillowy range of soft dunes, behind which stood one palatial beach house after another. I put up a hand to shield my eyes as a warm gust of wind dashed across us, peppering my sun cream-coated legs with a swarm of grit. The air was deliciously salty, the roar of the sea a beckoning call; this was the world at its most poetic, and I was entranced. Lost, for the longest moment, in the undulations of nature.

'Pretty impressive, right?' Tallulah turned to face me, her smile, as ever, wide beneath her sunglasses. She'd done her best to tie back her wayward hair, but the errant breeze was already whipping it away from its fastening. Yelping as the skirt of her dress was lifted up almost to navel height, she clamped it back down with a laugh.

'Impressive and windy,' I remarked. 'I'm very glad I wore shorts.'

Given that my own hair had reached a frustrating in-between length, I'd pulled it into two low pigtails, before tugging my faithful cap down on top. When it came to make-up, I'd done little more than apply brow and lip gel, and now wished I hadn't bothered with the latter – it felt as if half the beach had adhered itself to my mouth.

We'd picked up a takeaway cup of coffee each from the café on the corner of South Main Street, and now carried these and our overstuffed straw bags down to the shoreline.

'Shall we just walk until we get tired and sit down wherever we end up?' Tallulah asked, slipping off her sandals and hooking them over a finger. I was happy to go along with this, and as we strolled, our toes leaving indentations in the wet sand, I led her successfully off the topic of my book and onto hers, asking her about her process, which craft books, if any, she used, and what her long-term ambitions were. Like me, she was a dedicated disciple of my father and his 'rules', which I had first heard him mention back when I was sixteen and had ditched school for the day to watch him being interviewed at an author event in London.

Asked by the panel chair to discuss how he approached a new novel, my father had confided that he was a strict plotter, and that as far as he was concerned, there were four rules you had to follow if you wanted to make it as a writer. Sitting up a fraction straighter in my seat, I'd prepared to note them down.

'Number one,' he said, 'is never write for yourself. Write for the readers and for the market. If you treat writing self-indulgently, you'll never get anywhere.'

The interviewer looked as if she might interrupt, but he'd continued talking.

'The second thing is to make sure your characters act, don't react – you want them to be active, not passive. Nobody cares what they might be thinking or feeling, only what they're doing.'

I'd noted this down, even though I'd heard him say it many times before.

'The third rule is to believe in yourself and your ideas. If you don't think your novel is any good, chances are nobody else will either. You need to give it the hard sell – never apologise or be self-deprecating. People don't respond to it well, trust me.'

The woman asking the questions nodded politely, urging him to continue.

'The final one?' he said. 'Well, that's simple: avoid flashbacks. In order to keep the story going, you need to stay in the now, not harp constantly back to the past. All that backstory stuff is just filler. So, stick to the now.'

I had felt triumphant as I headed back to Cambridge later that evening, aware that I'd be in trouble for sneaking off but knowing it had been worth it. Because from that moment on, I had it – the formula that would guarantee me writing success – and I'd tried my hardest to adhere to it ever since.

'Your dad is such a pioneer,' Tallulah said, pulling me back from my sojourn into the past. 'Every book I've read about how to plot a novel goes on and on about backstory, but I think JB's method makes far more sense. Setting a story wholly in the present lends it that urgency.'

'Hard to do, though,' I said, and she sighed forlornly.

'Right? I'm so glad it's not just me. I find it so hard to ignore what the characters are telling me, demanding that I pay attention to what they're feeling all the time.'

I knew exactly what she meant. There was a strange kind of alchemy to writing, a blending of what was in your own subconscious with that of your chosen protagonist, but my father had long maintained that in order to tell a good story, you had to learn how to push those insistent voices from your mind.

'He's your mentor now, don't forget,' I reminded Tallulah. 'By the time summer's over, he'll have taught you all his tricks.'

She smiled, but for once, it did not feel authentic. Stopping to readjust the strap of her bag, she pointed ahead to where a trio of surfers were making their way towards the water. 'Let's set ourselves up over there,' she said. 'I love watching the boarders, reminds me of the trips we used to take when I was a kid.'

'Did you holiday here?'

'God, no. My parents could never have afforded to bring me and my brother here. We had to settle for Nags Head in Cali.'

'I'm sure I've been to a pub with that name,' I said, and was gratified to get a laugh.

The surfers had paddled beyond the breaking waves by the time we'd rolled out our towels, set down our bags and unpeeled the greaseproof paper from around the chickpea salad wraps that Tallulah had prepared that morning. We watched them as we ate in companionable silence. One of the figures was far more skilled than his companions, the effortless contortion of his body making each manoeuvre look seamless, while the others spent more time tumbling off their boards than they did riding them. It was only when they began to ride the waves back in again that I was able to see their features more clearly, and went still as I recognised a thick, untidy beard.

'Oh my God!' Tallulah clutched my arm.

'What?'

'That guy there, he reminds me of . . . No, it can't be him.'

'The one who looks like one of his parents could have been a yeti?' I asked. 'That's the man I met yesterday, the one who knocked me over. Tom. The stuntman,' I added when she appeared unable to speak. 'Do you recognise him?'

'That's not a stuntman,' she murmured, her voice pinched with excitement.

'That is Cellan Thomas.'

I I

At a loss for how else to respond, I laughed. 'Cellan Thomas as in the famous actor? No, it really isn't.'

Tallulah's grip on my arm had grown tighter. 'It is him!' she practically squealed.

I felt like reminding her that she was thirty-five, not thirteen. This is what Tom must have meant when he told me he was often mistaken for someone famous – Cellan Thomas must be that person. When I explained this to Tallulah, however, she shook her head roughly from side to side.

'No, no, no,' she insisted. 'He's the real deal. I'm sure of it.'

The surfers had reached the shoreline, and the one woman of the group was wringing water from her long, dark-red hair. I stared at the man beside her, willing him to look over in our direction, but he was preoccupied with untangling his ankle leash. All three were in wetsuits, but as I continued to stare, the two men unzipped theirs to the waist. I saw a flash of defined muscle, a scattering of dark hair, and averted my eyes as heat flared across my cheeks.

'Go and say hi,' urged Tallulah.

'I don't want to interrupt his conversation,' I said, rather lamely.

Tallulah made a tutting sound. 'He won't mind. If he really is the guy who crashed into you yesterday, then he at least owes you the time of day.'

'He definitely is that guy,' I corrected firmly.

'Well, then.' She gave me her most winning smile. 'Think of it as book research.'

I'd wanted to see him again for this precise reason, to ask him for some insider knowledge about what being a stuntman entailed, but now that I was confronted with him, it felt like an odd request.

'If you don't go over there, then I will,' Tallulah threatened happily, starting to raise a hand. 'I could simply wave him over here and—'

'Stop!' I grabbed her hand and yanked it down. 'I'll go over, just give me a second.'

Tallulah considered me. 'Teeth,' she instructed, and I opened my mouth into a rictus grin. 'Good, all clear, no spinach. Now eyes. Yep, all clear. No mascara gloop.'

'I'm not wearing any mascara,' I said, wishing now that I'd put some on.

'You need to lose the hat,' she said, knocking it off my head. 'And pull these out,' she added, tugging the toggles free so my hair fell loose around my shoulders. I glanced back towards the surfers.

'They're leaving,' I said. 'Oh well.'

Tallulah gave me a not-very-gentle shove.

'Oi!'

'Now get,' she ordered, as a cowboy might to his dog.

I stood up, conscious that I would have to run if I wanted to catch up with him, and set off across the sand. It was soft underfoot, the going slow despite my attempts to hurry, and I staggered as the sand shifted away beneath me. When the group was only a few metres ahead, I called out, 'Excuse me,' and saw three sets of shoulders tense. The woman stopped and turned to face me, the two men continuing on without her.

'Can I help you?' she asked, the politeness of her enquiry marred by the icy tone in which she delivered it.

'I just—' I began, craning my neck to look past her. 'I wanted to talk to Tom.'

'Tom?' She looked at me blankly.

'Yes, Tom. I met him yesterday. I gave him a lift home – Great Plains Road. I know him,' I persisted, as she folded her arms across her chest.

'Tom!' I called, then shouted it again, more loudly this time.

Both men stopped, and then at last, he turned. It was impossible to miss the change in his expression when he realised that I was not, as he'd presumably feared, a crazed fan.

'Honor,' he said, as if testing out the word.

'Yes,' I said, and waved at him quite unnecessarily.

Passing his surfboard to the man next to him, who stared at me in confusion, he made his way over, running a hand through his wet hair as he did so. There were droplets of water in his beard, and he was wearing sunglasses again, although this pair were the wraparound style, with blue mirrored lenses.

'Are you OK?' he asked. 'How's the knee?'

'Sand-encrusted,' I said, and he glanced down with a grimace. 'How are the balls?'

He laughed, and I noticed his female friend's eyes widen in shock.

'Oh, they're fine,' he assured me. 'Thank you for asking.'

'My friend over there,' I said, pointing towards Tallulah, 'seems to think you're a famous actor, so I guess it really must be true what you told me about being mistaken for someone else.'

He lowered his chin, taking a step backwards. 'Who does she think I am?'

'Cellan Thomas. You know, the actor. But you're not him, are you?'

The woman cleared her throat. 'We should get going,' she said. 'You've got that ... thing, remember? And Gunnar will—'

'It's OK,' he said, folding and unfolding his arms.

Tallulah was on her feet and heading over to join us. I could smell the orange blossom scent of her perfume in the air and wondered if she'd doused herself in it before seeking out an introduction.

'Hey,' she said, as she drew closer. 'I'm Tallulah.'

'You're the one who recognised me?'

The smile she offered him was coy in the extreme. 'Guilty as charged.'

'Hang on a minute,' I said. 'Are you saying that you're not a stuntman, then?'

'Not exactly.' He looked from me to Tallulah, and then at the ground. 'I do my own stunts sometimes, but it's more jumping off a chair than out of a plane.'

I understood what he was telling me, but my brain would not allow the facts to gain any purchase. This man, standing in front of me, with what looked like a spot on his forehead and a large frond of seaweed stuck to his leg, could not be Cellan Thomas, Oscar-winning movie star. I had sworn at this man, had flashed my ugliest bra at him, had asked after his balls. All of a sudden, I felt very faint.

'Oh,' I managed. 'I see.'

I could not look at him, at Cellan. It was as if he had changed into a completely different person in the past few seconds, and I no longer knew what to say, or how I would find the courage to speak even if I did. I thought about the way I'd pulled his T-shirt up towards my mouth and wiped blood all over it, how I'd callously ridiculed his beard, which the poor man must have grown in an attempt to remain incognito. In a rush, details of the *Idol* magazine story about him came back to me, and I recalled what he'd said the previous day about sobriety.

'Honor, are you all right?'

It was Cellan who'd asked the question, and I tried my best to smile.

'I feel stupid,' I said. 'I should have recognised you.'

'And ruin this weird surprise?' he joked. 'I shouldn't have lied to you. I'm sorry about that.'

'It's OK,' I told him. 'At least the whole seven-hundred dollars for a bike thing makes more sense now.'

He laughed. 'True. Although before you get any ideas, that offer was a one-time thing and has now expired.'

'Dammit!'

'This is my friend Cherry, by the way,' he said, gesturing to the woman in the wetsuit. 'And that's Colton over there.'

The third surfer, whose hands were occupied with twisting his dreadlocks up in a topknot, nodded in our direction.

'Honor is the kind soul who came to my rescue yesterday,' Cellan explained.

Cherry offered me a watery smile. 'And you just happened to be here at the beach?' she said archly. 'That was lucky.'

'It was my idea to come down here today.' Tallulah's tone, by contrast, was pure honey. 'Not Honor's.'

'We should let you all get on,' I said hurriedly. 'I just wanted to say hello, and now I've said it, so . . .'

Cellan removed his sunglasses; his eyes looked different today, closer to amber than hazel.

'What are you both doing this evening?' he asked.

'Nothing,' Tallulah enthused. 'We're completely free. No plans.'

'That's not strictly true,' I told her, then, turning back towards Cellan. 'My father's arriving in a few hours and—'

'Her father is Jeffrey Butler,' interrupted Tallulah. 'The writer.'

'The Benedict Stamp guy?' asked Cherry, noticeably perking up as Tallulah nodded. 'Cool.'

'We were thinking of doing a cookout later on,' Cellan explained. 'Nothing fancy, just a few friends and some grilled shrimp. You should come, bring your dad as well.'

'Are you sure?' I asked.

'You heard the man,' answered Tallulah firmly. 'He's sure.'

Cellan shrugged.

Any moment now, I would wake up from this most bizarre dream. Because there was no possible way this could be real. This sort of thing did not happen to a person like me. And yet, here I was, standing on a Hamptons beach with one of the most famous men on the planet, gaping like the proverbial goldfish.

'Cellan, are you coming?' Cherry had started to walk away.

'Yeah, one sec,' he said. Then, addressing me, 'Aim for around eight, that way you won't miss the sunset.'

'OK.'

'And Honor?'

'Yes?'

'Sorry again, for the whole stuntman thing. It's not the best start, is it, lying to someone?'

'It's fine,' I began, only to falter as my mind snagged on his choice of words.

Not the best start.

Cellan could simply have said a brief hello and walked away, relegating our strange encounter to just that. Instead, he had not only apologised but also extended an invite to his home, presumably a sanctuary he kept hidden from the prying eyes of the wider world. Nobody talked about the start of something without envisaging a middle and an end, but what I didn't know and could barely allow myself to contemplate was what, exactly, those markers would look like for us. Friendship felt implausible now that I knew who he was, while anything remotely romantic seemed laughable in its absurdity. And yet, as I watched him walk away, smiling back at him when he turned to glance across at me one final time, I experienced a similar sensation to the one that had overtaken me the previous day, and could not help but feel exhilarated. I may only have known Cellan Thomas for a matter of hours, but in that short time he had already provided me with an essential element that had long been absent from my life.

Inspiration.

12

Any fears I had that my father would not take kindly to Tallulah and me accepting an invitation on his behalf evaporated within seconds. We'd arrived back at the house to find him lounging across one of the wicker-framed sofas along the rear porch, an open novel balanced across his chest. As Tallulah filled him in on our eventful afternoon, I watched his expression change rapidly from one of apathy to animation.

'Cellan Thomas,' he confirmed, 'invited you to a cookout?'

'I'm as surprised as you are,' I told him, but Tallulah was shaking her head at us.

'He thinks Honor's cute,' she said, with her standard lack of irony. 'Must be a nice novelty for him to come across a fellow Brit, especially out here.'

'I think it's more likely that he feels bad for causing me a multitude of injuries yesterday,' I said, raising my knee to examine the still-painful scrape.

My father shifted into a sitting position. 'Or,' he countered, 'he's wary of attracting any more bad press; hasn't the guy just been in rehab?'

My predilection to always agree with my father was quashed by an urge to defend Cellan, but I regretted it as soon as I saw his expression darken.

'You know what they say about smoke,' he said.

'That it gets blown up people's behinds?'

He frowned at me as if I had spoken in Greek. 'No, about there being fire. Rehab can damage an actor's public persona, make him more expensive to insure.'

'Or her,' remarked Tallulah, shaking the sand out from her beach towel. 'Drinks?'

I nodded. We'd been unable to locate the free shuttle buggy on the way back, so had walked the forty minutes from Coopers Beach to the house, and I was parched.

'He'll be on the hunt for a comeback movie project,' my father went on, looking thoughtful. Taking out his phone, he tapped on the screen a few times before stowing it back in his trouser pocket. 'Hollywood is all about taking the right role at the right time, and I'd wager that now is the time for Cellan to do one heck of a blockbuster.'

'That poor guy,' said Tallulah, who'd returned with a bottle of rosé and three glasses. 'I bet he has to ice his ears every morning on account of how much they're burning.'

I thought privately that if Cellan had iced anything in the past twenty-four hours, it would likely be some way below his ears.

'I'm going to head on up and lie down for a bit,' I said, sidling towards the door, wine in hand. 'Unless either of you need me for anything?'

'No, you go on up, honey.' My father waved me away without looking. 'Tally and I have a bit of work to do before we head on out to this party.'

'It's not really a party,' I began, but I'd lost my audience. Pausing by the open doorway, I watched them for a minute or two, saw the concentration settle over my father's face as Tallulah sat down beside him with her laptop. I thought about my own modest pages of work, saved in a hidden folder on my desktop, shrouded in the shame that had chased me since childhood, and turned away.

Once upstairs, I opened my own computer, clicked on the
web browser and typed 'Cellan Thomas' into the search bar.
There were over eleven million results, and I scrolled past
IMDB, Wikipedia and Rotten Tomatoes. He did not appear
to have any official social media accounts, but there were a
number of fan sites, most of which consisted of photos
pinched from glossy shoots with superlative-heavy captions.
Several of the self-proclaimed 'Cellanoids' had posted gush-
ing stories about their encounters with the actor, whom they
invariably described as 'SO generous, SO sexy, and SO
misunderstood' by everyone bar them and their fellow
disciples. I could not help but grin as I recalled the horror-
struck expression the man himself had made when confronted
by two such enthusiasts the previous day.

The majority of the news headlines that popped up
concerned either Cellan's recent rehab stint or the on-off
nature of his relationship with Wylie Brooke who, the internet
helpfully informed me, was currently in Europe promoting
her new range of healing candles. *Idol* magazine must have
been misinformed, as that story had hinted that the model
would be joining her famous beau very soon. It was hard to
examine pictures of Wylie for long without feeling woefully
inadequate by comparison, and the two of them together
looked impossibly glossy.

I trawled back through the results page, this time in search
of interviews he'd done with more reputable publications.
Rolling Stone had published one not long before he won his
Oscar, the journalist coaxing out a puff piece that touched
upon Cellan's experience of growing up in Cornwall, and
how his dyslexia had led him towards an acting career. He
discussed the same subject during a video chat with *Empire*
magazine and made appropriate sad faces while reading out
cruel tweets about himself on *Jimmy Kimmel Live*. I watched

endless reels of footage, but at no point did I recognise the Cellan that I'd met in the street. This celebrity version of him looked and sounded the same, but his manner was at odds with the easy one that I'd assumed was his default. On camera, he seemed twitchy and uncomfortable; there was a fixed stiffness in the way he squared his shoulders, and he chewed at the skin around his fingernails between questions. Intrigued, I continued to hunt through the listings until I found a podcast, wondering if he would come across as more relaxed in purely audio format, but again, he sounded very different from the man I'd spoken to not two hours ago. It made sense, of course, that he would keep a little of himself back, but it did make me ponder which, if either, version of Cellan was closer to the real him: the stilted yet friendly celebrity version, or the wisecracking boy-next-door who'd ridden pillion on my bicycle. It felt important to know.

Taking my wine from the desk to the bedside table, I began the task of choosing an outfit to wear, eventually narrowing it down to cropped white wraparound shirt, pale blue jeans, and the oversized silver pendant my mother had given me for my thirtieth birthday. Assuming we'd go on foot to Cellan's house, I opted for Converse on my feet, then rooted through my tangle of earrings until I located a favourite pair of hoops.

I took extra care in the shower, shampooing twice and allowing the conditioner its full three minutes of nourish time before rinsing it out. I'd shaved my legs that morning but ran the razor over them again in case I'd missed a few hairs, then gave my bikini line a quick neaten for good measure. Jojo often joked that preening before meeting up with a man was a sure-fire way to jinx yourself into the friend zone, but as this was very much not a date, I figured the odds might actually be in my favour.

'Why is there so much of you?' I grumbled to my hair, as I clipped it up in preparation for blow-drying. For the first time since university, I'd allowed it to grow past my shoulders, not giving in to the temptation to chop it all off when it had reached its current, awkward in-between length. Now, however, I wished I had. It didn't matter how many times I tried to convince myself that I could become one of those women who could transform themselves from slovenly mess to impeccably styled goddess with a few twists of a hair straightener and a smear or two of make-up, I simply had not been born with the skills required, nor the inclination to learn them. As if to prove my despairing point, the brush I was using got tangled in my part-damp hair, and no amount of yanking, fiddling, or swearing could free it. In the end, tears of frustration leaking out across my cheeks, I had no choice but to reach for the nail scissors and cut myself free.

This was why I could never base a novel character on myself; I was worse than a romantic comedy cliché. Those protagonists generally had a hidden talent or two at the very least – something to offer whichever desirable man they were introduced to in the first act. I had nothing but bad jokes, bad dance moves, and now a bald patch.

When Tallulah knocked on my door half an hour later, she found me changed into my pyjamas and watching an old episode of *The OC* on my laptop.

'It's seven-fifteen,' she said, as I swigged the last of my rosé.

'I know,' I said. 'But it's OK, because I'm not coming.'

'Of course you are.'

'No,' I said firmly. 'I'm really not.'

Tallulah swept into the room, arms folded across the front of her Boho-style dress. She was, I noted forlornly, a woman who had very much been born with a talent for self-primping.

'This what you're wearing?' she asked, picking up the cropped blouse. 'Cute.'

There it was again, that word she seemed to attribute to every situation.

'I was going to,' I told her. 'But now I . . . I don't feel up to it.'

'Honor,' she said, with a sigh that felt judgemental, 'this is one of those moments. You know the ones I mean?'

I thought I could guess, but I shook my head.

'My mother would call it a gift,' she went on. 'Every now and again, the universe drops a little sugar lump of joy in your path, and it's up to you to gobble it down.'

'Sugar is really bad for your teeth,' I pointed out, but Tallulah was not having any of my sullen tone.

'I bet you've just got a headache from too much sun and wine,' she said. 'You get up and dressed, and I'll fetch you a couple of Advil.'

'But I don't want to—'

Tallulah fixed me with a hard stare. 'JB is so looking forward to it,' she said. 'Between you and me, I think he's pretty impressed that you've got him an invite. I mean, I probably would have gone over and spoken to Cellan if I'd spotted him, but I doubt he would have said "Come on over for shrimp" if it wasn't for you. You did this, Honor – it's all on you.'

'He's impressed?' I asked, and she smiled.

'Very. You don't want to let him down now, do you? He's dug out that awful tweed jacket of his and everything.'

I made a show of shuddering and she laughed.

'That's more like it. Now, get your clothes on, and I'll help you with your ha—'

'No!' I practically yelled, my hand going protectively to the towel I had wrapped around my frazzled locks. 'That's OK, I can manage. Just give me ten minutes.'

It wasn't long, but even ten hours would not have provided enough time to grow back the hair I had lost. Pulling on my jeans, I stared around the room, searching desperately for something – anything – that would disguise what I'd done.

'Right,' I said when I spotted it. 'I suppose you'll have to do.'

13

The front gate was propped open when we arrived, and the three of us followed the faint sounds of music and chatter along a wide driveway paved with grey stone. The house at its end, which was craftsman in style with low-slung gabled roofs, a stone-column porch and neat rectangular windows, was imposing in size yet charming in its design.

Finding a note pinned to the front door instructing us to head to the pool, we made our way around the edge of an impeccably tidy lawn towards the rear of the property.

The crisp wind of that morning had dispersed as the sun began to droop, and the clouds that trailed the sky were thin and limp, as if wrung out from the exertions of the day. The skin on my face felt tight and scorched – a symptom of the hours Tallulah and I had spent at the beach – and my scalp itched beneath the patterned scarf I'd had no choice but to wear. Tallulah had assured me that it looked 'cute', but she was being kind. In truth, the person who'd come immediately to mind when I had stared glumly at myself in the bathroom mirror was Captain Jack Sparrow. When I'd joked to the other two that I should probably have accessorised my outfit with a parrot and wooden leg, however, neither had laughed. They had simply stared at me askance, seemingly both mystified, and I'd resolved to put the proverbial sock in it.

Sweet, languid smoke curled out through a cluster of potted lilac trees as we approached the pool. My father, who'd insisted on bringing a bottle of whiskey along despite my warning about the teetotal status of our host, sniffed the air appreciatively.

'Something smells good,' he said, striding ahead of me as Cherry stood up from a lounger. She was dressed in a tight-fitting pink tank top, micro hot pants, and a diamanté choker that sparkled a little too much to be cubic zirconia.

'You're Jeffrey Butler,' she said, extending a hand.

'Call me JB.'

Glancing towards me and Tallulah, she dredged up a rather wan smile before turning back to my father.

'You must come and meet Gunnar,' she told him, gesturing to a small group of people on the far side of the terrace. 'I told him you were coming along, and he insisted I introduce you.'

'Introduce away,' my father replied, making to follow her.

'Can you direct me to the restroom?' asked Tallulah, and for a moment, Cherry looked uncertain.

'Maybe use the one in the pool cabin,' she said. 'I don't think Cellan wants people he doesn't know wandering around indoors.'

To Tallulah's credit, she took this slight well, heading off in the direction of a small glass-fronted hut, while Cherry led my father away. Abandoned, I felt suddenly exposed, and wondered again what I was doing here among all these notable people. My father was talking away animatedly to a tall, silver-haired man wearing trendy, thick-framed glasses, and I could tell that he was completely at ease. The grand house had not fazed him, nor had its glamorous inhabitants, but then nothing much ever did.

Unsure where I should put myself, I stared across the wide gardens and saw what looked to be the top of a pergola in the distance, its wooden frame festooned with the same fairy lights that were wrapped around the trees on South Main Street. I figured that nobody would miss me if I ventured up there to admire the view. Cellan had yet to appear, and Tallulah had gone straight from the bathroom to my father's side.

The dreadlocked surfer I'd met briefly on the beach was manning the barbecue and lifted a set of tongs as I passed.

'Hey,' I said, and was rewarded with a smile.

'Colton,' he reminded me. 'Chow won't be long – just waiting on these seaside Tonys.'

'Cool,' I replied, wondering if a seaside Tony would come served in a 'kiss me quick, squeeze me slow' hat as opposed to a bun, then sniggering at my own wit.

'What was that?' Colton asked.

'Oh, nothing. I was just . . . nothing. Ignore me,' I trilled, hurrying away as he shrugged in bewilderment. If I wasn't careful, I would start to get a reputation as 'that mad Brit', and it would be nothing I did not deserve. Colton continued to stare at me as I backed away, and I was still facing him, doing my best to communicate my inadequacies through the medium of gesture alone, as I reached the pergola, so did not see the person sitting on the bench inside until I was almost on top of him.

'Oh,' I said, wheeling around. 'Hi.'

Cellan sat forward and arched his back until it clicked, grinning as I winced.

'You found my hiding place,' he said.

'I was actually hoping it would be mine,' I admitted.

Cellan considered me for a moment, then patted the empty space beside him.

'Come,' he said. 'Hide.'

'Nice view,' I said as I sat down, and it was. The sloping edge of the grounds banked down to be swallowed by the pillowy dunes beyond, a wire-cleft wooden fence the only barrier between grass and beach. The ocean that had roared so determinedly that afternoon was muted by distance, but its whisper was no less insistent.

'I like it,' Cellan agreed, stretching his feet out in front of him. I glanced down at his beaten-up Vans, which he wore with no socks, then allowed my gaze to travel up, taking in the ripped jean shorts and faded blue hoodie. There were two small hoops in his left ear that I'd not noticed before, and when he raised a hand to readjust his mop of dark hair, I saw the flash of several chunky rings.

'People have bought houses for less convincing reasons,' I offered, and he looked at me in surprise.

'You think I own this place?'

'You don't?'

'God, no – I'm only renting it. Works out much cheaper that way, believe me.'

'How much would a place like this go for?' I asked. 'Purely out of interest?'

Cellan took a deep breath before saying, 'I reckon about thirty-five or forty million dollars, something like that.'

I laughed. 'Is that all?'

'Ludicrous, right?'

'Oh, I don't know,' I said, once again admiring the view. 'If you can afford it, why not?'

'Because it's not home,' he said simply.

I thought about all the Cellan Thomas trivia I'd consumed over the past few hours, debating how to ask my next question without making it obvious that I already knew the answer. In the end, I needn't have worried, because he beat me to it.

'Home is back in Cornwall,' he said. 'I have an apartment in Los Angeles, but only for convenience. Most of the time, I let my mates use it. I'm only there when I have to be for work.'

'What's LA like?' I asked, wishing the headscarf wasn't making my scalp itch quite so much.

Cellan chewed over his response. 'It can be fun,' he said, sounding pragmatic, 'but it can also be a bit full-on. I prefer it out here on the East Coast; it's much more suited to that raggedy surfer boy that still resides in here.' He tapped a hand to his chest. 'And how about you, Honor? Where is home for you?'

'Cambridge,' I said, explaining about the tiny flat above the bookshop, and my job at the university.

'And that makes you happy?' he asked. 'No big dreams of becoming a stand-up comedian?'

'Funny.'

'Cycle stunt rider?'

'Really?'

'Or,' he said, warming to his subject, 'you could combine the two and join a circus.'

'Are you trying to say that I'm a clown?'

Cellan's brown eyes glittered. 'If the big, floppy shoes fit . . .'

'At least my shoes aren't full of holes,' I pointed out, and at that, he laughed. 'And, to answer your original question, I actually do have a big dream, and it has nothing whatsoever to do with clowning of any kind.'

'You do?' Cellan sat up a fraction straighter. 'Do tell.'

But I didn't want to; all of a sudden, it felt ridiculous to have mentioned it at all. He might have asked, but there was no way he genuinely cared about the answer. Why would he? He was Cellan Thomas, A-list celebrity icon, and I was, well, a nobody.

'Maybe later,' I said, turning away so as not to witness his reaction. 'I don't know about you, but I'm starving, and I'm fairly certain you promised me some grilled shrimp.'

Cellan held up his hands. 'That I did. Come on then, I suppose it's bad form to hide away all evening, given that I'm the host.'

'It is,' I agreed. 'And you are.'

I stood up and he followed suit, yawning as he did so, and the two of us made our way back to the terrace, breaking off as we reached the pool. Cellan headed towards where Colton was removing steaks from the barbecue and putting them onto plates, while I made a beeline for Tallulah and my father, both of whom were talking intently to the older, grey-haired man.

'Hello,' I said tentatively, and Tallulah swung around, beaming as she saw me.

'Honor, there you are. We thought you'd gone.'

'No. I was just—'

'Never mind. You're here now, and you must meet Gunnar Hayes.'

She towed me forwards by the elbow until I was standing between the two men. My father, interrupted mid-flow, managed to hide his irritation well.

'Hey, honey,' he said, adding to his companion, 'This is my daughter.'

The taller man peered sternly at me through his glasses, then disarmed me with a broad smile. 'Honor,' he drawled, in what I took to be a Californian accent. He certainly had the tan and teeth to match. 'You're the gal that rescued my boy, Cef.'

'I think rescued might be a little bit of an overstatement.'

'Nonsense. I heard all about it – you, riding in like the Lone Ranger on that rusty steed of yours, pedalling him out of danger like that. Bravo.'

It was too ridiculous not to laugh, and so I did, apparently rather too loudly, because it prompted my father to put his arm around me and squeeze until I stopped.

'Gunnar here is Cellan's manager,' he explained, in a tone that left me under no illusion as to how important that made him. Behind me, Tallulah emitted a tittering sort of sound. They were all waiting for me to say something, but all I came up with was, 'Cool.'

Thankfully, Colton chose that moment to bellow across the garden that the food was ready, and so we all trooped obediently towards the barbecue, Tallulah hanging back and beckoning for me to join her.

'Can you believe it?' she hissed. 'Gunnar Hayes!'

'I know,' I said, even though I'd had no idea who he was until a few minutes ago. 'Who are all these other people? Do you know?'

Tallulah nodded with enthusiasm. 'Cherry, who we've met, is Cellan's publicist,' she said, 'and Colton is a stylist.'

I pictured the bedraggled Vans and suppressed a grin.

'What about the incredibly beautiful woman in the black dress?' I asked.

'That's Padma Sharma. I asked her what she did, and she was a bit vague about it, but I think she might be a life coach.'

I could not imagine Cellan hiring a life coach, but of course he had recently spent time in rehab. It was not a subject I felt comfortable broaching yet. But then, wasn't that exactly what writers should be willing to do? Ask the tough questions so that they might get closer to understanding the nature of human behaviour; why we do what we do, and how to make sense of it. I wished there were some sort of hand-book I could read that would instruct me in how a real author should behave. It came so easily to my father, but he had passed none of his natural talent to me.

We'd reached the others, and when I looked around at each of the gathered faces, it was Cellan's that stayed my gaze. He fascinated me, in part, of course, because of who he was and the status that role provided, but also because I had a sense of knowing him, almost intrinsically, as if his thoughts were replaying like an echo in my own mind. When he smiled at me, I felt it, a sensation I could not describe in words, because how can you truly hope to articulate the intricacies of a feeling? I was not a poet; I was barely even a writer – what chance did I have?

Someone passed me a plate, and I thanked them with a soundless murmur, staring down at the blackened shellfish skewer before raising my eyes and, once again, finding his waiting.

It was only by the slightest incline of his head that Cellan asked his question, and I replied with an imperceptible tilt of my chin. Without a word, he stepped out of the group and started to walk away, and before I could talk myself out of it, I followed him.

14

He had come to a stop alongside a low table, the top of which was littered with bowls of mixed greens, bread rolls and various condiments.

'Ambrosia salad?' he said, holding up a spoonful of something cream and lumpy.

'That depends.'

'On?'

'On what's in it. I mean, are we talking a potato base, or more of a coleslaw vibe?'

Cellan mulled this over. 'Well,' he said, 'it contains mandarin pieces, pineapple chunks, cherries, coconut and pecans.'

'That sounds—'

'And vanilla yoghurt, whipped cream and marshmallows.'

'Gross,' I finished. 'And definitely not something I would pair with prawns.'

Cellan let the gooey-looking salad drop onto his own plate, then forked up a huge portion into his mouth.

'S'yummy,' he said, between mouthfuls, to which I tutted.

'You've got cream in your beard.'

'I'll save it as a snack for later.'

'Nice.'

'I'm sure it will be.'

And here we were again; our game of mutual teasing seemingly impossible to avoid. Cellan helped himself to a second portion.

'Is it really that good?' I asked, bending over until my nose was inches from the bowl and sniffing it.

'Careful,' Cellan warned.

The end of my scarf had fallen forwards into the ambrosia, and he reached across to move it just as I veered away. Too late, I realised what was happening, and tried in vain to pin the silky material in place with both hands only to encounter damp, slightly flat hair instead.

'Shit,' he said. 'Sorry, I didn't mean to— What have you done?'

'Nothing.'

I snatched the scarf away from him with one hand, clamping the other over the small bare patch behind my ear.

'Is that a bald—'

'No!'

I backed away from him and collided with Tallulah, who, along with my father, had come across to join us. Jeffrey Butler, I noted in mild alarm, was still clutching his bottle of whiskey.

'Oh, good,' Tallulah said brightly. 'You've taken off that scarf. I did think it looked a little like one a fortune teller would wear.'

Whatever happened to 'cute'?

'I was just putting it back on, actually.'

'Aren't you going to introduce us?' prompted my father, and Cellan stepped forwards.

'Sorry,' he said, the very epitome of charm. 'You're Honor's dad?'

My father launched into a spiel about who he was, what he did, and how many books he'd sold, and I watched as Cellan nodded along politely. Tallulah then took her turn, correcting his assumption – which I was amused to hear him also make

– that she and JB were a couple, before explaining about the mentoring.

'And it's just so great that Honor here is writing a novel, too,' she enthused, as my father turned to me in surprise.

'You are, honey?'

I squirmed, exactly as I had as an eight year old and fought a strong urge to scowl at Tallulah. I had sworn her to secrecy after all.

'Sort of,' I admitted reluctantly. 'But it's probably all a load of rubbish.'

'Will you let me take a look?' he offered. 'Maybe I can give you a few pointers? After all, nobody can argue with global sales of over twenty million copies, can they?' He punctuated this statement with a brash bark of laughter, which landed like a slap across my face.

I longed for my father to show an interest in my writing, but I could not allow him to look at anything I'd done since being here in The Hamptons. It was all a jumble – an unspooling thread of feelings, emotions and cheap jokes that I knew he'd detest. The only other work – if I could even call it that – I'd done, was the diary entry describing how Cellan and I had met, and no amount of fame, riches or promises of adulation would convince me to show him that. Not in this lifetime.

'What kind of book is it?' asked Cellan, the sincerity in his tone making me want to weep with gratitude. When I waited too long to reply, Tallulah spoke for me.

'It's a romance, right? Oh, don't worry,' she hastened, taking in my shocked expression, 'I didn't sneak a look or anything, it was just a lucky guess.'

I could almost hear my father rolling his eyes.

'Don't make that face, Jeffrey,' Tallulah chided. 'The last time I checked, crime and mystery came below romance and erotica in the revenue rankings. Love story authors are the biggest earners in the US market.'

My father put the whiskey down on the table. 'Do you mind if I . . . ?' he asked, and Cellan shrugged.

'Go ahead,' he said, pushing a stack of red plastic cups along the table. I caught his eye and mouthed a 'sorry', but he shook his head, dismissing it as if it did not matter.

'The problem with the romance genre is that the plots are never realistic,' my father complained. 'Too many coincidences, and all that happy ever after baloney.'

I coloured, cheeks aflame.

'What's wrong with a happy ending?' asked Cellan, in a steady voice. 'Don't they offer an audience hope?'

My father scoffed. 'False hope,' he countered. 'A divorce takes place every thirteen seconds in America.'

Tallulah laughed nervously. 'Who says marriage equals love?' she protested. 'Some couples stay together forever and never make it legally binding.'

'I would never get married,' my father said, not without pride. 'It's the fastest route to financial ruin there is – after kids.'

'Jeffrey!' Tallulah admonished, as I stared fixedly at the ground. 'Your daughter is standing right there.'

'She knows I'm only kidding, right honey?'

He had grasped me again, his fingers pressed hard enough against my upper arm to leave a bruise, but I didn't pull away. I merely nodded, smiling weakly at the others to show that I agreed, and that it was all a big joke. Except it wasn't, not really.

Nobody said anything for what felt like an uncomfortable amount of time, and I saw Cellan's eyes narrow, as if he was contemplating his next remark carefully. My father, perhaps sensing he had made a conversational misstep, finished the whiskey in his cup and poured himself another slug, before turning to Cellan.

'How about you, Cef? Any plans to be a dad?'

'Excuse me.' Cherry had come across to the table in time to hear him. 'Cellan won't be discussing anything of a personal nature tonight.'

As she had on the beach, the publicist was careful to keep her tone light and airy, but the foundation of her instruction was gilded in steel. It was non-negotiable – of that, there could be no doubt.

'She's good, this one, I'll give you that,' said my father cheerfully. 'Being in the public eye can be like strolling through a minefield – you never know if what you say is going to blow up in your face.'

Given the number of minefields his character Benedict Stamp traversed in the books, my father's choice of metaphor was very apt, but I could see that it had not landed well with Cellan. Our host had put down his plate of food and folded his arms.

'I always go back to the advice my parents gave me growing up,' he said eventually. 'If you have nothing nice to say, it's better not to say anything at all.'

'Ah, that sounds like the British,' my father went on. 'Us Yanks are more of a "truth hurts, so deal with it" bunch.'

'No wonder the divorce rate is so high over here,' Cellan replied.

Tallulah giggled, and Cherry, who was examining the bowl of ambrosia salad and pulling much the same face as I had, sighed in exasperation.

'No personal talk,' she told him, waggling a finger. Then, to us, 'No offence, guys, but we don't know you. It's up to me to protect Cellan, so if I come across as a little uptight, it's only because I'm doing my job.'

I became aware then that I'd not said anything for a long time and opened my mouth only to close it again abruptly. Humour was my default whenever a situation became tricky, but it had abandoned me. There were too many live wires in this small circle, and I was worried what would happen if I inadvertently caused one to spark. Cellan, I observed, had retreated into himself, and stepping to one side, he beckoned over Padma the life coach. The woman did not so much walk as glide, her long skirt trailing along the honey-coloured stone of the poolside terrace. When Cellan offered to introduce her, she said that she knew everyone already, aside from me, and waited patiently for me to tell her who I was.

'I'm Jeffrey's daughter,' I explained, and she smiled although seemed confused. 'I'm English,' I added, guessing that my accent must have thrown her. 'My mother is . . . We live in England. I'm here visiting for a couple of weeks.'

'You're not staying for the whole summer?' Cellan sounded almost disheartened. 'Why not?'

'Oh, you know, I have stuff to do at home,' I lied. 'And I can't encroach on my father's hospitality for too long.'

Jeffrey, hearing mention of himself, butted into the conversation. 'What was that?'

'Honor was just telling us that she won't be here very long,' said Padma, casting a look in Cellan's direction. 'Which we're of course all very sad about.'

'That's her choice,' my father said, gammon-cheeked now from the whiskey. 'She knows she's welcome to stay as long as she likes.'

'I am?' This was news to me.

'Of course, honey. I love having you around; you bring me good luck. You're like a regular little mascot.'

I laughed. Because surely, that's what his words warranted.

'What's funny?' he asked, and then, turning to Padma, 'She's always chuckling away to herself, this one. I only wish she'd let the rest of us in on her jokes.'

'Oh, I don't know.' Cellan said slyly. 'I've heard a few of them, and we're all better off if she keeps schtum.'

Padma glanced from him to me, then back again, a smile playing around her lips. She'd painted them in the same crimson shade as her bindi, and in her swathes of black with contrasting gold jewellery adorning her fingers, wrists, throat and ears, she looked impossibly glamorous, yet not overdone. I recognised the same innate confidence in her that exuded from Tallulah and wondered if it was something that could be taught. People learned new languages all the time; perhaps I could be educated in the practice of self-love.

'And what is it that you do?' she asked, and I was midway through my reply when Cellan interrupted.

'She's writing a novel – a romance novel.'

Padma's dark eyes widened. 'That sounds exciting.'

'It will probably amount to nothing,' I began, but stopped as Padma shook her head.

'True confidence comes not from being right, but from not fearing to be wrong.'

'Easier said than done,' I muttered, and Cellan grinned.

'That's what I'm always saying to her,' he said. 'Drives her mad, doesn't it, Padma?'

'Perhaps the two of you could learn more from each other than I could ever teach?' she said, without a trace of sarcasm. 'And now that Honor will be staying here for the rest of the summer, there will plenty of opportunity to do so.'

'You're staying?' piped up Tallulah, turning away from where Cherry and my father appeared to be deep in conversation. 'That's such great news!'

'I don't know yet.'

I did not want to add that once back at the house, away from people he was set on impressing, my father could well change his mind. I'd always felt as if I was on borrowed time when it came to these annual visits, and that at any moment he would turn around and tell me he was too busy this year, that his schedule was set in stone and could not be moved around to accommodate his only child. As it was, I often spent the majority of my time in New York alone, wandering around the city as he worked on his latest best-seller. At least here in The Hamptons I wouldn't be alone. I had Tallulah, for some of the time, and now, however extraordinary it might be, it appeared I might have a friend in Cellan Thomas, too.

'What's to decide?' said Tallulah. 'Summer hanging out with all of us at the beach, or a flight home to rainy old England? No competition. Cellan, tell her she has to stay.'

'You don't have to say anything,' I protested. 'Don't let her bully you.'

But Cellan had given in to a smile, the first since the two of us had been interrupted by everyone else, and he waited until I looked at him to speak.

'I can't imagine that anyone could hope to tell you what to do,' he said, to which I pulled a face. 'But I do agree with what Padma said.'

'Which part?' I asked, aware that everyone around us had fallen silent.

Cellan did not seem to notice; his attention was solely on me.

'About us helping each other,' he said. 'I think she might be on to something.'

Padma pressed her hands together and rested her chin on her fingertips. 'I don't think,' she said. 'I know.'

And so, it was agreed. I would stay in The Hamptons for the summer at the behest of a Hollywood star. But while it was obvious to me exactly what I could gain from spending time with Cellan, who had already inspired me so much, I had no idea what help I could ever hope to offer him.

15

Jojo, when I rang her the following afternoon and let her know that I would not be home until the tail end of August, reacted in exactly the manner I'd predicted, repeating Cellan's name over and over incredulously, until I had no option but to tell her firmly to stop.

'But it's Cellan Thomas,' she repeated. 'How did this happen?'

'You know how,' I said, having opened the FaceTime call with the story. 'He ploughed into me when I was walking along, minding my own business.'

'This is incredible,' she enthused, blond topknot wobbling. She was clad in her typical Sunday afternoon uniform of men's jogging bottoms – likely pinched from a suitor – and an over-sized T-shirt from our decade-ago holiday to Zakynthos in Greece, which instructed its wearer to: *Drink triple, see double, act single.* For a while, the phrase had become her mantra.

'Dodie thinks so, too,' she added, angling the phone so I could see the sleeping form of her dog, who was stretched out on her back on the floor, all four paws akimbo.

'Yeah,' I agreed, unconvinced. 'She looks beside herself with excitement.'

'I think I might pass out,' Jojo went on. 'Is it too early to toast your good fortune with wine?'

'Definitely,' I said. 'Stick to tea if you please.'

'So, tell me more. What's he like? What does he smell like?

Is he as tall as he looks on screen? Does he have Hollywood teeth and an entourage? Is his girlfriend there, you know, whatshername? That awful waspish woman who pretends to cure people with bath bombs or whatever.'

'You mean Wylie Brooke?'

'That's the one.'

'No sign of her as yet, and no mention either, come to think of it.'

'Excellent,' Jojo said, getting up from the sofa and carrying the phone through with her into the kitchen, where she propped it up on the worktop. 'Keep talking,' she said. 'I'm just going to make a snack.'

'Boiled egg and salad cream sandwich?'

'You know me so well. What have you been eating over there?' she asked, adopting a twangy Texan accent. 'Bagel with cream cheese? Oatmeal with grandma's applesauce? A stack of pancakes with bacon and maple syrup?'

'I had the first one for breakfast today,' I admitted. 'And you're in no way amusing.'

She stuck out her tongue. 'Do you think we'll ever grow up?'

I sighed. 'Not if I can help it.'

'I bet you've been on your best behaviour around Cellan,' she said. 'None of your usual awful jokes, I hope?'

'Funny you should say that . . .' I told her, going on to explain about the beach meeting, and how Cellan and I seemed to have settled into an easy rhythm of traded jibes. Jojo dropped two eggs into boiling water, then fetched a loaf of bread from the fridge.

'Wow,' she said, when I'd finished talking. 'So, he's seen the real you?'

'A version of her,' I allowed. 'But I need to rein it in a bit, behave more like a thirty-two-year-old woman should, when conversing with an Oscar-winning actor.'

'Love how you casually dropped that in. My friend, y'know, the old Oscar winner.'

'It's true, though,' I protested. 'I want him to take me seriously, which he won't do if I'm simply myself.'

Jojo paused, butter knife in mid-air. 'What do you mean?'

'I mean,' I said, 'that being me is not going to be good enough, because I have never been good enough.'

Jojo came towards the phone and leaned forwards until her face filled the screen. I could see the Rorschach pattern of her irises, and a smear of toothpaste on her chin.

'Honor Butler,' she said gravely, 'you are more than good enough for anyone.'

'Jojo Tavner,' I intoned, 'you are more than kind to me, but you don't have to pretend. I know my failings and ignoring them is not going to help me get what I want.'

'Which is?' she asked, backing away to attend to her eggs.

'To write a prize-winning story,' I reminded her. 'Or have you forgotten about the competition?'

'No,' she said, swearing as some of the boiling water from the pan slopped onto her slippers. 'But I don't see how it relates—'

'Meeting Cellan has unblocked me,' I explained. 'I don't want to say too much at this stage, in case I jinx it, but I think I have the beginnings of what could be a great idea for a romantic comedy, one that brings a New Yorker and a Londoner together in a unique way.'

I could see from her expression that she was intrigued. 'Are you going to base your leading man on him?' she asked, enthused by the notion.

'No,' I said automatically, wincing inwardly as I realised this was not strictly true. If I sat down to write now, it was inevitable that Cellan would pour onto the page. There was no space in my mind for anyone else at the moment, fictitious or otherwise, yet I knew that if I set out to recreate a version of him for my own gains, I would be straying into morally murky waters.

'Are you sure?' Jojo said. 'Because he sounds like the ideal study to me. I mean, if anyone has a story worth telling, it's Cellan Thomas, and you just so happen to have been handed a front-row seat to his life. How can you resist?'

'You make it sound as if I'm some sort of tawdry tabloid journalist,' I protested. 'If I started to mine Cellan's life for character titbits, doesn't that make me dishonest?'

Jojo considered this for a moment. 'If you think about it, he hasn't exactly been one hundred per cent truthful with you,' she said, squeezing salad cream over her peeled eggs and reaching for a pepper grinder. 'Are you forgetting that he lied about being a stuntman when you first met?'

'He apologised for that,' I reminded her, only to falter. There was no escaping the fact that Cellan only admitted who he really was once he knew about my connection to the bestselling author, Jeffrey Butler; it could easily be that he was not impressed by me at all, and more by who I was related to.

'I just think that being a writer gives you a creative licence when it comes to this kind of thing,' she went on. 'Authors must base elements of their characters on the people they encounter all the time, even if they do it subconsciously. Cellan is an actor, he would understand that process, surely? And this competition is important to you. What was it you told me before you left? That you were going to make sure you won it, whatever the cost?'

'I haven't forgotten what I said,' I replied hotly, the implied pressure making me snappy. 'I'm just saying it's not as simple as picking a person and writing a story about them – that's not how it works.'

Jojo carried her sandwich and phone back into the lounge and sat heavily on the couch. 'I'm not here to tell you how to do . . . what you do,' she said, and I noted her reluctance to use the word 'job'. 'All I want is for you to value yourself more – and to have fun. I mean, if you don't manage to have a holiday fling with this man, then I may never forgive you.'

'Spoken like a true friend,' I said drily, and she smiled.

'The only advice I can give is just keep being yourself – don't rein the funny in, let it out. And don't ever go thinking you have to be someone else simply to be accepted, not by him or by anyone. Promise me.'

'I promise,' I said, crossing my fingers in my lap. I'd not moved from the wooden chair in front of the desk throughout the entire conversation, and my back was beginning to protest.

'I should go,' I said. 'Let you enjoy your sandwich in peace.'

'How many people am I allowed to tell?' she said urgently. 'About you meeting Cellan Thomas and basically becoming his best friend.'

I gave her a look. 'Nobody.'

'What? Not even my mum?'

'OK, her.'

'What about fish boy?'

'He's still in your pond?'

'What can I say, he knows how to show a gill a good time?' I groaned.

'And I like what he does with his rod—'

'Goodbye, Jojo.'

I hung up as she raised her enormous sandwich to her lips, winking at me lasciviously as she did so, and tossed my phone onto the small coffee table as the guilt began to trample its way through my high spirits. I had not been completely honest with Jojo, had not wanted to share my other reason for pursuing a friendship with Cellan. The truth was that when I, Tallulah, and my father had walked home together after the barbecue, it felt as if things had changed. I did not have to cast around for subjects to pique his interest, because he was the one asking me all the questions. For once, he had turned the full glare of his attention onto me, and I had basked in its warmth, enjoying the novelty of having impressed him – not through my ideas or opinions, or my writing, or my goofy humour, but because I had somehow befriended someone important. And I knew, without Jojo or anyone else having to spell it out for me, that I would do whatever it took to stay there.

16

Cellan had asked me to meet him outside the bakery on Windmill Lane, and despite setting off in plenty of time to get there early, he was waiting when I arrived.

It was a picture-book pretty day, the sky a cerulean blue canvas adorned with tufts of cloud. Purple perovskia blooms pushed their way through white picket fences, and the sun that shone across the trees dappled the smooth pavements with pebbles of light. Cats snoozed in the shade, bees fed lazily in window boxes, while the engines of the cars that passed seemed to purr with contentment.

'Hey,' I said, dismounting the bicycle that I had once again borrowed from the shed.

Cellan stood up from the step he had been perched on and took off his sunglasses. He was wearing a faded black T-shirt and pale blue jogger shorts above his trusty Vans and, as he drew nearer, I found my senses assailed by a fresh, clean scent. He had taken out the two hoop earrings he'd worn at the barbecue and replaced them with a single diamond stud.

'Thanks for coming,' he said, as if I would ever have refused his offer. 'This place does a great soft pretzel if you're game?'

'Sure,' I agreed, as he slid his shades back over his eyes, and put on the baseball cap that he'd been holding. His disguise, I realised, along with that beard of his. As much as it must be irksome, having to hide yourself away whenever you ventured outside, it would also be incredible to be that recognisable. Fame had always intrigued me.

The woman who served us either didn't notice who Cellan was, or didn't care enough to react, and within a few minutes, the two of us had our pretzels in a brown paper bag, along with a black coffee for me, and a cappuccino for him.

'I miss tea,' I confessed, and he nodded through a chewy mouthful.

'Me too. I have some bags at the house, I'll bring them next time.'

I experienced a thrill at 'next time'.

'Shall we walk?' I suggested. 'Unless you fancy another backy on the bike?'

'No, thank you,' he interrupted laughingly. 'Once was enough.'

I made sure the rickety contraption in question was locked up, and then the two of us set off in the direction of South Main Street. Aside from the occasional car, there was barely anyone around, and Cellan seemed nonplussed when I pointed this out.

'It's still early in the season – Memorial Day was only a few weeks ago. Don't worry, though, it will get busy. Really busy.'

'Do you think it's obvious that I'm an out-of-towner?' I asked, and Cellan hesitated for a moment while he appraised me. In an attempt to look less like an overgrown teenager than I had the first time we met, I'd worn a leaf-print smock dress and a pair of tan-coloured strappy sandals, which I had teamed with a new straw trilby.

'I'm afraid so,' he said, coming to a stop at a crossing. 'I've been living in the States pretty much full time for twelve years now, and no matter where I go, they always know I'm a Brit.'

'Or they just know you're a famous actor,' I pointed out, to which he frowned.

'Not at first.'

'Does it ever get less weird?' I asked, as the lights changed and a clicking sound started up. 'Being recognised by strangers?'

'Never,' he said, taking a sip of his coffee. 'You were a very welcome surprise.'

We rounded the corner and made our way past several quaint stores selling all manner of gifts, homeware items and foodstuffs. There was also a turquoise and pink-fronted pet shop, Little Lucy's Canine Couture Boutique, and I made a mental note to pop back there to buy something snazzy for Dodie. On Jobs Lane, we passed the elegant Ralph Lauren store, with its green awning and docile American flag, and I paused to peer through the window at the designer frocks and handbags.

'Seen something you like?' asked Cellan.

'Oh, only all of it,' I said with a sigh. 'A girl can dream.'

Cellan had taken a step back and was gnawing thoughtfully on his pretzel.

'It must feel powerful, to be rich,' I said. 'To be able to shop knowing that you could buy whatever you wanted.'

'Is that a question or a statement?' he asked.

'Maybe a bit of both. But don't feel you have to respond.'

'It's OK.' Cellan finished his coffee and scrunched up his empty paper bag. 'I'll tell you what it's like for me, but you might find that you're disappointed by my answer.'

I found that hard to believe and told him as much.

'I used to think that having money would make me happy,' he said. 'But then I made some, then a bit more, and then a lot more, and it didn't change the way I felt about . . . well, things, I guess. All that stuff we fill our homes with that we don't actually need. Take this for example,' he continued, going back to the window of Ralph Lauren and pointing at a simple white dress with capped sleeves. 'You didn't wake up this morning thinking about it, did you?'

Slowly, I shook my head.

'The only reason you want it is because you saw it. A few minutes ago, you had no idea it even existed.'

'But you could use that argument for anything,' I said. 'Even for people.'

'Ah,' he replied, 'but we're talking only about material stuff, the things that we have been coerced into thinking we need, thanks to all the years spent in a capitalist society. In reality, we don't need much at all, save for shelter, fuel and food. A capsule wardrobe should be enough to sustain us, and things like cars, phones and computers should not require an expensive upgrade every few years.'

'I get all that,' I said, 'but isn't there an argument that says it's OK to buy something simply because you love it?'

'But do you really love it, or have you been taught to associate pleasure with consumption?'

'I would argue that I really love books,' I told him, and Cellan grinned.

'OK, you have me on books. I'll allow those.'

'What about DVDs or movie downloads? You must be in favour of those?'

'Again, I'll allow it,' he said. 'But that's all.'

'So, you never go out and spend frivolously, simply because you can?'

Cellan stroked his beard. 'Once upon a time, maybe. But not anymore. These days I have a strict rule: unless I really, truly love it, I don't buy it. And you'd be amazed how much that one simple thing has curbed my spending.'

'You must have far more self-control than me,' I replied, remembering too late that he had recently fought a well-publicised battle against alcoholism. 'I mean, what you're saying makes sense, but I guess it's easier to view money casually when you have plenty of it. And what makes one person happy might differ wildly from others.'

'Do you think that dress would make you truly happy?' he asked. 'Because if so, I'll buy it for you. I'll buy you every dress in Southampton if that's all it takes.'

There was nothing in his manner that suggested he was joking, nor did he seem to be remotely annoyed with me for putting my side of the debate across. If anything, the conversation was entertaining him, but I felt cowed regardless.

'Please don't buy me every dress in Southampton. Some of them are absolutely vile. Have you seen the one that looks like a roll of toilet tissue would if it exploded inside a biro factory? No, thank you.'

'You sound upset,' he probed. 'I'm sorry if I came over a bit worthy – that's my small-town surfer boy coming out in me. Growing up, my parents didn't have a lot of spare cash, so my attitude towards money has always been a bit unusual.'

'I'm not upset,' I assured him, finding that now he'd apologised, I wasn't. 'And this is good, right? Happiness is what Padma wanted us to talk about.'

'True.' He laughed briefly. 'But, you know, Padma is not actually the wisest person in Southampton.'

'Oh?'

'No, there is one far wiser, and I happen to know that he's a big fan of dishing out advice.'

I rubbed my chin as I pretended to give it some thought.

'Nope,' I said. 'It's no good. I haven't got a clue who you mean.'

'Well,' said Cellan, 'I'm very glad to hear it. Because if you had, it would totally have ruined the surprise.'

I stared at him, still not understanding, then Cellan held out a hand.

'Come on,' he said. 'There's someone I'd like you to meet.'

17

'You're not funny, you know.'

I had followed Cellan in good faith as he led me up South Main Street, past the open cafés, and along the pristine sidewalk half-paved in terracotta tiles. There were more people milling around than there had been before, but aside from the odd smile of greeting, the two of us did not garner much attention. Cellan, in his disguise, could have been anyone, while I, of course, was no one. When he came to a stop outside the colourful window of Stevenson's Toys and Games, I was confused at first. And then I saw the machine.

'Don't tell me you've never seen the movie, *Big*?'

'Of course I have. Tom Hanks,' I added gravely, 'is an icon.'

'I know.' Cellan smiled wickedly. 'I've met him.'

Of course he had.

I turned back to face the machine, giving myself a moment to examine the Zoltar puppet inside. The man – well, he was half a man, given that only the top part of him fitted inside the large glass-fronted box – was dressed in a gold turban, canary silk shirt, swirly patterned waistcoat, and thick silver chain. There was a thin wooden flute tucked down the front of his trousers, and a light-up orb in his hands.

'He's got even more eclectic taste in jewellery than you,' I pointed out, as I clocked the plastic ruby ring and oversized gold hoop earring.

Cellan, who had come to stand beside me, made an amused-sounding grunt.

'Do you have a dollar?' he asked, motioning to the machine's payment slot. 'He speaks and everything – it's exactly like the one from the film.'

'That one caused all sorts of trouble,' I retorted, rooting through my bag for my purse. As soon as I'd fed in my crumpled note, Zoltar sprang rather jerkily to life, head nodding, hand moving slowly from side to side, and orb changing colour. Although I was expecting it, I was still startled when he spoke.

'The smallest, good deed is better than the grandest intention. Take it from me, the great Zoltar, intending shall get you nowhere, but doing, yes, that will bring you much, much reward. Provide Zoltar with more treasure, and I will provide you with the depths of wisdom.'

'Is that it?' I asked. 'Is that all the wisdom I get for my one hundred cents?'

'You get a keepsake, too,' said Cellan, as a small green card emerged from an ornate slot. On one side, there was the word 'Zoltar' and an image that reminded me of a tarot card, while on the other, a far longer version of what the puppet had just told me. I scanned the words.

'According to Zoltar here, I am a strong believer in fate, yet I feel that I have no control over my destiny. Hmm. He then goes on to say that, fortunately, I am destined to be very happy. Well, that's nice.'

'Anything else?' Cellan was peering over my shoulder.

'He worries that I'm irresponsible – ouch – and cannot tolerate slowness. Oh, and' – I said, starting to laugh ' – he says I will always live in a tidy atmosphere. He wouldn't say that if he could see my flat.'

'Messy, are you?'

'I prefer the term "organised chaos" if you please.'

'Noted.'

'I bet you have a team of people who you pay to tidy up after you,' I said, as I stowed my Zoltar card in my bag.

Cellan looked affronted. 'Absolutely not! I even do my own washing; I'm fully house-trained.'

'So am I,' I said. 'I just hate housework. I'd rather be reading.'

'Ah, of course,' he said, as we continued along the street. 'I was going to ask you about your book.'

'It isn't a book,' I replied. 'Not yet anyway.'

'How does it work then?' he asked. 'Do you just sit down, start writing and see what happens, or do you spend months planning everything before you begin?'

I gave him a sideways glance. 'Are you really interested?'

'I wouldn't ask if I wasn't.'

'You're probably better off asking my father. He's the expert.'

'I'd rather have your version.'

We had reached the top of South Main Street, where the Golden Pear café wrapped itself around the corner. I'd treated myself to a breakfast bagel here the previous day and smiled back as one of the waitresses clearing an outdoor table said hello. Seeing Cellan, she did a double take, her cheeks flushing with colour.

'Can I get you guys a seat?'

'No, thanks,' we said in unison, Cellan striding away towards the pedestrian crossing as I shuffled, waved and apologised for no good reason other than the fact I was British. The lights changed almost immediately, and I had to jog to catch up with him.

'I think she . . .' I began, and he nodded.

'It's OK. Doesn't matter.'

'Where are we going now?'

'You're going in here,' he said, as the wooden facade of Southampton's only bookshop came into view. 'Have a browse, while I go and pick something up from Citarella.'

I'd not been inside the bookshop yet, so was happy to do as he suggested, and stood for a moment or two outside, watching him walk away. He did so smoothly, but it was a steady tread as opposed to a saunter, a pace that communicated a message that he was not going to stop for a friendly chat. I wondered if a lot of celebrities had adopted a similar gait, learning through necessity to put their heads down and get to wherever they were going as soon as possible. Tiresome, certainly, but probably worth it when you considered the rewards.

The bookshop was a cluttered paradise inside, with overstocked floor-to-near-ceiling shelves, several display tables, and a small section towards the back that offered a range of stationery. A bright-faced girl of around eighteen greeted me from behind the till, and I had to step around the crouched figure of a second, older woman, who was busy removing a stack of hardbacks from a low shelf.

'Excuse me,' I said, then hesitated as I caught sight of the dust jackets. 'Can I?'

'Sure, honey – help yourself. We just heard from the guy's assistant that he's in town and is keen to pass by to sign a few copies. You might want to wait for one of those.'

Picking up one of the books, I turned it over, scanning the bio that was printed below a photo of the author and experiencing, as I always did, a pinch of rejection. It was where I wanted to be, in pride of place among the very best, next to the man whose opinion had always mattered more to me than any other.

'Don't worry, Dad,' I murmured, touching a finger to his face. 'I'm working on it.'

The woman stood up with some effort and bustled across to one of the low tables.

'Darn things are so heavy.'

'My mum complains about exactly the same thing,' I told her. 'She runs a bookshop in Cambridge.'

'Massachusetts?'

'England.'

There followed a flood of excitable chatter, as she demanded to see photos, discuss which titles sold the best, and made me promise to put both women in touch.

'We can send each other book recommendations,' she said, clasping her hands together.

Her glee was infectious, and I found myself scribbling down not only my mother's work email, but my personal one as well. Only when I saw Cellan loitering in the street outside did I extract myself, and the woman followed me to the door.

'My name's Rose,' she said, pressing a business card into my hand. 'Do pop in again, won't you?'

I promised I would, smiling to myself as I joined Cellan.

'Book people,' I said, by way of explanation. 'They are the very best.'

He'd taken off his sunglasses, and his hazel eyes softened as he turned them towards me.

Flustered, I looked away. 'Did you get what you needed?'

He held up a plastic container. 'Yep.'

I squinted at the label. 'Fish food? You really shouldn't have.'

'Well, you refused to let me buy you a dress, so . . .'

'How roe-mantic,' I drawled. 'Get it? Roe-mantic.'

Cellan shook his head. 'I got it.'

'Seriously, though – why the hell have you bought a tub of fish food?'

'That's for me to know,' he said slyly, 'and you to find out.'

Again, he led the way down South Main Street, only this time we walked along the opposite side of the street. There were more boutiques and a number of restaurants, tables dressed up like a wedding day in starched white cloth and flowers. Instead of heading right at the end of the road, Cellan crossed straight over and continued on towards a sweep of green bordered by trees.

'This is Agawam Park,' he told me. 'There's usually a fish market here on Sundays, but we must have missed it.'

'It's pretty,' I said, admiring the imposing stone arches of what looked to be a memorial. Several families had set themselves up with picnic blankets on the lawn, and a clutch of young children were pedalling around the perimeter on their bikes.

In the distance, I could see the shimmer of water, and raised an enquiring brow at Cellan.

'The lake,' he supplied. 'And the reason for this.' He shook the fish food at me. 'Better for them than the lumps of bread that people are always lobbing in there.'

'Lobbing,' I repeated with a laugh.

'What's wrong with lobbing?'

'It's just such a British word, like "golly" and—'

'Mate,' put in Cellan.

'Yes! And "chuffed".'

'What about "plonker"?'

'Nice one. And I would argue for "bollocks".'

He laughed. 'Such a lady.'

'Pretty sure your first word to me was "shit".'

'Oh yeah. Shit.'

I tutted. 'There you go again.'

We had reached the boundary of the pond, and Cellan rested his elbows on the top of the wooden fence that ran along its edge. Almost immediately, the surface of the water below began to darken, and the eager mouths of several fish came into view.

'Here.' He unscrewed the lid from the tub of food and offered it to me. I took a pinch of the pungent flakes and dropped them over the side, letting out an exclamation of delight as they were gobbled up instantly.

'What type are they – do you know?'

Cellan shook his head regrettably. 'My dad would. He came over here last summer and spent pretty much the entire week on the lake.'

'They look like carp to me,' I said. 'Although that is my standard go-to, if I ever spot anything bigger than a goldfish.'

'Do you spend a lot of time peering into ponds then?'

'Well, you know what they say about plenty more fish . . .'

I had meant it as a joke, but Cellan looked suddenly serious.

'You're single then?'

My reply seemed to snag in my throat, and instead of emitting words, I made a gargling sound, then coughed so hard that he took a few steps away from me.

'Sorry,' I spluttered. 'Must have inhaled some of the fish food. Give me a second.'

I turned away from him, bending over as I attempted to hack up whatever it was that was choking me, although I suspected it was nothing more sinister than embarrassment.

'I shouldn't have asked you that,' said Cellan when I'd regained control of myself. 'It's none of my business.'

'It's fine – I don't mind.'

'No, honestly, Honor. I hate it when people ask me direct questions like that; I loathe it so much, in fact, that I tell

Cherry to warn journalists off before I talk to them. I know I have a public persona,' he went on, grimacing slightly over the last word, 'but I've never understood the fascination around my dating life. It has nothing to do with acting.'

I stared at him for a moment, trying to gauge whether he was being straight with me, but I saw no trace of humour on his features, and could detect no hint of sarcasm in his tone.

'You really don't get it?'

'No.' He laughed in exasperation. 'I really don't.'

'It's because people idolise you,' I said. 'They want to know everything about you – favourite colour, first pet, who you may or may not be romantically involved with . . . All of it. You must have known this before you became famous.'

'I didn't set out to be famous,' he protested, kicking a stone through the dirt. 'All I wanted to do was act.'

'In major blockbuster movies,' I pointed out gently.

'All I did was follow Gunnar's advice. Fame was an unfortunate perk of the jobs I was being offered.'

'But it's a privilege,' I said, my voice low but firm. 'Plenty of people would love to be in your position. I would do anything to be as famous as you.'

Cellan looked up in surprise. 'Really?'

It was too late to take it back. I raised my hands in a show of surrender.

'Maybe not anything,' I allowed, 'but essentially, yes. Fame equals success, doesn't it? And I have always wanted to be successful.'

Cellan considered me, his free hand tugging at his beard, and then he shook his head. 'Here,' he said, handing me the tub of fish food. 'You do the rest. I've just remembered I have a call. A meeting. I'd better go.'

'Right now?'

'Yes. Sorry. My bad.'

'Wait,' I said, confusion knotting my brow. 'I'll walk back with you.'

But Cellan was already striding away, and from the speed of his departure and the haste with which he'd put a sizeable amount of distance between us, it was clear I was not invited to follow.

18

I had two choices: let him go and risk never see seeing him again or give chase.

I gave chase.

'Hey,' I called, shouting his name when I got no response. Cellan stopped and swung around in exasperation. A young mother sitting on a picnic blanket a few yards away paused in the process of feeding bits of muffin to her toddler and eyed us curiously. I'd outed him, I realised with a jolt. No wonder he was glaring at me. But almost as soon as the contrition struck, so did the frustration. I might have yelled his name out across the park, but he'd stomped off with barely a backward glance, leaving me with limited options.

'What did I say?' I asked. 'Why are you running away?'

'I'm not,' he said, before gesturing for me to follow him. For the few minutes that it took us to reach the road, I remained silent, retracing our conversation in my head. The subject of fame had been bad idea; that much was obvious.

'Sorry,' I said, at exactly the same moment he did. We both smiled.

'Do you really have a meeting?'

'Yes,' he said uncertainly, drawing up the word and my eyebrows along with it. Catching sight of my expression, he grinned. 'I really do – but not for an hour or so. I have time to walk you back to the bike.'

I started to ask him another question, but Cellan cut across me. 'I feel like we've talked way too much about my life,' he said. 'It's time you told me more about yours. Like, what made you want to be a writer for example?'

My standard answer to this question was that my father was the person who inspired me – but the truth was a little different, and I wanted to be honest with Cellan.

'I never wanted to be a writer per se,' I told him, pausing as we crossed onto Hill Street and headed west. 'A writer is what I am. At least, that's how it's always felt. I was telling stories from a very young age, and writing has always been my creative outlet, how I make sense of the world. Am I talking in riddles?' I said, when Cellan did not respond.

'You are. I was trying to think of something original and intelligent to say, if you'll only give me a minute.'

'Probably take longer than a minute,' I quipped, thankful that we'd returned to previous form and were once again trading light-hearted chat.

Cellan tutted at me. 'Having a way of expressing yourself is such an important thing,' he said. 'When I meet people who aren't into the arts at all, as in, not even reading one book a year, actively disliking art and the theatre, and never listening to music simply for pleasure, I feel as if I'm conversing with an alien. It's like, "Dude, how do you relax?"'

'Maybe they watch movies?' I suggested. 'Or I'd hope they would, after meeting you.'

The bakery was only a short way ahead of us; I could see the bike where I'd left it, tethered to the railings outside, and felt sadness like a heavy weight across my chest. I did not want this day, walk, encounter, date – whatever it was – to end.

'So,' Cellan mused, 'you don't think I have it in me to be smart or unique, but you do rate me as an actor?'

I stopped and faced him, pretending to consider his question carefully.

'I liked you in that one about the Scottish rebels going to war with the English.'

'A lot of women say that. Is it the kilt, the scraggly beard, or the dodgy accent?'

'The scenery,' I said, delighted to elicit a genuine laugh. 'But I didn't mind the beard – it was better than the one you have now.'

Cellan touched his hand to his chin, a self-conscious gesture that made me feel immediately guilty. 'This is all my own,' he said regretfully. 'The one the make-up team gave me was far manlier.'

'Acting must require an incredible amount of concentration,' I went on. 'And self-control. I would be terrible at it; I'd continually get the giggles.'

'That does happen.' Cellan had started walking again, and I had no choice but to follow. 'Nothing infuriates a director more – well, maybe except lateness. A film production schedule is like a tower made of matchsticks; one missing piece, and the whole thing is at risk of collapse.'

'Right, so tardiness and laughter are big no-nos – anything else I should know?'

'Why?' Cellan eyed me suspiciously, 'are you thinking of retraining?'

'Well, I figure being an actress could potentially be more fun than a student support assistant.'

'You're a writer, though,' he said. 'That beats both.'

'I'm not.' I'd said it so forlornly that he turned to look at me properly. We had reached the bakery, but I made no move to unlock the bike.

'Not what – a writer? Yes, you are.'

'Unpublished,' I reminded him.

'For now.'

He looked on the verge of placating me further, but suddenly I was loath to let him. I was being self-indulgent and, as my father often proclaimed, nobody wanted to spend time with a whinger.

'You never answered my question,' I said. 'About the acting – are there any rules?'

'Do you genuinely want to learn?' he asked. 'Because if you do, I can teach you.'

'You'd do that?'

Cellan shrugged, lifting a tatty trainer to nudge at the wheel of my bike. The clouds chose that moment to part, and his diamond earring sparkled as it caught the light.

'Sure,' he said. 'I can put you to the test, see if you have any potential.'

'You won't make me do anything interpretive, will you? I'm still mentally scarred from the time I had to pretend to be a tree in primary school. Everyone else wafted around in circles with their hands in the air, and I just lay on the floor. In my head, I was a felled oak, but my teacher accused me of cheating.'

'Sounds interpretive to me,' Cellan remarked, as I crouched to remove the chain lock from the bike. I was horribly conscious of time ebbing away; a clock set to rotate at twenty times its regular speed.

'Traumatic,' I corrected him. 'Those things stay with a person.'

'Noted. What if I can promise you no trees?'

'I'm not pretending to be a cat either – or a donkey, or any animal for that matter.'

'OK, so, basically what you're saying is, "Cellan, please don't make me do anything that has the potential to cause ridicule."'

'Nutshell.'

'OK. That I can do. I'm tied up the next few days, but if you're around on Wednesday then—'

'I am.'

Cellan stumbled backwards in mock surprise.

'Funny,' I deadpanned. 'If I'm eager, it's only because I'm following the advice of your friend.'

'My . . . who?'

'Zoltar,' I said, smiling sweetly at him as I put my bag in the bike basket. 'What was it he said? "Intending shall get you nowhere, but doing, yes, that will bring you much, much reward."' I'd recited the words in the same spooky voice used by the puppet and waved my hand around for good measure.

'Impressive.' Cellan fought down a smile. 'The fact that you can remember lines is encouraging.'

'What about the accent?' I asked hopefully, but Cellan had been distracted by his phone. It was the first time I'd seen him with a mobile, and it was only in his hand for a few seconds before he slipped it back into the pocket of his shorts, a frown just discernible around the layers of sunglasses, hat, and facial hair. It was probably the person he was supposed to have a meeting with, or a member of his staff reminding him about it. I pictured Cherry, remembering how determined she was to protect Cellan, and wondered what she thought about him spending his morning with me.

'You need to go,' I said, before he had the chance to.

Cellan smiled, grateful but sheepish. 'I'm late,' he said. 'A director's nightmare.'

'Thank God you look good in a kilt.'

'Wednesday?'

'It's all yours.'

Cellan folded his arms. I thought he would move when I pushed away from the kerb, but he didn't. Instead, he remained in the spot I had left him, and when I reached the corner and turned around a final time, he was still there.

Cellan Thomas.

Movie star.

Watching me.

19

The house felt oddly quiet when I let myself back in. Not the low hum of a dwelling recently vacated, but a taut silence, as if all the rooms inside were holding in a collective breath.

'Hello?' I called, reaching out a hand to stop the screen door from banging shut behind me. 'Anyone home?'

Nobody replied, and I could not detect so much as a murmur from upstairs. Tallulah and my father must have gone out. Heading to the kitchen, I glanced around in case either of them had thought to leave me a note but was unsurprised when I found nothing waiting. There were tell-tale signs of life in this part of the house at least. A jar of damson preserve was on the worktop, a knife sticky with residue in the sink, and when I opened the fridge in search of a snack, I discovered a half-drunk bottle of champagne and, chuntering to myself, retrieved a spoon from the drawer and slid it into the neck. My father was not usually a daytime drinker, so I could only assume that he'd had cause for celebration. Probably broken a new sales record, I thought, feeling all of a sudden deflated.

Taking off my new straw hat, I tossed it onto the table along with my bag and pulled out my phone, thinking that I would put on a podcast. I was at least three episodes behind on a new book review series called *Take it as Read* and had been waiting for the opportunity to catch up. I knew what I should be doing was writing; noting down the details of my

day with Cellan while it was still centre stage in my mind, yet
any urge I'd felt to sit down with my laptop on the cycle ride
back had been replaced by edginess, the sense that I was
missing something important.

The clock on the wall was ticking, its circular surround the
same dark rosewood as the cabinets. This was not the most
attractive room in the house, but it far outshone the cramped-
into-one-corner rectangle of lino that constituted my food
preparation area at home. I wondered what Cellan, with his
palatial beachside rental and Los Angeles apartment, would
think if he ever saw inside my poky Cambridge flat, letting
out a laugh that promptly stalled in my throat when I heard a
creak of floorboards above me, followed by a door being
softly opened and closed.

'Tallulah?' I called tentatively, as I put my hat back on to
hide the bald patch. 'Is that you?'

'Afraid not,' boomed a voice, just as my father came into
view on the landing.

Despite the balmy heat of the late afternoon, he was
wearing faded brown cords below a long-sleeved shirt and
had slung a mustard sweater across his shoulders. 'Will your
old dad do?'

He seemed in an extremely chipper mood.

'Less of the old,' I said, as he slid his watch over his wrist.
Seeing me looking, he paused for a moment on the bottom
stair.

'I have to take it off when I'm working. Damn thing is
heavy enough to give a guy repetitive strain injury.'

'Were you at home alone?' I asked, only to stall once again
as a door banged shut somewhere above us. My father's gaze
flickered upwards for only a second.

'Must be the wind,' he said. 'It gets stuffy if you don't open
the windows.'

'Didn't you hear me calling a few minutes ago?' I persisted, following him back along the hallway towards the kitchen.

'No, sorry, honey, I didn't hear a peep. Must have been in the zone. When I get lost in the action, you could let a bomb off next to me and I wouldn't so much as blink.'

'You're lucky,' I said honestly, as I recalled the many times I'd settled down to write, only to be distracted by the notifications on my phone, or people passing by under the window or, in truth, pretty much anything. My mother should have named me Procrastination – it would have suited me perfectly.

'Concentration can't be taught,' he said, filling a glass with water from the tap. 'It's one of those gifts you're born with.'

'Or not,' I intoned. Then, before he could reply, I asked, 'Is the new book going well, then?'

'I was actually doing a final read on the screenplay of my latest,' he said, with a sigh of pride long enough to inflate several balloons. 'The production company are ready to hit go on the project just as soon as we get some serious talent attached, and while we have the usual guy signed up as Benedict again, we still need to cast Marty, the son. Whoever it is will inherit the franchise, so there's no room for screw-ups. We need someone with real star power.'

'Is it a good script?' I asked, watching as he extracted a tub of olives from the fridge and speared one with a cocktail stick. The spoon inside the champagne bottle clattered against the door, but my father did not seem to notice. He was too deep in thought, giving my question serious consideration.

'Average,' he concluded. 'They brought a woman on board – part of a new drive to test sensitivity, or some clap-trap – and she's added things that have no merit. To be honest, it's a waste of my time, and therefore a waste of everyone else's dollar – but this is what Hollywood is all about nowadays: endless hoops weaved out of damn political correctness. And you know what I'm always telling you: to see the world from the top, you got to be prepared to walk along the tightrope.'

I failed to stop my face from creasing into a frown, and he gave me a pitying look.

'It's a metaphor, honey.'

'I know what a meta—'

'Anyway, tell me about your day. Cellan do a good job of showing you around town, did he?'

My father popped in another olive, chewing as I told him a few highlights. I left out any mention of my own faux pas, but I did tell him about feeding the fish.

'Sounds as if you've made quite the impression on him and, I have to say, I'm more than a little impressed. You may not have inherited my grade-A concentration skills, but I'm definitely staking my claim on your charm; that is all thanks to me.'

'Charming? Me? I don't think—'

'Oh, honey – come on. Cellan's a smart kid.'

'What do you mean?' I asked, as the last of the olives disappeared. 'Smart how?'

But my father was rummaging in the fridge again, muttering something about pickles. 'Darn it,' he said. 'Tally will have to go to the store.'

'Where is she, by the way?' I asked. Despite my keenness to have my father all to myself, I found that I missed her easy presence, the way she played umpire when his caustic remarks made me wince.

'Oh, out having her nails done or some such.'

'Really?' This puzzled me. 'I didn't think she was the nails type.'

'Maybe it was her hair, then. Truth be told, honey, I wasn't paying much attention when she stuck her head around the door. I was in the zone, remember?'

'Do you want me to make you a sandwich?' I asked. He'd taken out the bread, the cheese, and some rather wizened tomatoes, and was staring at them hopefully.

'Would you, honey? That would be swell.'

'No probl—'

'Slap plenty of relish on there, won't you?'

'I will. Do you want any crisps, I mean chips, on the side?'

'Sure. Whatever you think. I'll be outside.'

The hinges on the ancient back door squeaked in protest as he pulled it open, and a few seconds later I heard him dragging a chair across the wooden patio outside. Assuming he'd done so in order to sit in the shade, I was touched to find that he had, in fact, been pulling up a seat for me, which he patted as I handed him his plate.

'Sit,' he said. 'Talk to me about your novel. It's a romance, right?'

He had fished his glasses out from his shirt pocket and put them on – a clear sign that he'd re-entered work mode.

'It's not much of anything yet,' I confessed, torn between the desire to tell him my plan and the inkling that to do so would be a bad idea. 'But I think it has potential.'

'Have you started? Can I see anything, give you some pointers?'

'No! I mean, yes, I have, but it's all very rough. Nothing is at reading stage yet.'

'Well, as soon as you have something, I'm here to help. It might not be my preferred genre,' he went on, as I pulled an 'are you sure?' face, 'but I do know good writing.'

'I don't want to take up any of your time,' I mumbled, and reaching across, my father put a hand on my knee.

'You're worth it, honey,' he said. 'You're more valuable to me than anything else.'

Tears swelled, hot and unexpected.

I had felt like many things to my father over the past twenty-four years – at worst an inconvenience, and at best a rather tiresome houseguest – but I had never, not once, felt precious to him.

'Thank you,' I managed. 'That means a lot.'

My father removed his hand and picked up the sandwich I'd made him.

'Love you, honey,' he said, and I felt myself unfurl with happiness.

'Love you, too, Dad.'

We both swung around as the back door opened and Tallulah appeared.

'Here you both are,' she said. 'Like two seeds in an apple core.'

'Isn't it two peas in a pod?' I replied, and she grinned.

'Nobody likes a cliché, right, JB?'

'Lesson one,' he agreed.

I was about to ask her where she'd been when Tallulah began firing questions at me: she wanted to know 'everything about your date – oh, come on, it was *so* a date', asking me to relay every word, every nuance, every look that had passed between myself and Cellan, until my father threw his hands up in surrender.

'I'm out of here,' he said. 'Leave you girls to your gossip.'

'There's nothing to tell,' I protested, but he was already on his feet.

'Don't worry about preparing any food tonight,' he told Tallulah. 'I'm taking both of you out somewhere special, so make sure your glam rags are on by eight p.m. sharp.'

'Glad rags,' I corrected, like an irritating little pedant.

My father barked with laughter. 'Nope,' he said. 'I used the word "glam" on purpose. This place is hot news. You'll want to look your best, trust me.'

'OK,' I said, with the requisite amount of enthusiasm. Glam was all well and good if all your hair was present and correct on your head. I waited for him to go back inside before I took down the scaffolding on my smile. Tallulah, who, I noted, had also gone from sparkling to subdued in the space of a few seconds, slumped on the patio steps by my feet and stared out across the garden. I inspected her for any signs of a manicure or blow-dry, but as far as I could tell, she'd had neither.

'Bad day?'

Tallulah did not seem to hear me, and when I repeated the question, all I got in response was a 'huh'. I went to sit beside her, unfastening my sandals and chucking them over my shoulder with a snort of relief.

'Remind me never to go out in anything but trainers again.'

'Sneakers,' she murmured.

'Whatever. Potato, potarto. My feet are bloody killing me. What's your excuse?'

'For what?' she asked mildly.

'That frown. If the wind changes, it'll get stuck like that.'

'Nothing a little Botox won't fix.'

'Well, good luck affording any of that around here. I saw a dress in a shop down the road earlier that cost three thousand dollars.'

Tallulah tried to smile.

'If there is a Botox clinic,' I said, 'do you think it also offers hair transplants?'

'Hair transplants?' Tallulah looked at me sharply. 'Why on Ear—? Oh. Oh my God!'

'I know,' I said, the hat I had just removed clutched in both hands. 'It's bad, isn't it?'

'How did you?' she asked, examining the hairless oval in more detail.

I told her about the incident with the hair brush, and she sighed.

'Well, at least this explains that godawful scarf you wore to the cookout. I honestly thought you'd chosen it because you thought it looked nice. Jeez.'

'Will you please help me to cover it up?' I begged. 'I feel like a less-sexy Friar Tuck.'

Finally, I'd managed to make her laugh, so hard that she resorted to wiping the tears from her eyes as she fiddled around with my hair, twisting pieces this way and that.

'I think I can do something,' she said. 'What are your views on braids?'

'On thirty-two-year-old women? Yuck. But you know what they say about beggars.'

Tallulah laughed again. 'I can tell you're a writer,' she said. 'You have so much natural wit. If I tried to write a joke, it would take me a week, and even then, I'd leave off the punchline.'

'At least you'd never be the punchline.'

I had meant it as a compliment to her, but Tallulah's face seemed to fall once again.

'Where were you earlier?' I asked gently. 'Da— JB was a bit vague on the details. You don't have to tell me,' I added when she didn't immediately reply.

Tallulah sighed. 'I had to take a phone call, someone from home.'

'Has something happened?'

'Kinda.' She smiled in an attempt to reassure, though whether it was for my benefit or her own, I couldn't tell. 'Now, we should head on up, get started on your hair.'

'Tallulah, if there's something wrong . . .'

'No.' She shook her head, unwilling or unable to meet my eye. 'Everything will be fine. It has to be.'

20

It took us a little over thirty minutes to reach Three Mile Harbor which, as my father was quick to inform us, got its name not from its size or the depth of water surrounding it, but because of its distance from East Hampton. The Dall'Acqua restaurant at its northernmost tip was illustrious enough to boast its own marina, where patrons who chose to arrive by water had the option to moor their yachts and would apparently do so in plentiful numbers once the season got into full swing.

The sun had begun to set, the sky around it a riotous orange smeared purple by torn shreds of cloud. Below, the beach was painted silver, the grasses that bordered it sprigs of the darkest green. Night was waiting in the wings with its palette and brush, ready to transform the world into shadow.

Despite dressing in one of the nicest outfits I'd brought with me from home – a white floaty number with broderie anglaise detailing – I still felt woefully far from chic as I glanced around at the other diners. The men wore deck shoes with bare feet, polo shirts with the collars turned up, and belted chino shorts ironed to a stiff crease. Their female companions lounged in Missoni midis or brash Gucci blouses atop skin-tight white jeans. Hair styles were coiffed and high-lighted, wrists and throats adorned with gold, and there was barely a guest seated that did not have half their face obscured by oversized sunglasses. It reeked of money and privilege, and I adjusted myself, accordingly, raising my chin and relaxing my shoulders in an attempt to look as if I belonged.

My father stepped ahead to speak to the hostess, who greeted each of us politely before leading us through the restaurant and out onto the wooden deck beyond. We passed tables laid with white cloth and flowers, weaving in and out until we reached what I could only assume was the most coveted spot, right at the very front, overlooking an undisturbed sweep of water. A man was waiting for us, and I experienced a small jolt of surprise as he stood up and raised a hand.

Gunnar Hayes had swapped his black glasses for a more subtle rimless pair, and his thick, grey hair looked damp, as if he'd not long ago showered. When he leant across the table to kiss my cheek, I was almost asphyxiated by a waft of lime and cedarwood.

'Honor,' he said, clasping a hand to my shoulder so firmly that my knees buckled. 'Great to see you again.'

'Likewise,' I said, mystified by his presence. 'Are you waiting for someone?'

Gunnar glanced at my father, and the two men exchanged a knowing look.

'I thought it would be nice if Jeff and I got to know each other a little better,' he explained. 'And, as he told me the three of you come as a set, here we are.'

Tallulah was smiling so broadly that she was in danger of floating right off the deck.

'This place is just awesome,' she said, sliding gracefully into the chair that my father was holding out for her. 'Like something you'd see in a magazine.'

'It's a neat spot,' Gunnar agreed. 'But the striped bass is what keeps me coming back.'

'We should let you order for us,' gushed Tallulah. 'As you're the host.'

'I wouldn't dream of making a woman's decision for her,' he replied. 'Reckon it'd be a safer option sticking my hand into the lobster tank up there.'

I had clocked the rather macabre display to which he was referring on the way in and had mentally crossed shellfish off my menu options as a result. Seafood was one thing, seeing food while it was still alive and swimming quite another. When I said as much to the table at large, Gunnar rolled his eyes.

'You're not one of these so-called vegans, are you?'

'No,' I said, debating whether to challenge his use of 'so-called'.

'Well, that's a relief. Every place you go in LA now, it's mushroom this and lentil that. Finding a decent steak has become near-on impossible, and don't even get me started on all these milk substitutes.'

Tallulah and my father were nodding along, and I knew I should do the same. Gunnar Hayes was a powerful man; impressing him was the sensible option, but I could not quite bring myself to capitulate. Instead, I changed the subject.

'How long have you been coming to The Hamptons?' I asked.

'Oh, forever.' Gunnar clicked his fingers to summon a passing waitress and ordered sparkling water and a bottle of 'your best Chablis, make it ice cold' for the table. 'Ever since I was a boy. And I tell you what, it's changed an awful lot between the seventies and now. Back then it was little better than feral in places, and now it's New York's answer to Ibiza – a place to see and be seen.'

It occurred to me then that with both Gunnar and, to a lesser extent, my father, in tow, our small group had potentially become one worth seeing. I stole a glance around at the other diners, but nobody was gawping in our direction – not even subtly. I could only assume that perhaps when you regularly ate at places like Dall'Acqua, the celebrity sightings became commonplace. I had only ever seen one famous person before this summer – an Australian soap actor who was in Cambridge doing pantomime back in the early noughties, and who Jojo had managed to get a snog from when he did a personal appearance at our local nightclub. 'Gross,' she'd proclaimed afterwards. 'Tongue like an adder.'

The waitress was back with our drinks, and I was pleased to see my father – the evening's designated driver – refuse the wine.

'I should probably consider cutting back,' Gunnar said with a sigh, before proceeding to top his own glass up to the brim. Tallulah, who had not said much since we arrived, took such a large sip of her own wine, it caused her to choke.

I escaped to the bathroom to check that my complicated arrangement of plaits had not come undone, marvelling at the marble basin surrounds and gold-plated taps. There was a full-length mirror propped against the wall, its burnished antique glass making my still-pale skin appear sun-kissed, and I paused for a moment to examine myself. When was it, I wondered, that we transitioned from peering at our reflection through our own eyes to fixating instead on how we must look to others; when our standards for what was 'acceptable' switched from the everyday to the unreachable. I found it hard to recall a time when I had stared into a mirror and not found something to criticise, whether it was the width of my thighs, the protrusion of my stomach or, in this case, the outright oddness of my hair. It was exhausting. And here, in The Hamptons, immersed as I was in the lives of the far more attractive, wealthy, and successful, that sense of being someone who lacked had never felt more acute. It would be an interesting topic to explore in a novel, if only it was not such a passive trait. I knew what my father would say – that readers want an external not internal battle – and ground my teeth in frustration at the propensity of my own mind to lead me in completely the wrong direction.

I must try harder, be better.

'Honor,' said Gunnar when I finally rejoined the others. 'I was about to send out a search party.'

'Just admiring the facilities,' I told him, reaching for my wine.

'How's your book coming along?'

I flushed. 'It's not.'

'Not finding The Hamptons inspiring?'

'It's not that,' I said, meeting Tallulah's eye. 'I suppose I lack discipline. I need to be locked in a turret or something, with nothing but pen and paper, and no Wi-Fi code.'

'That's all I started with,' said my father, who had rolled up the sleeves of his blue-and-white striped shirt. He had cut himself shaving, I noticed; there was a bud of dried blood on his jawline. 'I still write longhand on occasion – feels more authentic somehow, and the written word has the added bonus of never getting lost when your damn machine decides to crash, as mine did not long ago. I lost forty thousand words of a book. Never got them back.'

'Heavens.' Tallulah had actually gasped. 'I would die if that happened to me.'

'I was pretty grouchy for a few days,' he told her. 'Bashed around my apartment like a moose with a broken antler, then started all over again. Fortunately,' he added, tapping a hand to his forehead, 'my memory is damn-near perfect, so I was able to recall most of what I had already written.'

'That's because you're amazing,' she replied dutifully, and I caught the flicker of something pass across Gunnar's face.

'Life nowadays is full of distractions,' he said, turning his attention back to me.

A gull had landed on one of the wooden posts that protruded from the water in the marina, and from where I was sitting, it looked as if it was perched atop Gunnar's head. I suppressed a smile.

'It's never been easier to get nothing done,' he said.

'Everyone needs a little downtime,' I replied neutrally.

'That's the problem with you Brits; you're inherently lazy – no offence.'

I stuttered out a denial, but he was having none of it.

'It's not your fault; it's been bred into you. All those years of the Empire, of making everyone else do the hard graft while you sat back and collected the profits. It's why us Americans so often have the upper hand – we're motivated to work harder.'

I finished my glass of wine and Gunnar, discovering that the bottle propped in the ice bucket was empty, motioned to the waitress for another.

'I say this to Cef all the time,' he went on, his extravagant hand gestures almost knocking over the table's decorative shell centrepiece. 'To be a big name in this game, you have to be prepared to keep working. Idle too long, and you're in danger of sinking faster than a stone into a bathtub.'

'But Cellan's done loads of films,' I said, more puzzled than defensive. 'Wasn't *Mr Right* his seventeenth? Not bad going, when you consider that his first proper acting role was only thirteen years ago.'

'Someone's been cramming their stats,' murmured my father.

The conversation was halted then by the arrival of our first course, which I saw to my horror was six fresh clams apiece, and a vast platter of oysters. The wine churned unpleasantly in my stomach, reminding me that I hadn't eaten since the soft pretzel of that morning, and I snatched up my sparkling water, hoping it would douse the nausea.

'Tuck in,' urged Gunnar, his hand huge as it picked up the tiny spoon propped in the dish of seafood sauce. I didn't care how much lemon, tomato or black pepper was on offer; there was still no way I was putting one of the slimy morsels into my mouth.

'Delicious,' Tallulah said, as if on cue. 'They're so fresh here; I can taste the ocean.'

'Go on, honey.' My father nudged a plate of clams towards me. 'You can't summer in The Hamptons and not sample the local seafood; it's pretty much a law here.'

Keeping one eye on the empty ice bucket in case I needed a place to vomit, I gingerly lifted the open shell towards my mouth and tipped.

'You have to wriggle it off a bit,' said Tallulah, passing me a fork. 'That's it, now just swallow.'

The clam slithered across my tongue, and I felt my throat constrict in reluctance.

'Do I chew?' I asked, although it came out as more of a muffled whimpering sound.

'God, no!' Tallulah frowned as she leaned towards me. 'Just open up and let it down.'

It was easy for her to say. I tried my best, but the clam snagged on my teeth and, feeling as if I was about to choke, I threw my head forwards and ejected the poor creature forcefully into my lap.

'Gross,' she proclaimed, as Gunnar started to laugh.

'No harm done,' he said, as I wrapped the offending item up in my napkin. My eyes were watering with the effort of not being sick; I dared not even sip water. 'Cuisine like this is for the seasoned few. Not everyone has a sophisticated palate.'

I waited for Tallulah or my father to defend me, but neither one did.

'Sorry,' I muttered when I was able to speak.

The waitress, who must have witnessed the entire performance, deftly removed all trace of what I had spat out and brought me a clean napkin. I did not dare look at my father. He should have left me back in Southampton, where I could have eaten a burger and chips up at the bar of the Publick House without anyone's condescending gaze on me. I did not fit in here, among these people, in a setting expressly designed for those who knew how to behave and could decorously consume raw shellfish without causing a scene.

As I always did when I was with my father, I felt wrong; a wooden peg bashed into a hole one size too small, its presence causing cracks to form. Thankfully, none of the others seated at the table were currently paying much attention to me, so I was able to dab at my eyes discreetly, taking deep breaths behind my hands until my heart rate began to steady. By the time I'd recovered enough to tune into the conversation, it had moved once again to the subject of Cellan.

'You'd think he would have his pick,' Gunnar was saying. 'But he's had a bad run of luck in his dating life.'

'Oh, I don't believe that for a second,' Tallulah protested. She'd eaten all her clams, and there were four empty oyster shells balanced in a neat stack on her plate.

Game, set, and match to her, I thought glumly.

Gunnar shook his head. 'Trust me,' he said. 'The problem is that the girls turn up expecting a movie star and end up disappointed when they discover how down-to-earth the kid is.'

'Is that a bad thing?' I asked, and Gunnar shrugged.

'Sure it is. His good nature is his biggest flaw; he's too trusting. And it's bound to get him in deep kimchi sooner or later. He can't see that he's an asset now, like a Bugatti or a Cessna – the guy still thinks of himself the same as the rest of us, but of course he's not. It's my job to remind him of that, even if he doesn't always like what I'm telling him.'

'But there are plenty of good-natured famous people,' I pointed out. 'What about Chris Martin from Coldplay? And Cher. Didn't she save some orphaned elephants?'

'That's not who Cef is,' Gunnar argued. 'His brand is edgier, and more enticing. The guys need to admire him, and the girls need to want him – that's what sells.'

'But if it's not who he is . . .'

Gunnar appraised me pityingly. 'No offence, honey, but you've only met the guy, what, twice?'

'Four times,' Tallulah corrected, and I grimaced.

'You don't know him,' he said. 'Nobody can know anyone after a few days, and I've spent almost every day with the kid for the past decade. I know what's best for him.'

'Which is?' I asked, genuinely interested to hear his reply.

'Work, to put it bluntly. I'm on the lookout for the right project, and I have the feeling I'm getting warmer.' Gunnar topped up his wine glass before offering the bottle to Tallulah. When she went to fill mine, however, I shook my head. I had embarrassed myself enough already and did not want to risk doing or saying anything else that might annoy this man – or my father, for that matter. If Gunnar thought I was bad news, he would find a way to put a stop to my friendship with Cellan, while my father could easily withdraw his invitation to let me stay on at the house. I needed both of them onside and, in my father's case at least, I wanted more than that.

'You're not going to whisk Cellan away from The Hamptons right away, are you?' asked Tallulah. 'Not when we're all only just getting to know each other.'

Gunnar smiled at her indulgently. 'Don't you worry,' he said, and then, turning very deliberately to face me. 'I've told Cellan he can have the summer to play hooky, fool around, get whatever he needs to out of his system, but then, after that, the party's over.'

21

Wednesday arrived, and with it a bout of summer rain.

I woke to the sound of it lashing against the windows and groped blearily for my phone. The previous night, I'd stayed up late attempting to write more of my novel, bashing my way clumsily through a chapter involving my stuntman hero Patrick and a complicated challenge that saw him having to drive a motorbike through a wall of flames. Of course, I had no experience of such matters, nor had I done the requisite work of shaping Patrick's character before diving into the story, so didn't get far before giving up and reverting instead to my diary entries.

As soon as I started to write about the time I'd spent with Cellan, it felt as if a tap had opened, the words spilling from me in a torrent so fast that my frantically tapping fingers could barely keep up. It felt indulgent to describe him in such superlative detail, yet the mere action of doing so bolstered my mood, reminding me that I could do this, that I had the skills required if not the plot to go with them.

When it felt this good, and flowed this naturally, the simple act of writing itself was enough to sustain me, and I kept going long after I should rightly have slept.

Now, I felt gritty-eyed and hollow from lack of slumber. It also occurred to me, as I pulled the shower curtain around the roll-top bath, that despite inviting me to spend the day with him, Cellan had not been in touch to arrange a time or place to meet. I hadn't felt comfortable asking for his number, and he'd not requested mine – nor did he know where I was staying. I had no idea what to do: stay put or go across to his house. To that end, I was grateful to the continuing rain for having made that decision easier, because no way would I be venturing out in a downpour – not even for Cellan Thomas.

Nobody else was up when I crept downstairs twenty minutes later and tossed some coffee into the pot. The shower had energised me slightly, but the brain fug still lingered. Crossing from the stove to the fridge, I caught sight of a dark shape at the window and screamed louder than I ever had in my life.

The figure lowered its hood, and a sheepish grin emerged through the gloom.

Cellan.

'Bloody hell, man – are you trying to kill me?' I asked, opening the back door, and ushering him inside.

'I tried knocking at the front,' he protested mildly.

'What with, a feather?'

'I can't help it if I have soft delicate hands.'

'All the better to perform CPR on me when I collapse with a heart attack.'

'I didn't want to wake the whole household.'

'So, instead you chose to sneak around like a burglar? Makes perfect sense to me. This is America, remember. I could have had a gun.'

'But you're not American,' he reminded me, 'and so you wouldn't.'

'My dad probably has,' I told him, although without much conviction. Jeffrey Butler might write books about an unhinged, trigger-happy mercenary, but I liked to think the two had little in common.

'How did you know where to find me?' I asked, as he tugged absently at the drawstrings of his hood.

Cellan smiled. 'My spies are everywhere.'

'You found out from Gunnar, right?'

'Actually, no – it was Cherry. She makes it her business to know where everyone that I befriend lives. She also gave me your address in Cambridge, just in case.'

'Just in case of what?'

'In case I decide to send you an invitation to next year's Oscars or something.'

'Really?' I asked, the word coming out as a squeak.

Cellan looked at me seriously, then said, in a purely deadpan tone, 'Of course not, but only because my mother would never forgive me. I took my sister this year, and Mum is next on the list.'

I had seen the photos online and assumed the auburn-haired woman in the ruched lamé gown was an ex-girlfriend. Cellan, I knew now, had been dating Wylie Brooke at the time of the Academy Awards, but clearly he'd decided not to take her with him.

'I hate all that celebrity gossip nonsense,' he went on, making me wonder if I had just articulated my thoughts. 'And a good way of guarding against it is by taking family members out to public events. That way, the hacks have nothing to speculate over.'

'Or,' I countered, holding up an empty mug as the pot started to bubble, 'it makes them even more curious, because they can tell you're trying to put them off the scent.'

'Yes, please to coffee,' he said, deftly changing the subject. 'I should really have picked up a couple on the way over – some refreshment for the journey.'

'I can make this to go,' I said. 'Pretty sure there's a couple of reusable cups in the cupboard. But can we wait for the rain to stop?'

'No need.' Cellan ran both hands through his hair. He was

wearing a blue and green plaid shirt unbuttoned over a grey T-shirt, and a silver chain hung slack across it. Unusually for Cellan, he did not have either his hat or his sunglasses, but his fingers kept moving as if to adjust each in turn regardless.

'I brought my car,' he explained. 'Well, I say car. It's more of a truck really – and it's not mine, it's Colton's.'

'Where's your car?'

'I don't actually have one. I used to have . . . well, far too many. I sold them all, and now I hire vehicles if ever I need them.'

'Or borrow them.'

'That too.'

'How about planes?' I couldn't help but ask. 'Any private jets gathering dust in hangars?'

Cellan visibly shuddered. 'God, no. Who do you think I am?'

'Erm, a world-famous global megastar,' I replied sweetly. 'An undoubted gazillionaire with enough cash in the bank to buy an island, let alone a plane.'

Cellan put his head on one side. 'I think you're overestimating my level of success.'

'OK, OK,' I said, passing him a steaming mug. 'Millionaire then.'

'Like I said the other day,' he told me, mock stern. 'Money doesn't really mean anything in the end, except perhaps security. If anything, money equals pressure.'

I rubbed my fingers together and he frowned.

'What are you doing?'

'Playing the world's tiniest violin.'

Cellan narrowed his eyes at me over the rim of his mug.

'If money could buy a person new jokes, I'd give you all of mine.'

'You're sweet,' I told him. 'But a box of Christmas crackers will only set you back about a tenner.'

'Even the really fancy ones from Fortnum and Mason?'

'I don't think those contain jokes. More likely inspiring literary quotes, or recipes for posh eggnog.'

'Sold.'

He smiled and so did I, feeling the warmth of our shared humour trickle through me. When I was not with Cellan, I found myself questioning the bond of friendship that was forming between us, believing it impossible that he would choose to spend time with me. Yet here he was, standing in the middle of my kitchen, making that very choice, and I would have been lying if I did not acknowledge how wonderful it felt.

'So,' I said, leaning back against the worktop, 'where are we going in Colton's truck?'

Cellan put his mug down on the table and said solemnly, 'I'm taking you to the end of the world.'

'That sounds . . . depressing.'

'You'll love it.'

'How far away is it?'

'About forty-five minutes if we take the scenic route.'

I frowned at him confused, and I could tell he was trying hard to suppress a smile.

'There's no need to make that face,' he said. 'It's fun at the end of the world, you'll see.'

'Do I need to write a quick will before we go, or—'

'No!' He laughed. 'But you might want to bring a sweater or jacket – the weather out there can turn on you without warning.'

'A sweater,' I repeated. 'You really have been in the States too long.'

'Maybe I'm just warming up.'

'Literally, or figuratively?'

'Can't a man do both at the same time?'

The look he gave me then felt loaded with something more potent than simple humour, and I wondered if he, like me, had become aware of a charge in the atmosphere.

'Anything else I need to do?' I asked, turning away before he saw me blush.

The coffee I'd made was revolting, and I tipped most it away down the sink. Cellan followed suit, wiping his brow with an exaggerated 'phew' gesture as he did so, which made me laugh.

'There is one more thing you need,' he told me.

'Oh?'

'A new name.'

'What? Why?'

'Because today we are not going to be ourselves. I'm not going to be Cellan Thomas, and you're not going to be Honor Butler.'

'Suits me,' I said. 'Never liked her much anyway.'

Cellan's face registered his dismay, but he didn't argue. Instead, he asked if I had my phone handy.

'It's upstairs. I'll go and get it, along with a sweater,' I replied, saying the last two words in a thick Southern accent. When I returned, Cellan had washed up both coffee cups and was drying his hands on a tea towel.

'That'll do nicely,' he said, nodding his approval at my choice of a salmon-pink hoodie, which I had zipped up over my ripped denim shorts. Thanks to Tallulah, who had taught me how to arrange my hair over the bald patch, I no longer needed to include a hat with every outfit, but I had snatched up my Cambridge cap as I left the bedroom, thinking it would provide a little extra protection if the rain continued.

'What did you need my phone for?' I asked, tapping in my passcode, and holding it out to him.

'Your passcode is one, two, three, four, five, six?'

'What's wrong with that?'

'Oh, nothing.' Cellan's brow knotted with consternation. 'If you're happy for any Bob, Dirk or Larry to gain access to your phone.'

'Pretty sure you mean Tom, Dick and Harry.'

'Them as well.'

'I'll change it.'

'Make sure you do,' he replied, opening up my browser app and typing something into the search window. 'Ah, here we are.'

I moved until I was close enough to see.

'Fantasy name generator?'

'Have you never used one of these before? I assumed writers must.'

'We do have brains and imaginations,' I pointed out drily. 'That's sort of the point.'

Cellan was still scrolling, dismissing options to choose a pirate name, an aristocrat name, or an exotic dancer name, before stopping at 'Southern American'. Pressing a finger to the 'get male names' button, he grinned as a list of options popped up.

'Billy Bob,' he said. 'That'll do. Now, it's your turn.'

'Decisions, decisions,' I mused. 'Would you say I'm more of a Randa Lynn or a Chastity?'

'Hopefully not the latter.'

'Ha-ha. What about Wilma?'

He shook his head.

'Mary Lou? Betty Sue? Billie Jean?'

Cellan reached an arm around me to tap the button, and again I caught the fresh, clean scent of him.

'We have a winner,' he proclaimed, and I squinted at the screen.

'Bambi? You're not serious.'

'What? It's a cute name.'

'One to really fawn over.'

'Dear oh dear.'

'Don't you mean doe a deer?'

'Please stop talking.'

'I will as soon as you tell me a) where we're really going; and b) why the hell I have to change my name to that of a Disney cartoon character?'

'So many questions,' he said with a sigh. 'I only have one for you, but it's an important one.'

'Which is?' I asked, turning from my phone to face him. He was still standing close behind me; so near that I could feel the heat of his breath. A beat passed, where neither of us said anything, and then Cellan spoke.

'Do you trust me, Honor?'

I looked at him, saw the merriment that danced in eyes, a playfulness that he seemed to save purely for me.

I did not need to consider my answer; it was the easiest I had ever given.

'Yes,' I told him. 'I trust you.'

22

It did not take long for Colton's Chevy Silverado to chew up the miles, and within a few minutes of me clambering into the passenger seat of the truck's pristine cab, Cellan had driven us out of Southampton and onto the highway.

The rain had blessedly stopped, but the morning's downpour had left a slight chill in the air, and I was glad of the extra layer I'd put on. Seeing me snuggle into myself, Cellan reached across and switched off the air conditioning, then rolled down his window and rested his elbow on the frame. The silver chain he was wearing had caught on one of the buttons of his shirt, and I suppressed the urge to reach across and unhook it for him. Allowing my gaze to roam, I took in his long dark lashes and straight nose, the flicker of his eyes as they moved from the mirror to the highway, the tapered length of his fingers and flash of chest hair above the neck of his vest. I liked the way he drove – one hand on the wheel, the other caressing the gear stick – and, realising that I was straying into gawp territory, I made a concerted effort to look away and take in the view instead. Clumps of trees were broken up by quaint shuttered houses, while private driveways snaked ribbonlike from the road into the forests beyond. I was on the ocean side of the car, which revealed itself in flashes of sun-tipped blue, just visible past the undulating pattern of the dunes.

Fully expecting us to head west, in the direction of the city, I was intrigued when we reached the crossroads on the outskirts of town and Cellan turned the opposite way. I knew from our trip over to Dall'Acqua at Three Mile Harbor a few nights ago that East Hampton was too close to be our final destination, and Amagansett was only a few miles further.

'Is this place we're going to in Montauk?' I guessed.

Cellan glanced across at me. 'Maybe. Have you been before?'

'Nope,' I said. 'This summer is my first in The Hamptons. I've been coming to New York every year since I was sixteen, but we never went to the beach. JB has always maintained that he is more of a city man, at least until now.'

'Perhaps he's mellowing?' Cellan suggested, and I nodded.

'He does seem . . . I don't know . . . different out here. He can be horribly grumpy at times, but on the whole, his mood this year has been up.'

'Glad to hear it. I did think that he was a bit . . .'

'A bit what?' I asked, but Cellan had stopped at a junction and, with a wave of his hand, ushered three drivers out ahead of us.

'Dismissive,' he said. 'Of you, I mean. All that stuff he was saying about romance novels surprised me. In my experience, fathers dote on their daughters. I know mine does.'

'Jeffrey Butler is not the doting sort. But honestly,' I went on, conscious of a sudden need to defend my more complicated parent, 'I think he's only disparaging about my choice of ambition because he worries that I don't have what it takes to succeed. It's up to me to prove to him that I do – that's partly why I'm writing this book. Or trying to.'

'Ah.' Cellan fished out his sunglasses from where he'd propped them in the cup holder and put them on with one hand. 'So, you have been writing? That was going to be my next question.'

'A bit.' I shifted uncomfortably on the dark leather upholstery.

'Can you tell me anything about the story? Who are your main characters?'

I was forced to look away then, sure that if I didn't, he would see humiliation painted across my face.

'I was thinking of making him a stuntman,' I said, in a small voice.

Cellan laughed as if I had told him a joke. 'I suppose that's marginally better than an actor.'

'I thought you loved your job?' I exclaimed, turning once again to face him.

Outside, the sun was breaking through, the clouds that littered the sky dispersing like soap suds.

'I enjoy researching the roles I'm hired to play, and getting under the skin of a new identity, but there's plenty about the job I find challenging. I guess, in the end, it's like most careers. There are elements people like, and others they find tedious.'

'You're right,' I agreed, thinking of my tiny office back at the university; the desktop computer that should have been condemned several decades ago; irate parents calling because they'd not heard from their student offspring in a day or so, and wanted me to track them down. And then I pictured all those half-finished novels languishing on my laptop, all those promising starts that had amounted to nothing but reminders that I was unlikely to achieve the one thing I wanted more than any other, to become the published author of a successful novel. Unless, I resolved, with renewed determination, I kept trying. Writing about Cellan might end up steering me away from what I needed to create in order to enter the competition, but I had also never been more invested in what I was putting down on the page. My father had told me once that had it not been for Benedict Stamp strolling uninvited into his mind all those years ago, then he may never have become a novelist at all. 'Without a good hero, honey, you've got nothing.'

Cellan, I knew, was a good hero. But I could not base my novel on him.

'You're being unusually quiet,' he prompted.

'Just thinking,' I said. 'You should try it sometime.'

He tutted out a laugh.

'Will you tell me more about what it's like?' I asked. 'Being an actor, I mean.'

'I hope you're not shamelessly plugging me for plot ideas?'

'No.' I gave in to a smile. 'My character is a stuntman, remember?'

'If Cherry were here, she'd be taping my mouth shut right about now,' Cellan said. 'But I suppose I can tell you a few things. It's not as if you're going to sell them to the *National Enquirer*, is it?'

'Definitely not,' I agreed, pleased that on this score, at least, I could be wholly truthful. I settled back in my seat as Cellan spoke, listening as he recounted stories from his early days in the theatre, how he'd fluffed lines and missed cues; he told me what it had felt like to walk onto a film set for the first time, and of the surreal sensation he experienced whenever his face appeared on a billboard or poster. As he talked, I studied him, the way he rubbed his forefinger and thumb together as if comforting himself; the nod of his head when he remembered a detail correctly; the roll of his eyes when he couldn't. He was a smorgasbord of idiosyncrasies, and I wanted to savour every morsel of him.

Midway through a particularly juicy anecdote about an extremely well-known actress who threw a tantrum after an underling dared to make eye contact with her, Cellan realised we'd crossed the boundary line into Montauk, and abruptly pulled over.

'Why are we stopping?' I asked, peering nonplussed through the open window. There was nothing around us save for scrubby grass, asphalt, and acres of blue sky.

'Before we go any further, we need to get our story straight.'

'Our story?'

'Yes. We're not us today, remember? I'm Billy Bob, and you're . . . ?'

'Bambi,' I said, in a desultory tone that amused him.

'Billy Bob and Bambi are a couple,' he decided, adopting a Southern twang as he said, 'here on vacation from Fairfax, Virginia.'

'Why are you doing a voice?'

'This, my little lady love, is how we speak.'

I pulled my mouth into a thin, tight line.

'What's the matter? Don't go all sluggin' on me now.'

'I don't understand what's happening,' I said, laughing helplessly as he contorted his features into a frown.

'You wanted an acting lesson,' he said, returning to his normal voice. 'This is it.'

'And I have to be Bambi all day?'

'You sure do, my sweet slice of peach pie.'

I put my head in my hands.

'That's not the spirit,' he cajoled. 'It's time to turn that frown upside down.'

I raised my eyes to his. 'Dear God,' I said. 'You actually are a Billy Bob.'

'Come on,' he prompted, again reverting to his British accent. 'Give me your best Southern Belle impression.'

'What shall I say?'

Cellan considered.

'Repeat after me: "Good lord, this Hamptons place is hotter than a goat's butt in a pepper patch."'

Laughing, stumbling over my words, I did as he'd instructed.

'Hmm,' he appraised. 'Nobody'll be handing you a Bafta anytime soon, but it wasn't a bad effort.'

I put up my hood and pulled the drawstrings until only my nose was visible.

Cellan took his hand off the wheel and slid a finger into the gap, gently tugging until my eyes and mouth emerged.

'Now, I don't know about you,' he murmured, Billy Bob once more, 'but I have a hankerin' for pancakes. I'm so darn hungry, I could eat a pair of britches.'

He pronounced it 'hawngree', and I agreed that I was too.

Cellan grinned in triumph.

'Well, then,' he drawled. 'As luck would have it, my sugar muffin, I happen to know of a right good place not far from here.'

Resistance, I knew, had become a moot point. I could either embrace my new identity as Bambi and really run with it, or risk coming across as the very poopiest of party poopers. Taking a deep breath, I pushed back my hood, plastered on a smile and took a deep, fortifying breath.

'I must be madder than a bullfrog with a bee sting,' I muttered, with enough of a twang to elicit a smile of delight from my companion. 'But I'm game if you are.'

Cellan turned the key in the ignition; his whole demeanour had seemed to transform over the past few minutes, as he'd gone from hopeful to giddily excited, and it was impossible not to be drawn in by his obvious enthusiasm.

'I hope I don't live to regret this,' I said drily, as we pulled back onto the road, but Cellan was shaking his head.

'At the very least,' he said. 'This will become a day you'll never forget.'

And, as it soon transpired, he could not have been more right.

23

Norma's Pancake House was everything a classic small-town American diner should be – cheap, cheerful, and ever so slightly chaotic. The hostess that greeted us did so from the opposite side of the room, with a wave and a yell that we should 'sit where you like, sweeties'.

'Booth?' Cellan turned to me. 'Or bar?'

Whenever I ventured into establishments such as this in New York, I was usually alone, and so would sit up on a stool by the counter so as not to swindle a whole table from other patrons. Today, however, I had someone with me.

'Booth,' I said, leading him towards one.

The seats were upholstered in wipe-clean blue laminate, the table shiny pine, and there was a large wooden fish mounted on the wall. I cast my mind back to the extravagant shell centrepieces at Dall'Acqua, where there had also been candles, flowers, and glasses made from crystal. And while that place had wowed me, here at Norma's, with its ancient sugar tumbler, sticky tub of maple syrup, and tin can of napkin-wrapped cutlery, I felt far more at home.

Sliding into my seat, I took a moment to glance around, taking in the photos on the walls of famous visitors, which were interspersed with others of proud-looking men, beaming as they held up their catch of the day. The fan on the ceiling thrummed, dishes were crashed, and shouts echoed from the kitchen, while behind it all, the faint yet unmistakable baritone of Bruce Springsteen filtered out from a large juke-box in the corner.

'I love this place,' I enthused, and Cellan's eyes crinkled over the top of his menu. He'd unearthed his baseball cap from the truck when we parked up but had drawn the line at wearing sunglasses indoors. Not that it mattered. Nobody appeared to be paying much if any attention to us – most seemed to be locals, their heads bent forwards over a newspaper or their phones, a cup of coffee at their elbows.

'I'm glad,' he said, mercifully speaking in his normal voice. 'It's a favourite of mine.'

'Do you always order the same thing?' I asked, but Cellan looked affronted.

'Of course not. I'm a man of adventure, not a creature of habit.'

'Whenever someone uses that phrase, I picture Gollum dressed as a nun.'

He laughed. 'And that is why.'

'Why what?'

Instead of answering, he merely smiled, then reached across and tapped my menu. 'What are you going to have?'

There were a large number of pancakes to choose from. Adopting my best Bambi drawl, I started to read them out.

'Jeez,' I said. 'I'm stumped. Should I go for the potato stack with sour cream and applesauce, or the Hawaiian with pineapple chunks and coconut syrup?'

'Well, there's a puzzle,' Cellan replied, taking up my baton and easing back into Billy Bob. 'I was just ponderin' on that, my little soda pop, and my belly's tellin' me we should say to hell with it and order a couple of Norma's specials.'

My eyes widened as I read the list of toppings.

'What you thinkin', sugar?' prompted Cellan.

'I'm thinking that ham, bacon, eggs, green tomatoes and potato might be a little much for my delicate constitution.'

'Ain't nuthin' wrong with a few 'maters and 'taters.'

'Now you're actually talking like Gollum.'

Cellan did not miss a beat. Putting down his menu, he screwed his features into a scowl and muttered the 'what's 'taters?' line from *The Lord of the Rings* movie. It was such a perfect impersonation that I raised my hand to high-five him, only to miss and knock off his cap. He was still rooting under the table to retrieve it when the hostess arrived.

'What'll it be, poppet?'

'Er . . .' I stammered, stage fright holding Bambi hostage.

Cellan re-emerged, hat pulled down over his eyes.

'Morning, ma'am,' he said easily, the very epitome of Southern charm. 'I'm going to try some of y'all's Special Pancakes, and my lovely girl Bambi here will go for the . . .'

'Banana stack,' I told her, choosing something at random.

The woman scribbled a note on her pad.

'You both want coffee?'

'The hottest and wettest you got, please.'

I suppressed a smile.

'Coming up.'

The hostess turned on her heel and hurried away far too quickly to hear my tut.

'What?' Cellan said.

'Hottest and wettest.'

'There's nothing rude about that,' he protested mildly. 'I can't help it if you twist it into something else in that sordid brain of yours.'

'Sordid?' I exploded, swiping at him with the menu.

'Yep,' he reiterated cheerfully. 'Sordid, dirty, filthy – whatever you want to call it. Are you sure you should be writing romance? Wouldn't erotica be more up your alley?'

I snuffled out a laugh. 'Up my alley?'

'What's the matter with you, woman? Here I am, making innocent remarks about hot, wet alleys, and you're turning them into something grubby.'

'You're an idiot,' I said, adding, as Bambi, 'A hot dang fool.'

'As long as I'm hot,' he said slyly, the corner of his mouth twitching up into a smirk.

We had strayed somehow into openly flirtatious ground, and I could feel the heat of a blush as it stole across my cheeks. Cellan continued to stare at me, steadily and without reserve, until the same heat began to spread out from somewhere far deeper inside me. I became aware of how close his legs were to mine under the table, of how easy it would be to slide my knee forwards, so it nestled between his. I imagined the grip of his thighs against mine, his hand sliding until his fingers found the soft cavern behind the joint, his thumb stroking, probing.

'Here's your coffee.'

I pressed myself back against the foam seat, nodding a thanks to our waitress as she deposited our drinks. She'd also had the foresight to bring a jug of tap water, which I reached for gratefully and decanted into a glass, before downing it in several noisy slurps.

'Thirsty?' Cellan raised an eyebrow.

'Very. Is it me, or is it really hot in here?'

Without breaking eye contact, he poured a measure of sugar into his coffee and picked up the pot of cream.

'It's you,' he said.

24

'Do you think we got away with it?'

Cellan paused with the key in the truck's ignition.

'Oh, absolutely,' he said. 'We were faultless.'

'You were. I feel like I took it too far.'

'What, you mean telling our waitress that we lived somewhere "over yonder"?'

'No. When I told her I was "full as a tick at a donkey farm".' I groaned, rubbing my stomach, which had rounded considerably on account of the pancakes I'd consumed.

'That was inspired,' he said. 'You know, a lot of people would have played this kind of role safe, but you've really gone for it. I'd say that warrants at least three stars on the chart.'

'What do I win if I get to ten by the end of the day?'

The truck's engine fired, a deep rumble that made my body quiver against the seat.

Cellan considered. 'I'm not sure yet,' he admitted. 'But I'll come up with something good. Now, are you ready to see the end of the world?'

I pulled a face. 'Sure. Why not? I mean, at least I can face my maker knowing I had a good last meal.'

Cellan chuckled as he steered us away from the kerb towards the main road, leaning over the wheel to check for oncoming traffic. The pace of life in Montauk seemed ever so slightly busier than in sleepy Southampton; there were more people on the streets and a greater volume of cars and taxis. The feel of the place was different. It was still quaint, but earthier somehow, less pristine. Not that I could gauge much about the village from the brief flashes of shopfronts, cafés and parkland I saw through the open window as we sped past. And, with his thick beard, cap pulled down, and his sunglasses once again obscuring his face, I did not think anyone glancing at the Silverado would gauge who Cellan was either.

Any residual rain clouds had long since burned away, the sun a white-hot throb against the windscreen. Unhooking my arms from the confines of the seat belt, I unzipped my hoodie and managed to wriggle out of it, checking the position of my low-slung pigtails as I did so. It was not a style that I would ever have considered had circumstances been normal, but I'd not been wholly displeased with how it looked that morning. I told myself that Bambi was the sort of woman who relished a cutesy hairdo.

A silence had fallen between us but it was not the uncomfortable kind. We were relaxed enough in each other's company not to feel obliged to fill every conversational lull with chatter, and it was nice, I realised, to simply be here beside him. I was in a bubble that I never wanted to burst, would be content to float around in forever given half the chance. Then again, I countered internally, wasn't this kind of nonsensical daydreaming tantamount to self-sabotage? Hadn't I heard Gunnar Hayes say only a few nights ago that he'd given Cellan carte blanche to 'fool around' this summer? Whatever it was that was growing between us felt real, but how far could it conceivably go? The summer would end, Cellan would be swallowed up once again by his celebrity life, and I would return home to ... to what? Disappointment, frustration, boredom. I needed more than that; I wanted what Cellan had – respect, success, wealth, and even, whispered a voice so indistinct that it barely registered, love, too.

I closed the door on that thought, hard and firm. There was no time for it yet, no space. I had made a choice many years ago to sideline relationships until my life looked the way I wanted it to, and I could not, would not, allow myself to be led off course.

'Honor?'

I'd been staring out through the windscreen, seeing nothing, the scenery a blur indistinguishable from my own meandering thoughts. Hearing Cellan speak, however, made everything snap abruptly back into focus.

'Yes? Sorry. Miles away.'

'Slipped into a food coma, did you?'

I groaned. 'Probably. I don't think these shorts have ever been tighter.'

'We're almost there,' he said. 'If you look up to the right, you'll see something quite remarkable come into view any second.'

I did as he instructed, gazing past the confines of the truck to the smooth grey tongue of the highway, and the misshapen green banks beyond. Warm air rushed in through the open windows as we rounded a bend and then, all of a sudden, I saw it, the unmistakeable outline of a lighthouse.

'Wow,' I murmured, catching the twitch of Cellan's beard as he smiled. 'That really is impressive.'

'Completed in 1796,' he told me. 'The first lighthouse ever to be finished in the state of New York.'

'Thanks, Wikipedia,' I replied, to which he laughed.

'Last time I was here, I brought my folks with me, and my dad made us go inside. There's a whole museum set-up, and you can climb to the top of the tower.'

'I bet the view from up there is quite something,' I mused, craning my neck as the lighthouse loomed ever larger in front of us.

'It is,' Cellan confirmed. 'But actually, I prefer the one from ground level. You'll see what I mean.'

The road curved round to the left and flicking up the indicator, Cellan steered the truck into a large car park, before aiming for an empty space in the corner, far away from all the other cars. It must have become second nature to him, the process of slotting distance in-between himself and the general public, and it occurred to me how sad that was. The man I knew seemed to like people and be interested in them, yet his fame had at some stage become a barrier that kept Cellan on one side, and those fascinated by him on the other. Was the payoff enough? I hoped he thought so.

Having clambered out of the truck, I tied my hoodie around my waist and took my phone out from my bag. Cellan, who was checking the angle of his cap in the wing mirror, leapt across in front of me just as I took a photo of the lighthouse.

'Funny,' I said, showing him the screen. 'You look like a ball of hair that's been fired out of a cannon.'

'Here,' he replied, holding out his hand for my phone, and then extending his arm. 'We need a selfie of Billy Bob and Bambi to commemorate this special day in our lives.'

'Well then, all right,' I simpered in my best Southern drawl. 'But only because it's you askin', my soggy-bottomed slice of pilchard pie.'

The face that Cellan pulled in response to this description made for an hilarious photo, and grinning, he raised his hand again, snapping picture after picture as I first attempted to smile neutrally, before giving in to helpless laughter, and finally resting my head against his shoulder and arranging my features into what I hoped was a vaguely attractive expression. Cellan scrolled through the results.

'All ridiculous,' he surmised. 'And I really do need to shave.'

'At last,' I crowed. 'The man sees sense.'

'Happens to all of us eventually. Now, did you put sun cream on this morning?'

I nodded. 'Yes.'

'Good,' he said. 'Because we're off to the beach.'

'Not the lighthouse?' I asked hopefully, following him across the car park.

Cellan hesitated for a moment before replying. 'It looks to be a bit busy,' he said, indicating the other vehicles. 'Do you mind if we—'

'No, of course not. Sorry, I should have thought. I keep forgetting that you're, you know.'

'Billy Bob?'

'I wish I could forget that.'

'I just . . .' He paused again, chewed for a few seconds on his thumbnail. 'It only takes one person to . . . and in a place as small as that . . . Well, I don't want the afternoon to be hijacked, that's all.'

'No, no, no,' I replied, hastening to reassure him. 'I completely understand. I don't need to see inside the lighthouse; it's nice enough looking at it from here.'

'You're sure? Because I can just wait in the truck if you want to go in?'

I laughed then at how preposterous this situation was, at the idea of a world-famous celebrity actor sitting alone in a car park, waiting for me to poke around a museum.

'I'm sure.'

'Cool. Thanks for understanding.'

'My pleasure,' I said, and then, adopting Bambi's voice to lighten the mood, I added, 'Anything for you, my curly cooked shrimp.'

'For someone who was appalled when I suggested this whole acting charade, you seem to be doing incredibly well,' he mused. 'I'd wager there's a lot more to you than you let on, Honor Butler.'

'Bambi,' I reminded him. 'And wouldn't you like to know?'

'I would,' he agreed, his tone dropping low enough to stir something in me, that same insistent tug that had pulled at me in the diner, when we'd been so tantalisingly close. I started to reply, but the joke I'd planned felt too clumsy. There was a nice moment here, and I didn't want to ruin it. Cellan looked at me expectantly as I stuttered then fell silent. I wanted him to take off his sunglasses; it was impossible to know what a person was truly thinking if you couldn't see their eyes.

'You said something about a beach,' I prompted.

'I did.' He sounded almost relieved. 'It's this way.'

The lighthouse was perched up on the cliff to the right of us, but Cellan continued straight on, leading me along a wide, stony pathway flanked by leafy shrubs. Sharp needles of sea grass sprung up in patches by the verge, while determined butterflies flitted past us to land on daisies speckled gold by pollen. I could not see the ocean, but I felt it like a cold breath in the air, the gentle purr of its waves coaxing me onwards. We passed a wooden pole with a neat box attached, the sign on its front encouraging us to 'discard old fishing line here'. Someone had left their bicycle propped against a low fence, and when I glanced towards Cellan, he ruefully shook his head.

'Don't be getting any ideas, you.'

A gap in the hedge revealed a flash of the deepest blue, and without discussion we increased our pace, walking with purpose now as opposed to the saunter of before. The sea has that power, the ability to draw you to it, knowing that when it does, you will become enraptured by its size, its might, its mystery. The night sky felt fathomless, but the ocean was unknowable – a vast, dark body that managed to be both beguiling and chilling. I suddenly knew then that I wanted the sea to play a part in the story I was writing. Ever-changing, always beautiful, it also had the potential to become a metaphor for the man beside me, who was so open yet closed at the same time. Cellan, I suspected, had so far only given me a carefully curated version of himself. There was so much more I had yet to discover.

Instinctively, my hand went out in search of him, the desire for physical contact overwhelming the reserve that had so far prevented me from seeking it.

Realising too late what I was about to do, I pulled my arm back just as my fingers grazed his forearm, and he turned, one quizzical eyebrow raised.

'There was a bug on you.'

'Thank God you were here,' he said lightly. 'It might have consumed me whole if not. The next people to come along this path would have found a hat, some shorts, and a pile of bones.'

'Maybe that's exactly what happened to the owner of that bike,' I suggested. 'Death by mossie.'

'Anything's possible.'

The path narrowed as we continued to talk, telling each other horror stories about the various deadly insects around the world. Cellan revealed that during a shoot in Australia once, in a camp not far from Uluru, he had got up in the night to visit the Portaloo and flipped up the toilet seat to find a redback spider crouched below.

'I screamed so loudly that a local pack of dingoes started

howling,' he said. 'The production assistant had to prise me off the ceiling, limb by petrified limb.'

'I shouldn't laugh,' I said, then did so regardless.

'Thanks for the sympathy.'

'Be careful,' I warned, 'or I'll have to get my tiny violin out again.'

Cellan made a 'pfft' sound as we reached the soft sand coating the dunes. The path forked, giving us an option of going straight down to the beach on the same route, or cutting up across the cliff side.

'Down?' Cellan asked, and I nodded.

We reached the shoreline a few minutes later, and I paused for a moment to look back up towards the lighthouse, so proud on its natural pedestal. The beach was a mix of sand, shingle and pebbles, the palette earthy hues of greys, reds and browns. The ocean stretched out ahead of us, the waves it tossed inland breaking into spray as they collided with the jagged edges of rocks. Gulls cackled together like friends over a shared joke, and the air smelt rich and wild. Aside from a lone man fishing some distance away, we appeared to have the place to ourselves, and when I pointed this out, Cellan sighed with pleasure.

'That's because it's the end of the world,' he reminded me.

'You keep saying that, and I keep furrowing my brow. Please can you explain what you mean before I collect any more unwanted lines on my face.'

'It's how the locals refer to this area. Where we're standing now is on the easternmost point of New York State, right on the tip of the South Fork. Other than Block Island, which is ahead of us, there's nothing else out there but the Atlantic Ocean.'

'And eventually Europe,' I said, but Cellan was shaking his head.

'That's exactly what I thought, until I was enlightened by my dad. He told me that there are actually many routes you could take, including to Morocco, the Bahamas, and even Australia, depending which way you were facing.'

'I don't ever want to go to Australia,' I muttered. 'Not after that story you just told me.'

'Might take you a while if you set off from here. Bit of a swim.'

'Brave the sharks to reach the spiders. Sounds sensible.'

'You might meet a friendly whale on route and hitch a lift.'

'Now that would be whaley fun.'

'Dear oh dear,' Cellan said, his shoulders shaking with mirth. 'I might start carrying a little cymbal and drum around with me, so I can badum-tish all your worst puns.'

Leaving the shadow of the lighthouse, we picked our way over the rocks, skirting the jut of an adjacent cliff and emerging onto a clearer patch of beach. A small white sailboat was just visible on the far horizon, an artful smudge of cloud at its wake. Catching sight of a speckled cockle shell, I bent to scoop it up, examining the fan-like surface for damage. That anything could survive unscathed in such a place surprised me, but this little specimen had made its journey to land with barely a scratch to show for it. I slipped it into the pocket of my shorts, glancing up to find that Cellan had wandered off ahead. As I watched, he came to a stop beside a bleached trunk of driftwood and lowered himself onto it.

I inclined my head, a silent question that he answered by patting the empty space beside him. He was beckoning to me because he wanted me there, had chosen to bring me here, to this spot so unadorned by anything but nature. In doing so, he was showing me another part of himself, telling me that the surfer boy from Cornwall was still present, still demanding of his time and attention, still the intrinsic heart of him, despite all the privilege of fame. I wondered then how much any of us really change from the person we are in the beginning. Cellan had put in the work, done the therapy, and found his way back to the boy he was once – but had that process led him towards true happiness, or away from it? Knowing the answer was important to me not just because of the lesson I might stand to learn, but because of the simple fact that he, Cellan, mattered to me.

More and more.

With every passing moment.

25

'You look very at home here,' I said as I sat.

The breeze blowing in across the water felt cooler than that which had flooded in through the open windows of the truck, but the sun was strong enough to override any chill I might have felt. The heat here was dry and sharp, despite being only fifty miles from New York City.

'I was born by the sea,' Cellan said, folding his arms and resting them on his knees. 'I guess there's a peace in that, a feeling of security in the familiar. Where were you born?'

'In a very large hospital called Addenbrookes, overlooking some other, slightly less big buildings, and perhaps a railway line, if you squinted.'

'But Cambridge is nice?' he asked. 'I've never been, but I assume it's like Oxford.'

'Parts of it are nice,' I allowed, bending to pick up a pebble that had a crack running through its centre. 'The university buildings, the river, some of the surrounding villages. There are a lot of characters in the city, a real zany bunch of eccentrics.'

'Makes sense.' Cellan said slyly.

'I'm not zany,' I protested. 'If anything, I'm astoundingly dull.'

'Don't give me that.'

'What? It's true. My life is exceedingly mundane most of the time. Visiting the end of the world with a Hollywood star who has convinced me to become Bambi for the day is not an average Wednesday in the life of Honor Butler, I can assure you.'

He had bristled slightly at 'Hollywood star' but managed to dredge up a smile of acknowledgement.

'You dad must have taken you to some glamorous parties over the years?'

'Nope,' I said, sniffing in an attempt to show nonchalance. 'Unless you count dinner the other night.'

From his expression as I filled him in on the details of my evening at Dall'Acqua, it was clear that Cellan was only just hearing about Gunnar's aim to become buddies with my father. I thought it best not to mention what Gunnar had said about Cellan's disastrous dating history, nor his remarks about the 'party being over', yet even having left those details out, Cellan still finished up looking suspicious.

'He said he had a project for me?'

'Not exactly,' I said, cursing myself internally for having mentioned the meal at all. 'If I'm remembering it rightly, all he said was "I'm getting warmer", or words to that effect.'

'Shit.' Cellan snatched up a stone from between his feet and threw it with some force across the beach.

'Something the matter?' I asked, although it was plain there was.

'No.' Cellan grimaced. 'Yes.' He turned to me and removed his sunglasses; his eyes beneath the peak of his cap appeared onyx black. 'It's just that . . .' He stopped abruptly, chewing over his words. 'This conversation,' he said, 'it won't go any further, will it? I mean, you won't share anything I tell you here today with anyone else?'

I itched to shatter the awkwardness with a joke, but his expression told me I mustn't.

'Of course not,' I said, thinking of the diary entries hidden inside multiple folders on my laptop. I knew that I would write down everything that I saw, heard, and felt today, but I had no intention of letting anyone else read any of it. 'If you ask me not to, I won't say anything to anyone.'

He studied me for what felt like a long time, eventually giving in to a sigh.

'It's just that I spoke to Gunnar after I— At the start of the summer, I told him I wanted to find an indie project, maybe even do some theatre, a West End show back in the UK. The way you tell it, the work he's got in mind is on a far bigger scale.'

'I have no idea what he was hinting at,' I told him honestly. 'Maybe he was just trying to impress us?'

'Gunnar doesn't need to impress you,' Cellan replied. Then, seeing my face fall a fraction, 'Sorry. That sounded insensitive. What I should have said was that Gunnar thinks of himself as a person other mere mortals have to impress, not vice versa. You don't get to the status he has in the industry without some serious ego attached.'

'He certainly has that in abundance,' I agreed, and Cellan shrugged.

'I wanted someone with clout; and to be fair to the guy, he has always looked after me. It was him that intervened when . . . well, when I needed an intervention.'

Cellan's stint in rehab was one of only a few topics neither of us had discussed, and the fact that I'd read about it in a magazine made me feel horribly – if misguidedly – disloyal. He seemed stricken having brought it up, and I turned very deliberately away to give him a few minutes of composure.

'I'm sure Gunnar wouldn't line you up for anything you didn't want to do,' I said, more to offer him comfort than because I believed it was true. 'In the end, he works for you, right?'

Cellan did not look convinced. 'We shouldn't be talking shop,' he said, standing up so quickly that the log wobbled.

'Boring of me. Let's discuss something else. I know!' he added triumphantly, spinning around as I hauled myself inelegantly to my feet. 'Beach erosion.'

'Nothing boring about that,' I tempered.

'There really isn't. I mean, take this beach, for instance – at some stage, perhaps even in our lifetimes, if the people of East Hampton don't get the help they need, then this beach will crumble away and be taken by the sea.'

'The end of the world will end?'

'It's not funny.'

'I'm not laughing,' I protested, pursing my lips together and staring fixedly at the ground.

Cellan raised my chin with his finger. 'Doesn't it make you sad, the thought that all this could be gone?'

'A bit,' I allowed, 'but the planet is changing all the time, has evolved over thousands of years into what we see and experience now. Nothing stays the same forever.'

He slumped as if my words had become pins and punctured him.

'You're right about that,' he said grimly. 'Progress has become a buzzword, but the rate at which everything seems to be hurtling forwards makes me want to pull the emergency lever and beg to be let off.'

'Then where would you go?' I asked, and Cellan did not hesitate.

'That's easy,' he said, making a wide arc with his arm before letting it swing down to his side. 'I would come here.'

We stayed on the beach at Montauk Point until our bladders insisted that we move, I having refused with some stridency to 'pee in the sea', as Cellan suggested.

'I can't believe you gone done said such a thing, Billy Bob,' I scolded, to which he replied, 'What's so wrong about piddlin' in the sea? You a sissy now?'

'Rather be a sissy than a piss-sea,' I'd replied, and had been rewarded with a resounding 'badum-tish'.

'Are you in a hurry to get home?' he asked, once we were back in the truck.

'Not at all.'

'Good.' Cellan tapped both his hands on the edges of the steering wheel. 'Some friends of mine who live out here are having a gathering tonight on Ocean Beach. It'll be a bit of volleyball, a bonfire, maybe a sunset surf if we're lucky – you'd be welcome to come as my guest.'

'Really? I wouldn't be cramping your cool, Hollywood style?'

Cellan looked down at his tatty shorts. 'You're right,' he deadpanned. 'I am extremely cool.'

'Don't take the piss.'

'I already did that, in the men's bathroom over by the lighthouse café.'

'I mean it,' I said. 'I don't want your friends to judge you for turning up to their party with me. A nobody,' I clarified.

'Oh, Honor,' he said, the words rushing out on the tide of a weary sigh. 'First of all, my friends are not the judgemental type; and second, you are not a nobody. You are a somebody. You are to your family, your friends, your colleagues, and to me. So, stop with the self-effacing silly talk. Please.' He slid the key into the ignition, turning again to face me. 'Will you?'

'Will I what?'

'Oh, for God's sake,' he cried, banging the back of his head against the seat, and emitting a drawn-out 'aarrgh'. 'Stop putting yourself down,' he reiterated. 'For me.'

'Fine,' I said meekly, as he exhaled in relief. 'But only because it's you.'

26

It was nearing four by the time we cruised into Montauk Village, and the abrasive heat of the day was beginning to soften. Cellan parked the truck in a small car park behind the pharmacy, before handing me the keys.

'Do you mind?' he said. 'For safekeeping.'

'No probs,' I told him, slipping them into the zipped compartment of my bag. 'I may behave like an idiot a lot of the time, but I'm pretty good at looking after things.'

He smiled. 'Good to know.'

We emerged onto a wide tree-lined street much like those in Southampton, only here the houses near to town were smaller and more compact. Upon closer inspection, I realised that a few of them were, in fact, doubling as small businesses, and their owners had bashed signs into the lawns advertising services such as bespoke jewellery, beauty treatments and portrait painting.

'Fancy having your palm read?' Cellan asked, as we passed a tiny dwelling with a multicoloured bead curtain strung over the door. 'My treat.'

'What, so they can tell me I'm going to meet a tall, dark, hairy stranger? That's already happened.'

'It's handsome – tall, dark, *handsome* stranger.'

'Impossible to tell,' I remarked coolly, 'what with all the hair.'

'I will shave this off,' he said, tugging disconsolately at his beard. 'But only when the time is right.'

'You mean when you start tripping over it.'

Cellan put an arm out to stop me mindlessly stepping into the road, where I would almost certainly have been flattened by a passing car, and made a tutting sound. 'Less joking and more following the green cross code, please.'

To hide how flustered I was to have had my boobs collide with him momentarily, I asked, in the manner of a sleeve-tugging toddler, how far it was to the beach.

'About five minutes,' he said, pointing towards a wide circular patch of green lawn. 'That's the main hub of the village. We head across that and follow the road straight down until we reach the sea.'

He set off and I followed, his pace slower and less laser-focused than it had been as we strolled together through Southampton, where I'd been so sure he was doing his best not to engage with anyone else. I didn't know if it was the more laid-back atmosphere of Montauk that had relaxed him, or the Billy Bob guise he'd adopted, but either way, it was nice to see. I had only been to Cellan's home county of Cornwall once before – an ill-fated trip to Polzeath with Felix, during which we had argued continually about my reluctance to settle down – but I could still appreciate the similarities between that area and the one we were in now. Montauk had the same stores selling beach gear and accessories, the same troops of surfers carrying their boards barefoot through the streets, and the same sun-kissed smiles on the faces of those we passed. Southampton was all neatness, while Montauk had more of rustic charm, although that was not to say that this hamlet exuded any less prosperity than its more obviously upmarket neighbours. There were still displays of wealth on show, from the gleaming sports cars idling at the kerb to the minuscule Chihuahuas strutting along in Burberry booties.

A construction of large wooden arrows signposted the names of various shops and restaurants, as well as more general information such as 'seafood' and 'art', while smaller signs advertised the hire of mopeds, bikes, paddleboards, kayaks, wetsuits and surf boards. The pavement crunched under a coating of sand, gulls stalked across vacated café tables, and the aroma of fresh coffee filtered out from open windows. It was also busier here than anywhere else in The Hamptons I'd yet visited, while the age range seemed to veer from very young babies in arms to elderly locals sitting on covered porches, arms folded as they watched the steady flow of people passing by.

Nobody looked at Cellan with any kind of recognition, and I guessed it was partly thanks to his current get-up, which ensured he fitted seamlessly in with the beachgoing crowd. They were all wearing hats and shades, too, and many of the men also sported long beards to match their long hair.

When I glanced at Cellan, I saw that he was smiling – not at anyone, as far as I could tell, or in response to somebody else who'd smiled at him, but simply because he was happy. This made me feel happy, too, so much so that for a fleeting moment, I was able to forget just how nervous I was about meeting his friends. When we reached the outskirts of the village, however, and I saw the wooden steps leading up through the dunes, my earlier wobbles returned.

'Wait,' I said.

Cellan removed his foot from the bottom step and turned back to face me.

'What's up?'

'The people hosting this party – who are they? They're not, you know' – I lowered my voice – 'celebrities, are they?'

'Yes,' he said solemnly. 'They are, in fact, Beyoncé and Rihanna.'

I pulled a face.

'Bollocks! I went too A-list, didn't I? I knew I should have stuck to someone more believable, like Tom Hanks.'

'Oh my God – stop pretending he's your friend.'

Cellan chuckled. 'OK, OK,' he said, rocking from one foot to the other. 'It's not his party either.'

A gaggle of teenage girls bustled past us, flip-flops flapping against the wooden steps as they giggled and flicked their hair. I stared after them, watching until they had crested the dunes and were out of sight.

'If I am about to meet someone famous, I'd like to be prepared,' I said to Cellan. 'You know what I'm like; I'll end up saying something totally inappropriate otherwise.'

'Locryn and Maddy are definitely not celebrities,' he clarified. 'Although I wouldn't be surprised if their son, Peran, becomes a world-famous surfer one day.'

'One day soon? How old is he?'

Cellan's lips moved as he silently counted. 'Seven,' he said. 'Going on eight this October.'

'And they're all British?'

'Locryn is. He and I grew up together. Maddy used to come over to Cornwall to visit her grandparents most summers, which is how she met us. She was born here, and Peran, the lucky little blighter, has dual nationality.'

'I see. So, they aren't just any friends, these are your best friends?'

Cellan considered this. 'I guess so,' he said. 'Definitely my oldest friends. I'd say Locryn knows me better than anyone else does.'

'And they're here all year round?'

'Most of it. They run a surf school, so they do most of their business during the summer, although there are a few diehards that brave the breakers even when it's freezing out here. I'm not one of them,' he added, before I could ask.

'Nowhere near good enough, despite surfing all my life. You have to keep at it, stay fit, and I don't get anywhere near enough free time these days.'

'Will you be surfing today?' I asked, but Cellan shook his head. 'In denim shorts? You must be kidding.'

'You could always go commando,' I suggested, but the rest of my sentence trailed off as the two of us reached the top of the wooden steps and I saw the view for the first time. The beach here was nothing like its shallow, stone-covered cousin a few miles along the coast; it was wider and straighter, with the kind of pale golden sand that would not look amiss in the pages of a glossy travel brochure. There had been barely another soul down by the lighthouse, but easily a hundred or more people were here. As well as the surfers, who were either standing in huddles by the shoreline or paddling out beyond the swell, there were numerous groups of youngsters playing music or kicking a ball to each other.

Cellan stooped to remove his shoes, and I followed suit, sighing with pleasure as my bare toes sank through the warm sand. It was impossible to progress at any kind of speed, and the pair of us waded rather than walked from the bottom of the steps to the harder, flatter sand beyond.

'Oh, good,' Cellan said. 'They're not far; do you see that volleyball net up ahead?'

I wrinkled up my nose as I squinted. 'I won't be expected to play, will I?'

'Are you any good?'

'Terrible,' I said morosely, to which he grinned.

'Forewarned is forearmed, I suppose.'

'The last time I played, my ex smacked a ball right into my face – so hard that I thought he'd broken my nose, which would probably have been a good thing, given how wonky it is. I could have had it set straight.'

Cellan scrutinised me, his expression one of bemusement. 'You nose is not remotely wonky,' he told me firmly. 'It's actually quite neat, as noses go. Like Pinocchio's was, before he told all those lies.'

I gasped with pretend offence. 'It is not neat – it veers slightly to one side. And my left eye is larger than my right,' I added.

'I see. Anything you do like about yourself?'

I thought for a moment. 'My ears. Not too big, not too small. They can stay.'

'And the rest?'

'I'll replace it all when I'm rich, piece by piece, until I'm a really sexy Frankenstein's monster.'

'You,' he said, deftly stepping around an angrily squawking gull, 'are a weirdo. Did anyone ever tell you that?'

I smiled up at him. 'Constantly – especially my best friend Jojo. According to her, I've been single so long that it's warped my brain. If she had her way, she'd order the NHS to give out dating app memberships on prescription.'

'You're not a fan?'

I exclaimed in disgust. 'No. What about you?'

It took Cellan a long time to answer, and we had almost reached the outer boundary of the makeshift volleyball court before he finally spoke. 'Dating apps aren't really an option for me.'

'But if they were,' I pressed. 'If you weren't, you know – would you try them?'

Cellan looked at me, and although I could not see his eyes, I could feel the weight of their gaze as he fixed them on my own.

'I don't think choosing to date a person based solely on what they look like is ever a good idea,' he said. 'There's a lot more to it than that.'

'Such as?'

'Connection,' he said simply. 'Impossible to predict, futile to deny.'

'But how can you tell?' I persisted. 'How do you know if what you're feeling is real?'

Cellan looked at me for a long moment. 'You just do,' he said.

27

I opened my mouth to respond, but my answer was obliterated by a yell of 'Thomas'.

A woman ran across the sand and hurled herself into Cellan's arms, the shock of it causing him to stagger backwards.

She let go in order to examine him, her hands on either side of his face, nose an inch from his, and then she laughed. 'Jeez. I barely recognised you under all this scruff,' she said, in an accent that could only have heralded from New York. 'Is it real or stuck on?'

'Maddy,' said Cellan, removing her fingers from his beard and rotating her in my direction, 'this is Honor.'

She beamed at me. I knew from what Cellan had already told me that she was around the same age as him, but with her windswept bob, freckled complexion, and dungaree shorts worn over a bright blue bikini, she seemed far younger.

'Hey,' she said easily, stepping across to hug me. 'Cef said he might bring a friend along. It's great to meet you.'

'Likewise,' I said, muttering something about not wanting to intrude.

'Oh, stop,' she said. 'We're happy to have you. Have you guys eaten? There's some cold meats and salad in the cooler, and I picked up a stash of those NA brewskis you like, Cef. How about you, Honor? You want a beer? Or I have sodas? There might even be a bottle of Jack rolling around in the truck.'

She had said all of this in a single, uninterrupted flow, and for a moment, all I felt able to do was stare uncomprehendingly.

'We can sort ourselves out—' Cellan started to say, only to break off as man in a black wetsuit bounded towards him. Tall and lithe, with sun-bleached hair and the broad shoulders of an Olympic swimmer, he looked like the human equivalent of gold bullion.

'Bloody hell, Thomas. Is that really you?'

'Bloody hell, Locryn – it really is.'

'What's all this?' the man said, tugging affectionately at Cellan's beard. 'You about to audition for the part of a marooned pirate?'

'Yo ho ho,' Cellan replied, giving his friend a gentle thump of greeting before introducing him to me.

'Your Honor,' he said, affecting a slight bow as he offered me a hand.

It was impossible not to blush, and I did so ferociously.

'Where's Peran?' Cellan asked, as Maddy and Locryn ushered us across to where they had set up a small encampment of blankets, deckchairs, and assorted picnic detritus.

'Out doing his thing with some of the older kids.' Locryn sounded proud. 'He'll be along once he gets tired.'

'If he ever does.' Maddy put a familiar hand on my arm. 'My boy never stops,' she confided. 'Either of them.'

Hearing this, Locryn blew her a kiss, and after executing a perfect pirouette, she pretended to catch it.

'I should have warned you about these two,' Cellan said, as Locryn passed me a can of Bud Light. 'Soppy as a dunked teabag, always have been.'

'Says the guy who used to come up with love poems for the girls he had a crush on and leave them under their beach towels,' teased Maddy.

'You did?' I exclaimed.

Cellan took off his sunglasses and rubbed his eyes. 'Afraid so. Locryn used to write them down for me because my spelling was so bad.'

'His ratio of success was poor to non-existent,' Locryn informed me. 'But he was consistent, I'll give him that.'

'How bad were these poems?' I asked, as Cellan pulled down his hat until his features were completely obscured.

'I seem to remember one that went something like: "Sunsets are red, the sea is blue, you're a straight ten, I'd like to kiss you",' said Locryn.

'Oh, wow.' I started to laugh. 'No wonder you got rebuffed.'

'When the poetry didn't work, he would build them elaborate love symbols in the sand,' Maddy went on. 'Teddy bears and hearts, that sort of thing.'

'That is . . .' I searched for the word. 'Tragic.'

'Isn't it?' agreed Locyrn, not without a certain amount of glee. Cellan was still hiding behind his hat, but I could see his shoulders shaking. 'Imagine what all his adoring fans would say if they knew. I keep threatening to sell the story; it's the only way to keep him in line.'

'That's cruel,' I said, and Cellan promptly reappeared.

'Thank you, Honor. At least I know who my real friends are.'

'As in cruel to the readers of whichever tabloid buys the story,' I clarified succinctly. 'Inflicting poetry that bad on them.'

Cellan groaned, Maddy clapped, and Locryn let out a bellow of laughter.

'Well played, Honor,' he said, offering me his palm to high-five. 'Very well played indeed.'

'I despise all of you,' Cellan grumbled, but he was smiling.

Maddy produced paper plates, and we all sat and helped ourselves to the contents of several foil containers. I had thought after the pancakes that I would never be hungry again, but I could not resist the blood orange and fennel salad drizzled with honey, nor the succulent chunks of watermelon swimming alongside salty blocks of feta. There were chewy slices of sourdough to dip in olive oil, black pepper crackers topped with fresh crabmeat, and spongy morsels of zesty lemon cake. I washed it all down with several Bud Lights, while Cellan dug into his stash of non-alcoholic beers, raising a toast to 'the enduring beauty of poetry' which made us all laugh.

Peran appeared half an hour after Cellan and I had arrived, coming in from the ocean with his surfboard dragging through the sand behind him, cheeks pink from exertion and his shoulder-length blond hair trailing sodden down his back. He had his mother's freckles and his father's wide grin, and after saying a rather timid hello to me and letting Cellan hoist him giggling into the air, he swiped a box of chicken drumsticks, collapsed into a deckchair, and began chomping through them one after the other, a blissful expression on his cherubic face.

Watching him, I was reminded suddenly, painfully, of Felix, and how he had pleaded with me to consider the idea of starting a family with him. I had been adamant in my reply, refusing even to contemplate such a life-altering decision until I had achieved my own ambitions. Felix had warned me that I would end up regretting my choices, but I had not reached that stage. Not yet.

The dregs of beer in the bottom of my can were warm, but I drank them anyway, my eyes catching Cellan's as they so often seemed to.

'You OK?' he mouthed.

I nodded, smiled. And it wasn't a lie. I was OK. I was better than OK. I was perhaps the most OK that a person could be.

The setting, the scenery, the sound of the waves – all of it was faultless. And then there were the people or, I countered internally, the person. The cautious voice in my head – the one urging me to be mindful of who Cellan was, what his status meant, and how far removed we were from each other's everyday lives – was insistent, but I was not in the mood to be naysaid by anyone, not even myself. I wanted only to enjoy this day for what it was, rather than all the things it might never be.

Thus resolved, I stayed where I was, knees tucked underneath me on the blanket, sipping a fresh beer as the day was swallowed up into the chrysalis of night. The sky that had been blue faded slowly into marbled pink, and I watched as Maddy started to build a bonfire. Cellan had moved a little way off and was talking in a low voice to Locryn and two men he also seemed to know from our assembled group, while others clinked glasses, lounged quietly, or played a game of catch across the volleyball net. Having exhausted his box of chicken and been helped by his mum into a hooded towel and grey pyjama bottoms, Peran had fallen asleep, his small perfect feet half-buried under the sand.

I was content to be a spectator and enjoy my position on the front row of a sunset that held every promise of being spectacular. Shifting to one side, I untied the sleeves of my top from around my waist and put it back on. As the sun had dipped, so had the temperature, and there was a docile breeze rolling in across the water.

Maddy was crouched at the base of her firewood stack, arranging a number of rocks in a circle around it.

'Do you need any help?' I called to her, but she shook her head.

'I got this. You kick back, relax.'

Her system was methodical, but effective, and soon enough I heard the rough click of her lighter. The bonfire crackled as the flames rose, coughing out sparks that fluttered into the cooling air. I watched, momentarily entranced, my senses stirred into life by the scent of burning timber, the whispering waves, the halo of gold around the sinking sun. There was only one thing that could improve a moment such as this, and he, I saw, with a rush of pleasure so acute that it seemed to seize the air in my lungs, had begun walking towards me.

Cellan stopped when he was a few feet away. He had taken off his sunglasses and cap and mussed up his dark hair.

'Room for a little one?' he said.

I scooted across the blanket. 'Plenty.'

There was sufficient space for him to maintain a modest distance, but instead he sat close enough for his knee to end up propped against mine. Bringing my hands – which had turned hot and clammy – into my lap, I started fiddling with the ripped bottom of my shorts, tugging at the frayed strands. Cellan, in contrast, was a study of stoicism; I could not read his expression.

'Are you warm enough?' he asked. 'You've got goosebumps.'

I followed his gaze to my bare legs. 'So I have.'

'Here,' he said, unbuttoning his shirt, 'use this.'

I started to protest, but Cellan ignored me. 'There,' he said. 'Better?'

'Much,' I told him. 'But won't you be cold?'

'If I am, I'll start dancing around the fire.'

'Will you recite some poetry while you do so?'

'You're not ever going to let me live that down, are you?' he said.

I smiled triumphantly. 'Nope!'

'Oh, come on, you can't tell me you've never done anything embarrassing in the pursuit of love.'

'As hard as it is to believe,' I said archly, 'I haven't. I don't make a habit of falling in love all that often, though, so perhaps that's why I've made it to the age of thirty-two unscathed.'

'All that often?' His tone was one of enquiry.

I twisted a denim thread around until the tip of my finger turned purple.

'Once,' I said. 'Once was enough for me.'

'He broke your heart?' Cellan guessed, and for just a moment, I considered letting him believe it.

'No,' I said, my voice small. 'It was the other way around. I was the heartbreaker.'

A pensive silence followed.

'He wanted to settle down, get married, start a family – all the boxes you are traditionally supposed to tick with a partner.'

'And you didn't?' Cellan asked.

'I wanted to wait. I know what I'm like,' I went on, sighing helplessly. 'Or I thought I did then. Being a mother would have consumed me, and I guess I was too selfish to accept that. There were things I wanted to achieve first – does that make me sound like an awful person? It does, doesn't it?'

'Absolutely not.' Cellan's tone was frank. 'It sounds sensible to me.'

'Felix, my ex, his argument was that if I loved him, then I should have been willing to put us and our future first, above what I wanted for myself, but I don't know. That never sat right with me, that idea of love limiting a person. Surely, it should be the opposite way around?'

Cellan didn't answer straight away, but when I turned to face him, I found that he was nodding in agreement.

'One of life's great sadnesses is that sometimes you have no choice but to hurt the people you care about,' he said. 'You can't make yourself love someone, and you shouldn't, for their sake as much as your own.'

My mind went briefly then to my parents, who had never loved each other. Their relationship, if I could even call it such, had been fleeting in the extreme, the union that had created me brought about by nothing more than proximity, a bottle of red wine and, according to my mother at least, a momentary lapse of judgement. Neither of them had tried to turn their encounter into a meaningful connection, because both knew it was pointless. If it had not been for me, chances are, they would never have seen one another again.

'You can't make someone love you either,' I said, with more desolation than I had intended.

Cellan relinquished a sigh, his hand going to rest across my own. I made myself stop fidgeting, and felt the nervous energy spread instead into my chest, where it bashed around like a moth trapped in a jar. Lifting my chin, I took a deep breath and closed my eyes.

'It's so beautiful here,' I murmured. 'At the end of the world.'

'I told you it was.' Cellan's reply was barely audible, and when I angled my ear down, he moved a fraction closer to me.

'Can I ask you a personal question?'

'Shoot.'

'You clearly love Montauk, and your best friends live here, so why have you rented a house in Southampton?'

'I can see why that might seem like an odd choice,' he conceded. 'I guess, I thought it made sense to be slightly closer to the city – or that's what everyone told me.'

By 'everyone', I had to assume he meant Gunnar, Cherry and the others.

'I'm very glad I listened to them, too,' he went on. 'If I hadn't, I might never have met you.'

'And you would have been spared all my groan-inducing jokes as a result.'

Cellan's hand was still in my lap, and my breath caught as he slid his fingers tentatively through mine.

'That's true,' he said, adding in conspiratorial whisper, 'but I actually like your jokes.'

'You do?'

'Mm-hm. Just don't tell anyone, you'll ruin my street cred.'

I leant towards him, returning the pressure of his fingers as he rotated his thumb against my knuckles. The beers I'd drunk had made everything feel hazy and unreal, but I could not deny the sensation of him, the heat that I could feel in every part of me. There were voices chattering, the hiss of the fire, the steady drone of the sea; beyond the shoreline, the horizon was splattered with vibrant hues of purple and orange. Nature was insisting that I gaze at it – that I listen, smell, taste and acknowledge – but I was helpless to obey its call. All that mattered now was him.

Cellan was near enough that I could taste the warm sweetness of his breath; his fingers had crept to my wrist and were stroking, so tenderly that I had to glance down to check if what I was feeling was real.

'Are you trying to tickle me?' I said, exhaling sharply as he nudged his nose into the space behind my ear. I was liquid, alive with sensation; heat pulsed through me.

'Is that what you think I'm doing?' he murmured.

I answered with a soft 'hmm', unwilling to speak again in case he moved away from me. From somewhere nearby, music started to play.

I felt him smile against my neck. Disbelief stole in then and began its sneering taunt. *Things like this do not happen to people like you.* And yet, when Cellan whispered my name, I made myself turn towards him, knowing I was lost.

'Eww – are you two kissing?'

I veered backwards out of the embrace so quickly that I almost sent Cellan flying. We both spun round to find Peran, awake from his post-chicken slumber, grinning at us from the deckchair.

'No,' I said primly. 'Absolutely not.'

The boy put his head on one side. 'Are you sure?'

Cellan was smirking. Getting up onto his knees, he made a grab for Peran's bare feet only to end up having sand kicked into his face.

'Gee,' he spluttered, rubbing at his eyes. 'Thanks for that, you little psammead.'

Cackling with laughter and delighted to have hit his mark so effectively, Peran sprung up off the chair and ran to where the others were gathered by the bonfire. I heard the word 'smooching', followed by raucous cheers, and wondered seriously how far I would have to dig to reach Australia.

'Oops,' said Cellan, as I hung my head.

'I think the word you're searching for is "bollocks".'

'Please don't mention those, not at the moment.'

I glanced up in time to witness him rearranging the front of his shorts, and blushed.

'I think,' he said, as Locryn mused aloud which word Cellan could choose to rhyme with 'Honor' when he wrote me a poem, 'that it might be a good time to head off. What do you say?'

I was on my feet in seconds.

'I say yes.'

28

We half-ran, half-stumbled across the sand, my hand in Cellan's as the two of us gave in to helpless laughter. By the time we reached the steps, I was out of breath – more from laughter than exertion – but Cellan did not give me time to recover.

'Come on!' he said, pulling me up behind him. His palm felt hot and dry. I gripped him tighter.

We had strolled down the beach without attracting so much as a glance a few hours previously, but now every pair of eyes seemed to be on us, following us, intrigued by us.

'Hold up,' I cried, as we thundered down the opposite side of the steps to the road. 'I want to put my shoes on.'

Cellan shook his head. 'No time. Here.' He crouched with his back to me. 'Get on.'

'I'm not letting you piggyback me.'

'It's that or a fireman's lift.'

When I didn't immediately move, he made as if to stand and I yelped in alarm.

'OK, OK – I'm getting on.'

There was nothing remotely sexy about a piggyback, but my body seemed to think otherwise. Almost as soon as my legs were wrapped around Cellan, and his hands were on my thighs, the same throbbing urgency that had taken over down on the blanket began to course through me once again. I was glad that Cellan could not see my face but guessed he must be aware of my heart beating. I could feel his, and it was pounding.

'Where's your hat?' I asked.

Cellan froze. 'Oh, shit.'

'We can go back?'

'No, no.' He shook his head and continued walking. 'Maddy will keep hold of it for me until I next see her.'

'Your hair smells nice,' I told him, sniffing it appreciatively.

'Thanks.'

'And you're actually quite muscular, aren't you?' I added, moving my hands across his chest in an exploratory fashion. 'Well done you.'

He grunted. 'You have fantastic legs,' he said. 'But then, I knew that already.'

'Been looking, have you?'

'Yes.'

There was something in the tone of his 'yes' that made me pause, and the silence that followed felt loaded. Cellan carried me all the way back through the centre of the village, past the busy outdoor tables of restaurants, the open doors of noisy bars, and an ice-cream parlour with a queue snaking out and along the block, until eventually we reached the truck.

'You have the keys,' he said, but it was a moment before he relinquished his grip on me. I slithered to the ground as decorously as I could manage, dropping my eyes immediately to my bag when he turned, flustered under the weight of his gaze.

There was a click and a flash of headlights as the truck's central locking system disengaged, and Cellan opened the passenger door.

'I'm just going to put my shoes on,' I said, hopping up sideways onto the seat.

Cellan reached down and took hold of my feet in his hands. 'They're all sandy.'

There was a wedge in my throat, and a pulse began to thrum somewhere deep inside.

'It's OK,' I said, but Cellan's hands had already begun moving, his fingers featherlight as he brushed the sand from between my toes. There was nobody else in the car park, and the sun had vanished from the sky, its canvas now a rich, clear indigo. I knew that if I searched I would find stars, but not even their beauty was enough to draw me away from Cellan. He had one of my feet in each of his hands, his fingers caressing.

'Do you think anyone recognised you?' I said, my voice uncharacteristically quiet. 'On the beach?'

Cellan thought for a moment, his dark eyes seeking mine. 'Maybe,' he said.

'Bugger. Sorry.'

'What are you apologising for? It's not your fault.'

'I know, but—'

'No buts.'

He smiled, and so did I. His hands had moved, each one now cupping my ankles, his forefingers stroking my calves. He took a small step closer to me, and the gap between my legs widened. I wanted to hook my feet around his back and drag him forwards until he was pressed hard against me, my need for him now so palpable that it almost pained me.

'Probably a good thing that Peran woke up when he did,' I said.

Cellan raised an eyebrow. 'You think?'

I bent my knees, drawing him nearer. 'Yeah. Don't you?'

'I think,' he said, taking another step towards the truck; towards me, 'that if he hadn't, then I would have kissed you.'

'Exactly! And that would have been— Well, you know.'

'Would have been what?' He was smiling at me in bemusement.

'Mad. Crazy. Utterly loop-the-loop bonkers.'

'And why is that?'

'Because you're—' I gestured wildly with one hand. 'And I'm—'

'You're what?' he prompted, hands now on my knees. I allowed myself to fall backwards until my head collided with the gear stick.

'Me,' I said, in a small voice.

'Honor.' It was an instruction. I levered myself up and found that Cellan had moved right into the open doorway of the truck. He had let go of my legs, allowing them to lie slack against the seat, but his hands still danced across my skin.

'Yes?'

'Did you want me to kiss you?'

I stared at him, searching for any trace of humour, any clue that he might be winding me up. But Cellan was not laughing; he was merely watching me intently, his hands now resting, palms up, against my inner thighs. I made myself breathe.

'Yes.'

He smiled then. 'Thank God,' he said. 'It would have been seriously awkward if you'd said no.'

I laughed in relief. 'What can I say? I'm only human. I have eyes in my head and blood running through my veins. I mean, it's not as if I'm a special case – anyone in my position would be up for it. I mean, look at you. Even with that beard, you're a decent eight out of ten, and—'

'Honor?'

'What?'

'Please shut up.'

'Why?'

'Because I really want to kiss you.'

'Oh.'

'Is that OK?'

'Yes, but—'

I did not get to finish. In a single, determined movement, Cellan had slid both his hands underneath me and lifted me off the seat. I responded by wrapping my legs tightly around his waist as he pinned me against the side of the truck. For a moment, we simply stared at each other, then we both moved at the same time, lips colliding timidly at first, then greedily, as we let ourselves fall joyously into the kiss. It was not the chaste kiss of two strangers, it was noisy, and playful, and hot. I raked my fingers through his hair, arching my back as his mouth moved to my throat.

'You taste wonderful,' he murmured, before kissing me again, on and on until all I could feel, all that I knew, was pure sensation. We writhed against each other, hardness and dampness and longing making my legs buckle; when one of us started to slow, the other probed deeper, each of us reluctant to stop, yet fully aware of what would happen if we did not.

I felt Cellan move, readjusting his position and hoisting me higher in his arms. He could not touch me anywhere without putting me down, and I knew he wanted to, knew it because I yearned to do the same.

'Hey,' I whispered, putting a hand against his chest. 'We can't. Not here.'

He nodded, resting his forehead against mine as he calmed his breathing.

'I know. I'm sorry, I just want—'

'Don't be.' I kissed him lightly on the corner of his mouth. 'I just want, too. We should—'

'Go home? Yeah, I know.'

With a sigh, he lowered me slowly to the ground, and I blinked as the world came back into focus. It felt like coming inside from a blizzard, and I staggered slightly, foal-like on my unsteady legs.

'Are you OK?' he asked, clutching my arm as I careered towards the still-open door of the truck.

'No.' I laughed. 'I am way better than OK.'

Cellan patted me on the bottom as I climbed into my seat.

'Well, then,' he drawled, suddenly Billy Bob again, 'buckle up, Bambi, my delicious slice of pumpkin pie, because you're in for the ride of your life.'

29

There was no discussion, we simply headed straight for my house.

I spent the majority of the journey back to Southampton twitching with a mixture of desire, disbelief, and excited trepidation. Not once had I so much as considered having sex with a man the same day I kissed them for the first time. But I told myself that this was not a normal day, and Cellan was definitely not a normal man.

I continued to steal glances across at him, drinking in every delectable detail and reliving every sensation I had felt when he'd picked me up and pinned me to the truck. Any earlier reserve I may have felt had been eradicated by pure, unequivocal lust, the type that cannot be disobeyed. I had forgotten how powerful it could feel. All I knew, all I was sure about, was that I wanted Cellan Thomas.

Despite it not being particularly late, there were no lights on in any of the windows as we pulled up outside, and I could not hear any music or sounds of voices either.

Cellan glanced across at me.

'They must be out,' I said.

He smiled. 'Good.'

Outside the truck, everything felt magnified – the crunch of our shoes on the gravel driveway, and the feel of Cellan's hand, hot in mine. We reached the door and I took out my key, wincing and then giggling as the screen door creaked on its ancient hinges. There was nobody here, I reminded myself, nobody to hear us creeping around like a couple of teenagers, although knowing this made little difference. Once in the hallway, Cellan slid his arm around my middle and pulled me gently back against him, his beard tickling my ear as he whispered, 'Where?'

'Upstairs,' I said, in a hushed voice that melted into a low moan as he began to kiss my neck. 'Top floor.'

'Where are you going?' he asked, as I moved away from him towards the kitchen.

'To get some water. I won't be a second.'

The beers I'd drunk at the beach had left me dehydrated, and I didn't relish the thought of a dry mouth, not when it was about to spend the next few hours exploring every inch of Cellan's body. The thought of that alone was enough to make me feel lightheaded and clumsy, and when I reached into the cupboard, my hand slipped.

There was a loud, glass-shattering crash, followed swiftly afterwards by another, even more disconcerting sound – that of hurried feet across floorboards. The door was flung open, and my father appeared, a large paperweight clutched in one raised hand.

I ducked, cringing against the wall.

'It's me!' I squeaked.

My father lowered his arm. 'Jesus Christ, honey, you almost gave me a heart attack. Why are you sneaking around in here in the dark?' He switched on the light, and I cringed again, blinking furiously as he came further into the room.

'I thought you were out,' I said.

'Even more reason not to sneak, in that case,' he said, giving me the once over as he placed his makeshift weapon on the table. 'Been at the beach, have you?'

He was clad only in boxer shorts; the hair on his chest, I noticed, beginning to grey.

'In Montauk,' I clarified, bending to retrieve the dustpan and brush from beneath the sink.

My father watched me sweep up the broken glass in silence, waiting, I presumed, for me to continue speaking. I wondered if Cellan had heard the commotion, or if he was, even now, undressed and waiting for me.

'I should let you go back to sleep,' I said, attempting to step past him. My father put out an arm. From somewhere in the house, I heard a door being quietly shut.

'Are you still writing?' he asked.

The question took me by surprise. 'Er, yes,' I stuttered. 'Well, kind of.'

He smiled rather grimly. 'That's what I thought.'

'I've been researching,' I replied, somewhat unconvincingly.

My father rubbed a hand through his hair. It had been sticking up at all angles when he burst into the kitchen, and this did not improve matters.

'Are you feeling all right?' I checked. 'You're not going down with something?'

'Now, why in the heck would you ask me that? Do I look ill?'

His reply had been delivered rather gruffly, and I bit my lip before replying.

'It's just that . . . it's not even ten and you're in bed.'

'When you work as hard as I do, you need rest. Books don't write themselves. If you're going to have a shot at becoming a novelist, Honor, then you're going to have to start prioritising worktime over playtime.'

'You're right,' I told him, staring dully at the floor. 'I've been avoiding it; I hit a problem, and instead of tackling it, I try to swerve it altogether.' I glanced up to find that my father's eyes had softened somewhat.

He folded his arms and let out a contemplative sigh. 'Are you sure that writing is what you want to do?'

I started to reply, but he shook his head, silencing me.

'I want you to think before you answer – really think.'

And so I did; I thought about how, when an idea took hold of me and inspiration ran like fuel through the cogs in my mind, the words would then flow from me onto the page as if I was possessed. I had tried to describe the process to people before, those who had never felt the inclination to write, and usually likened it to something banal, such as scratching an itch – but it was more than that. It was magic. And those moments, where I became unchained from one world and lost in another, were the ones that made all the other, stickier parts of the process tolerable.

'I'm sure,' I said, and this time he smiled.

'OK then.'

'I should . . .' I said, motioning to step around him, but before I had the chance to say anything else, the door to the kitchen opened and Cellan appeared.

'Oh,' he said, as my father jerked round in surprise. 'Hello, Mr Butler.'

I saw a look of incredulity pass across my father's face, but he recovered his composure quickly. 'Call me Jeffrey, please – or better yet, Jeff.'

'Shall do,' agreed Cellan, catching my eye as I mouthed a 'sorry' behind my father's back. 'I was just seeing Honor home,' he explained, without elaborating further.

'I was fetching him a glass of water,' I said hurriedly, adding to Cellan, 'I dropped it.'

My father looked at each of us in turn. 'Well, don't let me hold you kids up,' he said, crossing to the cupboard and taking out a glass. 'Now that I'm awake, I might treat myself to a nightcap. Can I tempt you, Cellan?'

'No,' I said, causing both men to look at me askance. 'Sorry, I just thought that . . . You said that you . . .'

Cellan frowned for a moment before realisation dawned.

'Have to go,' he said. 'Yes, I did say that. Don't worry about the water,' he assured me, 'I'm only ten minutes from home after all.' He was already backing out of the room. 'Night, Jeff – sorry to have disturbed you.'

My father raised a hand. 'Don't mention it, Cef – come any time.'

'I'll see you out,' I said, and followed him along the hallway. As soon as we were both through the door and standing together on the front lawn, I let out the groan I had been holding in and allowed myself to collapse against him.

'I'm so sorry,' I moaned. 'If I wasn't such a lumbering idiot, he never would have woken up.'

Cellan chuckled. 'It's OK,' he said, dropping a rapid kiss on my forehead. 'Breaking that glass might have been a blessing.'

'What do you mean?' I pulled back to look at him uncertainly.

'Don't make that face,' he chided, stroking my cheek. 'I like you, Honor. And I don't mind waiting.'

'I do,' I said hotly, and he laughed.

'I overheard what your dad was saying, about the writing, and I feel bad. I have clearly been dragging you away from your work.'

'You really haven't,' I assured him. 'I came willingly.'

Cellan responded with the twitch of a smile. 'Gunnar has some script he wants me to read,' he said, his hand now on my shoulder. 'That will take up most of tomorrow, so why don't you use the day to work on your book, then we can do something on Friday?'

'Something?' I echoed hopefully, and Cellan shook his head in amusement.

'Head on over to mine after lunch; I'll kick everyone out for the afternoon.'

'Just like that?'

'Well,' he said, taking my hand and raising it to his lips, 'there have to be some advantages to being – what was it you called me the other day – a global megastar. Yes, that was it. For once, I'm going to exercise my power of celebrity.'

'For me?'

'Yes.' He kissed my fingers. 'For you.'

30

Sleep was impossible, so I unplugged my laptop and moved it from the desk in my room to the bed, where I propped myself up on a fort of cushions and started typing.

I recorded everything that had happened during the day, from the conversations Cellan and I had shared to the heated embrace in the car park, feeling my body once again begin to burn with longing as I recalled how it had felt to kiss him. Once I was done, I closed the file and opened what existed of my novel, making myself read through the passages I had written, excavating each for any sections of prose worth saving.

Instead of worrying that my central character was not doing enough, I concentrated on who he was. What had made him decide to pursue his choice of dangerous career? How had his tendency to take risks affected the relationships in his life, and which moments in his past had fuelled his belief that loneliness equalled strength? I filled one page of my document, then another, pleased with how much more rounded my conflicted protagonist was becoming. If I could fall for Patrick and feel genuinely concerned about him, then hopefully my eventual readers would, too. Loving a figment of your own imagination was a safe option – a character would never let you down, would always be there in the same carefully curated guise you had constructed for them. It was an intoxicating thought, and one that continued to spur me on as the hours passed.

Slumber eventually crept in and whisked me away, but I was woken not long after seven a.m., by the sound of voices under my open window and the aroma of freshly brewed coffee. Having showered and dressed, I wandered out to the sun-dappled garden and found Tallulah and my father enjoying an al fresco breakfast of boiled eggs, toast and fresh fruit. There was a folded copy of the *East Hampton Star* in front of her, while he was ensconced in *The New York Times*.

'You look beat,' said Tallulah, as I collapsed yawning into a chair. I rubbed my eyes, taking in her immaculately applied make-up, neatly styled hair, and pale pink halter dress.

'And you look whatever the opposite of that is,' I replied. 'Special occasion?'

Tallulah glanced at my father who, other than giving me a brief smile over the top of his newspaper, had yet to say anything. He was also attired more smartly than usual, I noted, in neatly ironed shorts and a new-looking Ralph Lauren polo shirt.

'We're heading into the city,' she said, reaching across for her glass of juice. She had taken to squeezing oranges and grapefruits every morning, which she did by hand using the ancient metal press we had unearthed from the back of a shelf in the pantry. 'Jeffrey has a lunch and is letting me tag along.'

'Oh,' I said, trying my best to sound gracious. 'That sounds fun. Will you be driving?'

'We thought the train would be better,' Tallulah said, between sips.

'Can't be late,' said my father, folding the *Times* into a neat square. 'Important people don't like being made to wait.'

'Is this about the movie adaptation?' I guessed, and he nodded.

'Got it in one, honey.'

'Any more news on who you might cast as Marty?'

'You want an egg?' Tallulah interrupted. 'I can boil you one.'

'Thanks, but I'm fine,' I said distractedly, not looking round. There was something in my father's expression that I could not read – a kind of shiftiness I was not used to seeing from him. There was nothing coy about Jeffrey Butler, or certainly not that I had ever witnessed.

'Are you seeing Cellan later?'

Tallulah was not going to give up on her campaign of distraction. I sighed, turning to face her as my father noisily buttered a slice of toast.

'Not today,' I said. 'He's busy – and anyway,' I added, realising too late how reliant this made me sound, 'it's actually a good thing, because I was going to write all day.'

Tallulah beamed. 'That's so exciting!'

'Is it?'

'Of course, it is! How's it coming along? Have you reached the first plot point yet, or are you still setting up your world?'

'I, er . . .'

'Why don't you go and get your computer, honey?' said my father. 'I have an hour or so free right now, I can take a look at what you've done so far.'

'Really?'

The thought of my father reading my work made me feel almost as sick as the dread that he would never want to. The last time he had done so, it had taken me years to recover enough confidence to try again.

My father tapped at his watch. 'Tick, tick, tick – time is money.'

I fetched the laptop, and my father retreated with it to the porch, a plate of toast and jam balanced on top of his coffee cup.

'It's the file labelled "At Risk Of Injury",' I called after him. 'On the desktop.'

He raised a hand of acknowledgement.

'Oh God,' I moaned, rearranging my chair so it faced away from the house. 'I can't watch.'

'I bet he'll love it,' Tallulah said, although with less conviction than her statement warranted. The smile she offered me was plastered on, her usually bright eyes dull.

'How are you?' I asked. 'Is the thing at home—'

'All fine,' she said, going for bright and breezy but ending up somewhere closer to brittle. Bending over, she scratched absent-mindedly at her ankle.

'I keep getting bitten,' she said. 'Damn little critters can't seem to get enough of me.'

'You are a tasty dish,' I pointed out, but she didn't react. I tried again. 'How's your writing going?'

'Oh, y'know, it's going. Not sure to where, but it's going all right.'

'Has JB been helping?'

Tallulah smiled properly at last before replying. 'Tons. He's so generous with his time, especially when you consider how busy he is.'

I thought about my encounter with him in the kitchen the previous night, how he had scolded me for skiving work in pursuit of more frivolous activities.

'He does work hard,' I agreed. 'That's always been his focus, ever since I was a child.'

'What is the score with him and your mum?' she asked. Then, when I paled, 'You don't have to tell me if it's too painful or whatever.'

'No.' I swallowed. 'It's not, it's just that ...' I glanced quickly over my shoulder to check that my father was not listening. He looked to be completely absorbed in what he was reading, which lifted my spirits a fraction. 'We've never actually talked about it, not he and I, anyway. My mum is the one who told me what happened.'

Tallulah waited for me to continue, her foot tapping away beneath the table. I picked up a slice of melon from the plate of fruit and contemplated eating it for a second before deciding I wasn't hungry.

'It's no big secret,' I said. 'He came over to the UK to promote his third novel – the first two had sold really well, and the publisher was keen for him to do events, network with other authors, that sort of thing. My mother worked as a publicist then, and it was her job to look after him on the tour. They got on well and . . . she looked after him a little too well on the final night.'

Tallulah's eyes widened.

'That's right,' I said, forcing out a rather hard laugh. 'I am the result of a one-night stand. Born out of wedlock and everything, quite the scandal – or it was as far as my grandparents were concerned. I think if he could have, my granddad would have flown over, kidnapped Jeffrey and dragged them both down the aisle.'

'But that's not what happened,' said Tallulah.

'No. For one thing, my mother refused to tell anyone who the father was at first, and then when she did, there was a worry that it would lead to her getting the sack.'

Tallulah sat forward in her chair, seemingly riveted.

'Oh,' she gasped. 'You mean because—'

'Because my mum had done the one thing that you're not supposed to with the talent you're paid to shepherd around the place. She told me it was one of those "everyone knows, but nobody mentions it" situations.'

Tallulah nodded. 'And then?'

'My mum wrote to JB in the end, got a letter passed on by

his agent over here in the States, but it took a while to reach him, and in the meantime, I was born. Once a baby arrives, the focus goes completely onto them, and so it was true for me. My grandparents went from trying desperately to reconcile my mum with Jeffrey to being terrified that he would swoop in and steal me away – which of course he didn't. He replied, saying that while he was happy to provide support, he could not see himself having an active role in my life. His life was in New York, there was no way it could work.'

Tallulah had clasped her hands together and was tapping them against her chin. 'And your mum was OK with that?' she asked.

'As far as she was concerned, it was the perfect solution. They stayed in touch on and off over the years and eventually, when I was eight, he came back to the UK and we met. I can still remember everything about that day,' I said, wistful as I pictured myself, hollow-stomached and twitchy, approaching the tall man in the restaurant. 'I was terrified yet elated by the reality of him, this man that had made me.'

'Sounds like a great premise for a novel,' Tallulah suggested, but I shook my head.

'He would never forgive me if I wrote about him.'

'It would be your story, not his,' she pointed out gently, but I was adamant.

'Even less reason to bother. Who the hell would be interested in a story about me?'

Tallulah started to protest but was interrupted by the scrape of a chair. My father was coming back, and I looked from him to her, gripped by a sudden panic.

'You won't tell him I told you?' I hissed.

She shook her head, smiled, but didn't say anything. Dread gnawed at my stomach, but it was too late to take it back. Why had I been so open? Outside of my immediate family, the only person I had ever spoken to about this subject was Jojo and, to a lesser extent, Felix.

My father put the laptop down on the edge of the table, obscuring his copy of *The New York Times*, and lowered himself with a sigh into his chair.

'You've certainly been busy,' he said.

'Oh, Jeffrey,' admonished Tallulah. 'Don't be all cryptic – put the poor girl out of her misery and tell her what you thought.'

My father allowed the silence to stretch, his arms folded and his fingers drumming against his sleeve. 'I love all the descriptive stuff,' he finally said. 'The way you talk about New York feels new, and unique to you, which is hard to do. So many people write about the city without ever capturing its essence, but you've managed to do that.'

'I have?'

'You may only be fifty per cent a New Yorker, but she's worked her way right into your bones, I can tell.'

I did not think I could recall a time where I had ever felt more proud of myself. It did not last long.

'What about the characters?' asked Tallulah, and at this, my father's eyes clouded over somewhat.

'This Patrick fella you've come up with, who is he based on?' he asked.

I took a breath, feeling colour flood into my cheeks.

'Nobody.'

'Well, in that case, maybe you should think about trying that tack,' my father went on. 'Guy's a bit of schmuck; a bit soppy; a bit' – he frowned – 'too fond of gazing towards his own navel, if you catch my drift.'

I winced.

'Thing is, honey, if you're writing a romance, you need a hero that women are going to have the hots for right out of the blocks, otherwise why would they keep reading? In my experience, women prefer men that act, rather than those that sit around all day thinking about what they should do.'

'But he has to have flaws,' I argued, overcome by a fierce need to defend my character. 'How can he go on a journey towards bettering himself if he's perfect in chapter one?'

'Then give him a real quest; something tangible that he must battle against to win the woman. You don't see Indiana Jones wallowing in self-pity over how his parents raised him, and I don't remember James Bond ever taking a day off from killing bad guys to have a therapy session.'

'James Bond is a deeply flawed character,' I muttered.

'That's as may be – the key is that he's a doer. You can have your hero struggle with as many internal things as you like, as long as he's doing more exciting things at the same time. Your guy strikes me as passive, and he needs to be active. Give the poor dude some agency – and a bigger pair of nuts.'

'He is a stuntman,' I argued weakly. 'I do plan to have some meaty action scenes in there, but I wanted to set up his character first.'

'Listen, honey, you don't have to take my advice,' said my father. 'I mean, what do I know anyway, right? It's not as if I have any players in this game.'

His sarcasm caused my shoulders to droop, and I looked away from him, staring hard at a dribble of coffee that had stained the white tablecloth. Tallulah made a sympathetic sounding 'hmm'.

'This is your novel,' she said kindly. 'How you go about writing it is up to you – Jeffrey's just pointing out that there are different ways of tackling it.'

'Exactly,' he said, flashing me a smile as I raised my eyes. 'And if I were you, I'd spend the day thinking about it. Turn off your phone, go for a walk, and see where your mind goes. Never fails for me.'

'OK,' I mumbled. 'I'll try.'

'That's my girl, now if you— Shoot!' he broke off, having glanced at his watch. 'We'd better light a fire under our feet, Tally, if we're going to make that train.'

Having promised to clear up the breakfast things, and assuring Tallulah that no, of course I didn't mind her abandoning me for the day, I waved them off and trudged back upstairs to my room. It would have been easy to collapse into a sobbing and self-pitying heap on the bed, but what would that achieve, in the end? I was fortunate to have my father on hand, a writer at the very top of his game – how many other aspiring authors could say the same? How many of them would do anything to be in my position?

Walking into the bathroom, I faced myself in the mirror and gripped the sides of the basin until my trembles subsided.

This time, I decided, I would not flounder.

I would keep going, keep tweaking, keep shaping until I had something not only worth entering into a competition, but good enough to win it, too.

31

It was not until I ventured out to the Southampton Publick House that evening that I thought to switch off the 'do not disturb' function on my phone. I'd obeyed my father's advice and sought inspiration in silence and solitude, though it had done little to alter the trajectory of my character. Trying to force a plot onto the novel that did not feel authentic to either him or me was proving difficult, and I had ended the day frustrated and in desperate need of a drink to take the edge off.

'Thanks,' I said to the bartender, as she placed a glass of Pinot Noir down in front of me. Of all the bars and restaurants in the village, this one was the most typically American – and I liked it all the more for that reason. There were booths upholstered in brown leather, TV screens showing all manner of sports, and cocktail shakers sat upturned in a row along the polished bar top. Most of the walls were wood panelled, and the food being ferried out from a hatch-fronted kitchen was arranged in red plastic baskets. I did not feel as if I stood out here, as I often did in the more expensive eateries, and the staff were friendly and willing to chat.

Picking up my alcoholic reward for a day of fruitless hair-tearing, I swiped at my phone to unlock it and almost choked as a slew of messages appeared. All of them were from Jojo, and she had also tried to call me three times. Certain that something awful must have happened, I steeled myself for a moment before opening WhatsApp.

Are you there? said the first message, sent a little over two hours ago.

Pick up! said the second, while another begged, *Honor, seriously, where are you?*

She had given me ten minutes to respond, before sending yet another flurry of texts.

> Are you trapped under something heavy?
> Is that something You Know Who?
> And by that, I don't mean Voldemort, btw.
>   I mean CT!
> OK, still no blue ticks. Have you gone into
>   hiding?
> I can't believe you're not answering the
>   phone to me. I need answers!

Three missed call notifications were listed below, and then Jojo had sent another message, this time containing a link to a Twitter account belonging to someone named @Beachy_Babe88.

Is this you? she'd written.

Taking a large, fortifying sip of wine, I clicked the link. The tweet that appeared was only a few lines long, but what it said still caused most of the blood in my head to drain down into my stomach.

Pretty sure I just saw Cellan Thomas running along Ocean Beach with a girl, and they looked pretty cosy. Anyone else see him?
#CelebritySighting #MontaukBeach #CellanThomas.

The tweet had been liked over five hundred times, and there were numerous replies. I scanned the first few. Someone named @Hot_Montauk_Mama had replied saying she had seen someone she'd thought was him, too, while another, rather strident sounding user with the handle @Future WifeOfCellan, condemned the sighting as 'nonsense', before stating that it was common knowledge Cellan had returned to Los Angeles after leaving rehab. Scrolling down, my heart leapt again as I recognised the account belonging to *Idol* magazine, which had asked both the users who'd claimed to see Cellan to follow them so they could send a direct message. There was a similar request from *US Weekly*, as well as the *New York Post*.

I took another sip of wine and returned to WhatsApp.

> Honor? I'm starting to get worried now. Have you been kidnapped by jealous Cellan fans? Are you tied to a stake above a Hamptons beach bonfire about to be roasted alive for your transgressions? Seriously, though – call when you get these. Love you.

She had then left it almost an hour before messaging again, this time with another link attached:

> Bloody *Idol* magazine are running the story – look!

I became vaguely aware that the woman behind the bar was asking me a question and glanced up dazedly from my phone.

'You want another?'

Somehow, my glass had emptied itself. I stared at it for a moment, confused.

'Please – and make it a large one.'

The woman raised an eyebrow. 'Coming right up.'

Angling my phone so that the man perched on the stool beside mine would not be able to see the screen, I clicked the second link, mouth dropping open at the headline: CELLAN 'CHEATS' ON WYLIE AT WILD HAMPTONS BEACH PARTY.

Hardly 'wild', I thought, remembering the alcohol-free beers and a guest list that included seven year olds, although the mention of Wylie made me go cold. According to the story that followed, 'numerous' sources had seen Cellan 'cavorting' with several different women – including a blonde, who, the apparently scandalised journalist had written, 'threw herself at the actor as if she was feathers and him tar'. Knowing that this must refer to Maddy, I allowed myself a half-smile that was promptly wiped out by the sentence that followed.

> Supposedly teetotal Cellan was then seen swigging from bottles of beer, dancing, and being generally raucous, before kissing several women. Sources tell Idol, 'He was having the time of his life and he didn't care who knew it. No woman was off limits, and he seemed to have his pick of the party. The woman he disappeared with at the end of the night was a bit average, but then he seemed very drunk by that point.

A bit average!

I inhaled more wine.

There were, thankfully, no photographs of the two of us together, but the online piece had used plenty of Cellan, and even more of Wylie and him together. *Idol* went on to say that it had reached out to the former actress, but she had declined to comment, before repeating a lot of the stuff that had been reported before about their relationship, subsequent break-up, and Cellan's stint at a rehab facility. Right at the end of the article, there was an ominous box-out urging readers to get in touch if they had any idea who the mystery woman was and promised *Idol* would continue to update the story as soon as more facts came to light.

Hating myself, I switched back over to Twitter and searched for Wylie Brooke. She had not tweeted anything for several weeks, and all her Instagram story contained was a link where followers could buy her latest range of 'soul-calming bed linen'. Cellan did not have an official account, but there were hundreds of posts including more speculation followed by a hashtag of his name. A few seemed concerned by news that he had fallen off the wagon, while others were plotting to fly over to Montauk on the off chance of bumping into him. Someone calling themselves @Cef4Eva had condemned the rumours, defending her hero and pointing out that if he wanted to kiss loads of women, then that was up to him, and that if Wylie hadn't been such a controlling bore when they were a couple, then he might never have been sad enough to get drunk all the time in the first place.

This tweet had then been attacked by Wylie's own army of fans, who lambasted Cellan for breaking his ex-girlfriend's heart, before piously wishing whoever 'this new woman' was luck, because she was going to need it.

On and on the tweets went, unspooling a mixture of adoration, rumour and hatred that left me feeling drained and sad. None of these people knew Cellan, yet they felt as if they had every right to scavenge through the few scraps of his life that had been made public, and formulate an opinion based on little more than an outline of a person at best. I liked to think that Cellan would be able to laugh about all this, but instinct told me that he wouldn't – especially not the claims that he was drinking again. This would hurt him, and the day and night that had meant so much would be tarnished as a result.

I had to see him, I realised. Not tomorrow afternoon as planned, but right now.

My phone started to ring. Jojo. I hesitated for just a moment before answering.

'Hello?'

'At last! Where have you been? Did you see my messages? Tell me it's you who was kissing him on the beach – it was you, wasn't it?'

'No. OK, maybe.'

She started whooping.

'Stop,' I said. 'It's not funny.'

'No,' she agreed. 'It's not, it's bloody incredible. You and Cellan Thomas, snogging on the beach, making it into *Idol* online.'

'Shhh,' I hissed.

'Why are you shhh-ing me? I'm at home in bed, and who do you think Dodie's going to tell? She's not Pongo from *101 Dalmatians* – she's not going to head out and bark news of your hook-up all over Cambridgeshire.'

'I know,' I said. 'I'm sorry. This has all been a bit of a shock.'

'Not to me,' she said, sounding self-satisfied. 'I knew something would happen between you, although if I'm honest, I thought you'd do it somewhere a little less public than a crowded beach.'

'We did,' I protested, then baulked as I realised my error. 'I mean, we didn't. Nothing happened on the beach. Those so-called sources couldn't have seen what they say they did, because none of it took place.'

'But something *did* happen?'

I sighed, pinning the phone against my ear so I could root for my purse. Having peeled off a twenty and tucked it under the base of my half-drunk glass of wine, I hopped down from my stool and headed outside.

The night was balmy, and I could see a faint twinkle of stars in the inky black sky.

'It's a long story,' I told Jojo, turning in the direction of home. 'I'm not sure where to start.'

'That's easy,' she replied, and I imagined her settling down to get comfortable.

'You can start at the very beginning.'

32

Any urge I may have had to rush around to see Cellan had dissipated by the time I reached the house. Jojo, having listened in thrall to my account of the previous day, agreed that the best course of action was to stick to the original plan.

'The less bothered you are by all of this, the less concerned he'll be,' she said, sounding far more confident than I felt. 'These kind of things happen all the time to celebrities; he'll be used to it.'

I hoped she was right. I wanted nothing more than to pretend I hadn't even seen the story, but that did not stop me trawling through the comments below it, finding myself growing increasingly angry at the dismissive way people who did not know Cellan were willing to demonise him. On many occasions, I started to type a response, but every time, good sense took over before I posted it.

When I realised how late it had become, I sent Tallulah a message to check on her and my father's whereabouts, which she replied to within minutes:

> Lunch turned into dinner, so we're staying over. Hope the writing went well ☺ xxxx

The four kisses at the end made me smile despite everything, and taking advantage of the momentary mood-boost, I switched off my laptop and phone, and read until I fell into a fitful sleep, my dream turning into a nightmare of endless corridors and blacked-out windows. Waking early, I took as much time as I could getting ready, only to find that I still had hours to trudge through before I was due at Cellan's house. I decided to go for a cycle ride around the village but found myself heading straight for the outskirts, once again pedalling my way along the brilliantly named First Neck Lane before turning onto Great Plains Road.

There was something undeniably optimistic about the blueness of the sky, and the clouds bunched together at its edges glowed white as if freshly laundered. The breeze that chased jaunty leaves into open drains often felt intrusive, but today I found myself entertained by the tumble and spin. It was a comfort to bear witness to the world and all its many cogs continuing to turn, and I felt confident that this minor hiccup would turn out to be nothing more than an amusing anecdote. Cellan would not be fazed by a trivial item of gossip, nor by me arriving at his door three hours earlier than planned. All I knew was that I could not wait any longer to see him, no matter how much he teased me for it. Dismounting from the bike, I wheeled it across to the closed gate, and pressed the intercom button on the panel.

There was a crackle of static, but nobody said anything.

'Hi,' I croaked, coughing to clear my throat. 'It's Honor – I'm, er, here to see Cellan.'

There was a pause, and then the line went dead. Deliberating whether or not to buzz a second time, I relinquished a small 'phew' as the gate began to wobble, and then opened, revealing the pale-gold driveway beyond. It took me a few minutes to reach the house, and as I neared, I saw Colton's Chevy Silverado parked off to the left and a flashy black sports car beside it, which I did not remember seeing before. Perhaps Gunnar's, I thought, or maybe even

Padma's. It was the kind of sleek vehicle I could imagine the glamorous life coach driving.

Propping my own shabby mode of transport against the low wall that encircled the lawn, I made my way to the front door and gave it a tentative knock, wondering as I did so why I suddenly felt the urge to turn and run. But there was no time to change my mind because I could hear the steady tread of approaching feet, could see a crack of light as the door began to open. Ignoring the twisting sensation that had taken hold of my guts, I readied myself to greet Cellan with a joke, something silly that I knew would make him laugh, but whatever I had been about to say was swept away in a tidal wave of complete and utter horror.

It was not Cellan who had answered the door, it was Wylie Brooke.

Tall, fair, and with the kind of willowy figure that could only be maintained by avoiding all unhealthy foods, Wylie looked, in person, even better than she did on her Instagram account. Her ice-blond hair fell to her elbows, a thin, gold band the only thing holding it back from her face. As far as I could tell, she was make-up free, but her skin glowed with vitality, as did her wide green eyes. She was wearing a muted blue maxi dress covered in tiny flowers, a delicate shell necklace, and several turquoise-stone rings.

'Hi,' she said, when I didn't. 'Honor, is it?'

The smile she gave me felt sincere enough, and I dredged up one of my own in reply.

'Yes,' I stuttered. 'Sorry, I wasn't expecting to—'

'See me? No, I guess you weren't. I can't quite believe I'm here either, to be honest with you. Do you want to come in?'

I raised a hand to steady myself on the doorframe.

'I'm not sure if I should . . . I wouldn't want to intrude,' I finished lamely.

'Is Cef expecting you?'

'Yes,' I said quickly, worried that she might assume I was some kind of stalker. 'And no. That is to say, he told me to come later. I'm early because . . . I should go.'

I turned to leave but Wylie called me back. 'Wait a sec,' she said. 'Let me go see if he's awake. We were up so late, and you know how terrible he is in the mornings.'

I knew no such thing, and so I replied with a tight-lipped smile. 'Please,' I said, my voice brittle, 'don't wake him up on my account.'

Wylie frowned. At least, it looked as if she had, although not a single line creased her alabaster skin.

'Well, don't run off,' she said, beckoning to me as I backed away. 'Come in and wait. I was just about to make a smoothie; I brought Cellan some supplement powders from my new Clean and Supreme range, and they make the most delicious drinks. Honestly, you'll feel like a new you, I promise.'

This week had gone rapidly from extraordinary, to thrilling, to outright surreal, and I was finding it hard to keep up.

'When did you get here?' I asked, interrupting her mid-flow as she extolled the virtues of turmeric. Wylie looked momentarily taken aback, but she recovered her composure within seconds.

'Late last night. I drove out from the city after a TV slot.'

I wanted to ask her why; had she been invited, or come of her own volition? One thing was certain, however, and that was the fact she'd spent the night here – and she was comfortable enough to wander around answering doors and making smoothies. She had also, I registered apprehensively, offered to check if Cellan was awake, which meant that not only did she know the location of his bedroom, but was happy to stroll right into it, too.

'I really can't stay,' I said. 'I just remembered that I'm supposed to meeting someone – my dad!' I prattled on, slapping a hand against my forehead to illustrate just how foolish I was. 'He was in the city last night as well, some meeting about a movie, you know, all very important and exciting.'

Shut up, Honor. Shut up.

'Shall I tell Cef you passed by?'

'Yes, I mean no – it doesn't matter.'

I had reached the bike now and almost knocked it over in my haste to get into the saddle.

'It was great to meet you, Honor,' called Wylie.

I raised a hand but didn't turn around.

'You, too!' I lied.

Heart hammering in my ears, throat constricted by shock, I pedalled furiously down to the still-open gate and tore through it, crashing down the kerb and veering wildly into the middle of the road. Fortunately for me, there were no cars passing, but a man mowing the opposite verge paused to gawp at me.

'Shit,' I said aloud. 'Shit, shit, shit.'

I could not face going back to the empty house, nor into the village where curious stares would undoubtedly follow me, so instead I took the wide road that led past the lake towards Coopers Beach. The sun bore down on me and I spluttered as a swarm of sand was blown up from beneath my wheels. The undergrowth that banked the highway was a tangle of life, and in any other circumstance I might have slowed to admire the sprigs of beach heather and bearberry. Today, I could not see past my own desire to escape, the humiliation that snapped at my heels too vicious to ignore.

It was clear to me that Wylie Brooke was here in The Hamptons for one reason, and that was to claim back her man. She'd seen the story about the 'average' girl and had been propelled by jealousy or hurt or both back into Cellan's apparently eagerly waiting arms. And who could blame him? I thought dolefully. No man would turn down a woman like Wylie – she was stunning. It might have been easier to bear if I was justified in disliking her, but I couldn't even do that, not after she had been nothing but sweet to me.

I wished that Tallulah was with me. She knew Cellan and had become the person I talked to most about him as a result, often providing me with good advice and cheering me up when I scarpered down another burrow of self-doubt. I considered calling Jojo, but decided I couldn't face it, not when she had been so gung-ho the previous night, buoying up my confidence and making me believe I had nothing to worry about it. As it turned out, I had more to contend with than a story on a gossip site, which was, after all, just that. Wylie Brooke, on the other hand, was very much real, very much here, and very much superior to me in all the ways it was possible to be.

Having locked up the bike and propped it against one of the many wooden bollards that bordered the gaps between the dunes, I took off my shoes and stomped morosely across the beach and down to the water's edge, not caring how many gulls I scattered in the process.

'Same to you,' I muttered, as one particularly large bird squawked angrily in the air, its beady black eye narrowed in distaste. I could see the terns circling in the distance, dark slashes on a canvas of blue, green and gold, and let out a sharp gasp as the waves tossed icy pebbles across my bare feet. It was better here by the ocean where the natural rhythm of the tide eased my frantically racing heart. I had tired myself out getting down here, but it was more than just exercise that had left me lightheaded. I was scared, I realised, fearful that I had lost him. But then, whispered a crueller part of my subconscious, in order to lose somebody, they must first belong to you. And Cellan was not mine; he never would have been.

I wandered without purpose for a while, periodically picking up stones and hurling them into the water. Coopers Beach was not yet occupied by its daily influx of sunbathers, and the only people I encountered were dog walkers and joggers, the latter mostly shirtless men slick with sweat. A cocker spaniel wandered across and sniffed at my toes, but when I bent to scratch behind its ears, a red-haired woman in oversized sunglasses called it back. She looked vaguely familiar, perhaps an actress although I could not be sure, and did not reply when I called out 'lovely dog' in her wake. Nonplussed, I continued, passing a deserted lifeguard tower that brought to mind images of a red-shorts-clad David Hasselhoff running in slow motion across the sand. If Cellan had been with me, I would have done an impression for him; the thought made me want to weep.

I had been walking for what felt like hours, although I knew, in truth, that I had not travelled very far from where I had left the bike. I could still see the dip in the dunes that marked the beach entrance and toyed with the idea of going back. To where, though – and to whom? Frustrated at my own indecision, I turned inland and trudged up the sandbank to where the beach flattened out, before sitting down heavily on the ground. I did not care that the hem of my dress was wet, nor that the sun was most likely searing red patches onto my shoulders. All I wanted was to sit and think, and be allowed to dwell on the predicament I had ended up in. It was a hole I fell into so far that I did not hear anyone approaching until their shadow had fallen across me.

33

'Hey.'

It sounded like Cellan.

I blinked, raising a hand to shield my eyes from the glare of the sun.

It *was* Cellan.

I must have been doing my finest goldfish impersonation because he smiled and said, 'It's OK, you know. I'm not a ghost.'

'What are you?' I stammered. 'How did you . . . ?'

'I fancied a walk,' he said, crouching onto his haunches beside me. He was wearing his beloved Vans, Bermuda-style patterned shorts and a Ramones T-shirt. 'You know my house is just up there, right?'

I squinted past him.

'Oh yeah. I'd forgotten,' I said, even though I knew he was unlikely to believe me. 'I really had,' I added when he looked bemused. 'I've only ever been to this beach once, and you have to admit, all these over-the-top houses start to look the same after a while.'

'I like to think mine would have had a lasting impression on you.'

'I met Wylie,' I said, deciding to wade straight in.

Cellan shifted until he was in a sitting position, his eyes on the ocean.

'You did,' he agreed. 'She told me.'

'Are you—?' I stopped, shook my head, tried again. 'I assume you're back together.'

He started to laugh, and I turned to him.

'What's so funny?'

'You,' he said, turning to face me. His eyes looked baked by exhaustion, the skin around them dry and tight. 'You are.'

'I'm not trying to be funny,' I protested, before adding, in a slightly more mollified tone, 'For once.'

'When you assume—' he began.

'You make an ass out of you and me – yeah, I've heard it before.'

'Am I the ass in this situation or is it you?'

'It's definitely you,' I said, placing deliberate emphasis on the last word.

Cellan pressed a hand to his chest as if struck and rolled over onto his back.

'Man down,' he croaked. 'Leave me, save yourself!'

When he didn't sit up again, I shuffled around until I was on my stomach and propped myself up on my elbows. Cellan had come out without any sunglasses, and his eyes were shut. As I stared at him, he opened one a crack, and smiled at me.

'Wylie and I are not back together,' he said.

I experienced a rush of giddy relief.

'You're not?'

'Nope.'

'But then why is she here, in your house, having stayed the night?'

Cellan turned over onto his side and started digging his fingers through the sand. 'I'm guessing you saw the story?' he said, and I nodded. 'Well, so did Wylie. She assumed I'd fallen off the wagon and was worried about me. When I didn't answer my phone and she couldn't get hold of Gunnar, she panicked and drove out here.'

'Where was Gunnar?'

Cellan frowned. 'At some dinner, I don't know. That's not what matters. All you need to know is that Wylie is a friend, and a good one at that. It was me who screwed up our relationship, not her; she's actually been very forgiving.'

'She did seem nice,' I admitted, as Cellan's hand came to rest against my arm.

'She is.'

'And you're sure you don't want to give things another try with her?'

He shook his head. 'Definitely not. Wylie's a sweetheart, but we are not compatible in that way.'

'How do you know for sure if you haven't tried?'

'We did try,' he pointed out. 'Her harder than me, granted. She by no means got the best version of me, but even when I was' – he paused for a moment, features constricting – 'even when I was drinking a lot of the time, I knew it wasn't right.'

It was the first time he had mentioned that stage of his life to me, and I felt compelled to reach out and take his hand. Cellan stared for a moment at our entwined fingers.

'You wouldn't have liked me then,' he said. 'I was poisonous.'

'Like botulinum toxin.'

'Who?'

'It's the most toxic natural substance on Earth, commonly found in Botox.'

'Remind me never to have any.'

'You don't need it,' I said lightly, and he smiled ruefully.

'Tell me that when I'm sixty, and the sun damage has really started to show.'

'If I still know you when you're sixty, I definitely will.'

'You will,' he said with a nod. And then, 'Listen, I'm sorry about that bloody story. I should have been more careful.'

I muttered something self-deprecating about being 'average' and he rolled his eyes.

'Articles like that are litter-tray lining, the lot of them.'

'So, you're not annoyed at having been seen with me?'

Cellan's grip on my hand became tighter. 'No, of course not. Is that really what you think?'

'I don't know what to think,' I told him honestly.

'I'm not embarrassed by you, or ashamed to have been seen "canoodling" with you, or whatever it was that stupid story said – I'm just very aware of how quickly these things can spiral, and while it's unfortunately part of the bloody job for me, it doesn't have to be the same for you.'

'I assumed you came up with the whole Billy Bob and Bambi thing so that nobody would know who either of us were.'

'I did,' he agreed. 'But mostly it was done to protect you.'

'You don't need to protect me,' I assured him, feeling stung by the implication. 'I can take care of myself.'

Cellan let his fingers drop from mine and went back to gouging sand.

'All I mean,' I said, cringing as a gull landed less than a foot away from our heads, 'is that I accept who you are, and the fame side of things doesn't scare me – at least, not enough to convince me not to spend time with you.'

'It is a lot,' he said quietly, almost regretfully. 'That world is . . .' He blew air into his cheeks.

'I can only imagine,' I said, fanning out my arms and resting my chin on my hands. Cellan moved closer, and I shivered as he stroked a lock of hair from my cheek. 'But I do know that it's a part of who you are, and how can I ever know you properly if I haven't seen both sides of the coin?'

'You want to see my yin and my yang?'

I grinned. 'Definitely your ying-a-ling.'

Laughing now, Cellan pulled me gently around until our faces were level and pressed his nose against mine.

'Are you sure?' he said. 'You're certain you want to do this?'

I did not know if he was referring to the celebrity side of his life, or intimate parts of his anatomy, but given that I was more than happy to become better acquainted with both, I nodded with enthusiasm.

'I'm certain.'

'Because once you're in, that's it. And you will forever be associated with me.'

'How could that ever be a bad thing?' I said, genuinely puzzled by the seriousness of his tone.

Cellan closed his eyes briefly, his mouth set in a contemplative line.

'Honestly,' I assured him. 'What's the worst that could happen? They've already deemed me "average", and I promise I didn't cry about it . . . much.'

My attempt to lighten the mood did not land as expected. Cellan still looked troubled and had now started tugging at his beard.

'I understand if you don't want to be seen with me,' I said, in a deliberate and shameless ploy at provoking a reaction. It worked; Cellan jerked as if I had poked a finger between his ribs.

'It's not that.'

'You think people will judge you for canoodling with a nobody.'

'No.'

Inching forwards, I pressed the lower half of my body against his, feeling him stir almost immediately. He gazed at me, letting out a moan that sounded half like desire and partly like defeat.

'I want to know you better,' I murmured. 'That's the only thing I care about.'

His lips were so close that I could feel the sweet heat of them, but Cellan did not kiss me. Instead, he leapt in one fluid movement to his feet, pulling me up along with him.

'If we're really going to do this,' he said, 'then I say we do it in style.'

34

Gurney's Resort and Seawater Spa was situated in Montauk, part way along the Old Highway that stretched from Southampton to the tip of Long Island. Given that it was the only luxury hotel in The Hamptons set right on the beach, it was also fully booked – at least, it was until Cellan told the woman that answered the phone who he was.

We drove there in the sleek, black convertible I'd seen parked outside the house that morning and which, it transpired, belonged to Wylie. She had seemed only too happy to wave us off, assuring us that she would stay at the house and 'catch up on my socials'.

'Do you want me to let Gunnar know where you are if he passes by?' she'd asked, and Cellan had shaken his head.

'No need – he'll find out soon enough.'

I'd sent a quick message to Tallulah, but other than explaining that I would not be back until the following day, I did not elaborate. To do so felt like too much of a risk, as if by writing down what I was about to do, I would somehow jinx it.

Cellan kept his hand on my knee as we drove, only removing it to switch between gears or flatten his wild hair. Having not been back to the house, I had nothing with me bar my rather beaten-up old handbag, while Cellan had chucked a small leather holdall into the boot.

When the Gurney's sign came into view ahead of us, Cellan braked and pulled smoothly over to the side of the road.

'Last chance to bail,' he said, turning to me. The sunglasses he usually wore had been replaced by Ray-Bans, and with the black denim shirt, diamond stud earring, and collection of heavy silver rings, he looked far more of a celebrity than usual.

I smiled. 'Still game if you are?'

Cellan revved the engine in reply, and a thrill of anticipation roared through me that was every bit as strong as the Mazda's impressive horsepower. Rooting with nervous hands through my bag, I found my own sunglasses and put them on, then smeared on lip balm. It was the best I could do with the limited tools I had at my disposal, but I told myself that it didn't matter. Cellan was the star; he was the one people would be looking at. All I had to do was stay quiet, behave myself and try to commit everything to memory so I could write about it later.

'Here we go,' Cellan said in an undertone, almost more to himself than me, and I felt all the air tighten inside my chest as he steered us down a wide, open driveway. A canopy had been put up outside the entrance, and as soon as Cellan eased to a stop, three valets in navy blue and cream uniforms hurried out to open the doors.

'Ta,' said Cellan casually, passing the keys and what looked to be a fifty-dollar note to one of the men. He made no move to take the small holdall himself, instead stretching out his hand and grasping mine, as another valet opened the boot.

Inside the air was cool and the lighting dim; someone stepped forwards to offer us a damp towel on a tray, a second welcomed us and thanked us for choosing Gurney's, and a third hovered with champagne.

'No, thank you,' I said, promptly forgetting my plan to say nothing, then almost colliding with an enormous, potted monstera. Cellan did not break stride, and I had to jog a few steps to keep up with him. An almost imperceptible hush seemed to fall over the cluster of staff behind the check-in desk as we approached, and I was sure I saw the eyes of the youngest woman widen as she realised exactly who it was that had just arrived.

'Cellan Thomas, checking in.'

He had opted for the most outwardly cool-headed receptionist, and after she had tapped a few keys, checked Cellan's driving licence and asked if we had any further luggage, she passed across two key cards.

'Top deck,' she told a hovering valet, who smiled briefly before leading us through the lobby. Unlike most of the hotels I'd been in, which had lifts that took you up, Gurney's instead had a warren-like network of stairs that took you down, across and around. The resort itself was sprawled across several buildings on various levels, with a spa at one end, blocks of rooms, suites and bungalows, and a Beach Club at the front. As well as two restaurants and a coffee and juice bar, there was an outdoor cocktail bar, numerous shops, and a fitness centre. The decor was tasteful and understated, low sofas in muted earthy tones, vases of dried flowers, and strategically placed table lamps, and everything smelt faintly of a watered-down incense.

I followed Cellan through a glass door and out onto a terrace laid with low tables and squashy chairs. Vast white umbrellas of starched canvas provided pools of shade for lounging guests, most of whom did not bother to look up from their iPads or newspapers as we passed. Two young women, who were perched up by the bar with a bottle of rosé in an ice bucket in front of them, appeared to do a double take as they clocked Cellan, one grabbing the other and whispering fervently into her ear. I tried not to stare back, but it was hard to fight the compulsion to at least acknowledge them. When I caved in and offered a timid smile, however, it was not returned.

'Did you see . . .' I started to say, but Cellan was focused solely on reaching our room, and answered by merely squeezing my hand a little tighter in his. We left the terrace, headed over another, emptier wooden deck, then crossed a set of steps and were swallowed up into a low-ceilinged corridor. I glanced up, counting the spotlights as we walked – two, three, four, five – and then the valet stopped.

'Here you are, sir. Ma'am.'

Ma'am.

I stifled a childish urge to laugh.

The door was opened, and Cellan ushered me inside ahead of him, taking his holdall from the valet and slipping the man what I guessed was another sizeable tip. Only when the lock was clicked shut, and the two of us were alone, did Cellan finally bring his lips to mine. Closing my eyes, I kissed him back, feeling as I did something warm beginning to melt deep inside. Cellan put his hand on my waist, pulling me into him and burying his face in my neck.

'You smell nice,' he said, voice muffled. 'It's not perfume, it's . . . I don't know.' He sniffed me again, harder this time, and I wriggled to one side as his beard started to tickle. Cellan made a lunge as if to grab me, and I let out a yelp, twisting away and running the few steps from the doorway into the room, only to stop as I took in what I was seeing.

'Oh my God,' I breathed. 'It's huge!'

He came to stand behind me, resting his chin on my shoulder.

'The room?' he asked. 'Or the bed?'

'Both! I'm pretty sure this one room is bigger than my entire flat, and the bed is practically a cruise ship.'

'Ridiculous, right?'

Cellan stepped around me and flopped down onto the vast mattress. Even with both his arms outstretched, there was a good two feet of space between his hands and the edge of the bed. It had been piled high with pillows and scatter cushions, each carefully chosen to tone in with the tawny furniture and cream walls. As well as two bedside cabinets and the largest television I had ever seen, there was a pale oak chest of drawers and desk, several tub chairs upholstered in plum velvet, and a long, tan leather sofa. After tossing my bag down on circular, dark-wood coffee table, I slid aside the blinds covering the glass doors at the far end of the room and gasped.

'We've got our own terrace out here!' I exclaimed. 'And another bed, just for sunbathing on!'

After struggling to work out the complicated latch system, I got the doors open and hurried outside. The balcony was large, square, and decked entirely in soft wood, with a futon-style lounger in its centre and raised beds of plants bordering either side. There were no rooms above ours, but when I peered over the side, I could see straight down onto the balconies below, and quickly averted my eyes as a woman strolled out and began rubbing sun cream onto her bare chest. All that was visible ahead was the wide golden stretch of beach, beyond which churned the ocean; mighty, boundless, and searingly blue.

'You have to see this view,' I called, but there was no reply. 'Cellan?' I said, going back towards the door, but the bed was empty. Struck by a sudden fear that he had changed his mind about this entire escapade and abandoned me here alone, I ventured further into the room and was about to call his name again when I heard the sound of a tap running from inside the bathroom.

'Never mind,' I said loudly, in case he had heard me calling, and retrieved my phone from my bag. There was no way that

I could not archive the majesty of this hotel room, and as I wandered around making first a video and then taking photos, I told myself that it would be something to show my children one day. If I ever had any. Sliding open a large teak door that I assumed masked a wardrobe, I was surprised to find a small kitchenette, complete with sink, basket of snacks, and a number of assorted glasses. 'What have we here?' I murmured, still recording, and crouched to inspect the contents of a mini fridge. As well as the standard range of soft drinks, there were miniature bottles of red and white wine, champagne, and a whole host of spirits and mixers. A small menu had been taped to the inside of the fridge, and my eyes widened as I saw how much even a can of Coke would set us back. Set him back. Cellan had assured me on the drive over that this mini soirée of ours was his treat, and outright refused to listen when I had attempted to argue.

'It's not a big deal,' he'd said, and I had to conclude that, to him, it genuinely wasn't. Given that I hadn't eaten since very early that morning, I was almost tempted to crack into the five-dollar packet of pretzels but managed to resist.

There would be time to eat later, I thought. Perhaps after . . .

The bathroom door opened, and I swung around in time to see Cellan emerging from inside, a towel pressed up against his face.

'I wasn't raiding the minibar,' I said, holding up both my hands.

Cellan lowered the towel, the beginnings of a smile on his clean-shaven face.

'Your beard!' I cried. 'Where is it?'

'Down the plughole, mostly,' he replied, laughing at the expression on my face.

'You look like a dog that's just been given the keys to a sausage factory.'

'Interesting choice of simile,' I said, taking a step towards him. 'Can I?'

'Feel free,' he said, jutting his face towards me. The skin across his jaw was pale and smooth, and for the first time since he had crashed into me that day on South Main Street, I could see the exquisite sharpness of his cheekbones.

'You've got a bum chin,' I informed him, sliding my thumb gently into its cleft. 'I'd never noticed it before.'

'You mean to say you haven't been trawling the internet for photos of me and spent endless hours drooling over them? Way to kick a man when he's beardless and vulnerable.'

'You look' – I began, throwing my phone in the direction of the bed to free up my other hand – 'different. Younger. More . . .'

'Like a seal?' he suggested.

'I was going to say distinguished, but sure, seal works just as well.'

He pressed his lips together into a smirk.

'What made you do it?' I asked. I'd let my hands fall from his face so I could see him better, but Cellan caught hold of one and laced his fingers through mine.

'I told you I would,' he said. 'When the time felt right.'

35

'Where first?' Cellan asked, after I'd dragged him outside to admire the view. 'Beach, pool, spa? I can book you in for a treatment if you like?'

'What are you saying?' I asked, pretending to be affronted. 'Skin not glowy enough? Toenails in dire need of a polish?'

'I just thought you might enjoy a bit of a pamper.'

'Nah.' I balanced both my elbows on the edge of the balcony, closing my eyes as a breeze lifted strands of my hair. 'I'd much rather spend time with you.'

'Beach, then? I'll call down and get one of those cabanas reserved for us.'

'Just like that?'

'Just like that.'

'I don't have anything to wear on the beach,' I lamented, looking down at my striped cotton sundress in dismay.

'You don't have a bikini on under—?'

'Nope. Only my best underwear, and I'm not getting sand on that.'

Cellan's brows had shot up at the mention of 'best', but he did not comment further.

'Did you bring trunks?' I asked.

'I did,' he said, rather sheepishly. 'But don't worry,' he added, keen to appease my disappointment, 'we'll just get you something to wear.'

Scooting back inside, he called reception, and I heard him securing us a slot at the beach club.

'Please don't worry,' I tried to say, but Cellan stuck his tongue out at me.

'A Dior pop-up?' he said into the receiver. 'Perfect. We'll be right down.'

This time when we walked together across the terrace bar, it felt as if everyone was staring, and a few shameless people raised their phones in our direction. My instinct was to cringe and hide, but for once, Cellan seemed unfussed to have been recognised. He still moved in the same determined pace that he had during our wander around Southampton, but there was a wide smile on his face that had eradicated any stand-offishness, and when a young couple stepped into our path and asked if they could take a selfie with him, Cellan appeared only too happy to oblige. Thanking them for their kind comments about his performance in *Mr Right* – 'I sobbed so much at the end, Mikey had to take me out for froyo afterwards to cheer me up, didn't you, babe?' – Cellan then politely refused their offer to buy both of us a drink and told them to have a great vacation.

I didn't like to contemplate how many other guests had managed to take a photo while we'd been standing there, but aside from keeping on my sunglasses, there was not much else I could do to disguise myself. We were way past the point of Bambi and Billy Bob.

The Dior store was situated one level down from reception, between the lobby and the entrance to the seawater spa. The immaculately dressed young man who sauntered forwards to greet us did so without so much as a flicker of recognition, and I wondered if the staff at the front desk had called to forewarn him.

'I feel like Julia Roberts in *Pretty Woman*,' I hissed to Cellan, as the assistant wafted off to source bikinis in my size.

'The scarf on that mannequin costs eight-hundred dollars; I think we should go.'

'You said you wanted to see the other side of my life.'

'Yes, but—'

'This is it,' he said, picking up an oversized straw hat and plonking it on my head.

'You're enjoying this, aren't you?' I muttered, trying for a scowl that was beaten into submission by a smile just as our attentive helper returned.

'I've hung the garments in the fitting room for you, ma'am. Please do keep your panties on when trying the briefs.'

'Yes, of course, thank you,' I blustered.

Cellan coughed and I shot him a look.

'Don't.'

'What?'

'You know full well what.'

The assistant tittered as if he was on the joke, and leaving them to it, I made my way to the curtained cubicle at the back of the shop, resolved to choose whichever of the swimsuits was the cheapest and get out of there as fast as possible.

Dismissing the first bikini, which looked like a metre of floss that had been dipped in gold paint, I selected a cerise one-piece with an intricate pattern depicting a lion eating a snake and wriggled my way into it. Cut high on the leg and eye-wateringly low in the back, the costume could never have been described as modest, but I was surprised how well it flattered the contours of my body, cinching me in at the waist and around the chest. The material felt strong and supple, and the fastening had been fashioned from proper metal as opposed to the painted plastic of the supermarket-bought bikini I had left hanging to dry over my bath back at the house.

With some difficulty, I unhooked the tag, squinted down at the price, and winced.

'Any good?' Cellan asked, when I emerged a few minutes later. The sales assistant was tending to another customer, so I judged it safe to say, 'Yes, but they cost one thousand-two-hundred-dollars apiece.'

'So?'

'So? So, my friend Jojo's puppy cost less, and she's a pedigree.'

Cellan folded his arms. 'Do you want me to tell you how much I got paid for my last movie?'

'No, I—'

'Ten million dollars.'

'Oh.'

'After tax.'

'Shut up.'

'True story,' he said, as I gaped at him. 'I mean, a lot of that is tied up in various charities I support, granted, and I have to give fifteen per cent to Gunnar, but I'm pretty sure that leaves me with enough to buy you something to wear on the beach. Is it the pink one you like?'

'How do you know that?' I asked, my mind still reeling as it tried to work out what ten million dollars amounted to in relatable terms – six big Cambridge properties without a mortgage attached, enough interest in the bank to live off, holidays to the Moon.

'Pink suits you,' he said. 'Goes with that English rose colouring of yours.'

'But it's so expensive,' I wailed. 'It feels almost obscene.'

Cellan went to take the swimsuit from me, tugging when I refused to let go.

'Julia Roberts wouldn't cause a scene like this,' he said, then swore as one of the straps pinged open and the buckle struck him hard across the back of his hand.

'For that,' he said, sucking air past his teeth and shaking his hand ineffectually, 'I should make you accept the eight-hundred-dollar scarf as well.'

At the mention of 'scarf', my hand flew automatically to the still stubbornly bald patch behind my ear, which was currently obscured by carefully positioned hair. Cellan, thankfully, did not see – he was already on his way to the till, and a few minutes later, I found myself in possession of a very sleek Dior-branded bag.

'Thank you,' I mumbled, taking it from him. 'It's the nicest thing anyone has ever bought me.'

'You know what the best thing about it is?' he said, as we made our way back through the lobby and headed towards the steps that would take us down to the beach.

'What – how skimpy it is?'

Cellan swivelled wide eyes in my direction. 'No, but that is a definite bonus. The best thing about it is that you didn't want it at all.'

'I don't get what you—'

'You needed it,' he said triumphantly. 'Therefore, I manage to treat you and prove my point at the same time.'

I pulled a face. 'If you say so. Weirdo.'

Several people stopped to stare at Cellan as we followed the signs directing us to The Beach Club, and again I was left to marvel how unfussed he suddenly seemed. This was not the same man who had tried to buy my bike off me in Southampton, just so he could outrun a few teenage girls, but then perhaps it was because of where we were. Gurney's Resort was an exclusive kind of establishment, and thus I assumed that many of the guests here were likely to be wealthy types who valued their privacy and would therefore be reticent about approaching us.

Unlike the three other beaches I'd been to since arriving in

The Hamptons, the broad sweep of sand here had been ploughed flat and was clear of leaves and pebbles. As well as a large, square open bar and seating area, sunloungers had been set up in rows facing the ocean, each with a pristine white and orange Gurney's branded umbrella. Beyond these, situated directly below the block of rooms Cellan and I were staying in, were the even more plush four-poster cabanas, each of which had white curtains around a raised double mattress. Having requested towels from a hovering member of staff, Cellan pulled the curtains closed and told me that he would stand guard while I got changed.

Doing my best to balance on the makeshift bed only to wobble – a lot like Bambi, ironically – I managed to get into the new Dior costume, before settling myself down against the heap of orange and navy-blue striped cushions.

'Ready!' I called, smiling as Cellan's head appeared through a gap.

'Wow,' he said, eyes roaming over my body. 'You look . . . wow.'

'Stop gawping,' I faux-scolded, chucking a pillow half-heartedly at his head. 'You'll make me blush.'

Cellan continued to look at me steadily as he unbuttoned his shirt, only dropping his gaze when he tugged off his jeans.

'Nice trunks,' I said admiringly. 'Very . . .'

'Tight? I know,' he said, folding his discarded clothes before coming to lie down beside me. 'I usually wear my boardies, but I figured as we were coming somewhere posh . . .'

'You definitely look the part,' I assured him, allowing myself the indulgence of taking him in. He had caught more of a tan than I had, but our colourings were not dissimilar. I could see from the paler patches at the top of his legs where his shorts would usually end, and there was what looked to be the top of a tattoo just visible above his waistband. He was lithe rather than thickset, with enough muscle definition to suggest an active lifestyle but not an obsession with lifting weights in the gym.

'You're going to have to stop looking at me like that,' he said in a low voice. 'Dangerous thing to do when I'm wearing shorts this tight.'

'You can always roll over,' I pointed out, and with a groan, he did just that.

For a few minutes, we lay together in companionable silence, each listening to the roar of the waves and the occasional indignant call of a gull. When a waiter appeared and asked courteously if we required any refreshments, Cellan promptly ordered two club sandwiches complete with fries, a couple of root beers, and a bottle of sunscreen.

'It's like you have magical powers,' I observed, as the latter object was delivered to us mere moments later.

'Turn over,' Cellan instructed, kneeling up and giving the bottle of lotion a vigorous shake.

'Are you going to cream me up, Scotty?'

'I am,' he agreed. 'I want your skin to live long and prosper.'

He started on my back, the sun cream cold enough to elicit a small 'oof' of surprise as he squeezed it out between my shoulder blades. At first, I found it impossible not to tense up, but as his hands continued downwards and the pressure of his fingers increased, I started to relax.

'You've got so many knots,' he murmured.

'Probably all that hunching over a desk I've been doing,' I said.

'Book going well, is it?'

I was glad he could not see my face. 'Bits of it. I showed a few chapters to my father, and he had some thoughts.'

'That sounds ominous,' said Cellan, his fingers now working cream into my upper arms.

'Not really.' I sighed. 'OK, maybe a bit. But it's not as if I can ignore his advice.'

'Why not?'

'Because he's the expert,' I said glumly. 'I'd be foolish not to listen to him.'

'But he writes action thrillers, right?'

'Yes, but—'

'And the majority of his readers are men, right?'

'Actually, it's a seventy-thirty split.'

'That's still a majority, unless my dyslexia is mistaken.'

'It is, but—'

'All I'm saying,' Cellan went on, pausing mid-application. 'Shall I do your legs, too?'

'Please.'

'All I'm saying,' he repeated, shuffling down the mattress until he was level with my knees, 'is that your audience is different from his. You're writing in a different genre, for potentially different readers, so it makes sense that your books would be nothing like his. You should never doubt your instincts,' he added, smearing a large dollop of lotion up my inner thigh. 'If your heart says that what you're writing is good, then chances are, it is.'

'If only that were true,' I muttered, then sighed with pleasure as his thumb grazed the underside of my buttock.

'Am I being too firm?' he asked.

'With the cream? No.'

'Good,' he said lightly, picking up my foot and starting to massage lotion between my toes, 'because I'm very much starting to enjoy myself.'

We fell into silence once again, and I closed my eyes as his hands continued to roam. Every time he ran them up to the top of my thighs, his fingers strayed further, until eventually he rested both gently on my bottom.

'This OK?' he murmured, to which I smiled sleepily.

'Yes. But I feel bad. It must be your turn soon.'

'All in good time,' he said.

The food arrived, and the two of us fell on it like ravenous hyenas, stuffing in fries and licking tomato seeds and mayonnaise off our fingers.

'You've got a little something on your face,' Cellan said, before wiping a great dab of tomato sauce across my cheek.

Extracting a soggy piece of lettuce from my sandwich, I flicked it onto his bare chest.

'You can take the animal out of the zoo . . .' he drawled, and this time I retaliated by fishing an ice cube from my glass of root beer and posting it down the front of his shorts.

Cellan yelped, tipping a large portion of his fries onto the sand as he tried in vain to fish it out. Almost immediately, there was a commotion of squawking, and a flock of gulls descended, snapping up the chips before either of us had time to react.

'Bloody hell,' Cellan said, peering gingerly around the curtain. 'It's like a scene from an Alfred Hitchcock movie out there.'

I knelt up beside him to look.

'Wait till they discover we've got bread in here.'

As I muttered the words, a gull bashed its way through the curtain on the other side of the cabana, closely followed by two more. Abandoning what was left of my sandwich, I staggered unsteadily to my feet and made a run for it, not stopping until I reached the shoreline. A green flag had been propped up in the sand, and when I glanced up at the closest lifeguard tower, a woman sitting atop it gave me a nod.

'I can't believe you left me to the birds!' said Cellan, who had just caught up with me. I went to reply, then shrieked as he ran forwards and gathered me up into his arms. I was slippery from the sun cream and wriggling like a worm on a hook, but Cellan's grip was strong, and a few moments later, I found myself summarily dunked in the ocean.

'That'll teach you to—Whoa!' he yelled, as I threw myself at his legs, toppling him over just as a wave crashed across both of us. I managed to stand up only for Cellan to body tackle me once again, this time not letting go as the two of us flailed, limbs entwined. Only when we'd put some distance between ourselves and the shoreline, did I deign to stop fighting him.

'I've got a wedgie,' I announced, then laughed as Cellan immediately slid his hand around to investigate.

'So you have.'

Somehow, my legs had ended up around his waist, and I caught my breath as he pulled me closer in against him. The sea was freezing, and already my teeth had started to chatter.

'Cold?' he said, and I nodded.

Cellan wrapped his arms around my back and hugged me tightly.

'Better?'

'A bit.'

His grip on me slackened and I moved until my mouth was level with his. Cellan's whole body seemed to stiffen, and then he kissed me very gently on the lips.

'I can think of other ways to warm up,' he said, and I wondered if my heart would bash its way right through the front of my chest.

'Oh?' I managed, and he smiled, fixing me with a look that left me under no illusions as to his meaning. Another wave hurtled ashore, this time spinning the two of us around on the spot, and I spluttered with laughter as the salty water flooded into my eyes, ears, nose and mouth. Cellan, whose dark hair had been flattened against his forehead, gave in to a coughing fit so intense that I was forced to thump him on the back.

'This is not,' he said, gulping down mouthfuls of air, 'in any way romantic, is it?'

'No,' I agreed, peeling a large frond of seaweed off my leg. And then, my words rushing out before my shyness got the better of me, I said, 'Shall we go back to the room and . . . warm up?'

Cellan smile of reply told me all I needed to know.

'I thought you'd never ask,' he said.

36

Wrapped in yellow beach towels, we ran dripping up the wooden steps, our clothes bunched up in our hands and my Dior bag bouncing between us.

Cellan opened the door and we fell laughing into the room, his hand leaving mine only long enough to lock it behind us. We had left the balcony doors ajar, and after crossing the room to close them, Cellan led me into the bathroom and switched on the shower. It was a walk-in, all gleaming chrome and white-brick tiles, and the water that fell was hot and strong. Without bothering to take off my swimsuit, I followed him under the torrent and tipped back my head. There was a nook in the wall for the complimentary toiletries, and having selected the body wash, he squeezed some into his palms. A rich, tart scent of mandarin filled the space, and I turned to find that the glass wall had completely steamed up.

Cellan was behind me, the water cascading over his face. For a moment, we simply stood and stared at each other. The soap washed away through his fingers, and he ran his clean hands through his hair.

'Here,' I said, over the sound of the shower, 'let me.'

I reached for the bottle of gel, and he acquiesced at once, closing his eyes as I started to run gently scrubbing hands across his body. My brain was shouting over the din of my incomprehension that yes, this was happening; I was in a shower with a movie star. Those were the facts, but it felt cut-throat to reduce Cellan to those terms, to look on him as an actor first and a man second, so I shoved the thought away. In this space, right now, there were two people that could have been anyone; who we were outside of this room had ceased to matter; reality, with all its interruptions and complications, had ceased to matter, as had the past and any future that might come knocking. All I cared about, all I was focused on, was the present.

Taking a step back, I dropped the bottle of shower gel, waiting until Cellan opened his eyes. He went to move towards me only to stop as I raised a hand to my shoulder and hooked my fingers under the strap of my swimsuit. Without breaking gaze, I lowered first one side, and then the other, easing the wet material down over my hips before letting it fall to the floor.

Cellan's hands were already on his waistband, and in one deft movement he had removed his trunks. I looked at him, all of him, eventually trailing my eyes back to find his waiting, a smile playing around his lips.

'Are you warmer?' he asked.

'Much.'

The water continued to fall, the steam rising until the mirror above the basin turned our reflections to sludge.

'You're beautiful,' he said.

'So are you.'

Cellan stepped out from under the water, then shook his head, covering me in droplets.

'Nice try,' I told him. 'But I'm already wet.'

Our eyes met again, and this time I failed to hold in a nervous laugh.

Cellan turned to switch off the shower, then walked slowly past me, his finger trailing against my stomach as he went.

'Where are you going?' I asked.

He stopped, pausing in the open doorway. The half of his body that was now bathed in sunlight glistened; he had not bothered with a towel.

'Follow me.'

'What are you?' I said lightly. 'The Penis Piper.'

Cellan raised his eyes heavenward. 'Don't make me come and get you,' he warned.

Feeling a thrill of intense desire course through me, I hurried after him. Cellan was at the far end of the room, closing the blind, and I admired the neat curve of his buttocks and his long, strong legs. Coming over to join me by the foot of the bed, he stood in front of me for a moment and I waited, aware suddenly of being very warm. He did not seem to be in any rush, but every part of me was burning to be touched by him; it was a need that felt urgent and fierce – and I feared it would consume me if he did not move soon. There would be nothing left of me for Cellan to take, and I wanted him to have all of me.

'Is it OK if I kiss you?' he asked, and bringing up his hand, he touched it gently against my collarbone. 'Here?'

I could only nod; my throat felt full, my cheeks flames.

Cellan dropped his lips to the spot his fingers had been. I started to tremble.

'And here?' he murmured, caressing first the hollow of my throat, then my neck, and then my shoulder. When his palm grazed my breast, I let out a small moan, and Cellan bent forwards, taking my nipple in his mouth before moving slowly across to the other. Every movement he made, he did so with care, his eyes constantly returning to mine, checking that I was still there with him, that I was comfortable with everything he was doing to me.

Timidly, I reached across and started to run my hands down his torso, chasing the rivulets of water through his soft chest hair. Cellan's mouth was becoming more insistent, and as his fingers strayed downwards, I parted my legs, inviting him further, closer, deeper. I moved my hands up into his hair, combing my fingers through until he raised his mouth to mine. There was a beat of stillness where all I could hear was the rasp of our breath, and then he was kissing me, and his fingers were inside me, and I was liquid heat, need, hunger.

Cellan broke away and lifted me onto the bed before dropping to his knees, his hands sliding beneath my bottom, his head between my thighs. Extracting one hand, he slid a tender thumb against me and began to rotate it, slowly at first, his eyes never leaving mine. It had been so long since anyone had touched me in this way, and no man had ever reduced me so expertly to such useless yet glorious mush. I started to rock against Cellan's still-probing fingers, arching back only to lurch forwards again as his mouth took over. Whatever was building inside me, it was too big for this moment, and for this room; I tried to wriggle away, but that only seemed to make him more persistent, and I let out a moan as the ripples of pleasure hurtled through me. Lightheaded, disoriented and weakened by pure sensation, I fell back against the bed, laughing helplessly as Cellan flopped down beside me.

'You,' he said, stroking a tangle of still-wet hair off my cheek, 'taste even better than ambrosia salad.'

'Is that so?' I said, placing a hand on his stomach and sliding it down. Cellan shut his eyes briefly as my fingers closed around him, and then he smiled.

'Most people would take that as a compliment,' he murmured, his breaths becoming shallower as I rolled over onto my stomach and began to kiss my way down his body, finding new delight in every inch of him. When I took him in my mouth, Cellan made a sudden, convulsive movement, and I knew he was already close.

'Wait,' he pleaded, pressing himself hard against the mattress. 'Please.'

I slowed, but did not stop, waiting until he had regained control before driving him back to the edge again and again, turned on by how much he wanted me, slick with renewed desire for him. Cellan appeared lost, as I had been, torn between a need to release and the urge to remain right on the edge of it. When I was sure he was about to let go, he stopped, wrenching himself out from under me and climbing off the bed.

'What's the matter?'

'Nothing.' Cellan was staring around the room. 'Where are my jeans?'

'By the door. You're not going to put them on, are you?'

Cellan had found the errant trousers, and snatching them up, began to dig through the pockets. 'Bollocks,' he said a second later, and darted into the bathroom.

'Are you just looking in the mirror and calling out the things you can see?' I enquired.

Cellan laughed. 'Aha!' he cried triumphantly, and a moment later he had bounded back into the room and chucked a box of condoms into my lap.

'Nice,' I said, 'but I actually prefer chocolates.'

'I'll remember that for next time,' he said, smiling at me wickedly. 'Now, where were we?'

37

Hours passed before we finally broke apart, both of us sated in a way that rendered us loose-limbed and giggly. After wrapping himself in one of the Gurney's Resort terry cloth robes and passing a second to me, Cellan made two cups of proper English tea in our small kitchenette area, and we carried them outside to watch the sunset.

A shawl of velvety cloud was tossed over the darkening sky, through which glowed flashes of sapphire, amber and violet. A murmur of voices and music filtered up from the Beach Club, and one lone man with a rake was tending to the sand around the now-empty cabanas. The ocean appeared grey in the fading light, each wave that rose and fell was shrouded in blackness, while on the far horizon, a navy sweep of water was illuminated by the last rays of the day. We could no longer hear the chatter of the ever-present gulls, but the giant's snore of the incoming swell continued. As I so often did when I tuned in to the sound of the sea, I felt grounded and at peace.

'This tea is pretty decent,' I remarked, having taken my second sip.

'There's no need to sound so surprised,' Cellan replied, bringing his own cup to his lips. 'When I was growing up, it felt like all I ever did was surf or make tea. My mum is a big fan of a Thermos, and I used to fill about six of them with tea every morning to share with my mates.'

'You were lucky to grow up on the coast,' I told him. 'Cambridge can feel so claustrophobic. We have the river but being able to go punting is not the same as catching a wave.'

'Catching a wave,' Cellan repeated. 'Check you out with the lingo.'

'Two days in Montauk and I'm talking like a local.'

A faint trace of stubble was already starting to show around his jaw, and I had to resist the urge to lean over and kiss him. Cellan, seeming to sense this, smiled at me.

'I guess I did have a good childhood,' he allowed. 'I'd say I was pretty content a good sixty per cent of the time.'

'What about the other forty?'

Cellan drank some tea.

'I wasn't a big fan of school. Being dyslexic makes everything academic much more difficult, and I hated being made to sit still for hours on end, you know? I wanted to be outside, going places, exploring caves on the beach, just moving around. It's part of why I leant into acting, I suppose; I wanted to satisfy that need I had to be active. Plus, you don't have to do an awful lot of writing in drama class.'

'There must be some reading involved?'

'You mean scripts?' he said, and I nodded. 'I used to get my sister to dictate them onto cassette tape for me and learn them by listening. I would study for days, memorising not just my own parts, but everyone else's as well. I still work the same way now.'

'Who does your recording nowadays, Cherry?'

'God, no.' Cellan laughed. 'She would never have the time nor the patience. I just use an app on my phone these days unless the production company provides an audio file. The same goes with books – I listen rather than read, so please make sure there's an audiobook version of yours when it's finished.'

'Hmm,' I said, noncommittally, keen not to dwell too long on that particular subject. 'What was your first ever lead part?' I asked instead.

'Jack,' he said. 'From *Jack and the Beanstalk*. I was fifteen and it was the local pantomime. I remember that opening night so well, how nervous I felt before going out onstage. I'd bought my parents tickets, but then my dad didn't make it because there was some lecture or other that he wanted to attend.'

'A lecture? That sounds—'

'Boring? That's what grumpy teenage me said at the time. My father is an intellectual, always learning, always debating, always reading – I think he used to look at me and wonder if there had been a mix-up at the hospital.'

'He must be so proud of you, though?' I protested, and at this, Cellan looked away towards the horizon.

'Proud probably isn't the word I'd use. I think he's more perplexed by this strange world I live in than anything else. He and my mother, they seem to think it's all a lot of nonsense. Even when I've won awards, they kind of pat me on the back and say, "Oh yes, well done on winning that tin pot accolade that means nothing – come back and see us when you have a master's degree in astrophysics."'

'I'm sure they're not that bad,' I said hopefully, but Cellan looked pensive.

'It's not their fault,' he said, shrugging as if unaffected. 'I've wasted so many years worrying about what they think of me, and in the end, I had to let it go. Fact is, I have to live with me, and I need to be passionate about what I do, even if it seems silly to other people. It was one of the many lessons Padma taught me, when I first started working with her.'

'Did you meet her recently then?' I asked, thinking fondly of the beautiful dark-haired woman who had been so quietly encouraging towards us.

'While I was in rehab. She was one of the regular alternative therapists that came by, and the only one I really connected with. Drinking used to be the thing I did to feel better about who I was, and she made me understand that in order to break that habit, I would need to find other ways to accept the man I have become, and the life I have chosen to live.'

'That makes sense,' I agreed, putting a hand on his arm. 'And if it helps at all, I happen to like the man you are.'

Cellan looked at me, his hazel eyes turned gold by the setting sun.

'It does help,' he said. 'It helps a lot.'

'Have you ever spoken to your parents about it?' I asked. 'Told them how they make you feel?'

'No, although me and my sister talk about it a lot. She's more like them in terms of her interests, but she also understands how frustrating they can be, and how narrowminded. Perhaps it's simply a symptom of that generation,' he said. 'How about your parents? I mean, I know JB . . . is well, a bit old-fashioned in his views.'

'You know that from meeting him twice?'

'He wears it proudly,' Cellan pointed out. 'Rather like I once wore my Scout badges.'

'He does make me cringe sometimes,' I confessed, feeling horribly disloyal. 'The way he talks about women can be' – I put my head briefly in my hands – 'aaargh!'

'What about your mum?'

I smiled as an image of her came to mind, dark hair piled up untidily, straining tote bag of books slung over one arm, notes scribbled to herself across the back of her hands, because she still hadn't worked out the simple beauty of asking Siri to set reminders on her phone. When I started to describe her to Cellan, his features softened.

'She sounds like you,' he said. 'I hope I get to meet her one day.'

'Me too,' I said, although inside I was reeling. I had been doing a very good job of obeying Jojo's instructions to 'live in the moment for once' all day, refusing to acknowledge the doubts that had attached themselves stubbornly to my subconscious ever since Gunnar's proclamation about Cellan fooling around for the summer. I told myself that it didn't matter if these few weeks were all we ever shared, because a short-term dalliance was all I could realistically have ever hoped for. Cellan Thomas was still a celebrity actor who lived in Los Angeles, while I was still Honor Butler, a nobody who lived above their mum's shop. A relationship did not feel possible – but then why, I mused, as I searched his expression for traces of contrition, was he alluding to a future that apparently included the introduction of my mum?

'Is there a stepdad in the picture?' he asked, sipping the last of his tea.

'She's dated a bit,' I told him. 'But nobody that ever sticks. The problem with my mum is that she seems to attract the bookish geeks of the world, which would be fine, if they were remotely her type. You'd think they would be, given her chosen profession, but if her history of ex-partners is anything to go by, then what she really likes is an ageing rocker, complete with tattoos, long hair, and stories about when he was once a roadie for the Rolling Stones.'

'That doesn't sound much like JB,' Cellan said with a laugh, and I shook my head.

'No, he was most definitely a misnomer.'

'What about you?' he prompted. 'What is your type?'

'Oh, you know.' I sidled in closer to him. 'I'm quite fussy. Oscar-winning actors only, please – bonus points if they happen to have an odd name.'

'Hey, what's wrong with Cellan?'

'It's not spelled right – where's the "F"?'

He tutted. 'You should have seen the variations of spelling I got as a kid. I feel like it was my duty to become famous, if only so I could educate the world on the matter.'

'That's a better reason than most,' I agreed.

The sun had set as we had been talking, and the sky was steadily merging from the deepest blue to black. There were no stars visible yet, but I could see the trails of yellow-bulbed lights that were strung above the hotel's terrace bar. Each of the tables had a firepit as its centrepiece, and from here the flames looked like dropped puddles of gold. Seeing me staring, Cellan slid an arm around my waist.

'Do you want to go and get a drink?'

'No,' I said, allowing myself to nestle against him. 'I want to stay here – preferably forever.'

'In this moment, or this hotel room?'

'Both.'

'You'd soon get bored.'

'Of this room? Are you kidding? It's bigger than my flat. And this view – nobody could ever get bored of that. If I were rich enough, I'd move into a luxury hotel full time.'

Cellan was shaking his head.

'Are you telling me you've never been tempted by the idea? Would staying here forever really be so bad?'

'This is not reality,' he said, in a measured tone. 'It's a bubble. A very nice bubble, granted,' he added, as I frowned in dismay, 'but a bubble all the same. Things like this feel amazing because they're an occasional treat. If you lived this experience every day, eventually you'd become blasé about it. As creatures, we're built to go out and sample as many different sights, sounds and experiences as possible – not much chance of that when you're trapped in one room.'

'Oh, I don't know,' I said slyly. 'I would argue that I've seen, heard and experienced quite a lot in this room.'

Cellan affected a gasp and pressed a hand against his chest. 'Young lady!' he exclaimed. 'You'll make me blush.'

'Bit late for that.'

Cellan pulled me back into his arms and buried his face in my neck.

'You smell like mandarins,' he said.

'Do you find that a-peeling?'

He groaned. 'I bet you have fun, don't you, writing romantic comedies? It's the ideal outlet for your questionable humour.'

'It can be fun,' I allowed, 'but mostly, it's like trying to juggle a pineapple and a carton of eggs while tap dancing naked, in a storm.'

'That I would pay good money to see.'

'I wish it were you judging it.'

Realising too late what I had said, I promptly fell silent, but Cellan's attention had already piqued.

'What do you mean by judge?'

I did not want to tell him about the competition; it felt amateurish somehow. But Cellan was looking at me with such sincerity, a kindness in his gaze that told me he cared, that he was genuinely interested, that he would be supportive.

'This book that I'm writing, it's for a contest,' I began, explaining how Jojo had talked me into entering, and how I had been trying, and mostly failing, to produce three chapters and a full synopsis ever since I arrived in the States. I had to give Cellan credit – he did not, as many others had, question why I did not simply ask my father to knock on a few industry doors on my behalf. He merely listened, waiting for me to finish before he spoke again.

'It sounds as if you're under a lot of pressure,' he said. 'Once you attach a deadline to anything, it immediately becomes more stressful.'

'That's true,' I allowed. 'But if you never did, then nothing would ever get done. And I'm a professional when it comes to procrastinating. My laptop is full of novels that I've started and never finished; I'm always enthusiastic at the beginning, then either lose interest or confidence in my ability to write it – usually both. I figured if I could cobble together three passable chapters and a plan that might have a shot at winning me this competition, then I would have no choice but to see the novel through to completion, because there would be a deal attached, and money changing hands, and someone in an office waiting to read it.'

'I see.' Cellan looked thoughtful. 'So, you have essentially bought your own whip, and are cracking it over your shoulder?'

'Yes,' I said. 'And nice imagery, by the way. Are you sure you don't want to enter as well? I'd never forgive you if you beat me, obviously . . .'

'You write the book,' he said. 'I'll star in the movie adaptation of it.'

The willingness with which he trusted my ability as a writer punctured my smile, and Cellan frowned.

'You don't have to cast me if you don't want to.'

'It's not that.' I paused, debating how much to tell him. How would he react if I admitted that, save for a few rough chapters that I had cobbled together of my stuntman romcom, I had made very little progress, and that I had, in fact, been spending most of my free time compiling diary entries of all the moments he and I had shared instead? It was embarrassing to admit on two counts, because not only did it paint me in a rather obsessive light, it also illustrated my almost total lack of work ethic, and that frustrating predilection I had to veer into procrastination.

Cellan was still waiting for me to continue, watching me in that intense way of his that made me feel equal parts seen and scrutinised.

'You really believe this competition will change your life, don't you?' he said.

'Yes.'

It was an easy question to answer.

'I think if I got somewhere with it, it would help me feel more worthwhile. It would prove to everyone that I can become a success on my own terms – and I include myself in that,' I added. 'I want people to be proud of me, but I want to feel that way for myself, too.'

'In that case,' Cellan said, glancing for a moment or two up to where the stars were now beginning to emerge in the oily sky, 'you should do whatever it takes to win.'

38

The following morning, after a leisurely room service breakfast of pretzel croissants, fresh fruit, and the best strong black coffee I had ever tasted, we checked out and Cellan drove us back to Southampton. Having pulled up outside my house, he leaned across to open the glove box and took out a mobile phone.

'It feels a bit late in proceedings to be asking for your number,' he said, smile fading as a flood of messages poured onto the screen.

'Shit.'

'What's the matter?' I asked.

'Gunnar's on the warpath,' he said, with a slight grimace. 'Seems I missed a meeting yesterday.'

'Oops.'

'Oops,' he agreed. 'He'll get over it.'

I reeled off my number and he tapped it in, saving me under Bambi.

'I'd ask for yours, but my battery is long dead.'

'I'll send you a message when I get home,' he promised, sounding distracted. 'We'll do something soon, yeah?'

'OK,' I said, ignoring the voice inside my head that yelled, *'Soon? Soon when?'*

'Come here.' Cellan slid one hand around the back of my head and pulled me forwards, kissing me lingeringly on the lips. 'Very soon,' he promised.

I watched him drive away, trying my best to quell the uneasiness that was beginning to bubble away in my stomach, a sense that something was wrong. Clutching my Dior bag, which contained my still-damp swimsuit and yesterday's underwear, I turned and headed down the driveway.

'Hey, excuse me.'

A man had stepped out from behind one of the large conifers that bordered the property, making me jump so violently that I dropped everything I was holding onto the ground.

'Sorry,' he said, as I made a grab for my errant knickers. 'Didn't mean to scare you.'

'Maybe don't lurk in the bushes then,' I suggested sarcastically, taking a few deliberate strides away from him. Blond-haired and broad-chested with a decidedly ruddy complexion, he was dressed simply in blue jeans, dirty trainers, and a T-shirt bearing some kind of sporting logo. If I'd had to guess, I would have said he was in his mid-to-late thirties.

'I'm looking for someone,' he said, sounding apologetic, and for a horrible moment, I wondered if he was a journalist or photographer, come to doorstep me. 'Tallulah Marshall – I was told she's staying somewhere around here?'

I did not reply straight away, but the man must have noticed my flicker of recognition. 'You know her,' he stated.

'That depends on who's asking,' I said firmly. 'Are you a friend of hers?'

The man sighed. 'I should hope so,' he said. 'In there, is she?' He gestured towards the front door.

'I . . . er.' I shifted from one foot to the other, trying to decide what to do.

'Did she tell that you she was here?'

'In Southampton, yes. I wasn't sure exactly where, so I showed her picture around a few places in town, and some dude at the café told me he'd seen her wandering up in this direction a few times.'

'I'm sorry, who are you?'

The man looked downcast. 'Cole,' he said. 'I'm guessing she hasn't mentioned me?'

'No,' I told him.

'Yeah,' he muttered. 'That figures.'

'Listen, why don't I go inside? Tell her you're here.'

He went to follow me across the lawn, but I stopped, turning to him.

'Do you mind waiting here? I don't want to invite you in unless—'

'It's OK.' He went backwards a few paces. 'I get it. I'll wait.'

Checking over my shoulder before I inserted my key into the lock, I hurried inside and shut the door firmly behind me.

'Honor, that you?' called my father's voice from the direction of the back porch.

'Yes,' I called back. 'Is Tallulah out there with you?'

I heard words being exchanged, then footsteps, and Tallulah appeared in the hallway. 'Hey,' she said, slipping the pencil she was holding behind one ear. 'We were about to send out the sniffer dogs – where have you bee—?'

'Later,' I interrupted. 'There's a man outside, says he knows you. Cole.'

All the colour appeared to drain from Tallulah's face.

'Cole?' she repeated incredulously. 'Cole is here, right now?'

'A Cole is here, yes. At least, that's what he told me his name was.'

Tallulah hurried towards the window and gasped.

'Who is he?' I began, but she was already crashing through the screen door. I heard the murmur of voices, then almost immediately, the pitch of Tallulah's shot up. Putting down my bag, I went back outside and found her on the front steps. Tallulah's arms were folded, her cheeks aflame. The man, Cole, stepped towards her but she shied away from him.

'Careful,' I exclaimed, moving just in time to avoid being clouted. 'What's going on?'

'Cole was just leaving,' Tallulah said icily. I could tell from the rigid way she was holding herself that she was furious; it was unnerving to witness.

'Tal, come on, we have to talk.'

'No, Cole.' She shook her head. 'We don't. I told you everything on the phone.'

Cole's temper seemed to flare at that, but he managed to regain control of himself before he spoke again. 'Two weeks we agreed – it's been, what? Four? Five?'

'So?'

'So, Jackson needs you. I need you.'

'Hang on a sec,' I said, glancing from one to the other. 'Who is Jackson?'

'You kept him a secret, too, did you?' Cole's tone was acidic in its bitterness. 'Ashamed of us no doubt now that she's spending all her time with fancy rich folk.'

As if on cue, my father chose that moment to wander around the side of the house. Like Tallulah, he looked as if he'd been working. His shirtsleeves were rolled up, and his glasses were hanging by a gold chain around his neck.

'This him?' demanded Cole, advancing on my father with such purpose that both Tallulah and I rushed forwards to intervene. Far from looking alarmed, my father merely smiled at the newcomer in the way he might a fan who'd asked for a photo.

'I'm Jeffrey,' he said. 'Jeffrey Butler – feel free to call me JB, though. Most people tend to find that easier.'

He had not, I noted, offered Cole his hand to shake.

'I'd say it was good to meet you, Jeff, but unfortunately we're way past that.'

'We are?' My father remained outwardly bemused.

'Cole, stop it,' ordered Tallulah. 'You're behaving like a total asshole.'

Cole barked out a hard laugh. 'I'm the asshole?' he exclaimed. 'Well, ain't that just a thing?'

'Why don't we all just calm down and—' I began, only to be railroaded by Tallulah.

'Oh, I'm calm,' she seethed. 'But I'm also pissed as hell. We agreed, Cole,' she fumed, turning on him. 'When we spoke the other day, you told me to take as much time as I needed.'

'That was before I found out you'd been lying to me,' he threw back, more exasperated than angry. 'A group of writers, you said. All women. This fella here doesn't look much like a woman to me.'

'Honor's a woman,' argued Tallulah, as Cole glanced irritably towards me. I did not think there was much need to confirm this, so instead I explained who I was.

'And you're fine with this, are you?' he challenged. 'Your old man screwing a woman the same age as his own daughter?'

'Now, hang on a second here,' said my father placatingly. 'That's not what's going on. Whatever it is you think you know, you're mistaken. Tallulah has been doing a bit of work for me while I assist her with her writing, and that's about the extent of it.'

'Oh, c'mon, man – that's bull crap.'

I appeared to have lost the ability to speak and could only gape at each of them in turn. Tallulah had not once mentioned Cole or Jackson, who I had to assume were her husband or boyfriend, and possibly even child. And from the look of quiet dismay on my father's face, she had withheld the truth from him, too. Cole had begun berating Tallulah again, and I was forced to shout over them to be heard.

'Enough,' I said, glaring at them before moving to stand in front of my father. 'Clearly, this is a private issue between the two of you. If you can assure me that you won't start smashing the place up or hurl pots and pans at each other, then I suggest you go inside, have some coffee, and discuss this situation in a calm and rational manner. Jeffrey and I,' I went on, cutting across Tallulah's predictable protests, 'will go out for an hour or so and leave you in peace.'

'We will?' My father looked concerned. 'I'm not sure that's a good idea.'

'No, she's right,' Tallulah said meekly, either unable or unwilling to meet his eye. 'Me and Cole do need to talk. But we'll go out, you guys should stay here.'

'No,' I argued. 'We're already gone, aren't we, Dad?'

I turned determinedly towards the road, only for my father to wander off in the opposite direction.

'Just getting my cell,' he said, reminding me that my own phone still had a flat battery. It would have taken me less than a minute to run upstairs and fetch the charger, but I couldn't be sure that I'd get back down again before my father returned, and I was worried what Cole might to do him. While the man's simmering anger appeared to have subsided a fraction, there was no telling how fast his mood would turn if provoked, and Jeffrey Butler, as I knew only too well, was extremely adept at articulating whatever thought came into his mind, regardless of what the consequences might be. I wanted to extract him as much for his own safety as I did for Tallulah and Cole's privacy.

It was hard to look at her, knowing as I did quite how much she had kept secret from me. Tallulah was by no means my closest friend, but I had opened up to her about elements of my life, most pertinently the elements concerning Cellan and how I felt about him. Now, I felt rather foolish at the thought of being misled.

'Honor,' she said pleadingly. 'I'm so sorry about all this. I never meant to—'

'Don't worry about it,' I replied, although even to my own ears, I sounded far from convincing. 'It's fine. We can talk later.'

Cole was kicking at the dirt with his trainer, eyes resolutely lowered, and for a moment I felt almost sorry for him. There was a story here with far more intrigue than any plot I had managed to come up with so far, and as much as I wanted things to be resolved, I also burned with curiosity.

When my father reappeared, he had his phone pressed to his ear.

'Yes,' he said. 'I understand. I sure will. By five.'

Rather than waiting for me, he walked straight past the house and continued on in the direction of the road, leaving me with little choice but to hurry after him.

'One hour,' I said, looking over my shoulder at Tallulah. 'We'll be at the Golden Pear.'

I fell into step beside my father just as he was ending his call, and immediately started to apologise.

'Sorry if I came over a little bossy back there. I figured they needed some time.'

'That's OK, honey.' He offered me his arm, and I looped my own through it, aware as I did so that it had been years since the two of us had walked together in this way, traversing the streets around his New York apartment as he told me stories about his eccentric neighbours.

'Do you think Cole is her husband?' I blurted out, unable to hold the question in any longer.

My father's expression gave very little away. 'I don't know. But I'd like to think not.'

'Did she ever tell you that she was married?'

'No.'

'Why do you think she's never mentioned him? They clearly have history.'

'You'll have to ask her that, honey. I can't read minds, last time I checked.'

His sarcasm rankled, but I managed to suppress my irritation.

'And what about Jackson – do you think he could be her son?'

He flinched, the movement so slight that if I had not been watching him, I would have missed it.

'I don't think it's right for us to discuss her private business,' he said. 'Tallulah's a grown woman, and in the end it's up to her how much she chooses to share with us.'

He was right, but any shame I might have felt at raising so many questions was eradicated a few seconds later, when my father contradicted his own point.

'Are you going to tell me where you were last night?' he said, as we crossed over Eel Pot Alley and continued on along North Main Street.

'Isn't it obvious?' I replied.

We had reached the corner where an interior design store was situated, and there was a sign outside advertising a local Hamptons Greek night. The sunshine that was filtering down through the overhanging branches of the trees felt coarse against my skin, and I wished I'd had time to apply an SPF.

'You really can't guess?' I said, and my father sighed.

'I was concerned for your welfare when I didn't hear anything.'

'But you knew I was safe,' I protested mildly. 'I texted Tallulah.'

'That you were staying out, not that you were in a hotel with Cellan Thomas.'

'How do you—?' I stopped when I saw the look on his face. 'Know?' I finished lamely.

'Honor, honey, when was the last time you checked the news?'

He was frowning at me with what I took to be pity.

'I don't know – yesterday morning. My phone died.'

'This wild night the two of you had in Montauk,' he said, enunciating each word carefully. 'Did you honestly believe it would go unnoticed?'

'No, but—'

'Well, I'm afraid it didn't. You certainly caught yourselves some attention.'

'So?' I jollied, bemused by his sombre expression. 'It's not as if the whole world suddenly knows who I am, is it?'

My father did not reply for a long time, eventually turning so that my arm fell away from his. A car that was idling to let us cross drove on, and from somewhere distant I heard the toot of a horn.

'Sorry, honey,' he said. 'I'm afraid that's exactly what it is.'

39

The story, such as it was, had been reported everywhere.

While Cellan and I had been fooling around smearing ketchup on each other's chins and watching the sunset over the ocean, several of our fellow guests at the hotel had been busy uploading photos, videos and snippets of news to their various social media channels. It was impossible to glean exactly who had posted first, because each one had been shared or circulated thousands of times. As well as images of us strolling hand-in-hand through the lobby and across the bar, there was blurry footage of the two of us cavorting in the sea, and of Cellan chatting to the sales assistant in Dior while I hung back clutching a pile of swimsuits.

Headlines ranged from the contemplative: WHERE'S WYLIE? to the salacious: DIRTY WEEKEND and the more informative, CEF'S NEW GIRL A BRIT. Various 'sources' had been quoted as witnessing the two of us 'all over each over like a pox', which I thought was an unfortunate choice of metaphor, with yet more claiming that 'the actor looked starry eyed the whole time – either the guy is smitten, or he was high'. Another so-called 'insider', who according to the *New York Post*'s online site wished to remain anonymous, was quoted as saying, 'Put it this way, they were at Gurney's for one reason – and it wasn't the shrimp platter. After being seen heading back to their room at around three p.m., the pair did not emerge again until the following morning.'

Cellan and I had taken a risk, each of us fully aware that he would be recognised, but I was still taken aback by the speed with which the story had spread. Not only that, but there seemed to be a baffling amount of detail, including the price tag of my Dior gift, exactly what we had eaten down at the Beach Club, and how much Cellan had tipped the various valets. My assumption about the fifty-dollar notes had been wrong; he had, in fact, been shelling out one-hundreds.

My father, who had allowed me to borrow his phone while he went inside the Golden Pear Café to fetch us both some iced tea, now held out his hand.

'I'm almost done,' I said, logging into Twitter. My father did not have the app saved, so I had to gain access via the browser. Much of the speculation seemed to be centred around my identity and having failed to come up with much more than the fact I was British, fans and followers had begun expressing their opinions on the way I looked instead. Knowing full well that I should not continue reading, I nonetheless began to scour the replies with a reckless kind of intensity, my heart crashing ever harder against my ribs as the conclusions became more ruthless. According to Cellan's legion of admirers, I was 'dour', 'plain', 'moody', 'unsophisticated', and 'not a patch on Wylie'. The last one had stung. None of these people knew me, nor ever would, yet it still felt discombobulating and cruel to have them judge me so entirely on the strength of a few images.

'Jealousy, honey, pure and simple,' said my father, who had leaned across to take a look. 'They want what you have, and they'd cheerfully tear you down to get it.'

The 'it' in this particular scenario being Cellan, of course. I disliked him being referred to in those terms, but even I had to admit that my father had made a valid point.

'Here,' he went on, breaking off a large piece of sugared doughnut and holding it up to my mouth.

I shook my head. 'No, thanks.'

'It's pumpkin and butterscotch . . .'

'I'm sure they're delicious, but I'm not— I can't eat anything. I feel sick.'

My father snatched the phone from my hand and held it up out of reach. The screen showed a tweet from someone calling themselves @CellanMeSoftly, who'd created a gif of me almost tripping over the monstera plant in Gurney's reception area and added the caption:

Shame she didn't crack her ugly face open on the floor. #HandsOff #CellanThomas #DreamOn #Punching.

'I need to charge my phone,' I groaned. 'Cellan could have been trying to reach me. I don't even know if he's seen all this.'

'Honey, think about who he is. There's no way he hasn't been brought up to speed. Cherry will be all over this, trying to take back control of the narrative.'

'Should we call her?' I asked. 'Or go over there? Maybe we should go over there!'

'And be snapped by the paps? That'll only make the situation worse.'

I picked up my iced tea only to put it down again without taking a sip, the glass wobbling slightly on the green and white wicker tabletop.

'You think that—'

'Sure. It's a big story; you're a huge story.'

'Me? Why me? I'm not the celebrity in this scenario.'

'Don't be so naive,' he said, popping the last morsel of doughnut into his mouth. I waited while he chewed, taking deep breaths to quell my nausea. My father pulled a napkin from the holder, dislodging several more in the process. I watched dully as they were picked up by the wind and tossed into the street.

'Honey, it's exactly the fact you aren't famous which makes this story such a juicy one. There's a reason why mystery novels sell so well – it's because readers always want to know whodunnit.'

I put my face into my hands and groaned. I needed to talk to Cellan.

'I think we should go back to the house,' I said, rising quickly to my feet. 'I know, I know – it was my idea to leave in the first place, but that was before all this.' I gestured to his phone.

My father looked nonplussed. 'Chill your heels,' he said, taking what felt to me like a deliberately slow sip of his iced tea. 'When was the last time we did this – just me and you? I feel like we never talk anymore.'

Anymore? When had we ever?

I sat down, defeated as I always was by my father's will.

'I have a good feeling,' he confided, 'that all this is going to work out for the best.'

'All what?' I replied cautiously.

'This stuff with Cellan. As I said to you before, the guy is no dummy.'

'I remember,' I said, 'but I'm still no closer to understanding what you mean by it.'

'You're my daughter,' my father continued, 'and Cellan knows that, understands how it could benefit him.'

'Dad,' I hissed, feeling indignant, 'you can't just mention his name like that.'

'Why the heck not? If Cellan Thomas is happy to waltz around with you in full sight of anyone who might be looking, then I can't see why he'd be troubled by me talking about it.'

At a nearby table, a woman lowered her cup of coffee and stared at us.

'It wasn't like that,' I mumbled, although with less conviction than before. Because my father was right. Cellan had seemed completely at ease in the hotel, and perhaps I was overreacting to the fact people had noticed us. As long as none of the various publications discovered who I was, then the story would soon disappear.

Wouldn't it?

Having coveted the idea of fame for so long, it was disconcerting to find out just how uncomfortable it felt to be the sudden topic of strangers' attention. Cellan had warned me, telling me in no uncertain terms that I would not be able to go back once I had stepped into that arena, but I had not listened – not properly. From the outside looking in, it always felt as if the celebrity world was one of privilege and opportunity, which I guessed it was, but with that came a loss of anonymity, the sense that part of you now belonged to the world at large. I had thought I was ready, when in reality, I had absolutely no idea what I had let myself in for.

'I really do need to go,' I said, this time determined not to be swayed by him.

My father sighed deeply and pushed back his chair.

'I'm not sure I like this bossy side of you,' he said. 'You definitely don't get it from me.'

'No,' I agreed, as we headed back up the road. 'That trait is purely my own.'

We had been gone less than forty-five minutes, and I hoped that had provided Tallulah and Cole enough time alone to discuss their most pressing issues. What I did not expect to discover when we arrived back at the house was a lot of empty drawers, and a note propped up against the kettle with the word 'sorry' scrawled in Tallulah's loopy hand. My father stared at it for a long time, then went straight to his room and slammed the door shut behind him.

Thoroughly confused and more than a little upset, I headed upstairs to my own room and finally plugged in my phone. It took a few minutes until it had enough charge to switch on, during which time I paced in agitation, swearing under my breath. When at last the home screen lit up, I practically fell over in my haste to check it, ignoring the endless messages from Jojo, my mum, and a number of other friends who barely ever got in touch, until I found one from a number I did not have saved.

Hey Bambi, I read, smiling as I saw he had signed off with a blowing kiss emoji. Without giving myself time to waver, I pressed call.

It rang and rang, for so long that I started to walk once again in circles around the room, picking various items up uselessly and putting them down again. At last I heard a muffling sound, and then a woman's voice.

'Hello.'

'Cellan?'

'No, it's Cherry. Is that you, Honor?'

I sat down heavily on the small sofa. 'Yes – is Cellan around?'

'He can't come to the phone right now.'

She did not elaborate, but neither did she hang up.

'I was hoping to . . . Never mind,' I barrelled on. 'I can call back later.'

Cherry made a faint tutting sound. 'Probably best you don't,' she said matter-of-factly. 'We're just trying to work out next steps. Wylie is here, as you know, and we have to be careful how we handle this going forward. Cef's career is at a crucial stage, and you wouldn't want anything to derail him from his ambitions, would you?'

I'd thought my father was exaggerating when he mentioned 'controlling the narrative'.

'But Wylie is ... She lent us her car,' I pointed out, to which Cherry sighed.

'We have to consider public perception. As far as the media are concerned, Wylie and Cellan are still very much together, and we don't want to invite a third party into the mix until that situation has been fully resolved.'

'I don't understand what you mean,' I replied, my legs beginning to jiggle nervously. 'Wylie and Cellan haven't been together for a long time – he told me that.'

'Facts aren't what matter right now, Honor. I told you, it's all about perception. Now, please just allow me to do my job and look after my client.'

She hung up before I could reply, and I pressed the button to call back immediately, indignant fury rising like smoke inside me. This was Cellan's phone; how dare she speak for him? The call was cut off. I tried again, and this time it didn't even ring. Cherry must have removed the SIM card.

I stared at the screen, wondering how I could have gone from wrapped up naked in Cellan's arms to cut off from him completely. There was nothing to stop me going to the house, I knew, but it was obvious what would happen if I did. Cellan had his protective guard around him, and there was no way I would be allowed through the gate, let alone to see him. No, I had to trust that he would reach out to me as soon as he was able, even though it crushed me to hand all the power over to him.

But then, I had never had a say in how this story went; I was as useless at navigating the chapters of my own life as I was at constructing fictional ones, and never had that fundamental flaw in my character been more apparent than now.

40

I passed the next few hours in a fog of uncertainty.

Having texted first my politely intrigued mother and then a seemingly delighted Jojo, I had tried repeatedly to call Tallulah, initially getting the engaged tone and then an invitation to leave a voicemail. This I did, begging her to ring me back and telling her that whatever had happened, I would understand. In all the maelstrom of the story breaking online and being unable to talk to Cellan about it, I had not allowed myself much time to dwell on the fact that she had gone. And even though I knew she had kept elements of her life a secret, I respected her enough to appreciate that she must have had a good reason for doing so. Whatever the truth about Cole, I could not believe she was a bad person, and hoped that the message I'd left would convey that.

Going back on to Twitter was foolish, but I did it anyway. One kindly user had zoomed in on an image of my face purely to highlight all the things wrong with it, while another had pointed out cheerfully that if Cellan Thomas was in the market for slumming it, then at least it meant the rest of his fans had a chance. Hateful tears fell, and I brushed them angrily away, telling myself that it was all meaningless, and that I was stronger than this, yet nothing made me feel any less wretched. It had begun to dawn on me that sooner or later, the media would get hold of my name, and far from being excited by the prospect, I felt utterly sick. Irony, it seemed, was having a laugh at my expense. But then, if I had known what would happen, would I still have gone to that hotel with him? Yes, I thought helplessly. I would. Cellan was who he was, and if I wanted to spend time with him, I had no choice but to accept that.

Leaving my phone on charge, I made my way to the study my father had been using as an office, thinking that I would knock and offer to make him some lunch. There must be a part of him that blamed me for Tallulah leaving, and I did not want to give his feelings of resentment time to fester. When I reached the door, however, I heard the sound of his voice and, curiosity winning over restraint, tiptoed closer and pressed my ear to the wood.

'I can get all that to you,' he was saying, 'and then you'll announce when? Friday? Yes, that works. Talk soon.'

There was a long pause, during which I held my breath, trying my best not to make a sound. My father must have made a second call, because a moment later I heard him greeting someone.

'Are we on schedule?' he barked. 'Because the studio is keen to— Yes, I know. Very fortuitous; exactly the nudge we needed. Played right into our ha— Right? No, that's fine. This weekend, you reckon? I can deliver what you need, leave it with me.'

Nothing, it appeared, disrupted my father from his work, and feeling ashamed, I crept back to my room, where I picked up my laptop from the desk. Finding that I had left it switched on, which I never usually did, I yanked the power cable out from the wall and took both it and the computer downstairs into the lounge. I might not be able to see or speak to Cellan, but there was nothing stopping me from writing about him.

The diary I'd been keeping had become the place into which I funnelled all my feelings, and today it felt like a lifeline – something over which I had full control when everything else seemed to be in the hands of others.

I started with our arrival at Gurney's, describing how it had felt to walk in clutching his hand, and how he had shaved off his beard because it felt right. I wrote about the swimsuit and the seagulls, the way his hands had felt when he rubbed in sun cream, and how he had lifted me into his arms in the sea. When I reached the account of what had taken place between us in the bedroom, I almost stopped, but to not relive those moments felt inauthentic. If I was telling the story of us, I did not want to leave out any of it. I noted down the purely physical sensations, but then went into far greater detail when writing about the topics we had discussed after being intimate, making sense of the man as I did so, getting beneath the veneer he so skilfully plastered on for the majority.

Writing was a better escape than reading, or watching television, or riding a bike – it was all-consuming. And despite the fact that the subject of my journal was also the person at the very heart of my discord, the two felt like separate entities. One was an experience I would cherish forever, the other a problem I did not know how to solve. I kept my phone on the arm of the chair beside me, but neither Cellan nor Tallulah tried to call. It was only later, once the early evening arrived in England, that the handset sprung noisily into life.

'Mum?' I said, and then immediately burst into tears.

'Oh, you poor darling thing,' she said, as I tried and failed to gain control of myself. Putting my laptop on the coffee table, I pushed my way out through the screen door and sat down on the front steps. The air was hot and dry, the trees shivering in the breeze. I gazed up at the cotton-wool clouds moving slowly against the blue, and envied them their quiet, simple existence.

'Sorry,' I muttered. 'It's just the stuff online. Have you seen it? It's horrible. And Cellan isn't talking to me or isn't allowed to talk to me. I don't know. His publicist was pretty rude when I tried to call.'

'What is your father doing about it?'

'Dad?' I laughed bitterly. 'Nothing. He's not speaking to me either.'

My mother listened as I relayed the circumstances of Tallulah's flit, leaving out the part where Cole had accused her of sleeping with her mentor. I knew she would want to believe the worst of JB, and even now, given everything, I felt compelled to defend his reputation.

'Didn't you say before that Jeffrey is rather pally with Cellan's manager – what's his name again?'

'Gunnar,' I muttered.

'That's it. Can't you ask your father to drop him a line? Surely, he's higher up the food chain than this Blueberry person.'

'Cherry,' I corrected, with a chuckle that made me feel slightly better. 'But yes, you're right.'

'These people deal with situations like this every day,' she said soothingly. 'I may not have been a publicist for a long time now, but I do remember what it was like. So much of what is released to the press is pre-arranged and carefully scripted in advance, so I imagine Cellan was in for a telling-off when he got back. This is far more to do with his actions than yours, but I'm afraid, in this instance, you have ended up as collateral. If he hasn't been in touch, it's because he's feeling guilty. You know men cannot abide to take responsibility for anything.'

'Some men,' I replied, sensing that she was gearing up to criticise my father. 'Cellan's not like that, he's not irresponsible. Why are you sighing?'

'I'm not,' she lied. 'I'm simply asking you to be wary. I know you think you know this man, but how long has it been since you met him? Not even a fortnight.'

'You're always telling me to be more open,' I said hotly. 'Then, when I do decide to trust a man and let him into my life, you tell me I'm making a mistake.'

'No,' she said patiently. 'I'm just saying be careful. Cellan may seem as if he's making the right choices on your behalf, but he does have a history of behaving rashly.'

'That was different,' I protested weakly. 'He was drinking then.'

'Yes,' she agreed. 'And you have to ask yourself why that was.'

'I trust him,' I said again, more firmly this time. 'When he does open up about his past, it will be when he feels ready. I'm not going to put any pressure on him, because I don't feel the need to. He has a far better handle on his emotions than I do,' I added.

A blackbird landed on the grass in front of me and cocked its head to the side, watching me for a moment before lowering its beak in search of grubs.

'I'm glad he's put in the work on himself,' my mother allowed, sounding mollified but not yet convinced. 'And he clearly trusts you, which must be a difficult thing for someone like him. If he wants to see you, he'll find a way.'

'What if he doesn't?' I implored. 'What then?'

My mother hesitated before replying, and I watched as the blackbird extracted a worm from the mud. Seeing it trying to wriggle desperately away made me want to cry again, and I had to press my fingers hard into my eyes to stop myself.

'If he doesn't,' she said regretfully, 'then he was never worth your time to begin with.' There was a pause. 'Honor, are you there?'

'I'm nodding.'

'You know,' she said, 'when you broke up with Felix, you told me it was because you had a very clear idea about how you wanted your future to look, and I so admired you for that, Honor. It was a brave decision. Not everyone knows themselves well enough to trust their instincts, especially when following them means hurting those you care about. That single-mindedness is not a weakness, it's the opposite. Don't let yourself forget how strong you are, and how far you've come without any assistance from a partner.'

'How far I've come?' I laughed bitterly. 'I haven't achieved anything in the four years since Felix and I broke up, not one single thing. All I wanted, all I have ever wanted, is to make a success of myself, and I have failed at that over and over.'

'You're being too hard on yourself,' my mother protested. 'Have you ever really sat down and worked out what success actually looks like to you, in real terms? I know you want to be an author, but you could self-publish a book tomorrow and achieve that dream overnight.'

'I want to do it the traditional way,' I said firmly. 'I want my books in proper bookshops and libraries.'

'You know,' she went on, 'a great number of self-published authors do far better than their traditional counterparts; they often sell larger numbers and make more money.'

'I don't care about the money,' I said.

'Ah, so it's more about the kudos?'

'I just want someone professional to believe my writing is worthy of being published.'

'Someone,' she said gently, 'or *a* someone?'

Her question stopped me short, and I made myself consider if there was some truth to it. She meant my father, of course. He was the one I'd always wanted to impress, the person whose opinion meant the most, and I knew that anything other than a traditional route into publishing would be seen as lesser by him. But it was not a sentiment I shared – I did not think any less of those who chose to plot their own path. I was not my father, so why the hell had I been trying for so long to become like him? I had fallen back in love with writing on this trip, not because of a competition but because I'd found the courage to note down my innermost thoughts and feelings, had been inspired by life, my creativity unblocked by a simple need to tell my own story. If being the author my father thought I should be meant forever struggling, then wasn't I signing up for a miserable future, one that was dishonest and destined to flounder? I remembered what Cellan had told me about letting go of the expectations his intellectual parents had for him and accepting who he was. It was time I did the same.

'Oh, Mum,' I said, biting my lip. 'What the hell have I been doing all this time?'

'Trying,' she replied, and I nodded as the tears began to fall once again. 'And, darling, there is absolutely no shame in that. None whatsoever.'

It was too difficult to speak, so I didn't say anything, and my mother remained silent as my sobs subsided. Only when she was satisfied that my crying had ceased did she ring off, and for a while I simply sat motionless on the step, staring blankly at the flowerbed. Nobody had thought to do any gardening since we arrived, and weeds were beginning to poke through the earth, their tiny green leaves delicate yet determined. Was that my destiny, I wondered, to push forwards enough to be noticed only for fate to tear me out again by the roots? To be forever a beginning, and never an end? I did not want to keep failing, I wanted to know how it felt to see something through, and not to simply quit when things became difficult. Only then would I be worthy of the happiness that would follow.

I stood up at the same time as the screen door opened behind me, smiling tentatively as my father emerged. He no longer appeared to be angry or even sad – in fact, if I'd had to guess, I would have opted for elated, which made little sense. What could possibly have happened to bring about such a change in his mood?

I did not have to wait long to find out.

41

I had often pondered what it would feel like to be in the eye of a tornado, feet planted on the ground while a column of violently destructive air swirled around me. Given the events of the past few days, I no longer needed to imagine. I knew.

Releasing my name to the media had been the first rumble of thunder in the ensuing storm, and the responsibility for getting through it had fallen not to me, but to Cherry and her 'team'. As my father had cheerfully informed me on that afternoon in the garden, he, Gunnar, and the vibrant-hued publicist had discussed all the options and settled on the one they each believed was the most straightforward. Other than being made aware of the plan, I wasn't consulted and neither, it appeared, was Cellan. I'd not been permitted to speak to him, and every call I made to his phone was either ignored or answered by Cherry.

'You'll see him soon,' she kept telling me. 'It's all in hand.'

The *Mail Online* was the first to run the story, and it did so under the headline: CELLAN'S MYSTERY GIRLFRIEND IS FAMOUS AUTHOR'S LOVECHILD. As well as details of how and when Cellan and I had met, there was a lot of information about my father's career as a bestselling author, and the mutual respect the two men shared. While he had not been quoted directly, a 'source' close to the author had reportedly said, 'JB fully approves of the match, and is keen to welcome Cellan into the family'.

'It makes it sound as if we're getting married!' I bemoaned to Jojo. 'Who does this source think they are, Mrs Bennett?'

The feature reported incorrectly that I had a degree from Cambridge University and now worked in a bookshop. They'd also somehow got hold of a series of unflattering photos of me as a teenager, as well as a more recent one of me being licked across the face by Dodie, which someone had stolen from Jojo's Instagram. Most surprising of all were the nuggets of information that could only have come from Cellan himself, including how we'd visited the lighthouse in Montauk, and the names of Maddy, Locryn and their surf school. He'd even allowed Cherry to share the story about how he used to come up with poems for all the girls he'd had crushes on as a teenager, which had never been made public before.

My father had managed to ensure that the 'lovechild' element of the story linked back to his books and again, a 'source' had talked at length about how Jeffrey had 'delved deep into his own experience of non-traditional fatherhood in order to fully understand how his character, Benedict Stamp, felt when confronted by his long-lost son, Marty'. Given that my father had not ever thought to discuss the subject with me, this particular revelation came as a surprise.

The further the original story travelled around the various celebrity news sites, the more skewed the details became. Loathing myself, I read them all, poring over every word, every caption, every unflattering photograph, and all the many inaccuracies. I wondered if Cellan was doing the same and if he, too, was struggling to find anything to laugh about. I longed to see him purely so the two of us could roll our eyes about the media circus. I needed him to reassure me that this was exactly how things should be unfolding and tried not to be hurt that he hadn't contacted me.

In a separate, carefully managed story, which emerged a day later, Wylie Brooke was given her opportunity to comment, and I was touched by her assertion that I was both 'sweet' and 'kind'. She denied any crossover between Cellan dating her and whisking me off to Gurney's for the night, stating that the two of them had split 'months ago', and 'remain the closest of friends, with the utmost respect for each other'.

The aim of both articles was to dampen speculation, but it seemed to me as if the opposite were true. Now that Cellan's legion of fans knew who I was, the vitriol only increased, and I was dismayed by how many were quick to accuse me of using my famous father to gain access to the inner circle – despite the fact that details of Cellan knocking me over in the street had been widely shared, presumably at his instruction. All I could do was take the blows as they rained down on me; I was unable to reply, and powerless to intervene.

At the end of the third day, my phone rang, the sight of Cellan's name causing my heart to soar. When I answered with a breathy, 'at last', all I got in response was a bored-sounding sigh.

'It's Cherry,' she said, thus confirming my fears. I asked if I could talk to Cellan.

'He's not here.'

'In the room, or in the house?'

'We're both in the city.'

'Oh.'

'Listen, are you free this coming Friday? There's an event happening up here that we think could be a great vehicle for the two of you.'

When I asked her to explain what she meant by 'vehicle', she responded sniffily with a 'doesn't matter', before going

on to tell me about an upcoming artist named Su Lou, whom
Cellan had known for years, and whose first exhibition was
taking place at a gallery in Chelsea.

'I know your dad has a place right by there. We thought if
you both came, and the press got the photos they want of the
three of you, then we can start moving this thing to the next
stage.'

I didn't know what the next stage was, nor did I relish the
idea of posing for set-up photos, but I did want to see Cellan
– desperately, ardently, fiercely – so I agreed that I'd be there,
with Jeffrey Butler on my arm, at seven-thirty sharp.

All day I fretted, from the moment I woke, through the
entire car journey from Southampton to New York City, and
across the hours I whiled away in my father's apartment,
where I paced and fidgeted and eventually drove him
muttering into his office. Having come to the frantic
conclusion that I had nothing in my suitcase chic enough for
an exhibition, I took the E train to East 53rd Street and
walked the remaining six blocks to Bloomingdale's, my
favourite of all the large department stores on account of its
classic Art Deco design. Once inside, I panic-splurged over
four-hundred dollars on a Ganni maxi dress the colour of
root beer, which had cutaway panels on the back and waist, a
beaded embellishment in the shape of a diamond on the
front, and a high, crew neckline. Then I handed over my
credit card a second time to pay for a pair of black, soft-bow
sandals.

Accosted by an overzealous sales assistant as I wound my
way out through the cosmetics counters, I agreed to let him
make me over, then figuring that I may as well pull back the
throttle to its fullest extent, I found a hair salon with a free
appointment and let the stylist snip my long hair into a sleek,
shiny bob.

'I can fix that,' she said breezily, when I sheepishly drew my tiny bald patch to her attention, and snatching up her clippers, buzzed me in an undercut.

When I returned to the apartment to change, I stood for a while staring at myself in the bathroom mirror, trying to decide if Cellan would love or loathe my new look.

'Oh wow, honey,' said my father when I finally emerged. 'You look like a beauty queen.'

'I wish Tallulah were here,' I said, and his face fell. 'Still no reply?' I asked.

'Not a peep. You?'

'Nothing. She never picks up, and all my messages so far have been ignored.'

'She'll come around,' he said, in what I took to be an effort to convince himself as well as me. 'But, as far as tonight is concerned, it's all about us.'

Us, he'd said – me and him. We were finally a 'we', together as a unit. Standing on tiptoes, because even in my high heels, Jeffrey Butler still towered over me, I pressed my lips to his cheek.

'Come on then, Dad,' I said. 'Let's go and show the world exactly who we are.'

42

The evening air was balmy, and the heat of the city seemed to rise from the sidewalks, enveloping us as we walked. I had grown so accustomed to the slower pace of life in The Hamptons that the noise, chaos, and sheer number of people in New York felt like an assault on my senses. Where I once would happily have thrived, I now found myself cowering, stepping with curled lip over stains and spillages, and recoiling from shouts or the slam of car doors.

'It's so loud,' I murmured to my father, who was striding along beside me in dark suit trousers and a pale almond shirt, which he had changed into in order to complement my dress.

'Isn't it?' he beamed, chin aloft. 'The sweet cacophony of home.'

I had always had the sense that I could seamlessly slip in among the fibres of the city, but tonight I felt apart. Perhaps it was simply because I looked so different, and therefore was more aware of the searching eyes of those we passed, or maybe the past few days had taught me the value of being truly anonymous – a state I had never properly appreciated until it was lost.

'I don't know if I can do this,' I said, clutching an urgent hand to my father's arm. 'It feels like too much, all this. I wish I could have seen Cellan on his own first.'

He steered me off the sidewalk and under the awning of a grocery store, where stacks of flat peaches were on offer for three dollars a box.

'Honey,' he said, 'listen to me – this is just your nerves talking. I remember feeling the exact same way when I went to do my first radio interview, which must have been almost forty years ago. You think people are going to judge you, but they don't. Everyone is too damn worried what other folk are thinking about them to waste any time critiquing others.'

'People are already judging me,' I reminded him. 'Have you not seen Twitter? There was a post today asking followers to vote for who they'd rather kiss, me or a goat, and the goat won by a landslide.'

'Saddos and nobodies.'

'Actually, Jojo said she voted for me, which was nice of her.'

'None of those people are going to be at this shindig tonight, though,' he said, as I looked anywhere but at him. The urge to flee had become so overwhelming that I had begun to actively search for escape routes. 'Consider this a warm-up event for the real world. If you're going to keep dating this guy, you'll have to face it sooner or later.'

He had me there, and he knew it. I did want to keep dating Cellan if dating was even what we were doing. It was bizarre that we hadn't yet been given the luxury of time to discuss it. Instead, the status of our relationship had been decided by other people, some of whom did not even know us.

'Promise you won't move from my side,' I said, gripping his hand.

My father smiled easily. 'Of course not, honey. Why would I? You're the star of the show.'

'I think you're confusing me with Su Lou,' I said, to which he frowned, clearly baffled.

'Su who?'

I shook my head, allowing him, once again, to lead me along the street.

'You'll see,' I said.

The exhibition was being held at Plain Ashes Fine Art, a large rentable space on the ground floor of a nondescript brown-brick building on West 24th Street, a pebble toss from the High Line. A short section of red carpet had been unrolled by the entrance, where a woman with bejewelled horn-rimmed spectacles stood waiting, a clipboard and pen in hand. It was impossible to see who was already inside because the windows were frosted, but as my father reeled off our names, I peered over the woman's head in search of Cellan.

'Go on inside,' she told us warmly. 'The gold stickers indicate sold items, and reds are under offer. If you want to make a bid, please see a member of gallery staff.'

'Are we early?' I whispered, digging out my phone from my bag to check the time.

Aside from the two of us and three aproned staff clutching trays of champagne, the only people milling around were three rather sweaty-looking men who looked as if they'd come from the office, a peroxide blonde with a pillar-box red pout that clashed with her skin-tight pink minidress, and a small, neat Japanese woman, who smiled when I looked in her direction. This, I knew from an earlier google search, was the artist.

Su Lou created all her work from materials scavenged from the sea, her mission being to highlight the issue of ocean pollution, and the results were astounding. As well as a large seascape constructed from coiled layers of coloured rope, there were sculptures of distressed seabirds built from disposable lighters, a vast colour-wheel mosaic patterned with shards of plastic, and a human-sized leopard seal made solely of glass bottles. Glancing up, I saw a collection of fishing nets in various lurid shades strung across the low ceiling, while a tidal wave of plastic sunglasses, old iPhones, and snorkel masks reared up gracefully from a far corner. Everything had been carefully lit by angled spotlights, and a soundtrack of shifting water filtered out from hidden speakers.

'Wow,' I murmured, crossing the room to examine one of the sculptures in more detail.

My father squinted at the label, which had a red sticker attached. 'Albatrash,' he read aloud, before emitting a low whistle. 'Twelve thousand dollars – that's a lot of green to lay down on a heap of rubbish.'

Glancing around to make sure Su Lou was not close enough to have overheard, I hissed, 'It's not about the materials, it's about the craft, and the vision.'

The woman in the pink dress tottered past, pausing alongside the leopard seal and extending her arm to take a selfie. One of the gallery staff members, who was dressed in a white smock and had bright purple hair, hurried over to intervene.

'No photographs,' he said. 'Press only this evening.'

At the mention of 'press', I wheeled around in mild alarm, but other than a few more student-age arrivals, all of whom were dressed eclectically, nobody else had appeared. The nerves that had almost caused me to bolt continued to judder through me, and the next time a tray passed, I accepted a glass of fizz and drained half of it in a single gulp. My father, who did not like anything containing bubbles, asked the server if there was any whiskey available, and less than two minutes later, a tumbler containing a generous measure was placed in his hand.

More guests arrived, a small jolt of recognition going through me at the sight of Wylie Brooke, who wafted in amid a wall of flashing cameras and made a beeline for Su Lou. The two women clasped each other's hands as Wylie shook her long white-blond hair over one shoulder, marvelling in honeyed tones about how glorious the collection was, and how she couldn't wait to choose a piece for her new loft apartment. When Su Lou was called away to greet another influx of potential buyers, Wylie's gaze fell on me, and for a moment she squinted as if unsure of who I was. I smiled and saw the lift of her features as comprehension dawned.

'Honor,' she said, sashaying over in her vertiginous heels. She was dressed simply, in ultra-short black shorts and a primrose yellow bandeau top, and her skin seemed to glow under the bright spotlights. 'Love the dress – Ganni, right? And you've changed your hair.'

I patted my shorn locks self-consciously.

'It looks great,' she enthused.

'So do you,' I stammered. 'And thank you, by the way, for what you said about me. That was kind of you.'

I caught the shadow of what looked like confusion pass across her face, and then she laughed. 'Sure,' she said. 'I mean, Cherry came up with it all, I just signed off on it. You know how it is?'

I did not, clearly.

My father barrelled into the conversation before I had the chance to reply, introducing himself and remarking on the exhibition.

'Sublime, isn't it?' Wylie gushed. 'I just love Su Lou's whole ethos. She's so in tune with the planet, you know? You'll have to help me settle on which piece to buy.'

'We can help each other,' schmoozed my father, raising his glass of whiskey. 'Why don't you lead the way?'

'Dad,' I said through gritted teeth, as Wylie bent to get a better look at the leopard seal. 'You promised not to leave me on my own.'

'I'll only be across the room, honey,' he said, striding after

Wylie as she vanished into the now quite sizeable crowd. The sound of voices had drowned out the gentle percussion of the waves, and flashes were continuing to go off around the entrance, as more and more notable people were crossed off the guestlist. I recognised two women from a reality TV show, the model son of a famous British actor, and a man so tall he could only have been a basketball player. Nobody spoke to me, and having circuited the gallery several times, I paused not far from the door and drank three more glasses of champagne in quick succession.

Maybe Cellan had decided not to come. It was nearing nine p.m., and there was no sign of him. Thinking that I must locate my father soon, if only so I could convince him to leave, I inched my way around to the far side of the vast tidal wave and leant against the wall, wondering not for the first time how it was that I was here, at this party, with these strangers, and wishing I had a friend in tow. Tallulah would have enjoyed this, and I would have felt more confident with her by my side.

I was in the process of plucking yet another glass of bubbly from a tray when a buzz of excitement passed through the room. Flashes of stark blue light lit up the entrance, and I heard shouts of 'over here' and 'to me'. I did not need to hear Cellan's name being called to know he was here; I could sense him. My body had begun to shake, my mouth dry and my hands slippery. Propelled by the need to see him, I hurried out of the corner on unsteady legs, stumbling as my new sandals snagged between the floorboards. The lofty figure of Gunnar entered the room first, followed closely by Colton, who grinned widely as he greeted Su Lou. Cherry was next through the door, but rather than moving forwards she hung back, apparently waiting for someone.

More cameras clicked, and the woman in the pink dress,

who had pushed her way through the throngs of people to the very front, let out a small groan of pleasure as Cellan came into view.

It had only been a few days since I'd seen him last, but in that moment, the gulf between us had never felt wider. I watched, legs set as if in concrete, as he hugged Su Lou before dipping his ear towards Cherry. She had positioned herself like a bodyguard by his side, neatly poised to intercept anyone who approached. Wylie was ushered into the inner sanctum, my father trailing in her wake, and when Cellan clocked him, I thought I saw the briefest flash of irritation corrode his features. I wanted to walk towards him, but I could not seem to make my feet obey my brain. Already a queue of eager patrons was forming, and it wasn't long before I lost sight of him altogether. I drained my glass, then tucked my hair behind my ears, took my phone out of my bag and saw a message waiting from Jojo. I had sent her a photo of myself before leaving the apartment, with a simple 'Will I do?' caption underneath. Jojo had replied with a fire emoji, and the words: *swit swoo*.

I wish you were here, I typed rapidly, smiling despite myself, despite the weirdness, despite all of it. When I glanced up again, Cherry was standing in front of me.

'Found you,' she said, unsmiling.

'I wasn't hiding,' I replied, and giggled. Seeing the expression on her face, I promptly clamped my lips together only to start hiccupping.

'Oops,' I said, holding up my empty glass. 'Too much champagne.'

Cherry's gold nose ring caught the light as she frowned. 'Are you drunk?'

'Almost definitely not. OK, maybe a little.' I giggled again, wobbling on my heels until she put out a hand to steady me, muttering something disparaging under her breath.

'What was that?'

'I said, this isn't ideal – but you're here now, so we'd better get on with it.'

'Get on with what?' I asked, smiling at her expectantly.

'Your reason for being here this evening. Your father explained it all to you, right?'

'No, he—'

But Cherry had been summoned. When I made no move to follow her, she turned back, reaching out a hand with barely concealed impatience.

'Come on,' she said. 'Cellan's waiting.'

Aggravated by her curt manner, I folded my arms.

'Why can't he come to me?' I asked, and she took a deep breath.

'Because he's Cellan Thomas,' she said, as if it were obvious to everyone in the world but me. 'He doesn't go to people, they come to him.'

It was such an absurd thing to say that I laughed, which did little to lessen her irritation. I might not have known the man she worked for long, but I liked to think I knew him well enough to be sure of a few things – a key one being how amusing he would have found her statement. If he had been standing here beside me when she said it, I was ninety-nine per cent certain he would have laughed as much as me.

'You're really not going to play ball?' Cherry demanded, and I shrugged.

'If he wants me, tell him to come and get me.'

Giving me a scowl putrid enough to spoil milk, she stalked back towards the entrance. I saw her say something to Gunnar, who glanced in my direction, then she put a hand on Cellan's arm. Breaking off from his conversation with the basketball player, he listened for a moment, then went very still, his eyes searching across the assembled heads in the crowd until they settled on me.

I had expected a mouthed 'hello', a wave, perhaps a glimmer of the yearning that had held me to ransom all week long – but Cellan did not so much as smile. Something was wrong, I realised.

Something was very wrong indeed.

43

Taking a deep breath, I walked towards him, only breaking eye contact when I was forced to go around the three men in business suits. Cellan waited until I was a few feet away before stepping out from the small circle of people surrounding him.

He still was not smiling.

'Hi,' I said, the cadence of my voice making the word sound like a question.

Cellan fixed me with a steady gaze. There was a healthy regrowth of stubble across his jaw, and he had the bronzed complexion of someone who has spent a number of consecutive days in the sun. Dressed in a black shirt, dark jeans, and his preferred collection of chunky rings, he looked obscenely handsome, although I stopped short of telling him so.

'It's good to see you,' I went on, going to touch his arm and then thinking better of it. 'I was beginning to think you'd changed your mind about coming.'

'The thought did occur to me,' he said, in a measured kind of tone. 'But Su Lou's a good friend of mine. I didn't want to let her down.'

I tried not to let on how much it hurt to know that he'd not factored me into his decision and groped for something complimentary to say instead.

'I love her work. I'd buy every piece if I hadn't maxed out my credit card on this outfit.'

Cellan gave my dress a cursory glance. 'It's not your usual style.'

'That's kind of the whole point. I felt like a change.'

'Is that why you cut all your hair off?' he asked. 'To change?'

'You inspired me when you got rid of the beard.'

I had hoped this would elicit a warmer response from him, but Cellan merely rubbed a hand across the lower part of his face. People were talking all around us, an excitable chatter that only added to my feelings of unease. Cherry was deep in conversation with a doppelganger of herself, only with blue instead of red hair, while Gunnar was gesticulating with both hands as he held my father and Wylie captive in conversation.

'This feels weird,' I blurted, widening my eyes in bemusement as the blonde with the red lips sidled towards us. Ignoring me, Cellan accepted her proffered hand, holding on to it for a little longer than I would have liked. She was 'such a fan', the woman told him, before explaining how 'me and my girlfriends send each other gifs of you all the time, you know, when we're having a bad day at work or whatever. Never fails to perk us up'. Cellan laughed good-naturedly, then agreed not only to record a voice note for her to circulate on WhatsApp, but also to pose for a photo, which the blonde asked me if I would take.

'Honor won't mind helping out,' he said. 'She's a pro.'

What he meant by that I did not know. I was beginning to get the distinct impression that he was annoyed with me and could feel rising hackles battling against distress as I obediently took some pictures on the woman's phone.

'Nice lady,' he said, when she eventually strolled away.

'Yes,' I agreed. 'Very open. Brave of her to admit quite how obsessed she is with you.'

Cellan narrowed his eyes. 'On the whole, I think I prefer

honesty,' he said. 'At least you know where you are with truthful people.'

'Are you saying that I'm not an honest person?' I replied, shock making me snappy.

Cellan put his hands in his pockets. 'You tell me.'

'What exactly is it that you think I've done?' I exclaimed, but again we were interrupted by someone wanting a photo. The more charming Cellan was to the stream of people he had never met, the deeper my resentment towards him burrowed. As he preened and posed and pretended to enjoy himself, I stood quietly to one side, trying to work out exactly what I could have done to bend him so out of shape. At some stage, Gunnar cut in and said there was an official photographer milling around, who was keen to get a shot of Cellan with the artist, and while he went off to do that, I escaped to the bathroom, emerging after a few minutes to find Cherry waiting for me.

'You're needed for a photo,' she said. 'And please don't be a mule about it this time.'

'Me?' I said, too surprised to argue.

Finding myself ensconced moments later between Cellan and Wylie, I tried not to blink as the powerful flash illuminated our faces, or weep at the lack of tenderness in the arm that was slung around my shoulders. Cellan's smile was a rictus, his cosiness towards me false, and the outward bounce he was displaying straight acting. My father, by contrast, appeared to be having the best night of his life, nestled as he was beside Gunnar, Wylie, and the artist Su Lou.

'Is there any way I could get a copy?' I heard him ask the photographer, explaining that the picture of his daughter 'with two such great pals of mine' warranted both a frame and pride of place on his apartment wall. Overcome by a sudden dizziness, I leant forwards and placed both my hands on my knees, breathing in deeply as the alcohol, the lack of food, and the sheer peculiarity of the night's events threatened to engulf me.

'Hey.' It was Wylie, her hand warm in the small of my back. 'Are you OK?'

When I shook my head, biting my lip to stop myself crying, she helped me to stand and ushered me gently towards the back of the room. There was a curtained-off kitchen area that I had not noticed before and having filled an empty champagne flute with water, Wylie handed it to me.

'Sip this,' she said. 'It'll make you feel better. It's a shame I didn't bring any of my electrolyte powder pouches along, those things are dynamite when you've had too much to drink.'

'It's not the booze,' I mumbled. 'I'm just . . . Tonight, it's been a lot.'

'You mean that whole photo thing?' she said, wincing with sympathy as I nodded. 'Think of it as the means to an end.'

'Do you know what's up with Cellan?' I asked, loathing the fact I had to. 'He seems a bit . . . odd.'

Wylie picked an imaginary piece of fluff off her shorts. 'Cellan's always odd.'

'Moody, then. I feel like he wants to shout at me but can't because everyone's watching.'

Wylie's pretty face crumpled. 'Why would he want to shout at you?' she asked.

'That's just it,' I said pitifully. 'I don't know. The last time I saw him, things were great between us, but now . . . It's as if he's changed into a different person.'

'Cef's never enjoyed this side of the job,' Wylie explained, frowning as I sipped more of my water. 'To be honest, I'm surprised he let himself be talked into coming tonight. He could have viewed the exhibition any time, yet here he is at the launch. I assumed it was because he wanted to see you.'

'And he hasn't said anything?' I checked. 'About being annoyed with me?'

'Not a thing,' she assured me. 'All he ever said to me about you was nice stuff.'

I started to explain about the story breaking, and how I'd been unable to get through to him on the phone. Wylie listened with interest only to glance suddenly over my shoulder, and I turned to see Gunnar bearing down on us.

'Is Cef with you?' he barked, throwing his hands up when it became clear that he was not.

'He's not in the john either – dammit!'

Yanking aside the curtain, Gunnar stomped into the tiny kitchen and opened the fridge, glaring inside as if he half-expected to find Cellan crouched on one of the shelves. My father appeared a second later, Cherry beside him.

'Colton's checked the truck,' she said. 'No sign.'

'And he's not in the office or out front?' demanded Gunnar. Cherry shook her head.

'Dammit!' he fumed, before turning on me. 'He must have told you where he's going.'

'He didn't,' I said, shrinking under the force of his wrath. 'I barely spoke to him.'

Wylie went to say something, then stopped, her hand going to her mouth. Even my father seemed lost for words. I looked at each of the assembled faces in turn.

'Does it really matter where he went?' I said cautiously. 'I mean, Cellan is a grown man – if he wanted to leave, that's his decision, isn't it?'

Cherry spun around, hands pressed to her cheeks.

'Maybe he just went to get a coffee, or a slice of pizza,' I continued, 'and is coming straight back.'

'You really don't know him at all, do you?' she said accusingly. 'Cef wouldn't just up and go without telling one of us.'

'Not unless something upset him,' agreed Wylie.

'Or someone,' said Gunnar

It took me a few seconds to register the fact that they were all staring at me.

'Does he have his phone?' I asked Cherry. 'Why not just try calling him?'

'Like I haven't thought of that already,' she said sourly.

Ignoring her, I scrabbled through my bag for my own phone and pressed the button to dial Cellan, feeling my chest expand with hope as it rang. The call was answered, but before I could emit so much as a word, the line went dead. It was the confirmation I'd been dreading, and the cold, cruel fact of it struck me hard. I slumped back against the wall, defeated.

I knew then that Cellan had chosen to disappear, and he'd done so because of me.

44

With nothing to go on and no idea where to begin searching, I felt I had little choice in the end but to return home with my father. Even if I had trawled the city streets until I found Cellan, there was no guarantee that he would be happy to see me. If anything, the opposite was true.

Gunnar promised to let me know if and when they found him, and then he, Colton and Cherry had climbed into the Chevy Silverado and driven off into the night. Wylie, who was staying with friends on the Upper East Side, called herself an Uber and reassured me that she'd get the word out if Cellan got in touch.

All that was left to do was wait, and so I did, my phone on the sofa beside me, a pot of coffee stopping me from falling asleep. I'd brought my laptop into the city with me, so used this to keep tabs on Twitter in case Cellan had been spotted. Searching under the hashtag of his name inevitably led me towards more posts about myself, but even these had ceased to matter in the wake of tonight's events. I no longer cared what people thought of me. The only opinion that meant anything to me was Cellan's and knowing that I had somehow caused the light of his affection for me to dim was close to excruciating.

'Please call,' I texted. 'I'm here.'

At a little before three a.m., Gunnar rang to say that he was going to 'hit the hay', as he called it, explaining that

Cherry had managed to get through to Cellan for a few minutes, during which time he'd explained that he was fine.

'But then where he is?' I implored, as Gunnar stifled a yawn.

'The kid used to live in the city. He's probably hooked up with an old girlfriend.'

'Right,' I said shortly, his words landing like bullets in my chest. 'Goodnight then.'

Cellan was safe.

It should have been enough, but I felt wounded. If he had answered Cherry, why couldn't he have replied to me? I tried for what felt like the thousandth time to trawl through everything that had happened between the morning he dropped me off back in Southampton and the gallery party, yet all I was left with were reasons that I should be annoyed with him, not the other way around. The only thing that snagged, and the one point that I kept looping back to, were the details in that second exposé. I had assumed Cellan himself had been the one to share them, but what if he hadn't? It stood to reason that he would suspect me of having blabbed, but other than filing the information away in my diary, I had not mentioned it. Thinking it was worth a try, I picked up my phone and typed out another message.

'Glad you're OK. Just wanted to say that as far as the press are concerned, I haven't said or done anything. I promise. I'd even swear on banana pancakes, and you know how much I love those.'

I added two kisses, then deleted them in favour of a banana emoji and pressed send. The two grey ticks appeared, indicating the text had been delivered, but Cellan did not come online to read it. I had to hope that he was not, as Gunnar had so casually decreed, 'hooking up' with an old girlfriend, and that he was, in fact, asleep in a plush hotel bed

– exactly the place I had allowed myself to fleetingly fantasise about ending the night with him only hours ago.

The coffee had done the trick, and I felt twitchy and wired by caffeine. Hauling myself up from the sofa, I walked to the large window and stared out over the city. New York, in all her great, glittering, grinding beauty was spread before me, a night sky metropolis decorated with artificial stars. Somewhere out there, amid the machinations of eight million people, was a man who had come to mean more to me than I felt ready to admit. And although logic told me that I had lost him, I would not allow myself to believe it. I was not going to give him up as I had others.

I had pressed my face against the glass for so long that my breath had caused it to fog, and taking a step back, I raised my hand and drew a heart in the condensation.

An image of myself as an intrepid eight year old came into my mind, and I greeted her like an old friend. She was always the same, dressed in her smart new frock and shoes, her hair brushed, and her notebook of stories packed neatly into her bag. She was the version of me that had existed in the moments before Jeffrey Butler became not some imagined prince from a fairy-tale delusion, but a real, solid, kind, but also deeply intimidating man, and I had lost her on that day, inside that restaurant.

I could hear the sound of my father's snores, loud and regular, coming from his bedroom, and after tiptoeing past his door, I made my careful way into his office. The air inside was stuffy, the window closed, and a spider plant gasped for life on the sill. He had left his desk relatively tidy, the wood and green leather chair pushed in, a stack of documents in the out tray, all the many fountain pens stacked into a Yale mug. On the overstuffed bookcases that bordered the room, I found copies of his Benedict Stamp series in a multitude of languages, several special editions with sprayed-edge pages and embossed hardback covers, and his prized first edition of *The Wind in the Willows* – a gift from his late father – which was locked in a glass presentation box. There were also reams of notebooks in various states of disrepair, and I slid one out at random, taking a few minutes to flick through. My father's handwriting was barely legible, but he certainly had plotting down to a fine art, and I noticed that at the end of each planned scene, he had added the word 'kaboom' followed by a question mark. This, I knew, was to remind him that every chapter must end with something powerful enough to convince the reader to keep going. In Jeffrey Butler's case, this was often a literal 'kaboom', in the shape of a building exploding or a bad guy bursting in with a gun; in a romantic comedy such as the one I was trying – and failing – to write, the equivalent might be a first kiss, or even something as simple as a lingering look. No wonder, I thought, as I returned the notebook to its place on the shelf, that my father found my preferred genre so entirely tedious.

I had always tried to follow where he led, plot how he plotted, and craft stories full of adventure, because until this trip, I had never doubted that his was the perfect formula. In writing about Cellan, however, I had found myself veering more towards my character Patrick's internal struggles, and how what was going on inside affected his outward actions. It was the person that drew me in, not the kabooms, and surely a reader had to care about the protagonist for the external battles to matter? It was clear that I had been following a set of rules that were destined to make me fail.

My eyes strayed again to the bookshelves, to tome upon bestselling tome, the conflict that had for so long muddled my mind, calcifying as I argued back against logic. The fact was, Jeffrey Butler was not the only bestselling author in the world, and he did write predominantly thrillers. When I compared his style to that of the writers I had grown up reading – Jilly Cooper, Marian Keyes, Jane Austen – there could not have been more differences. Focusing on the emotions of their characters had not stopped any of those women from finding their tribe of readers, so why had I for so long held on to the notion that if I were to do so, then it would ostracise me from success? I knew why; it was because I had put my father on a pedestal so high, that in gazing up at him, I had lost sight of every other valid example. Even my own.

Switching off the light, I closed the office door quietly behind me and made my way back to the sofa, where I pulled my laptop towards me and started to read the diary entries that I had began the day I met Cellan. Viewing them through the lens of acceptance rather than criticism, I was able to find things that I liked, that moved me, and that made me laugh. My account of the time Cellan and I had spent together felt all the more special now that I feared it had been finite, and although I knew that nobody would ever see it but me, I took the time to tweak and refine. Those days, hours, minutes and seconds had been perfect, and I wanted my words to become a celebration of that.

I sat there until the pale-yellow light of day blended through the grey of night, the city below me stirring sluggishly into life as garbage trucks crashed, dogs barked, and locals called out greetings to one another as they wandered out in search of coffee. At a little after eight-thirty, my phone lit up with a message.

Cellan.

I need you, it said. *Please come.*

45

It took me thirty minutes to reach Brooklyn Heights, and having exited Clark Street Metro station, I ran down the block towards Fifty Henry Wine Bar, almost tripping in my haste to reach Cellan.

He was sitting, as he'd told me in his message that he would be, on a small wooden chair in the far corner, an untouched glass of whiskey on the table in front of him and a rather grim smile on his face.

'That for me?' I asked mildly, sliding into the seat opposite his.

'Enjoy a liquid breakfast, do you?' he replied. His voice sounded raspy, as if he hadn't spoken for a while.

'Depends on the liquid,' I mused. 'If it's milk turned chocolatey by Coco Pops, then I'm all for it.'

I was rewarded with slight shake of the head. Cellan had not slept, that much was obvious, and he was still in the smart shirt and jeans he'd worn to Su Lou's launch.

'I thought I would drink it as soon as it was put down in front of me,' he said. 'But I've been here nearly an hour now, and I've yet to take a sip. The staff must be thrilled.'

As he said it, a waitress who had been hovering at the bar headed over, and having given the small menu a cursory glance, I asked for two orders of eggs Chesapeake and a couple of strong black coffees.

'Hungry?' was all Cellan said, when the waitress had wandered away.

'We both are,' I said. 'And food makes everything better.'

Cellan's eyes fell to the glass between us, then back up to mine. 'Aren't you going to take it away from me?' he said.

'Is that why you summoned me here? I know you're a film star and everything, but I'd wager that even you could manage to lift a glass and take it to a sink.'

I was teasing him because the alternative felt too murky, a thread which I was not sure I wanted to pull. I did not need him to spell out for me what was happening here, because it was plain to see: he was teetering on the edge of a relapse into drinking alcohol, and instead of toppling over into the abyss, he had called me.

The waitress returned with our coffee. 'You all done with this?' she asked breezily, her hand hovering above the whiskey as she looked from Cellan to me.

'Yes,' he said, his fingers tapping against the tabletop. 'You can take that away now.'

As soon as the glass vanished from sight, his shoulders dipped with relief. I watched as he rearranged his features into a heroic half-smile, before reaching for the sugar and stirring some into his cup.

'You look awful,' I said, as he took a sip.

Cellan spluttered out a laugh. 'Gee, thanks for that.'

'No, I mean, you still look great, handsome, fit, whatever – but you're also a bit crusty, you know? Like I used to be every Thursday morning at university.'

'What happened on Wednesday nights?' he asked, mopping spots of coffee off his chin with a napkin.

'It was sports night in the union bar. Did I ever tell you that I was in the hockey team?'

'No, but now I'm a bit more scared of you.'

'You shouldn't be,' I told him. 'I was awful. But I was great at all the extracurricular activities, which mostly involved downing pints of Guinness and doing dares.'

'Guinness?' he pulled a face. 'You animal.'

'Takes one to know one.'

'Ouch.' He grimaced. 'I probably deserved that.'

I sipped my coffee and stared around, admiring the faded oak panels on the walls, the small vases of dried flowers on every table, and the neat carriage lamps set at intervals along the picture rail. There was music playing, so faintly that I had to strain my ears to hear it.

'Oh, it's Glenn Miller,' I said, starting to bop in my seat. 'I love him!'

Cellan looked puzzled at first, then he smiled – properly this time – and began to mouth along to the lyrics with me, the two of jiggling from side to side and him tapping out a tempo on the table.

'If there's a catchier tune than *Chattanooga Choo Choo*, then I've never heard it,' I said, only to let out a whoop of delight when the track ended and the opening bars of *In the Mood* sent me into an even more enthusiastic dance, complete with air-trumpet moves.

Laughing now, Cellan nodded his head, his shoulders going up and down in time to the music. 'We used to listen to him when I was growing up,' he said. 'My dad was obsessed.'

'Mine, too,' I said. 'He has all the albums on vinyl.'

'Jeffrey Butler has just gone way up in my estimation,' said Cellan, smiling as the waitress executed a perfect pirouette before putting our breakfast plates down in front of us.

'You were right,' he said, looking at the crab cakes topped with poached eggs and slathered in hollandaise, 'I am bloody ravenous.'

'When was the last time you ate anything?' I exclaimed, as he tucked into his food with gusto. He had polished off half the meal before I'd even finished grinding pepper over the top of mine.

'Some time yesterday morning. Wylie left me a whole load of her smoothie powders, so I had one of those.'

My facial expression made him grin.

'It was nice!'

'But was it substantial?'

'Well, no, but—'

'No wonder you're half-starved.'

'Thank you,' he said, lowering his knife and fork. 'For knowing what I needed, and for answering my message and, you know, for being here now. I feel awful about the way I behaved last night.'

'I'm glad you mentioned that,' I said, running my knife through the yolk so it oozed out over the crab cake. 'What happened? Did I do something?'

Cellan thought for a moment, his gaze fixing on something in the middle distance. 'I didn't enjoy not seeing or speaking to you this week,' he said, and I nodded urgently.

'Same! It was horrible. My father told me not to go over to the house, and Cherry barked like a dog at me every time I tried to call you.'

'She can be a bit like that,' he allowed. 'But it comes from a good place.'

'She doesn't like me.'

I had not posed it as a question, and Cellan looked pained. 'As far as I was aware,' he said, 'you were the one who'd said it would be better if we didn't speak. Cherry told me how upset you were by all the shit people were saying about you online, and I know I should have reached out, but I felt so guilty about it.'

'Hang on,' I said, interrupting him. 'Cherry told you what?'

'That you didn't want to see or speak to me.'

'I said no such thing!' I exclaimed, so loudly that an elderly couple glanced over in alarm. 'All I ever said to Cherry was how desperate I was to see and speak to you. She told me it was better for the narrative,' I muttered, putting unfavourable emphasis on the hated word. 'Sit down and shut up was very much the message coming through to me loud and extremely clear.'

Cellan picked up his coffee and put it down again without taking a sip.

'So, it wasn't you that spoke to the *Mail* journalist and told them all that stuff about my teenage habit of writing love poetry?'

'Of course not,' I said, feeling thoroughly confused. 'I would never betray you like that.'

At this, Cellan had the grace to look shamefaced.

'Shit,' he said. 'It must have been someone at the beach party – a random friend of Maddy and Locryn's. I was quite open about where we'd been earlier in the day, and bloody Locryn isn't exactly subtle when it comes to shouting his mouth off.'

'That does make sense,' I agreed, thankful to finally be crawling free from the kennel I'd felt confined to for the past twelve hours. 'Do you really think that if I had anything to do with that bloody story I would have handed over those hideous photos of me from the early noughties, when I believed it was acceptable to wear denim cycling shorts in public?'

'You did?'

'I was fifteen!'

'But presumably able-sighted?'

'Ha-ha.'

'Shit,' he said again. 'I've really messed up.'

'No,' I mumbled, giving him a begrudging smile. 'I'm here, aren't I?'

'I like it when it's just the two of us,' he said, sliding an arm across the table so he could take my hand. 'Last night was . . . I didn't enjoy myself. I never do when I feel like I'm on parade like that. I misjudged you and I'm sorry; I won't do it again.'

'It's OK.' I squeezed my fingers against his. 'I understand.'

My coffee had gone cold, which I decided was probably a good thing. I'd drunk so much of the stuff during the small hours that I was in danger of taking flight.

'Where did you go last night?' I asked, continuing to eat my eggs one-handed. 'You seemed to just disappear.'

'That was exactly my aim,' he admitted. 'All I wanted was to walk, and think, and get some space from everyone, and that's what I did. I walked all over the city for hours, not stopping, not looking at my phone, not talking to a soul. I didn't realise how much time had passed until I happened to glance down and see Barthman's Sidewalk Clock on Broadway, then I figured I should probably check in.'

'Gunnar called and told me,' I said, deciding not to mention the second part of that particular conversation. 'But that was three-ish – what did you do between then and when you contacted me?'

He shrugged, rubbing the fleshy part between my thumb and forefinger.

'I sat by the Hudson for a while, then walked along the waterfront there, just watching the lights, listening to the night traffic. I thought about you,' he added, hazel eyes flickering to mine, 'and tried to decide what to do about my career.'

I cocked my head.

'Your career?'

'Gunnar keeps on at me that this is a critical point. He's been pushing this script on me, but I don't know ... I guess I'm not really feeling it.'

'What's the part?' I asked, using my elbow to nudge my empty plate to one side. 'No, don't tell me – you've been asked to play a Louisianan named Billy Bob? Or a stunt bike rider!'

Cellan shuffled his feet under the table, his knee pressing against mine.

'It's an action film,' he said. 'I'd be playing the long-lost son of a mercenary.'

'But that's— Marty Stamp? You've been offered a part in JB's movie?'

'Gunnar says it's the right vehicle to relaunch me.'

I fell silent, struck momentarily dumb by a niggling sense of déjà vu. 'And you don't agree?'

'It's not the type of role so much as this particular script. Marty feels very two-dimensional to me. I listened to the entire thing, and I still feel no nearer to understanding him as a person. Usually, there's a lot of background stuff, but as far as I can tell, Marty is a carbon copy of his father, only angrier. And he treats women like crap.'

I knew having read the novel that he was not far wrong in his condemnation, but I could not help but be excited at the prospect of Cellan appearing in a film that had such close ties to my father, and therefore me.

'If you took it on, surely you'd get a say in how he behaves?'

'To a certain extent maybe,' Cellan agreed. 'But it would mean a long shoot abroad, probably in Morocco, and a whole load of gym time to bulk me up. I'd rather do something quieter first; ease myself back in with a small indie film or theatre stint.'

'And Gunnar disagrees?'

'Vehemently. As far as he's concerned, he knows what's best. And, as he keeps pointing out, when I get paid, he, Cherry and Colton, and all the other people who are counting on me get paid. This part could mean big money, whereas a smaller project could be peanuts by comparison. I have people depending on me.'

'That's a lot of pressure,' I said quietly.

'Yeah,' he said. 'Yeah, it is. And last night, I don't know, I just cracked. In the past when I used to feel like that, I'd just go out and get wrecked, drink until I felt better, numb all the anxiety with alcohol. And I almost caved in this morning, was so close to undoing all the work I'd put in, all that soul-searching and talking and understanding the way my brain ticks.' He tapped a finger to the side of his head.

'But you didn't,' I said, and he nodded, mouth set in a line as he fought down whatever emotions had risen to the surface.

'I didn't,' he agreed. 'I messaged you instead.'

A silence fell between us then that was filled by the buoyant trumpets of Glenn Miller and his band, as they set the elderly couple's feet tapping with a rendition of *A String of Pearls*. Unable not to join in, I started to sway gently in my seat, rocking Cellan's hand in mine.

'Can I give you a kiss?' I asked, still bopping.

He raised both brows. 'After coffee, eggs, crab cakes, and no toothpaste for the past, oh, thirteen hours?'

Pushing back my chair, I twirled on the spot, my fingers still clutching his, and sat daintily down on his lap. The waitress, who had arrived to collect our plates, clucked with approval as I buried my face in his shoulder to hide my blushes.

'Come here,' Cellan said, wrapping his arm around my shoulder and pulling me tight against him, kissing me on and on until the cheers and whoops of other diners made us both collapse with helpless laughter.

'I think we'd better get the bill,' I said. 'Before they throw us out.'

'We could go back to my hotel?' he murmured, but I shook my head.

'Later,' I said, catching his meaning and enjoying the shiver of anticipation it sent through my body.

'But first, I've got something that I want to show you for a change.'

46

Having located a New York souvenir shop and nipped inside to buy each of us a large, foam, cowboy hat, I led Cellan through the wide, tree-lined Brooklyn lanes down to the district of Dumbo, where we paused on Washington Street to admire the view of the Manhattan Bridge.

'I still don't see why I have to wear the pink one,' he grumbled. 'You get the traditional tan-coloured Stetson and I get the bubble gum one – how is that fair?'

'Life isn't fair,' I told him, angling my head so I could give him a quick kiss. 'And anyway, pink suits you.'

'Swap and I'll give you five-hundred dollars.'

'Nope.'

'A thousand – two thousand!'

'All right, moneybags, I get the idea. But my answer is still no.'

Continuing to badger, he trailed after me between the vast brownstones. It was a warm enough day for the city to be renamed The Baked Apple, and I could feel the heat of the cobbled road burning through the soles of my trainers. Cellan, dressed all in black save for the ridiculous hat, must have been boiling, and I wondered aloud if I should have let him return to his hotel after all.

'If we go into a room with a bed in it, no way will you prise me out of it again,' he said, sliding a hand into the waistband of my shorts and tugging me forwards. Unable to reach my mouth because of the angle of the Stetson, he planted a kiss in my cleavage instead and laughing, I squirmed out of his grasp.

'No more action until I get my poem,' I said, fanning my face with a leaflet I'd been given advertising Segway tours. We had turned our backs on the river now and were heading towards the Brooklyn Bridge.

Cellan's jaw worked as he mulled, and I watched his face light up as inspiration struck. 'Roses are pink, and so is this hat; please let me swap, I look like a twat.'

I tutted so as not to laugh.

'That is not a love poem. Try again.'

A cluster of pigeons were dancing in haphazard circles beside a hot dog cart, the vendor of which gave the two of us a bemused expression as we passed.

'Honor is pretty, Honor is cool; but wearing that hat, she looks like a fool.'

'I'm beginning to see why this poetry ploy never got you very far.' I laughed, joining the line of people spooling like lemmings into the stairway leading up to the bridge. Cellan let go of my hand as we moved into single file, and I felt suddenly, ridiculously, bereft. Once up on the pedestrian walkway, we stood to one side to let the steady stream of tourists pass by, waiting for a gap to open up.

'I've got it,' said Cellan, his impish grin making me roll my eyes.

'Go on then, hit me.'

He cleared his throat. 'The moment that I met Miss Honor, I knew, this is it – I'm a goner! So warm is her soul, and kind are her eyes, she even looks hot in a stupid disguise.'

I laughed, but he shushed me.

'I haven't finished.'

'Sorry. Please continue.'

Cellan gave me a very exaggerated wink. 'She's silly, and sexy, and gives the best head; she also likes books and is very well read.'

'I should really be filming this,' I said, and he feigned shock before carrying on.

'But the thing I like most, more than any other, is the way she has forgiven me, for being a tosser.'

He beamed with satisfaction as I laughed.

'That was great,' I said. 'Until the last line. I would argue that "tosser" doesn't rhyme very well with "other".'

'Ooof,' he said. 'Low blow.'

I patted his cheek. 'You'll live. Now, shall we listen to some music as we cross the bridge?'

Taking my headphones out from my bag and unknotting the cable, I passed one earbud to him and slotted the other under the brim of my hat, before plugging the wire into my phone. Having scrolled through my music library and found the track I had been looking for – *We Belong Together* by Ritchie Valens – I pressed play.

Cellan's face lit up, and taking my lead, we started to dance deftly forwards.

The majestic arches of the Brooklyn Bridge loomed high, its lattice of cables turning the clear blue sky above us into a chequerboard. The floor shuddered as cars roared beneath our feet, the distinctive shape of Manhattan coming into view through a haze of heat on the opposite bank. The song ended as we reached the midway point and the Statue of Liberty appeared, blurry but unmistakable, in the far distance. Cellan's fingers brushed against mine, and I felt the hairs stand up on the back of my neck, each one awakened, as I was, by his touch.

'I love this spot,' I told him. 'I know it's not exactly off the beaten track, but the Brooklyn Bridge has a sad yet romantic backstory. I always think about it when I come here.'

'Tell me,' he prompted.

'So, the bridge was designed by husband-and-wife engineers named John and Emily. They spent years studying how to build what was then to become the longest suspension bridge in the world, then returned to New York from Europe and began the project in 1869, I believe it was. Part of the construction included these underwater structures called caissons, which unfortunately caused several of the workers to suffer from decompression sickness.'

'You mean like the bends?' asked Cellan.

'Exactly. And sadly, Emily's husband suffered the same fate – he ended up blind, deaf, mute, and partially paralysed. Rather than give up the project, Emily saw it through to completion, all while caring for the man she loved and convincing others that he should retain his position as chief engineer. This was in the days before women were allowed to vote or own property, which makes what she did even more impressive. It was essentially just as much her achievement as his, yet his is the name that history associates with the bridge.'

'She sounds like quite a woman,' he said. 'And your knowledge is far better than mine. The only trivia I know about the Brooklyn Bridge is that when it was finished, twenty-one elephants were led over it in celebration.'

'You know,' I said, with a last lingering look out towards Liberty Island. 'I think I like that story even better than mine. Who needs acts of undying love and bravery when you have a stampede of pachyderms? Maybe I should write some into my book.'

'You might hate me for saying this,' said Cellan, as we made our way along the final stretch of bridge. 'But I'd be willing to bet that, elephants or not, your book will still be far better than anything your father could come up with, because you have what he hasn't got.'

'What's that then?' I asked. 'Terrible jokes?'

'Well, yes, there are those,' he allowed, turning to peer at me from under his pink hat. 'But what I was actually going to say, was heart.'

My plan had been to show Cellan the places in New York that I loved the best, those I went back to every year during my visits, the hideaways that I credited for getting me through long and often lonely weeks in the city.

I took him to Bryant Park, where we sat on the grass eating pistachio soft scoop ice creams and watching the birds as they flitted from branch to picnic table, to shrub. A bank of tulips in shades of pink, purple and white had been planted in the shade of the public library, while late-blooming daffodils peered out from tangles of ivy in the central beds. When one of the ping-pong tables became free, Cellan jumped up and dragged me over for a match that ended in mutual hysterics, as we each sent the ball flying into litter bins, people's lunches, and a hole in the trunk of a tree that contained a very put-out squirrel.

From there, we wandered all the way along Broadway to my favourite store, Strand Books, where teetering shelves groaned under the weight of old, new, popular and obscure titles. It smelt wonderful inside, of antiquated paper, binder glue and dust, and Cellan looked on bemused as I skipped excitedly from one tome to another, telling him what I had enjoyed most about each and explaining how their US jackets differed from those in the UK.

'Bookshops here feel far less snobby,' I said, as we came to a stop next to a table piled high with brightly coloured romantic comedies. 'There are still so many people that choose books they think they should read, rather than those they know they'll enjoy.'

'Sounds a lot like actors,' he said wryly. 'I have definitely taken jobs that I thought I should. If it were solely up to me, I'd probably go back to the theatre full time.'

'Really?' This surprised me. 'You'd never do another film?'

'Maybe. But not for a few years. There's something so much more rewarding about performing live to an audience than there is about being on set, surrounded by people who are paid to be there, rather than the other way around. With theatre, the audience changes every night, so even if you're performing the same material and reciting the same lines, the experience of it feels different. Movie work can become' – he lowered his voice – 'a bit tedious.'

'Careful.' I raised my hand to make the tiny violin motion only for him to grab it and stuff my fingers into his mouth.

'Gross!' I cried, wiping them against his shirt. 'Now I can't touch any more of the books.'

'No,' he said, drawing me closer, 'but I can think of other things you might like to.'

'But we're not done yet,' I protested, as he towed me through the shop and back onto the sun-scorched sidewalk. 'I wanted to show you a falafel place I like in Williamsburg, or I thought we could walk along the High Line – the last time I was up there, I saw a red cardinal.'

'All great, I'm sure,' he said, sticking out an arm. 'Taxi!'

'You know what Samuel Johnson said: if you're tired of New York, you're tired of life.'

'He was talking about London,' Cellan said, grinning as a yellow cab screeched to a halt beside us. 'But nice try.'

Hauling me into the car's blessedly air-conditioned interior, he took off his hat and balanced it on top of mine.

'St Regis Hotel, please,' he told the driver, and before I had the chance to do much more than buckle up, we were zooming away from the kerb. Taking back his hat, Cellan held it up for us to hide behind, and leaned across to kiss me, his lips pressing hard against mine as the taxi lurched around a corner.

'I want you,' he said, his voice a sensual growl as he started to kiss my neck.

'I want you too,' I said huskily, melting into him as his hand travelled up my thigh. New York passed by in a blur of noise and colour beyond the windows, but I barely saw a thing. I was focused solely on Cellan – the taste and feel of him, the trace of aftershave still clinging to him, the intensity in his golden-brown eyes and his need for me, so raw and unequivocal. In the midst of the fog that had become my conscious state, I was aware of a small pocket of dread opening up – the sense that a trap had been set, and that the two of us were hurtling straight towards it.

We arrived at the hotel and Cellan pressed his credit card against the contactless device, his other hand already on the door, eager to escape the confines of the cab. The St Regis Hotel was tall and grand, its facade cladded in white stone. Flags hung down above a canopied entrance, and the steps into the lobby were covered in a pristine red carpet. A gloved and top-hatted doorman stood aside to let us pass, and I found myself being whisked through a plush lobby. The floor was marble, the fittings almost predominantly gold, and the ceiling had been painted to look like a summer sky. I blinked, dazzled by a vast chandelier, and tried to concentrate on not allowing my jaw to hang open in awe. While Gurney's Resort and Spa had been the epitome of relaxed beachside luxury, the St Regis was refined old-world glamour with exactly the right amount of glitz to make it sparkle. It did not, however, feel typical for Cellan.

'This place,' I murmured, as he towed me towards a bank of gold-fronted lifts.

'I know,' he said with a mirthless smile. 'Cherry's choice, not mine.'

'Is she here, too?' I asked, suddenly fearful. Now that I knew for certain that the flame-haired publicist had lied to both of us in order to keep us apart, I was wary of running into her. I did not think I would be able to tolerate another one of her withering stares, not when she had caused me and Cellan so much torment this past week.

'Don't worry,' he said, reaching across to press the call button. 'Nobody is going to disturb us. I'm going to lock us in and take all the phones off the hook.'

There was a discreet 'ding' as the elevator arrived, and an extremely well-dressed family of four filed out, the teenage daughter doing a double take as she clocked Cellan.

'Told you not to take off the hat,' I said sotto voce, and Cellan laughed only to freeze in his tracks.

'Shit,' he muttered, making a move towards the closing lift doors. But it was too late; Gunnar had already seen us.

47

'There you are, kid,' he said, crossing the lobby in a few broad steps. As always, he looked impeccable, in a blue suit tailored to fit, his sweep of grey hair neatly coiffed. There was a copy of the *New York Post* tucked under his arm, and he was holding an iPad, its screen blank.

'Gunnar,' said Cellan shortly, gripping my hand a fraction tighter. 'I was just heading up to get some sleep – can this wait?'

Gunnar's eyebrow had twitched up cynically at the word 'sleep'. I felt a hot blush begin to steal across my cheeks and stared resolutely at the floor.

'I'm afraid it can't,' he replied, sounding regretful. 'There's been a . . . development.'

Cellan was no longer bothering to mask his irritation. The first elevator had been taken by another guest and, leaning back, he pressed the button once again to summon a second.

'Shall we go and sit down?' Gunnar suggested, to which Cellan let out an exasperated sigh.

'If this is work-related, I honestly don't have the mental energy to deal with it at the moment. I need a shower and a few hours' kip – surely, it's not life or death whether or not I decide on the part today?'

'This is not to do with the movie.' Gunnar's manner had become less genial. 'It's more of a personal nature.'

I swallowed; my skin felt clammy and my chest tight.

'What is it?' Cellan asked sharply.

'I really think it would be better if we—'

'Gunnar, seriously.'

'Why don't I . . . I should go,' I said hesitantly, trying to free my hand. Cellan held on tighter.

'Whatever it is, you can say it in front of Honor. We've agreed that there won't be any secrets between us anymore.'

I did not recall having had this conversation, although I was touched by the sentiment. Cellan must genuinely trust me, and that meant a lot.

Gunnar glanced at me without warmth. 'Let's go somewhere more private,' he said, and stalked away towards the front desk.

'Sorry about this,' said Cellan, throwing back his head in a gesture of frustration. 'Hopefully it won't take too long.'

Gunnar returned with a key card.

'They've said we can use one of the conference suites,' he said. 'Follow me.'

The two of us filed after him across the lobby in stony silence, and although I kept my eyes focused on the back of Cellan's dark shirt, it was impossible not to notice all the furtive glances and whispers. I was still wearing my oversized foam cowboy hat but took it off as Gunnar ushered us into a wide, carpeted room with long rectangular windows. There were rows of tables laid in black cloth, chairs pushed neatly beneath them, and another grandiose chandelier hung from the vaulted ceiling.

'I'll cut to the guts, shall I?' said Gunnar, tossing his newspaper onto the table and searching through the pages until he found what he was looking for, a double-page feature about Cellan and me, his not-so-mystery new girlfriend.

I peered down at it, eyes widening as I saw several of the

photos that I had taken in the car park below the lighthouse in Montauk.

'I don't understand,' I said, my attention snagged by a smaller boxout at the bottom of the righthand page, which at first glance appeared to be a review of Su Lou's exhibition. There was no photo, but a 'source' who attended the launch had reported that 'Cellan and his apparent girlfriend barely spoke. If I hadn't known they were involved, I would have assumed they were strangers. She was very drunk and almost fell over at one point, and he seemed embarrassed by her behaviour.'

I seethed at the audacity of this person.

'How did the press get hold of these photos?' Cellan said, tapping his finger against one of the selfies.

'I don't know,' I replied, panic winding its way, nettle-like, around my throat. 'I sent them to you last week. Could Cherry have intercepted them? She did have your phone, didn't she?'

Gunnar scoffed. 'Cherry runs everything past me,' he said. 'And this is the first either of us has seen of these.'

Cellan was still frowning down at the newspaper, his lips moving slowly as he read. 'What does it say here?' he asked, turning not to me but to Gunnar, who bent forwards in order to take a closer look.

'This might be tough to hear,' he said. 'Shall I read it out to you?'

Cellan appeared to have turned to stone and, dropping my hand, he folded his arms across his chest. 'Please do,' he said, the request brittle.

Gunnar placed a finger on the spot he was reading from and cleared his throat.

'A source close to the actor's new girlfriend tells the *New York Post*, "Honor has long had an ambition to become an author, like her father – the global bestseller Jeffrey Butler – and is willing to do whatever it takes. Ever since she met Cellan, she's been keeping notes, her plan being to write a book based on him."'

'That's not true!' I cried, but Gunnar ignored me and continued to read.

'Another insider reveals, "Cellan's friends all think he's fallen hard for Honor, and she's clearly using that to her advantage. Usually a private person, they say he's been opening up to her about his childhood, admitting that his father missed his first ever stage performance – as Jack in *Jack and the Beanstalk* – and that he fears his parents aren't proud of his achievements." He also told her in confidence about his experience of working with a very famous actress – who the *Post* cannot name for legal reasons – and an apparent tantrum she had on the set of a movie they did together. The source adds, "Honor has a record of everything he has said and done – including details of the intimate moments they shared – and is willing to sell it all to the highest bidder."'

The silence that followed this felt strained. I was overwhelmed by an urge to laugh, and only just managed to quell it.

'It's not funny, Honor,' condemned Gunnar. 'I'm guessing you didn't sign off on any of this, kid?' he said to Cellan, who had gone very pale.

'No,' he said, voice hoarse. 'I never talk about my family – especially not in a way that would hurt or embarrass them.'

'This is all nonsense,' I said, knitting my fingers together to stop them shaking. 'I have not been plotting to write some book about you. There must be other people that know that story about your father?'

'Only Padma.' He flicked his gaze to me. 'And you.'

'But I would never tell anyone,' I exclaimed. 'What about Maddy or Locryn?'

He shook his head. 'They wouldn't.'

'Well, someone must have.'

'What about the rest of it?' prompted Gunnar, who was staring at me with distaste, as if I was something unmentionable that he'd discovered languishing in the back of the fridge. 'Have you, or have you not, been keeping notes on Cef?'

'No!' I said, with enough conviction to crack the stern expression on Cellan's face. He wanted to believe me, but I knew I had to be honest.

'I didn't keep notes,' I said. 'But I have been keeping a diary. That's the truth, and that's the extent of it. I wrote it for myself, not for a book, or to sell to bloody journalists.'

Cellan looked uncertain, but Gunnar was not convinced.

'So, what? It all just magically turned up in some hack's inbox, did it? You have to admit, Honor, this looks more than a little fishy,' he said stonily. 'Information only you knew, photos that only you had possession of.'

'Neither of those statements is true,' I fired back at him.

'If she says it wasn't her, then it wasn't her,' said Cellan, coming loyally to my aid.

'Thank you,' I said triumphantly. 'Listen, I don't know who it was that spoke to the press, but I can swear categorically that it wasn't me. Nobody has used my phone but me; I always have it with me, and it's right next me when I sleep. Ditto my laptop,' I added, although this was not strictly the case. I had let others use that, but I could not believe that either of them would have done this to me.

Cellan was nodding, but he still looked unsure.

'There's more, isn't there?' he said, directing the question to Gunnar.

''Fraid so, kid.'

Putting the iPad down on top of the newspaper, he tapped in his passcode and opened the gossip site *TMZ*. This time, the headline was less conjectural: CELLAN GIRL ONLY IN IT FOR THE FAME.

'Oh, for fuck's sake,' I muttered, scrolling down to read the story. According to another 'insider', I had apparently arrived in The Hamptons with the sole aim of tracking Cellan down and seducing him.

'Honor knew he would be feeling vulnerable after all those weeks in rehab, so she decided to take advantage of his kind nature. She has always been obsessed with fame and success and is desperate to impress her father. Becoming Cellan's girlfriend is just the first step; she won't stop until everyone knows her name and doesn't care who she has to walk over to reach the top.'

'This is horse shit,' I exploded. 'A total fucking fabrication.'
'Keep scrolling,' was all Gunnar said.

'TMZ has managed to obtain footage taken by Honor during her and Cellan's recent wild weekend at thousand-dollars-a-night spa, Gurney's in Montauk, during which she can clearly be heard sharing her glee at having hoodwinked the actor into taking her along.'

When I made no move to press play on the video, Gunnar leant over and did it for me. I quailed in horror as the sound of my own whispering voice filtered out into the empty conference suite, and a wobbly film taken inside our hotel room filled the screen of the iPad. I remembered now that I had provided commentary while I made my way around, thinking it would be funny to send it to Jojo.

'Do you think these sheets are Egyptian cotton?' I heard myself say. 'Only the very best for me if you don't mind.'

I winced at my own stupidity and immaturity.

The footage panned over to the minibar, and I could be heard mumbling something about pretzels, before turning the phone so my face was clearly in view.

'Shall I empty the whole lot into my bag?' I giggled. 'Money is no object after all.'

Behind me, I felt Cellan shift. I dared not look at him, at either of them.

Having turned the camera back around, it caught the moment that Cellan had emerged from the bathroom, his shirt open and a towel covering the lower half of his face. The film blurred as I tossed the phone onto the bed, but it landed at the perfect angle to record the two of us kissing. Gunnar tutted, but I could not so much as blink, such was my paralysing fear and self-loathing.

'Care to explain how this found its way onto the internet?' prompted Gunnar, his self-satisfied tone snapping me out of my horrified trance.

'I have no idea,' I said quietly, looking desperately at Cellan. He still had his arms folded, and his face was set. 'I would never . . . that stuff I said, it was a joke. I was going to send it to my friend Jojo for a laugh.'

'But instead you sent it to *TMZ*?' Cellan countered icily.

'No,' I pleaded. 'I didn't. It wasn't me; I must have been hacked. People can do that nowadays, can't they? Stand next to you with some kind of device in their pocket which downloads all the data on your phone.'

'Even if that were true, it doesn't explain how these so-called diary entries got out,' said Gunnar drily. 'I'm afraid, as they say, you've been caught with your fingers in the bait tin, and now you're on the hook.'

The man really was obsessed with all things nautical.

'Cellan,' I said, grabbing his rigid arms. 'You know me, you know I wouldn't do this. Why would I? It makes me look like a complete—'

'User?' he suggested tersely. 'I know you're desperate to impress your bloody father, but there are better ways of going about it than shacking up with me. You think you'll be successful by association, is that it?'

'No,' I insisted, my voice wobbling treacherously, but Cellan merely shook his head.

'I trusted you,' he murmured, the hurt and confusion he so obviously felt manifesting itself cruelly on his open, handsome face. 'You made me believe that— How could you do this? How could you do this to us?'

The 'us' was too great a wound, and I felt myself buckle as sobs rose.

'I didn't,' I said beseechingly, but Cellan was walking away from me, ashen faced as he fought to stay calm.

'I can't do this,' he said. 'I don't— I can't see you again, Honor. I'm sorry.'

'No!' It was nearly a scream. 'Cellan, I didn't do this. You have to believe me.'

He had reached the door and turned to look at me one final time.

'I did believe you,' he said. 'I really, really did.'

The door closed behind him, and I lurched forwards only to be caught by Gunnar, his hand clamping around my arm.

'Let him go,' he said. 'Poor kid, he's been through enough crap.'

'Get off me,' I cried, twisting and pulling to get free. Gunnar did not move, waiting until I had exhausted myself before he spoke again.

'You were never in his league, honey,' he said. 'Like I said to you before, Cellan had a few things he needed to get out of his system this summer, and you provided a nice distraction for him. But that's over now. You didn't play by the rules, and this is the consequence.'

'What the hell are you talking about?' I raged, glaring at him. 'This isn't some stupid game, it's real life.'

'This is Cellan's real life,' he intoned. 'Not yours. For you, all this has been a fantasy. And if you've got even half the sense of your old man,' he went on, the menacing edge in his voice making me go cold, 'you'll respect Cellan's decision. The kid has made it very clear that he's done with you. Now, I have places to be, people to see,' he added, finally letting go of my arm. 'You give your father my best, won't you?'

I stayed where I was, motionless with defeat, while Gunnar collected his damaging pieces of evidence and left the room. I was too wrung out to cry, but I could feel the tears building like a tsunami inside me. Wrapping my arms around my shaking body, I hugged myself as tightly as I could bear and let rip a scream of anguish that seemed to echo off the walls. Crumpling over onto the carpet, I brought my knees up to my chest, rocking backwards and forwards as the sobs wracked through me. Something hard was digging into me, and I reached shakily into the back pocket of my shorts, confusion turning to even greater sorrow as I stared at my hand.

It was the speckled cockle shell I had picked up on the beach in Montauk, smashed into tiny pieces.

48

Such was my despair as I headed across the city that I did not register much beyond the few metres unspooling in front of me. I didn't stop to apologise when I bashed into people, nor did I give more than a cursory glance into the road before stepping out to a chorus of car horns. My sole focus had become finding out who was behind these devastating leaks, and I had a fairly good idea of where to start.

'Dad,' I called, as I let the apartment door bang shut behind me. A framed photo of my father laughing alongside a solemn-faced Stephen King fell off the wall and went crashing to the floor.

I ignored it.

'Dad,' I called again. 'Are you here?'

He emerged from his office as I reached the lounge area, dressed in beige cords and an olive-green shirt.

'Honor? What's with the ruckus?'

'Tallulah,' I threw at him. 'Where does she live?'

'Somewhere in New Jersey I think – why?'

'Because I need to speak to her, and she's still refusing to answer the bloody phone.'

'What's the urgency?' he asked. 'Is it something I can help with?'

'No, it's—' I stopped as a sob threatened to overwhelm me. 'I think Tallulah has been going through my private documents and selling information to the press.'

My father laughed in disbelief.

'It's not funny, Dad. There's a video and ... Cellan said that ...' I wrung my hands together. 'Stuff is out there that only I had, things only I knew, but I didn't tip off the press. The only other person who could have hacked into my phone or my laptop,' I said, making a grab for it and hurriedly tapping in my password, 'is Tallulah. And the more I think about it, the more it makes sense. Aha,' I said, turning the computer around so he could see. 'My photos and videos have synched automatically into my library on here, so she could have got to them without ever needing to touch my phone.'

'Slow down a minute here, honey.' My father scooted down beside me on the couch. 'What exactly are you accusing Tallulah of doing?'

'I don't know – spying on me for starters. She said she was a writer, but had you ever heard of her before this summer? More likely she's an undercover reporter, sent to infiltrate your life only to stumble fortuitously into Cellan's. Come to think of it, wasn't it her idea to rent a house in The Hamptons? She must have had insider knowledge that Cellan was there, too. Then, all she had to do was try and engineer an introduction, which, as it turned out, came a lot easier than she was hoping. I thought it was strange that she recognised Cellan so easily that day on the beach – she clearly knew he'd be there. Someone must have tipped her off. Maybe she and Cherry are in it together? Cherry's probably promised to get her into some parties if she helps tarnish my reputation. She's always hated me,' I added furiously.

'Tallulah doesn't hate you,' tempered my father.

'I meant Cherry.'

'I'm sure nobody hates you, honey.'

'Then why try to destroy me? What did I ever do to deserve my life being ruined?'

My father stuttered out a little laugh. 'You're exaggerating,' he said soothingly. 'So, a few photos and videos went out into the world – so what? It's not like you made a sex tape with the guy.'

I paled at the thought.

'I'm not going to let her get away with it,' I said firmly. 'I want to ask her why, and I want to see her face when she answers.'

'This has nothing to do with Tallulah,' he said, but I was not listening.

'Cole appearing when he did was ever so convenient, wasn't it? He never did say who he was, did he? I bet he's just some lackey employed by *TMZ*, and when he turned up, Tallulah knew she'd been rumbled, so she fled.'

'You've got this wrong,' said my father, so matter-of-factly that I paused mid-rant.

'How can you be so sure?' I demanded. 'I know you think she idolises you, but I thought you were grown-up enough to see past your own massive ego.'

'Hey,' he snapped. 'That's enough.'

I reddened at the telling-off, but I had gone beyond the point where I could be corralled by words alone. Taking a moment, I stood up from the sofa and went across to the window, desperately searching for solace among the Tetras-like landscape.

'We don't know her,' I said quietly. 'Not really. She could be anyone.'

'I know her,' he said, not looking at me.

I remembered Cole's shouted accusation, how he had been so sure that Tallulah and my father had been carrying on together. I thought of the champagne opened in the middle of the day, the sense I'd had on that same day that the house was holding its breath, how strange Tallulah had seemed when she finally emerged, mumbling something about a phone call from home. Then there was the night they stayed over in the city, and all the times I'd heard the sound of tiptoeing feet, as she presumably crept from his bedroom back to her own. The clues had been there all along, but I had not seen them. I had been too caught up in my own drama.

'You and Tallulah?'

My father closed his eyes briefly. 'Yes.'

My hands gripped the windowsill behind me. 'All summer?'

He shook his head. 'Nothing happened until we got to the Hamptons. Hell, you almost caught us the first time. I had to make up a story about her getting her nails done.'

'You didn't have to lie to me at all,' I pointed out, to which he gave me a scornful look. 'Really? Is that the kind of conversation you want to have across the dinner table with your old man? And even if I had wanted to tell you,' he went on, interrupting before I had the chance to argue, 'I wouldn't have known what to say. Tallulah and me, we never talked about what we were doing, we just did.'

'Actions outweigh words,' I intoned. 'That sounds about right for you.'

'Honor, listen, none of this,' he said, gesturing towards my laptop, 'has anything to do with Tally. I don't know why she upped and left the way she did, but she's a good person.'

'But then if Tallulah didn't—'

The truth, when it dawned, made me feel faint with nausea. 'You? You're the one?'

My father's phone started to ring from inside his office, the jaunty tempo of the *Pink Panther* theme tune grotesquely at odds with the mood that had fallen over the room.

'I should get that,' he said, making to stand. 'Might be important.'

'More important than this conversation?' I said appalled.

He didn't answer. I watched him hurry along the hallway, then heard the click of a lock. It was instinct, more than reasoning, that made me follow him, and having reached the closed door, I pressed my ear against the wood.

'He's going to sign? Well, at least some good has come from all this. You were right, he really needed that extra nudge, didn't he?'

There was a pause, during which I hardly dared breathe.

'It's not as if there wasn't enough green laid out for him. I know. Yeah, it's unfortunate, but she'll get over it. You know what kids are like. OK. Sure thing.'

I heard him ring off, but I did not bother to move from my position behind the door. When my father opened it a second later, he jumped as if Tasered.

'Who is going to sign what?' I demanded. 'And what's unfortunate?'

'Now, honey—'

'Don't "now, honey" me. You were talking about Cellan and your bloody film, weren't you? You and Gunnar have cooked this whole thing up for what? Manipulate Cellan into taking on a role he doesn't want?'

'I'd argue that he does want it, given how he's agreed to sign the contracts today,' said my father, stepping around me and stalking towards the kitchen. I stood in seething silence as he fetched himself a glass and tossed in some ice cubes, before topping it up with a large measure of Maker's Mark.

'He told me he hated the character,' I said, relishing the fact that I had something in my arsenal that I knew would hurt him. I no longer cared what he thought of me, and the sensation was one of a balloon having its string snipped. I was untethered.

'According to Cellan, Marty Stamp lacks depth, has no soul, and treats women like crap. Did you mean to base him on yourself?'

The look my father threw me was venomous.

'And I'm guessing I'm the "she" who will "get over it",' I went on, raising my hands to indicate sarcastic speech marks. 'Get over what exactly? The fact that my own father sold stories about me, or that the kindest, sweetest, and most wonderful man I have ever met no longer wants anything to do with me?'

'I gave Gunnar access to the diary you were keeping, but I didn't speak to the press until much later along, once the story was already out there. Cellan is the one who screwed all this up,' he muttered, taking his drink to the sofa, and sitting down heavily in the seat he had not long ago vacated. 'If he'd only agreed to the part sooner, then nobody would have had to resort to any kind of tactics. The problem is, the kid thinks too highly of himself, which I guess left Gunnar with no choice but to force him to question his own judgement.'

'By making it seem as if I was lying to him?'

'That was unfortunately a price he deemed worth paying – and after some initial misgivings, I began to see how it could benefit you.'

'How?' I mouthed, barely coherent in my astonishment, 'could this possibly benefit me?'

My father sipped his whiskey, neck flushed purple and face blotchy.

'You wanted success,' he pointed out. 'This is the fastest way to reach it. You won't have any trouble getting a book deal now that you've become a somebody. If anything, honey, you should be thanking Gunnar. I had to slog for years to get a gig.'

'I wanted success, yes,' I said despairingly. 'But on my own merit.'

'I read your diary,' he said laconically. 'Your dossier on Cellan was pretty damn detailed for someone who wasn't planning to use it for their own gains. You told me outright that you'd considered basing a character on him, so don't go pretending that you're the innocent victim in all this.'

Bruised by his accusations into silence, I sank into a chair and closed my eyes. I needed to shut out the world while I examined my own motives, picked apart what he'd said to see if there was any truth hiding beneath the surface. I'd collected what could be construed as notes on Cellan, but I never intended to use them for personal gain. It was more that I was collaging our time together into a memory that I could look back on once the summer had ended, pore over the account of our time together and allow it to inspire my writing. It had felt joyful, but did that make me, as Gunnar had declared, nothing better than a fantasist? A teenage girl trapped in the body of a thirty-two-year-old woman, one who had put life, love, everything aside to pursue the approval of a man whom now she could no longer bear to look at?

I had always done everything for my father. Now, I realised, it was time to stop. In handing over my diary to Gunnar and colluding with him so despicably, he had betrayed me in the worst possible way, and he didn't even seem to realise it.

My father was staring into his whiskey glass, but he raised his eyes to mine as I stood. 'Where are you going?' he said, as I bent to pick up my laptop, shoving it, my phone, and a nest of charging cables into my ragged tote bag.

'I don't know,' I told him, making my way towards the front door without a backward glance. 'But anywhere would be better than here with you.'

49

The leafy borough of New Milford lay towards the northern end of New Jersey, far enough away from Manhattan to feel separate, yet close enough to reap all the benefits of a big city. All this Tallulah told me in the few moments after I arrived at her house, which was a two-storey wood-panelled abode with a neat, tapered roof. The front garden was littered with toys, including a small tricycle, several push-along plastic trucks, and a rather moth-eaten football. A tyre swing hung from a tree, and on a hook just inside the front door, I noticed a child's red anorak.

Tallulah herself looked worn out. She was wearing faded denim cut-offs and a white tank top that had started to lose its shape, and there was what looked like ink stains on her fingers.

'Thanks for letting me come over,' I said, wiping my feet on the mat and following her into the bowels of the house.

'That's OK,' she said. 'You sounded kind of frantic in that message you left me. Coffee?'

I went to say yes, then changed my mind. 'I've drunk so much coffee over the past twenty-four hours. I don't think I can stomach much more of the stuff.'

'Thank God for that,' Tallulah said lightly. 'Because I've just remembered that we're out of filters. Listen, this place is a mess.'

'It's fine,' I said automatically, averting my eyes from the dirty dishes piled up in the sink, the cereal box tipped over on its side, and the remains of something that may once have been pork chops festering on the cooker.

Tallulah looked around.

'No,' she said. 'It's really not. Come on, we can walk and talk.'

The streets felt quiet after the bustle of Chelsea, and I moved to the side as a dog trailing its lead stopped to pee in a flowerbed. The threat of summer rain hung heavy in air that smelt faintly of woodsmoke and cut grass, the only sounds the soft slap of our shoes against the pavement.

'You seem different,' I said, as we reached the end of the block and crossed the road. There was a deli on the corner up ahead, with red awning and a cluster of chairs set up outside.

'Different how?' she asked, glancing at me.

'Subdued,' I told her.

Tallulah smiled sheepishly. 'I'm exhausted,' she said. 'Jackson has just turned three, and at that age the batteries just keep on going. He's adorable, but a lot.'

'Is Jackson your son?'

She turned to me, not shocked but amused.

'I guess it makes sense that you would assume that, but no, he's not mine. Jackson is my nephew.'

'Oh,' I said, drawing out the word as I joined together the dots. 'So, that means Cole is your . . . ?'

'Baby brother.'

'Right. I see. Well, I don't completely see.'

'You want anything?' We had reached the deli.

'Diet Coke would be nice – but I'll buy.'

Tallulah shooed me away. 'No chance,' she said. 'You came all the way out here. The least I can do is treat you to a soda.'

I waited while she went inside, taking a moment to assimilate.

'You look as if you're trying to work out a really tough Sudoku,' she remarked, emerging with a brown paper bag, a takeaway coffee cup, and my drink, which was blessedly ice cold. Clumps of off-white cloud had begun to mass in the sky, and Tallulah stuck out a hand as if checking for rain.

'I reckon we've got a bit of time before it starts drizzling,' she said, before gesturing to an area of green park on the opposite side of the road. 'Shall we sit?'

There was a bandstand set back from the pathway, its white painted boards and draped American flag reminding me of Southampton, and Tallulah let out a small groan of relief as she lowered herself onto its wooden steps.

'Feels good to take the load off.'

I cracked open my can and took a sip, recoiling with a splutter as the bubbles went up my nose. I felt calmer here, out in the suburbs, having put some distance between myself and my father. Other than telling Tallulah the headline facts in the rambling voicemail I had left her a few hours ago, I had yet to convey exactly what had transpired, and now I felt oddly reluctant to start. My head throbbed from thinking about it, the anger that had been so potent now depleting, leaving a residual numb misery in its wake. For at least the length of time it took me to finish my Diet Coke, I wanted to focus on someone and something else.

'Why did you just run away?' I asked, resting my elbows on my bent knees.

Tallulah had crossed her legs at the ankle, and her foot began to twitch up and down as she spoke. 'I guess I was embarrassed. It's never nice to be caught out in a lie. I knew you'd both think badly of me, and I simply couldn't face it.'

'Why would we think badly of you?'

Tallulah picked at the lid of her coffee cup.

'I was being selfish,' she said. 'Thinking I could put myself first and to hell with everyone else. I knew Cole needed me, but I just kept on pretending he didn't, like he would cope fine without me all summer.'

She must have seen the question in my expression – I wanted to know why it was her job to help raise her brother's son.

'Cole was married to my best friend, Hayley. She and I were besties from the first day of kindergarten, and I loved her so much that I didn't even mind when she hooked up with my brother. You'd think it would be weird, but I always understood why he loved her, and the day they got married was such a happy one for our families. Hayley and Cole tried for a baby for years; I took on extra work to help them pay for IVF, and my own parents cashed in their savings. When she finally got pregnant with Jackson and made it past those first twelve weeks, we were all overjoyed. He felt like a miracle.'

I had read enough novels to sense when a story was about to take a dark turn and braced myself. Seeing her like this had reminded me of the inkling I'd had, way back at the start of my strange American summer, that Tallulah was over-compensating for something sad or traumatic that had happened in her past. She took a moment to gather herself together, her fingers still picking at the plastic edge of the lid.

'The cancer got diagnosed when she was four months along, and of course she refused to start treatment until after the baby arrived. We all supported her decision, although in my angrier moments, I found myself wishing that the pregnancy had failed. And I know that makes me sound like a monster, but it just felt so unfair.'

'It doesn't make you sound like a monster at all,' I said. 'It makes you sound human.'

'She died six months after Jackson was born,' said Tallulah, turning to face me.

I touched a gentle hand to hers. 'I'm sorry.'

She nodded furiously, managing to keep her tears at bay, then groaned.

'Hell,' she said. 'It still hurts so much. You'd think it would ease, but ...' She shrugged. 'It's like someone has stuck a knife in me, and I'm supposed to just carry on, go about my business as usual, even though everything I do causes me pain. It doesn't seem to matter if I'm happy or sad, the agony of losing Hayley is this constant thing.'

I winced in sympathy.

'Cole went to pieces of course. He'd been so strong, and then as soon as she passed, all that fell away. He had this little baby and no money ... I gave up my place and moved in with them, tried the best I could, but I was struggling. Books and reading and writing had always been my solace, but I no longer had time for either; it wasn't until the start of this year that the fog cleared a bit, and I sent JB that message. I never expected for a moment that he would reply, let alone that we would—'

She stopped abruptly, looking at me fearfully.

'It's OK,' I said. 'I know that you and he were ... Well, I know a bit.'

'I'm sorry I never told you,' she said. 'It was complicated. We never gave what was happening between us a label, so even if I had blurted it all out to you one day – and believe me, there were times when I really wanted to – I wouldn't have known which words to use.'

'It's OK,' I assured her. 'I understand.'

Tallulah smiled briefly before continuing. 'Being with Jeffrey made me feel like myself for the first time in years. It was so nice to spend time with another adult and not be discussing diapers, or sleep patterns, or the best ways to deal with tantrums. I love my nephew, but motherhood was never something I wanted, and Jeffrey . . .' She trailed off, but I knew what she had been about to say.

'Understood that?' I finished, and she sighed. 'He didn't sign up for fatherhood either.'

'No,' she agreed. 'But he loves you.' She said this so fiercely that it startled me.

'He really does,' she went on. 'I know he's messed up, and you still need to tell me exactly what's happened, but underneath all the bluster, he's nuts about you.'

'I wish that were true,' I said, and Tallulah smiled encouragingly.

'It is true.'

I shook my head, and then, falteringly but thoroughly, I told her about the plan Gunnar had cooked up, and how my father had played his part in it.

'He did not say that to you!' she exclaimed, as I went over the conversation that I'd had with him shortly before I'd walked out.

I nodded grimly. 'He did.'

I'd shown her the video from Gurney's, at which she'd clenched her teeth with discomfort, agreeing that it looked 'pretty bad'.

'The worst thing is all the stuff I wrote about Cellan in my diary was like I was an obsessed fan or something. Even if I explain that it was my father who showed it all to Gunnar – which I can't do now without causing serious trouble for both of them, given how Cellan has agreed to star in this movie – I still have to come up with a valid reason as to why I was making such detailed notes of everything he ever told me.'

'But Honor, you're a writer – it's what we do.'

I frowned. 'It is?'

Tallulah put down her shredded coffee cup. 'Do you want to know the best thing that's happened since I ran out on JB? I've started writing. And I don't mean that claptrap I was pretending to enjoy drafting out in The Hamptons, but a real story, based on my real experiences, full of characters that feel real to me. That's why I look so darn awful,' she added with a laugh. 'I'm writing all the time, half the night and during every gap I get to myself in the day. Cole took Jackson into the city this morning to visit Central Park Zoo, and I should by rights have cleaned the house, but instead I went back to my notebook.'

'Until I interrupted you,' I said regretfully.

Tallulah pressed her shoulder against mine. 'You're worth it.'

I smiled, then let out a roar of frustration so loud that several birds flew out of the surrounding trees.

'Sorry,' I said, as Tallulah started to laugh. 'I'm just so . . . argh. I don't know what to do, or how to even start to fix everything that's gone wrong, or even if it's worth trying. Maybe I should do what Gunnar said and just accept that summer is over.'

'You mustn't do anything that awful man tells you to do,' she said firmly, and this time I laughed, albeit rather ruefully. 'I think the only way of making sense of all this, Honor, is to do what you do best.'

'Which is?'

Tallulah reached across and tucked my hair behind my ear. 'Write about it,' she said.

50

For three days, in the spare bedroom of Tallulah and Cole's house, dressed in borrowed clothes and armed with little more than my laptop, I wrote my story.

The world, as I was learning, could wait a while, and other than a few text-message exchanges with my mother and Jojo, I did not so much as glance at my phone. Nor did I look at any of the gossip sites or read any newspapers. When my father rang, late on the first evening, Tallulah answered, taking my mobile into the back garden and staying there for almost an hour.

'He understands,' she said upon her return. 'Says he's ready to talk when you are.'

Jeffrey Butler, it appeared, had finally learned how to be patient.

When I needed a coffee refill or a screen break, I ventured out of my box room and spent joyful half hours playing with Jackson, who was every bit as smart, kooky, and adorable as his aunt. Cole, although clearly broken was entirely decent, and I was forced to tell him off the third time he attempted to apologise. I understood why he had panicked at the thought of his sister being lured away but hoped that the two of them would find their way towards having a real conversation about the future.

'I've said I'll stay until Jackson starts kindergarten,' was Tallulah's response when I asked, adding that, 'by then,

I might even have finished something worth publishing.'

We didn't talk about her relationship with my father, but I knew they were back in regular contact, and often heard the trail of her laughter when she was chatting to him on the phone.

But while Tallulah's goal of securing a book deal kept her motivated, my own work was fuelled by a different yearning. As I wrote about my weeks with Cellan, I started to find clarity amid the mess and meaning in among all the miscommunications. Things became clear, chief among them my feelings towards him. I could not deny them any longer, and what was more, I didn't want to.

It was at the end of the third day that I had my idea.

Tallulah walked me to the first of three buses I would take to reach my destination, and I clung to her as we hugged, reluctant to let go.

'You know you can come straight back here if you need to?'

'Your generosity is humbling,' I told her. 'But if this doesn't work, then I think it'll be best all round if I go home.'

'You always told me that New York was your second home,' she reminded me. 'Maybe New Milford could be your third?'

I smiled. 'Maybe it already is.'

It was late afternoon by the time I got to the car park behind Main Street, and I took the passage alongside the hardware store, coming out at the exact spot Cellan had crashed into me on that first, fateful day. I did not allow myself to dawdle, instead continuing past The Fudge Company sweet shop, Tennis East sporting goods, and all the way up to the Golden Pear Café. Southampton was exactly as I'd left it – sun-dappled, beautifully adorned, and spotlessly clean – but I was changed. I no longer felt compelled to gaze wistfully into shop windows at garments I couldn't afford, hankering after a status that would allow me to buy them. Things and stuff were never going to make me happy; Cellan had been right all along.

Arriving at the house, I paused in the gap between the conifers and stared up at the weather-beaten boards and white-edged windows. The sky beyond the slanting roof was floured with sparse cloud, and birds sang jauntily to one another as they perched high on the power lines. Instinct told me not to bother knocking at the front door, and when I rounded the side of the house, I found my father where I'd known he would be, in a chair on the back porch. Hearing me approach, he turned.

'Hello,' I said. 'You're here.'

'You know I like to get my money's worth.'

The remark was light-hearted enough, but the tone in which it was delivered fell short of convincing me that he was in a jovial mood. He looked, now that I was standing right in front of him, depleted somehow. Not like himself at all. The jeans he had on were tatty, the T-shirt stained, and he was wearing slippers instead of proper shoes. From the inch of stubble on his face and the sallow tinge of his skin, I could see he'd been neglectful when it came to self-care and guessed it likely that he'd also been hitting the bottle. Jeffrey Butler was not accustomed to losing, and he did not wear it well.

'Tallulah told me you wanted to talk,' I prompted, putting down my bags before propping myself on the step.

My father's chair creaked as he got up and came to sit beside me. 'You're wearing one of her dresses,' he said.

'Didn't have much choice. I left most of my clothes here. We were only supposed to be in the city for one night.'

'I took your glam rags to the dry cleaner,' he said, and I had to smile at that.

'It's *glad* rags.'

'I figured it was the least I could do, after . . .'

'After?'

'I should never have read your diary, let alone showed it around,' he said. 'I overstepped, and I'm sorry.'

'Why did you read it in the first place?' I asked.

'Because I'm a nosy old bastard,' he replied, glancing at me hopefully only to look disappointed when he failed to elicit a smile.

'I didn't realise what it was at first,' he said. 'I thought maybe it was another book you were writing and then, once I began reading, I found that I couldn't stop. You really are a great writer,' he added, but I was not in the mood to be mollified by praise and motioned for him to continue.

'Gunnar had told me that Cellan was keen to toss in the towel on movie acting for good, and so he needed to find a way to make him question his own judgement – called it "a little nudge". I mentioned your diary in passing, said there seemed to be an awful lot of personal information about Cef in there, and he leapt on it right away, told me that all I had to do was send over a few excerpts and he would take care of the rest.'

My father shook his head. 'I told myself I was doing it for your sake,' he said, sounding wretched. 'But Tallulah has since made me realise that I acted like a selfish, self-interested prick.'

'She made you admit that?' I said in surprise. 'Go, Tallulah.'

He smiled rather ruefully. 'The pair of you have me all figured out, don't you?'

'If only . . .' I muttered. 'I wish you'd spoken to me about all this stuff, Dad, instead of going behind my back.'

'I should have, honey. There are so many things I should have done. My life is full of damn shoulds.'

'Tell me some of them.'

'Well, I should have treated your mother better for starters.'

I had not been expecting that. 'She always said it was amicable between you both?'

'It was,' he said. 'It is. But only because Jennifer accepted the fact that I was incapable of being a father. The day she told me she was expecting you . . . hell, I have never been so terrified in my whole life. It was easier for me to simply duck out and toss a load of money at the problem, but what I should have done was moved there, been there for both of you in a meaningful way, the way Tallulah has for her little nephew. All I had to do was be your dad, and I failed at it before I even tried.'

I had never heard my father put himself and failure into the same sentence; as far as I was concerned, the failure had always been on my side. I had failed to be enough for him, and then failed to impress him when we did finally meet. As I tried to explain this to him, he seemed to crumple.

'All this time, you've been feeling like a failure and so have I,' he said, shaking his head before rubbing a weary hand across his face. 'Every year when you visit, it feels as if you arrive with this flashing neon sign that reads: useless father.'

'I feel as if there's a flashing neon sign in your apartment that reads: disappointing daughter,' I said.

He shook his head slowly once again, raising a hand to fiddle with the chain attached to his glasses 'How could I ever be disappointed by you, Honor?'

'You always seem so critical,' I said, squirming with discomfort at having broached this previously undiscussed subject with him. 'And the older I get, the more you seem to avoid spending time with me. I always thought that if I could just get a book published, then you might begin to view me not as an equal, but at least a colleague. And I did try, Dad, I really did. I tried to be like you, but it never worked.'

'Well,' he said heavily, 'thank the lord for that. You don't want to be like me, honey.'

'But you're happy,' I protested, the last word falling rather flat as he raised an eyebrow. 'Or you were, before all this happened. You have your career, your success, a movie coming out.'

'What I am a lot of the time is lonely,' he replied. 'And I may have success, but it's all an act, all that bravado. I'm aware that my characters are two-dimensional, probably because I'm two-dimensional – one of those classic bone-headed bachelors that think the world must be at fault rather than them. Me and Tallulah have been talking,' he added, seeing my look of incredulity. 'That woman can read me like . . . well, I won't use the pun. I am a writer after all.'

I responded with a rather limp smile.

'She's made me face some things, about myself and how I've been handling life – or not handling it. It seems I have some work to do, and I wanted to start with you. I meant what I said to you before, honey – there is nobody that means more to me than you. And I should have respected the way you felt about Cellan, instead of using the pair of you. It's not like I didn't know you had fallen for him.'

He rubbed his hands across his face in agitation.

'I appreciate your apology,' I said quietly. 'But I can't simply forget what happened, and all the hurtful things you've said to me. I want to understand, and I want to forgive, but it's going to take some time.'

My father picked up my hands in his; they were warm and dry, stained with ink as Tallulah's had been.

'You've been writing,' I said, my voice breaking as I fought to contain my emotions.

'A new project,' he confided, squeezing my fingers. 'A love story.'

'What?' I exclaimed, pretending to fall off the step with shock.

My father smiled, and for a moment, he looked truly happy. 'Thought it was about time I tried something different, something braver,' he intoned, not looking at me.

'And how are you finding it?' I asked, stretching out my feet to be warmed by the sun. The grass had grown in the time I had been away, and I could see the purple hue of the thistles that bordered the walls of the old shed. Pollen motes hung in the air, insects darted, and from somewhere far away came the drone of a passing plane.

My father considered the question for a few minutes, and then he chuckled.

'I'm starting to realise that all this romance baloney isn't as easy as I thought.'

'Finally!' I said triumphantly, and he rolled his eyes.

'Would you take a look at it for me?' he asked. 'Maybe give me a few pointers?'

'Er, yes – I guess I could,' I said, thinking how futile an exercise it had been to try and plot my life. So many years I'd spent chasing what I thought was my next chapter, when all along I should simply have waited for the twist in the tale to come.

'Shall I fetch it now?' my father asked, getting to his feet, and pulling me up along with him. Standing one step below me, his face was on a level with mine; we were equal for what felt like the first time.

'It will have to be later,' I said. 'There's something important that I need to do first.'

51

In a bid to cheer me up following the total implosion of my
life, Jojo had begun sending me daily funny videos to watch,
things such as cats being scared by cucumbers, old people
dancing at raves, and a Bristolian lad falling over on a muddy
path, the latter of which saw me lay down on the floor in
Tallulah's spare room and weep tears of mirth. It was through
these forays onto YouTube that I became inspired to make a
video of my own, only mine would not be for likes or laughs,
but for a completely different purpose.

I had a story to tell, and an audience of one that I hoped
would want to hear it.

Having set up the laptop so the camera was facing me, I
arranged myself on a chair in the bedroom and took a deep,
fortifying breath. This was not within the remit of usual
behaviour for me, but I was determined to see it through. I
remembered what my mother had said to me all those weeks
ago – *Failure is only guaranteed if you don't even try. The only
way you can know for sure if anything will work out is by giving
it your best shot. That's all any of us can do. If you never try,
you'll never know* – and it was her words I had in my head as
I reached across and clicked the record button.

'Hey,' I said, braving a smile. 'I hope you don't mind me
sending you this. What I have to say is too long for a text
message, and I was concerned that if I called you, I'd be too

scared to say what I needed to, or that you would interrupt me with questions. That's if you even answered my call in the first place, which seems unlikely.'

I cleared my throat, trying my best not to focus on the image of myself staring back. I had never even filmed myself for a social media post before and was a very long way from my comfort zone.

'This talking to camera thing is quite hard, isn't it?' I went on. 'I have no idea how you do it for a living. You're probably wondering why I've chosen to put myself – and you – through this ordeal, and the truth is, I have a story I want to tell you. So much of this summer has been about other people's versions of us, whether that's our friends, the bloody press, or your many fans. The weight of expectation, of assumption, and all the pressure that has come with it . . . it's been a lot. I think we both lost sight of who we were, at least in relation to each other, because of all that noise. And that's why I wanted to tell you my version of events, right here and now, with no interruptions. I want you to know me, and to understand why I am the way I am. I need to explain how meeting you has freed me from all the stupid self-sabotage I've been inflicting on myself. I'd been doing it for so long that it had become an actual trait of my personality, one that would have corroded me entirely in the end.'

I paused for a moment, taking a few deep breaths as I prepared what to say next.

'In order to properly tell you my story of us, I have to share one about myself. And to do that, I have to start at the very beginning, with a little girl walking into a restaurant, about to meet her father for the very first time . . .'

Once finished, I didn't watch it. After checking the viewing options were set to private and copying the video link into my email, I copied and pasted it across from my phone into a message, typed out a few lines of text, and then, before my courage abandoned me completely, I pressed send.

An hour passed, and then another. I read the first three chapters of my father's new book – about a man who finds love in his mid-sixties – and was surprised how receptive he was to my feedback. Tallulah rang for a chat, then I called Jojo, content to listen as she updated me on how things were progressing with fish boy.

'I think we should start calling him Sam,' she said coyly, 'given that he's now my boyfriend.'

There was no reply from the recipient of my video message when I checked before we ate dinner, and nothing when the plates had been washed and tidied away. My father opened a bottle of wine as it started to rain, and we sat in the lounge with the windows open, a candle flickering on the table as the radio scratched out some jazz.

I went up to bed and fell into a dreamless sleep, waking to a blank screen and a heart less hopeful. A day unfolded around a schedule of blissful nothingness, as I wandered from room to room, picking up books only to put them down after reading a few lines. I contemplated baking a cake before cycling instead to the bakery, the air cool against my neck, thighs burning with effort. Zoltar stared motionless at me from his glass box, hydrangeas sang with colour, and all the while my phone lay dormant in my pocket, a stubborn reminder of all the things that could remain unsaid.

I began day three uncertain, ended it with a resolve to delete my social media accounts. I wanted to close the door on the prying eyes of strangers, and not provide any journalists or begrudged fans with a portal upon which to reach me should they ever want to again. It was a very small price to pay, and as soon as I had done it, I felt immeasurably better, as if I'd let go of all the worry regarding what other people thought of me. I knew myself now, and more than that, I accepted who I was. For the first time in my life, I could say with complete conviction that I liked the person staring back at me from the mirror each morning, and that alone felt like a huge achievement.

One more day, I told myself, and then I must accept what the silence was telling me, yet the thought of doing so made me feel weak with sorrow. Loathing myself, I returned to the internet, searching for any mention or suggested whereabouts, then took my bike out to the house on Great Plains Road, daring to dream but finding nothing but a locked gate, and a buzzer that went unanswered.

Five days after I had recorded my story, my father drove to New Jersey, coming back the following morning plump with all the happiness that I feared had become elusive for me. *Strange,* I wrote that night, as I had taken to doing when I could not sleep, *how it is possible to recognise love in the eyes of others, its glow radiant enough that it demands the attention of everyone within its orbit.* I thought about all its forms and trickeries, how much it hurt and how well it could heal. I wanted to ignore love, but how could I? It was the only reassurance I had that all this had been worth it. Because even if I ended up with nothing but my memories, I would still have love.

And that, I knew, would never fail to inspire me.

Then, on the seventh day, something unexpected happened.

I'd just returned from a walk to find my father stomping around the front garden in circles, his phone pressed to his ear and an aggrieved expression on his face.

'Can he even do that?' he was saying, as I propped the bike against a tree. 'I thought the contract was watertight?'

Noticing me, he flapped his hand to beckon me over, then grasped my shoulder. I was hot from my sojourn around the village and desperate for some water, but when I tried to move, he gripped me tighter.

'I guess so, in that case,' he said, blinking furiously. 'Go with Hemsworth.'

Liam, Chris, or Luke, I wondered, but this did not feel like the right moment to ask. My father said a brusque goodbye to whoever had called, then turned to me.

'What's happened?' I asked, peering at him. 'You look as if you're in shock.'

'Cellan damn Thomas – he's quit the movie.'

My stomach shrunk abruptly to the size of a walnut. 'What?' I stammered. 'When?'

'This morning, allegedly. The whole cast turned up for the first read-through and he was a no-show. Cindy, that's my contact at the production company, said she tried to get hold of Gunnar, only to be told that he no longer represents him. They eventually tracked down Cef's former publicist – you know that Cherry woman – and she passed on his number. Cellan then answered, and said he's very sorry, but there's a scheduling conflict and he would be returning his fee.'

'He's quit the film and Gunnar – and Cherry?'

My father released my shoulder so he could rub his chin. 'Honey, did you tell him about . . . you know? It's OK if you did, I'm just trying to understand why—'

'No,' I said truthfully. 'I didn't. I haven't spoken to him, not directly anyway.'

As I said it, my phone buzzed in my bag. We both stared at it.

'It won't be him,' I said, rooting through the mess of receipts, biros, sun cream, empty water bottles and notepaper until I located the handset.

It was him.

I watched the video, he'd written. *Can I see you?*

I hesitated, fingers poised and heart racing with a mixture of relief and anxiety as I desperately tried to come up with the right response. Closing my eyes, I waited until an image emerged, making me smile as it came to me. There was only one place that felt right, and only one message I needed to send.

Meet me at the beach.

52

The stones crunched underfoot as I picked my way across the beach, the only other sounds the swooshing tide, and the gentle whistling of the wind. Above the lapis ocean, the sky was a paint chart of blues. Silver-tinged clouds lay scattered along the horizon, while behind me the lighthouse stood tall and splendidly proud, on its plinth of earth and rock.

I hadn't expected Cellan to arrive before me, though I recognised the distant figure on the shoreline at first glance. His shape had become so familiar to me, a study undertaken without any purpose other than to know him, as well and as deeply as it is possible to know a person. I stood still for a moment and watched him, savouring the final vestiges of the hope that had, for so many days, kept me striving. Cellan stooped to pick something up and examined it, turning it over in his hands before tossing it back into the shallows.

There was nobody else on the beach. We were alone.

I made myself continue and tried to keep my eyes on him, though it was difficult on the uneven ground. Glancing down in order to seek a less treacherous path, I looked up again to find him staring at me and raised a hand. Cellan followed my gesture of greeting with another of his own, though his was more tentative. I became aware of trepidation running like oil across the calm surface of my optimism, and faltered, coming to stop beside a blanched trunk of driftwood. Seeing me pause, he hesitated, a questioning expression on his face that I returned with a smile. With a final, fleeting look out across the water, he turned and made his way towards me.

'Fancy seeing you here,' I said as he neared.

Cellan responded with a short laugh. 'I heard it's a good spot to catch porgies.'

'What are they – those pigs that swim in the sea around The Bahamas?'

He smiled. 'Exactly right.'

'You look nice,' I told him. 'I always did like you dressed like Forrest Gump when he does that long run across America.'

Cellan glanced down at his Billabong T-shirt, blue board shorts and bedraggled Vans.

'Well, you know how I feel about Tom Hanks,' he said. 'And I thought this would be better than a cowboy hat and a pull-cord that makes me say things about snakes in boots. You look nice, too, by the way.'

I pulled out the skirt of my plain white dress self-consciously. 'Not sure this would suit Tom Hanks, but OK.'

'Shall we sit?' he suggested, and I nodded, waiting while he lowered himself onto the makeshift bench seat first, before perching beside him.

'How did you get here?' I asked. 'So quickly, I mean? I got straight in my father's car the moment I sent you that reply.'

'Jeffrey came with you?' he said, momentarily aghast.

I laughed. 'No, you plank. I can drive, you know.'

'I was at Maddy and Locryn's,' he explained. 'Been hiding out there for a while now.'

'You quit the film,' I said, and he grimaced.

'I quit a lot of things this week – the film, the house in Southampton, Gunnar, Cherry . . .'

'Shaving,' I added, and he gave me a sideways look.

'I didn't think there was time. I did clean my teeth, though,' he said, peeling back his lips to show me.

'I feel so special,' I deadpanned, and Cellan let his mouth droop down into a sad arch.

'So,' he said.

'So,' I replied.

'I watched your video.'

'And?'

Cellan waited until I stopped fussing with the laces of my trainer. I knew he wanted me to look at him, but suddenly, I found I couldn't bear to. The story I'd told him was the most honest, most real, and most *me* body of work I had ever created – there was a lot more on the line here than my ego.

'I loved it,' he said quietly, seriously. 'I really did.'

There was a pebble half-buried in the shingle, its smooth pink surface incongruous among the myriad browns and whites. Stretching a hand, I picked it up, brushing away the speckles of sand with my thumb.

'I would never have been able to tell it had it not been for you,' I said. 'I thought I was suffering from writer's block all these years, but it turned out to be an honesty block. As soon as I took a long, hard look at myself instead of pretending everything was fine, it was as if something opened up inside me. I never expected to learn so much about myself from writing.'

'You didn't really learn it,' he said. 'You had all the answers already, buried deep in your subconscious. Writing is merely the method you used to locate them. I know, because it's the same with acting, and the main reason I want to choose more roles that challenge me. You can explore so many of your own emotions within the safe confines of a character, as long as that character has enough layers.'

'Marty Stamp single-handedly takes over a Russian submarine using just his bare hands in that film you just turned down,' I reminded him. 'Is that just an average Tuesday for you?'

'Ha-ha,' he said flatly, grinning at me. 'I meant a mental challenge, not a physical one. Besides, you've seen me attempting to be macho, and I'm rubbish at it.'

'Have I?' I exclaimed.

'See!' He laughed. 'You weren't even aware of it.'

'I'm barely aware of my own name most of the time, so you shouldn't take it too personally.'

'I hope you're still planning to enter that story competition,' he said, frowning as I pulled a face. 'Why not? You have buckets of talent. You could even enter with the story you told me – I don't mind how many people read about us.'

'I won't be doing any such thing,' I said meditatively. 'That competition asks for the three opening chapters of a novel, plus a full synopsis.'

'And?'

'And I can't write a synopsis, or any more of the story, come to think of it. I do feel as if I have a decent chance of writing my stuntman book, though, but I want to take my time, not have the pressure of a judging panel.'

Cellan's brow was knotted with confusion.

'Why can't you use what you've already done?'

'Because,' I said, making myself meet his eyes, 'I don't know how the story ends.'

The look he gave me was searching, the two of us close enough that I could see the tiny flecks of gold in his irises.

'I'm so sorry,' I said, my voice catching as the words thundered out of me in an untidy torrent. 'About the bloody video I took in the hotel, and all the things I wrote about you in my diary, and the fact that my laptop password is the name of the bookshop my mother owns, and my phone passcode is one, two, three, four, five, six. I'm a complete idiot and a total liability, who can't be trusted with taking out the bins, let alone with people's secrets. I want you to know that it wasn't me who gave all the information to the press, but that I am culpable, if not by intent, then by stupidity.'

I could not bear to look at him and buried my face in my hands.

Cellan waited a few moments, then gently pulled down my arms. Unable to hide my face, I closed my eyes instead, feeling the heat rise in my cheeks.

'Honor,' he said, so softly that I braved a peek at him. 'I know you weren't behind the leak.'

'Gunnar told you the truth?' I guessed, but he shook his head.

'No. I think he was happy for me to think it was you, hence why . . . well, it doesn't matter; the less said about him, the better. I didn't need anyone to tell me, I worked it out for myself, by process of elimination.'

'I see . . .'

'I was confused at first,' he admitted, looking rather abashed. 'I should have trusted you straight away, I know that, but when you've spent years around people who see you as a commodity, it becomes hard to believe that genuine folk still exist. And I knew how you felt about success, how much it meant to you to impress Jeffrey. All that stuff you said about fame, and how fortunate I was, it played on my mind. I'd be lying to you if I said it hadn't. But then I told myself to focus not on what you'd said, but what you'd done,' he went on, as I tried not to crumple under the weight of my own short-sightedness, 'and then it all became so clear. Nobody can fake what we shared. I mean shit, Honor, I'm an Oscar winner, and even I would struggle to pull off a performance of the calibre that Gunnar and Cherry were telling me you had.'

'Any excuse to mention that Oscar . . .' I muttered and was gratified when he smiled.

'I did need some time, though,' Cellan went on. 'I saw your message, and I decided to wait a few days, because I wanted to be sure of my own feelings. I had to let all the trauma of what happened, and all the changes I'd made to my life in the wake of it settle. But I'm through the other side of that now, and I'm feeling positive about the future for the first time in what feels like far too long. I don't want to be an asset,' he said firmly. 'And I don't want to act purely in the interests of others if it means I'm short-changing myself on all the things that matter.'

Was I one of the things that mattered to him? I could barely breathe for longing it to be so.

'It sounds as if we both needed some time,' I said.

Cellan leaned back on the log, his legs so much longer than my own. 'Yes,' he said simply. 'We did.'

'I have missed you, though,' I told him, dropping my eyes as he looked at me. 'Nobody else tolerates my awful jokes half as heroically as you do.'

'I'm not sure that's a compliment,' he said. 'But strange as it may seem, I have missed them – both you and the bizarre humour.'

'If anyone here is bizarre, it's you,' I rebuffed. 'What kind of man takes the woman he fancies to the end of the world on their first proper date?'

'That's easy,' Cellan said, his shoulder warm as he pressed against me. 'A man who can see that life as he knows it is over.'

We turned towards each other at the same time, noses colliding over shared laughter, and I slid a timid hand into his.

'I never used to believe that moments like this could happen to people like me,' I said.

Cellan squeezed my fingers. 'I never used to believe that people like you could happen to moments like this,' he said.

'That's the great thing about the future,' I murmured. 'It's impossible to predict.'

'Elements of it maybe,' he agreed. 'But one thing I can tell you for certain is that I have decided to go home.'

'To LA?'

'Not to LA, dafty – real home, Cornwall, and I want you to come with me for what's left of the summer. Meet my family, see where I grew up, maybe even catch a few waves. How does that sound?'

'It sounds perfect,' I enthused. 'I would say come and stay with me in Cambridge afterwards, but one glance at my hoarder's nest of a flat, and you'd be off along King's Parade in a cloud of dust.'

Cellan chuckled. 'It's going to take more than a bit of mess to scare me off, and anyway, Cambridge is an easily commutable distance from London. If I'm going to be scouting around for a theatre project, then I'll need to be close by.'

'You really mean that?' I exclaimed in delight, and he smiled.

'I really do.'

A beat of time seemed to stretch out as we stared at each other, while the wind skipped over the stones. Gulls stood, sentry-like, upon rocks part-obscured by the sea, and behind us through the dunes, tough scraggy grass was bathed dry by the dipping sun. Not a world's end, but the tip of a new adventure. One full of beauty, and of truth.

'What do you think will happen to us?' I asked, gazing at him in awe. My love for this man had become my beacon, the light that led me home.

'I don't know,' he murmured, lips brushing against mine as he bent to kiss me.

'But I bet it will make for a great story.'

Acknowledgements

I send my first thanks to you, reader. There are so many books out there by so many brilliant authors, and I am honoured that you chose this one. I set out to write a novel that would provide an escape from the worry that has clouded the past few years, a story with unashamed love at its heart and a good few laughs along the way. I hope it brought a smile to your face . . . and a hankering to visit The Hamptons.

To my agent Alice Lutyens, who doesn't bat so much as an eyelash when I tell her to 'put a rocket up my bottom', and persists in championing me to anyone who'll listen. You are a marvel, and I feel very lucky to have you steering the Broom ship. Thanks must also go to the incredible team at Curtis Brown – especially Flo and Liz – for helping my books travel as far around the world as their author does.

To my editor, Kimberley Atkins, for always knowing exactly how to finesse my stories and manage my bonkersness during the edit phase, and for doing it all with such joy, passion, integrity, and professionalism. Huge thanks also to my Hodder & Stoughton team – Alainna Hadjigeorgiou (for publicity), Olivia Robertshaw (for editorial), Alice Morley (for marketing), Kay Gale (for copyedit), Becky Glibbery (for yet another wanderlust-inducing cover) and Catherine, Sarah, Rich, Iman, and Lucy (for sales).

Thank you to my fellow writers, so many of whom I am fortunate enough to call friends. Special mention must go to

Tasmina Perry (for selling The Hamptons to me – you were right!), Clare Mackintosh (for coming all the way to Queens in New York to buy me pizza and give me career-altering advice), Cathy Bramley and Kirsty Greenwood (for Zoom writing sessions, laughter, and Harry Styles gifs), Katie Marsh (for being my best and most steadfast cheerleader), and Cesca Major (for energy, inspiration, Coldplay tickets and general awesomeness).

To Lisa Howells, Chris Whitaker, and Tom Wood – not even Maverick could be a better wingman. I love you all from the bottom of my heart (and that salmon jug).

To my Nearest and Dearest crew – Sara-Jade, Fanny, Louise, and Claire – thank you for keeping me perpetually stocked with cheese, gin, gossip, and brilliant books.

To Gemma Courage, for coming out to New York to help me research this book – let us never forget The Machine™, birthing turnstiles, great racks, one-in-one-out, bookish chat over afternoon wine, and the magic of Bleecker Street. And to my friends, you know who you are – thank you for always supporting my writing and me.

And lastly (but not leastly), I must thank my family – every single scattered, treasured, and wonderful one of you – for your patience, love, and support.

Mum, you are my first reader, favourite co-walking plotter, biggest champion, and the most important person in my life. Thank you feels inadequate when I consider all that you do – but know that I mean it. You are the one I do it all for, and always will be.

**What if your life worked out perfectly . . .
for someone else?**

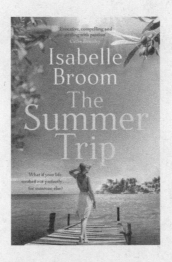

Discover Isabelle Broom's escapist holiday romance
The Summer Trip, available now!

'A tender, utterly romantic and evocative tale that will leave
you feeling as if you've spent a summer in Corfu'
Rachael Lucas

'This is a delicious, sun-splashed summer tale'
Woman's Own

Bookends

When one book ends, another begins...

Bookends is a vibrant new reading community to help you ensure you're never without a good book.

You'll find exclusive previews of the brilliant new books from your favourite authors as well as exciting debuts and past classics. Read our blog, check out our recommendations for your reading group, enter great competitions and much more!

Visit our website to see which great books we're recommending this month.

Join the Bookends community:
www.welcometobookends.co.uk

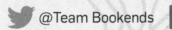 @Team Bookends   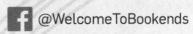 @WelcomeToBookends